Praise for the Mommy

DEATH GETS

"Waldman is at her witty best when dealing with children, carpooling, and first-trimester woes, but is no slouch at explaining the pitfalls of False Memory Syndrome either."

—*Kirkus Reviews*

"Waldman skillfully unravels the intertwined relationships . . . to reveal a cunning murder plot . . . Juliet and her patient husband make an appealing couple—funny, clever, and loving (but never mawkish). Waldman has an excellent ear for the snappy comeback, especially when delivered by a five-year-old." —*Publishers Weekly*

"A perky, enthusiastic, and infectious read."

—*Library Journal*

A PLAYDATE WITH DEATH

"Smoothly paced and smartly told."

—*The New York Times Book Review*

"Sparkling . . . [A] swift and engaging plot . . . Witty and well-constructed . . . those with a taste for lighter mystery fare are sure to relish the adventures of this contemporary, married, mother-of-two Nancy Drew." —*Publishers Weekly*

"[A] deft portrayal of Los Angeles's upper crust and of the dilemma facing women who want it all." —*Booklist*

THE BIG NAP

"Waldman treats the Los Angeles scene with humor, offers a revealing glimpse of Hasidic life, and provides a surprise ending . . . An entertaining mystery with a satirical tone."

—*Booklist*

continued . . .

"Juliet Applebaum is smart, fearless, and completely candid about life as a full-time mom with a penchant for part-time detective work. Kinsey Millhone would approve."

—Sue Grafton

"Juliet is a modern heroine refusing to quit or take another snooze until she feels justice is properly served."

—*BookBrowser*

NURSERY CRIMES

"[Juliet is] a lot like Elizabeth Peters' warm and humorous Amelia Peabody—a brassy, funny, quick-witted protagonist.

—*Houston Chronicle*

"Funny, clever, touching, original, wacky and wildly successful."

—Carolyn G. Hart

"A delightful debut filled with quirky, engaging characters, sharp wit, and vivid prose. I predict a successful future for this unique, highly likable sleuth."

—Judith Kelman, author of *After the Fall*

"[Waldman] derives humorous mileage from Juliet's 'epicurean' cravings, wardrobe dilemmas, night-owl husband, and obvious delight in adventure."

—*Library Journal*

"[Waldman is] a welcome voice . . . well-written . . . this charming young family has a real-life feel to it."

—*Contra Costa Times*

DEATH GETS A TIME-OUT

Ayelet Waldman

BERKLEY PRIME CRIME, NEW YORK

DEATH GETS A TIME-OUT

A Berkley Prime Crime book / published by arrangement with the author

PRINTING HISTORY
Berkley Prime Crime hardcover edition / July 2003
Berkley Prime Crime mass-market edition / June 2004

Illustrations by Lisa Desimini.
Design by Steven Ferlauto.

For information: The Berkley Publishing Group,
a division of Penguin Group (USA) Inc.,
375 Hudson Street, New York, New York 10014.

Visit our website at www.penguin.com

ISBN: 0-425-19712-3

Berkley Prime Crime books are published by The Berkley Publishing Group,
a division of Penguin Group (USA) Inc.,
375 Hudson Street, New York, New York 10014.

PRINTED IN THE UNITED STATES OF AMERICA

10 9 8 7 6 5 4 3 2 1

Acknowledgments

My sincerest thanks go to Diane at the breathtakingly beautiful Casa Luna for giving me a place to stay in Mexico; to Karen Gadbois and Susan McKinney for information on San Miguel; to Jean Rosenbluth for details of Los Angeles life and geography; to Clara Hennen for reading and commenting on the book; to Kathleen Caldwell for her unending support; and to Sophie, Zeke, and Ida-Rose for letting me get my work done. Thanks to Minouche Kandel and Dr. Eric Kandel's work on recovered memory. Any mistakes and misinterpretations I have made are entirely my own.

I feel special gratitude to Mary Evans and Natalee Rosenstein for shepherding my work so carefully. And, as always, thanks to Michael for making everything possible.

One

"DON'T be so *rigid*, Peter," I called after my husband as he went to answer the door. "Everybody loves breakfast-for-dinner. Breakfast-for-dinner *rocks*." My redheaded five-year-old, Ruby, and her younger brother, Isaac, nodded, slurping up their Cheerios with obvious delight. These were the very same Cheerios that, had it been morning, they would have left disintegrating in a sodden mess at the bottom of their cereal bowls. Kids are such suckers for a change of context. Breakfast-for-dinner. Pajamas to school. Chocolate syrup on their toothbrushes. Okay, maybe that last one would be going too far, but don't think I hadn't considered it. Anything to get them to brush.

"That's the last time I take you seriously when you offer to cook," Peter said as he came back into the kitchen. He was following in the wake of my best friend Stacy. Stacy is one of those women who was born to make the rest of us feel like we woke up a few hours late and have been scrambling to catch up ever since. She's a top talent agent at International Creative Artists. Her kid is a math prodigy and a soccer whiz, and competes all over the state—I'm never sure if it's the matches or the Math Olympics that keep them traveling. By them I mean Zachary and his nanny. Stacy's too busy to take a bus to Stockton for the semifinals of either algebra or foul-kicking.

In addition to everything else, Stacy is just about the most beautiful friend I have. All this gorgeousness isn't necessarily natural. She's a wizard at putting together a good-looking package. She has her hair done by a man who flies in from London once every six weeks, and her makeup is hand-churned from the urine of blind Parisian nuns. Or something like that. Anyway, it comes from France, and a tube of lip-stick costs more than a pair of my shoes. And I'm a sucker for expensive shoes. Over the years I've gotten used to feeling intimidated in the face of Stacy's perfection. I've even developed the ability to laugh about my lack of self-confidence. I accept the fact that flawlessness is pretty much out of the question for me. Hey, I'm happy if I manage to brush my teeth before noon. Makeup is *way* beyond me, and the only thing I can remember using a blow-dryer for in recent memory is to dry out a particularly nasty diaper rash. Isaac's, not my own. I'm ashamed to admit that it probably doesn't hurt my self-esteem that Stacy's marriage is, sadly, in a state of semiconstant upheaval; her husband has a weakness for tall, blond twenty-two-year-olds. Women who look just like Stacy did when they met. My marriage, albeit not necessarily the hotbed of romance it once was, is absolutely solid. Peter and I love each other, and have come to accept one another's flaws and failures. Well, except that whole cooking thing.

"Hey, are those real diamonds?" I said.

Stacy rolled her eyes at the question. Of course they were real. Stacy has an agreement with Harry Winston. She makes her movie star clients wear the jewelers' designs at the Oscars, the Emmys, and every other awards show, and in return they bedeck her in precious stones whenever she demands it. I've seen Stacy draped in ropes of rare, black Tahitian pearls worth tens of thousands of dollars. She showed up at a dinner for the president of our university in a choker so thick with rubies that she looked like she'd had her throat cut. She's even managed to snag a pair of ten-carat diamond earrings to wear to the odd movie premiere. I'd never before seen her looking quite so magnificent, however.

"Is that a tiara?" I asked. Ruby's head shot up from her bowl, and she stared at the glittering crown on my old friend's head. She jumped down from her chair and bolted out of the room. Weird little kid, that one is.

Stacy stared at me, tapping one pointy-toed, stiletto-heeled shoe. "It's a hairband," she said.

"A diamond hairband?"

"Yes, a diamond hairband."

"Are we wearing those nowadays?"

"We seem to be wearing pajamas nowadays. Might I ask why?"

I presented my bowl of instant oatmeal with a flourish. "Breakfast-for-dinner!" I said. Then, eyeing her burnt orange, floor-length, taffeta gown, I hugged my frayed flannel bathrobe around me a little more closely. I cursed myself for not looking harder for the belt for the bathrobe and instead resorting to cinching it with one of Peter's old ties. "Why are you so dressed up?"

"Think about it," she said through gritted teeth.

"You and Andrew are renewing your vows . . . in Vegas."

"No."

"Um . . . it's Oscar night and you're going to the Vanity Fair party?"

"No."

"You're a fairy princess!" Isaac piped up.

Stacy smiled at him, then glared at me. "No."

Suddenly, I groaned, overwhelmed with that all-too-familiar feeling of hormonal brain implosion. "You're going to the Breast Cancer Benefit that you invited me to last month. And that you reminded me about two days ago when we were at yoga."

"Bingo," Stacy said.

I smiled weakly. "I guess I don't have to finish my oatmeal."

As I tore through my closet trying to find something that even approached evening wear, I cursed my failing memory. "I swear this has nothing to do with you," I said, poking my head out and smiling weakly at my friend. She stood in the middle of my messy bedroom like Cinderella in the grimy kitchen, after the Fairy Godmother has dressed her, but before she's gone for her pumpkin ride.

"I know," she said.

"Last week I made it all the way to Ruby's school before I remembered that I was on my way to drop off the dry cleaning, not pick up carpool. How about this one?" I held up a pale green crepe gown I'd worn to my cousin Marcie's son's black tie Bar Mitzvah the year before. Stacy shook her head, and I went back into the bowels of my entirely unsatisfactory closet. It wasn't that there weren't enough clothes in there. On the contrary, the shelves and bars were overflowing. The problem was that nothing fit anymore. Two kids and a lifetime of physical sloth had made my once svelte body a thing of the past. The distant past.

"And yesterday I had to go back to the grocery store three times because I kept forgetting things. This?" I waved a dress at her.

"It'll do," she said.

"I blame the children," I said as I crammed myself into a cocktail dress that I'd last worn long before Isaac had made his appearance. If it weren't for the fact that every woman I knew was suffering from the same ailment, I would have seriously considered having an MRI. What is it about childbearing that lowers a fog over the brains of normally intelligent women? Here we all are, competent professionals, used to managing companies, handling crises, hiring and firing people, and now we stumble through our days with yesterday's underwear peeping out the leg of our slacks. Or maybe it's just me. Maybe all the other moms juggle carpool, lunchboxes, doctors' appointments, piano lessons, religious school, parent-teacher conferences, karate, diaper changes, soccer, and babysitters with the same aplomb they brought to graduate school and appellate arguments. Maybe I'm the only one with drifts of unwashed laundry taking over the living room and toilet paper stuck to her shoe.

I pinned a large broach to the bodice of my dress and stuffed my feet into a pair of three-inch black heels with silver buckles that had fit before I'd had two children and grown half a shoe size. They were too fabulous to throw away.

"Okay?" I said to Stacy, as I executed a limping pirouette.

"Hair? Makeup?" she barked.

"Right. Right." I ran into my bathroom and scrawled a bright red smile on my chapped lips. A little mascara and I was done. My hair, however, was hopeless. I wrapped a towel around my shoulders and dunked my head into the sink. I slicked my wet hair back with most of the contents of a bottle of hair gel and hoped that the cresting wave of eighties nostalgia had reached Joan Jett.

"Done," I said, coming out of the bathroom. Just then Ruby walked into my room, her hands behind her back.

"I found it, Mommy."

"What sweetie, what did you find?"

"My princess crown!" With a flourish she presented me with a silver plastic tiara. Much of the paint had chipped away, and one side had been chewed to a frayed stub.

"Wow," I said. "That would definitely complete my outfit."

"Now you can have a tiara just like Aunt Stacy's. Put it on!" my daughter ordered.

"It is not a tiara," Stacy said. "It's a diamond hairband." She had the grace to blush.

"Um, honey, I just did my hair. I'll put it on later, okay?" I said to my daughter. Her eyes began to fill, and her plump lower lip trembled. "Okay, I'm putting it on right now!" I said, and balanced the tiara on my head. "It's perfect!"

She smiled and said, "Don't take it off."

"You know why we're friends?" I asked Stacy as I disentangled the plastic teeth of Ruby's crown from my hair, and struggled to buckle my seatbelt while Stacy peeled out of my driveway.

"Because we know each other better than anyone else does, and that includes our husbands," she said.

"Nope. Because I make you look so good."

She smiled at me and, reaching over, pinched my cheek. "You look beautiful, Jules. Fix your pin so it covers up more of that stain."

Two

WE were just the wrong side of fashionably late to the benefit. The other women at Stacy's table, all of whom worked with her at International Creative Artists, were already taking delicate quantum-particle bites of their radicchio and fig salads. I noticed that most of them had pushed aside the Gorgonzola cheese. I wondered if it would be acceptable to scrape their plates onto my own.

Stacy and I made our apologies and sat down. She swept a practiced eye over the crowd. The yearly All-Girl Gala for the Cure, sponsored by the Breast Cancer Action League, was a chance for the women of Hollywood to do good while strutting their stuff, without having to bother finding a beard in a flashy Armani tux. The gowns were fabulous, and the dealmaking was formidable. Hollywood runs on an old boys' network, and it wasn't often that the women were given the chance to engage in the same kind of billion-dollar bonding. The Gala was one of the few times in a year where a young female director could catch a studio executive's eye without being upstaged by that week's boy wonder, or a woman with some money to spend could find a script worth investing in without having to funnel her cash through a patronizing tough-guy producer. Since I wasn't part of the Industry other than as the wife of a middling successful screenwriter, I'd never had a reason to go to the Gala. When Stacy invited me to be her date for what she called Babes for Boobs, I jumped at the chance to see the glitterati do what they do best—glitter.

"Miyake. Armani. Miyake. Valentino. Miyake. God help us—Versace," Stacy said, pointing a polish-tipped finger at the gowns gliding by our table.

"And yours?" I asked.

"Donna Karan."

"And mine?"

"Back of your closet, circa 1993. No, wait—1992."

"Man, you're good," I said.

I finished gobbling up my rare grilled ahi with mango cilantro salsa, and made my own perusal of the room. The lights were dim, in honor of the carefully sculpted cheekbones and Botoxed foreheads. Plastic surgery looks best in soft light. The tables were set with mint green china that matched the papered walls and complemented the gilded chairs. A lavish arrangement of white lilies and tuberoses spilled over the center of each table. The hum of conversation was pitched at a higher level than normal—there was no bass drone to disturb the soprano whirr. Noticeably absent was the noise of clicking silverware. I appeared to be the only woman eating anything at all.

At a table close to the front, I saw my friend Lilly Green. She was leaning forward, her perfect, pointed chin resting on one delicate hand. Her mouth was open in a warm and inviting smile that, if I hadn't known her so well, I would have assumed was absolutely real, signifying nothing so much as her complete absorption in and delight with her tablemates' conversation. The truth was most likely that she was bored—she usually was at events like this. Unlike other movie stars, Lilly would much rather have spent an evening playing Scrabble with her kids than reveling in the glitz of Hollywood.

But she was also invariably polite, and while not the kind of person either to suffer fools gladly, or engage in phony small talk, she also hated to hurt people's feelings.

Lilly caught my eye, and waved. I waved back. Stacy looked over at me. "Are you *ever* going to introduce me to her?" she asked.

"To whom? Lilly?" I pretended innocence but I knew exactly what Stacy was after—a client. I had gotten to know Lilly Green when she made her acting debut in one of Peter's slasher movies. My husband made his living writing screenplays that appealed to teenage boys and pretty much no one else. They starred cannibals and mummies, supernatural serial killers and bloodthirsty ghouls. Lilly had played a lovely young victim who turned into a homicidal walking corpse. Despite the part my husband had written for her, we became friends. She'd won an Oscar for her next film, and gone from B-movie starlet to full-fledged star. We'd remained close, but I have to admit that I'd grown a little uncomfortable around her. She tended to be surrounded by a retinue of managers, publicists, and assistants, and even though she was still the same, unpretentious woman who picked up Ruby every Wednesday and took her along to riding lessons with her own girls, because Ruby had once mentioned that she liked horses, it was hard for me to figure out how to interact with her. Maybe it all came down to my uncomfortable suspicion of my own motivations. Was I Lilly's friend because I liked her and had things in common with her, or was I her friend because I liked being friends with a movie star? I didn't really know the answer to that question.

"Introduce me," Stacy said, already halfway out of her chair.

"Okay," I said. "But you have to promise me you aren't going to try to poach her from her agent."

Stacy looked shocked, wounded, but I knew better.

Lilly had shaved her head for her most recent role, the Oscar-friendly tale of a mentally retarded woman with breast cancer, and the hair had just begun to grow back. If anything, her shorn skull highlighted her almost luminous beauty.

Next to her, Stacy, who always looked so impeccable, so perfectly put together, seemed a pale contrivance. After Lilly and I rubbed cheeks in an approximation of a kiss, I stroked the top of her head. "You have a mohair head," I said, and she laughed, although it seemed to me that it wasn't quite the belly laugh I was used to getting out of her. One of my favorite things about Lilly was how she invariably cracked up at my jokes. Peter says I'll like anyone who thinks I'm funny, and it's probably true. Although he's wrong that that's the only reason I married him; it was just as important that he makes *me* laugh.

I introduced Stacy, and Lilly politely shook her hand.

"So, what are you doing here?" I asked. "You hate parties."

She shrugged.

"Lilly's being honored tonight," Stacy said. "Didn't you look at the program?"

"Honored?" I asked.

"For dying of breast cancer on screen," Lilly said. "I guess they couldn't find a woman what was really sick to drag up onto the stage."

"You've performed a profound service," Stacy said. "Raising people's consciousness, increasing awareness. You certainly deserve the award."

"Maybe," Lilly said, although it didn't sound like she really believed it. I had to agree with her. Looking around the room, I wondered how many of the women were struggling in anonymity with the horrible disease from which Lilly had only pretended to suffer. Didn't they deserve acknowledgment more than she did? After all, when the cameras stopped rolling, she went home. The black cloud never disappeared from *their* skies.

"So, what are you up to, Juliet?" Lilly asked. "Still solving murders?"

I smiled uncomfortably. "Not murders." I shifted my weight. My feet had begun to ache in their too-tight shoes.

She cocked an eyebrow at me quizzically.

"Go ahead, tell her," Stacy said, prodding me in the side with her elbow. "Juliet's become a private eye!"

I blushed. I was still a little embarrassed about my new career. It's not that I didn't enjoy it—on the contrary, I was absolutely in love with the job. I'd finally succumbed to the entreaties of my good friend Al Hockey, whom I had met when I was a federal public defender and he was an investigator in the same office. We'd worked on a lot of cases together, and we stayed friends even after I quit to stay home with my kids. When Al hung out a shingle as a private investigator, he asked me to join up with him. As happy as I was with my new identity as sort-of-working-mother, I had the nagging sensation that there was something almost ridiculous about turning my fundamental nature as a nosy snoop into a career.

"Really? A detective?" Lilly asked.

"Well, an investigator. I don't have my license yet. And it's only part-time," I said. At the time Al had made his offer, I'd been slowly going crazy. I know there are women who skillfully and happily manage the transition from full-time, productive member of the work force to stay-at-home mother. I've met them in the park. Those are the women who swap homemade Play-Doh recipes and puree their own babyfood from organic produce they grow in their backyards. I'd rather be forced to *eat* the Play-Doh than make it. And I honestly can't remember the last time I served a vegetable that didn't come out of my freezer, unless pickles count. Don't get me wrong. I love my kids with a ferocity that sometimes scares me. I love their dirty little faces and stubby toes. I love the absurdly funny and piercingly insightful things they say, and the way they tangle their fingers in my hair when I lie down with them to take a nap. But the prospect of spending an entire day alone with them fills me with dread. Keeping two people with a collective attention span of three minutes entertained for an entire fourteen-hour day is a task that makes Sisyphus's look like playing marbles. Half the time I feel like hiring a nanny and getting my bored, frustrated, rapidly expanding butt back to work as a lawyer. I spend the other half convinced that there's a point to being there day after day, hour after hour, driving from playdates to piano lessons, doing endless loads of very small laundry, and clinging to sanity with one exhausted fingernail. Al's offer seemed like a way to do both—be with my kids, and do some work that didn't involve very short people and a very dirty house.

I had initially suffered from the delusion that it would be a breeze to work part-time while the kids were in school. However, I hadn't yet ever managed more than a forty-five-minute workday. By the time I dropped Ruby and Isaac off at their two different schools, and ran whatever errands were absolutely critical to the continuation of our existence as a family, I had exactly enough time to make two phone calls or write half a letter before I had to race off to pick them up again. So far Al had been remarkably patient with my glaring absence from our joint venture, although he *had* taken to calling me his invisible partner.

Lilly narrowed her eyes and leaned forward. "What kind of work are you doing?"

"Criminal defense work, primarily," I said. "Lawyers hire us to investigate their cases. You know, take pictures of the crime scene, track down witnesses, that kind of thing. And we've done some death penalty mitigation work, too."

"What's that?" Stacy interrupted. "How do you mitigate the gas chamber?'

"We dig up what we can on a defendant's background to help the lawyer convince the jury that executing him wouldn't be fair. You know, like if he was an abused child, or was really nice to his grandmother. That kind of thing."

Lilly stood up and grabbed my arm. Her face was flushed and beads of sweat stood out on her upper lip. "I need to talk to you," she said in a low voice.

"Um, okay," I said, taken aback by her vehemence.

Lilly glanced quickly around and met Stacy's eye. She bit her lip. "In private," she muttered.

Stacy raised her eyebrow and smiled stiffly. "I'll see you back at our table, Juliet," she said. "Nice to meet you, Ms. Green." But Lilly had already started to hustle me across the ballroom floor. I stumbled along, doing my best to keep from looking as though I was being dragged against my will.

"Hey Lilly, ease up," I said. "I can barely walk in these shoes."

She dropped my arm. "Sorry," she said. We'd come out into the hallway outside the ballroom. We were on the second floor of the hotel on a kind of mezzanine, looking out over the opulent lobby. The hall was empty except for a short line of women standing outside the ladies' room. A dumpy woman in a viciously patterned, skin-tight gown looked over at us. Her eyes widened and she jabbed an elbow into the side of the woman standing next to her. A ripple ran through the line, and within seconds everyone was either staring at Lilly, or very obviously and carefully *not* staring at her. I had a sudden insight into what Lilly's life must be like. These women were all in the movie business, and even they were incapable of treating her normally. How much worse must it be out on the street?

"Let's go in here," Lilly said, opening a door into an empty room and pushing me through. It was another ballroom, although a much smaller one. She pulled two chairs off a stack against the wall and motioned me to sit down.

I perched on the crushed velvet seat and poked at the matching curtain draped along the wall. "I haven't seen this much mauve since my cousin Dara's bat mitzvah reception at Leonard's of Great Neck."

"What?"

"Never mind. What's going on, Lilly? Is everything okay? Are you okay?"

"I have to talk to you about something," she said, worrying the silk of her skirt with agitated fingers. I cringed, sure she was going to tear through the gossamer fabric. The dress probably cost more than my monthly rent. This kind of anxiousness just wasn't like Lilly. She was not a nervous person—she had always exuded the kind of serene confidence specific to very beautiful, very successful women, even when it had looked like her career might begin and end with movies in which her heaving breasts were mauled by flesh-eaters.

"Sure, fine, but don't tear your beautiful dress, okay?"

She let go of her skirt and clasped her hands, as if that were the only way she could keep them under her control. "I want to hire you," she said.

I blinked in surprise. "For what? We don't have any experience doing domestic cases. Not that we *couldn't* do one, it's just that we haven't really done that kind of work. Yet." Lilly's ex-husband, Archer, had taken her for a rather remarkable amount of money when they'd divorced, and I figured she was trying to get some of it back.

Lilly ran a hand over her shorn head and looked around the empty room, as if searching for concealed paparrazi and gossip columnists. "It's not a domestic case. It's a criminal case."

I leaned back in my chair and looked at her. She had knotted her hands together so tightly that her knuckles were white.

"No one can know about this, Juliet."

"I'm still a lawyer, Lilly. Everything you say to me is in confidence." I waited.

After a moment she seemed to steel herself. She nodded once and looked up at me. "I want to hire you to help in a capital murder case."

I couldn't help it—I gasped. "Capital murder? Who? What case?"

Lilly paused again, and then finally said, "Jupiter Jones."

I felt a rush of something that I'm embarrassed to say was a lot like excitement. The rape and murder of Chloe Jones, the very young wife of the Very Reverend Polaris Jones, founder and leader of the Church of Cosmological Unity, had sent the entire city of Los Angeles into a tailspin. Mrs. Jones had been found raped and murdered in her San Marino home. For a while all of Southern California had been engulfed by paroxysms of terror, convinced that some new Manson Family had come to town. Movie stars decamped to their Aspen and New York lodgings. One televangelist crackpot made the national news by insisting God was exacting revenge for our city's hedonism; the Chief of Police blamed the city counsel's assertion of limitations on racial profiling; and the newly elected and xenophobically insane mayor insisted that the influx of illegal immigrants was responsible. When Jupiter Jones had been arrested for the crime, there had been a collective sigh of relief, and then a buzz of titillated horror because the culprit was the victim's own stepson.

I leaned forward in my chair. "What do *you* have to do with Jupiter Jones?"

Lilly bit her bottom lip and narrowed her eyes at me, as if to assess my trustworthiness. Finally, she spoke. "He's my brother."

My mouth gaped open in what surely must have looked like a caricature of astonishment—or a wide-mouth bass on a hook. "What?"

"Well, my stepbrother," she said, twisting her hands.

"How is it that the papers haven't managed to get hold of that piece of information?" It certainly seemed like something *The National Enquirer* might have been interested in printing. I could write the headline myself. CANCER STAR SISTER OF OEDIPAL MATRICIDE.

"I pay people a lot of money to keep things like that out of the papers. Anyway, my mother and Polaris were together years ago, when Jupiter and I were really little."

Now I was really confused. "Your mother? Your mother was married to Polaris Jones?" Beverly Green, Lilly's mother, was the first woman Speaker of the California Assembly. I could write that headline, too. POLITICAL POWERHOUSE LINKED TO NEW AGE CULT LEADER.

"Not my mom. I mean, not Beverly. Beverly is my stepmother. My real mother was married to Polaris Jones. A long long time ago."

"Your real mother? Who is she? Where is she?" I asked, putting my hand over the knot Lilly had made of hers in her lap.

"She . . . she died. When I was five. I don't really remember her. We were living in Mexico then—my mother and me, and Polaris. Except he wasn't Polaris. Back then his name was Artie. Jupiter lived with us, too. And a bunch of other people."

I raised my eyebrows. She shrugged. "It was kind of a commune, I guess. We all moved back here after my real mother died. I moved in with my dad and mom—I mean my stepmother. Artie and Jupiter came around a lot when I was younger, but after Artie became Polaris and The Church of Cosmological Unity got to be such a big thing, my parents really didn't have much to do with him. My mom had been elected to the Board of Supervisors by then, and I guess she figured it would look bad if she were associated with all those CCU nut jobs."

I could certainly understand that. It was hard not to be aware of Polaris Jones's church. Certain parts of the city were liberally sprinkled with navy blue billboards, painted with silver stars and Polaris's benevolent visage, and the stern warning that our extraterrestrial ancestors were watching our every move, and finding us wanting. I could never understand how anyone could be taken in by such an obviously ludicrous theology—not that I knew much about it—but I knew the CCU had a massive campus out in Pasadena, packed with disciples spending thousands of dollars on classes that would earn them the points necessary to achieve Primal Infinitude. Periodic newspaper exposés about its shady financial dealings seemed to have little effect on the CCU's popularity. I think even the Scientologists were getting a little concerned about the thousands of seekers of enlightenment bypassing their Celebrity Center in Hollywood and heading out to Pasadena.

"I don't get it, Lilly. Why do you want to hire me? What do you want me to do?"

She grabbed my hands in hers and squeezed tightly. "I want you to help Jupiter. They've charged him with capital murder, and I can't *bear* the idea of him on death row. I don't remember much about Mexico or my mom, but I do remember Jupiter. Neither of us spoke Spanish, so we were each other's only playmates. He was littler than I was, maybe two years younger or so. We did everything together. We even slept in the same bed. Honestly, when my mother died and I came to live with my dad, I missed Jupiter as much as I missed her."

"Does he know you're trying to help him?"

She nodded. "He called me from jail right after he was arrested. Artie—Polaris—won't speak to him. I guess that's understandable, but Jupiter doesn't have any money of his own. He lived with Polaris and Chloe. I hired his lawyers, and I'm paying them, but that's a secret. Nobody knows that except them, Jupiter, and me. And now you."

"Who did you hire?"

"Raoul Wasserman."

I whistled. I'd met the famous defense attorney only once, when we were arguing motions before the same judge. He'd swept into the courtroom like a queen bee surrounded by a swarm of busy little associates. He was empty-handed, which I soon realized was because one of the worker bees was carrying his briefcase for him. Another had hold of his cell phone. Wasserman must have been six foot five, at the minimum. I found out from Peter that in his day Wasserman had been one of the greatest Jewish basketball players ever to play in the NBA, not that there's a whole lot of competition for that title. He had thick black hair swept high off his forehead, and a quiet voice that nonetheless managed to resonate throughout the high-ceilinged room. Even the judge deferred to Counselor Wasserman, pushing his motion to first on the docket, and nodding and smiling throughout his oral argument. The poor U.S. Attorney who had the ill luck to argue for the government seemed to concede defeat before he even began, and it took only a few moments for the judge to exclude all the evidence that Wasserman wanted out of the case. The legend and his coterie buzzed out of the courtroom, leaving the rest of us defense attorneys feeling suddenly shabby and ill-prepared. We all lost our motions that day.

"If you've got *him*, why in heaven's name do you need *me*? I'm sure he's got a team of investigators working the case already."

She squeezed my hand harder. "Maybe. Probably. And he's the best, I know he is. But I don't trust him. He's . . . I don't know. Slippery. I need someone there to make sure he's doing what he's supposed to. You're my friend, Juliet. I know I can trust you."

I patted her hand, surreptitiously trying to loosen her grip on my now aching fingers. "I am your friend, Lilly. And that's just why I shouldn't be working on your brother's case. It might be a conflict of interest."

"Why?"

"Because I would be *his* investigator—part of his legal team—but *your* friend. Don't you see how that would be weird?"

"No, I don't. If I can hire and pay his lawyers, why can't I hire and pay you? I wouldn't be asking you to *report* to me or anything. I just want you on his defense team so I know for sure that there's someone there who is going to devote herself to Jupiter. Someone who isn't doing it just for the money, or for the notoriety."

I blushed. The frisson of excitement I'd felt when I'd first heard the name "Jupiter Jones" had certainly been because of the notoriety of the case. Every criminal defense lawyer dreams of catching the big fish—one of those high-profile cases that end up on *Court TV*. And I was still, at heart, a defense lawyer. It's kind of like being Jewish or Catholic. Once you're born into the religion, you're doomed, even if you stop going to services. I wanted this case—I wanted it bad. But could I do it? Was it ethical to represent a friend, or the brother of a friend? And did I want to work the hours this case would certainly demand?

"Please, Juliet. I need you. I really need you."

Lilly had always been there for me, even when I was asking for favors that seemed downright impossible. And she'd stayed my friend, even after she'd become famous. That counted for something, didn't it? Anyway, who was I kidding? As soon as the words "Jupiter Jones" had left her lips, I was hooked.

"Let me talk to my partner," I said. "If he thinks it's okay, and if Wasserman goes along with it, we'll take the case."

Lilly flung her arms around my neck. "Thank you so much," she said.

I hugged her back. "Don't thank me yet. Let's see what Al and Wasserman have to say, first."

"Oh my God!" she said, leaping to her feet. "My award!"

We rushed back into the banquet hall just in time for Lilly to step up to the podium, receive her Tiffany crystal bare torso of a woman with only one breast (could I really have been the only person who thought that was in shockingly bad taste?), and give a gently humorous and profoundly moving speech about the inspiration cancer survivors provide the rest of us. Lilly was a consummate professional. You would never have known, looking at her on the stage, so beautiful that she almost glowed, that, moments before, she'd been pale and frightened, begging me for help.

Three

I'M as macho as the next mother, but I am simply not able to get my children dressed, fed, and out the door in the morning while crouched over the toilet seat, vomiting. The morning after I gobbled up all that Gorgonzola cheese and rare ahi tuna, I had to wake up my husband to help me juggle food poisoning and carpool. Peter works at night. Every evening after we put the kids to bed, he takes a thermos of black, bitter coffee into his office and hangs out with zombies and flesh-eating cheerleaders until dawn. Then he staggers to bed, and loses consciousness until noon. That morning, though, he was awakened earlier than usual by the lovely sound of me gagging and crying for help.

Even his toes looked tired. That was the only part of his body visible to me as I lay on the cool tiles of the bathroom floor. "What's wrong?" he said, his voice scratchy and barely audible. He cleared his throat. The sound of the phlegm rattling around made me heave again, and I bent back over the toilet.

"Are you sick?" he asked.

"No. I'm just cleaning out the toilet. With my face."

"Right. What do you need me to do?"

I waved in the general direction of Ruby and Isaac.

Half an hour later, when I'd finally managed to splash some cool water onto my face and stagger out of the bathroom, I found the children sitting in front of the TV, eating hotdogs. They were wearing shorts and T-shirts, and their hair stuck out in tufts all over their heads.

"Hotdogs?" I asked my husband.

He shrugged and said, "Dinner-for-breakfast."

"Shorts? In the middle of winter?"

"Hey, they insisted. When they freeze, they'll get the message that they should listen to their father when he suggests warmer clothes."

"Hair?"

"Ruby said it's 'Bed-Head Day' at school."

"What, did Congress make Bed-Head Day a national holiday while I was in the bathroom? They go to *different* schools. How can they both possibly have Bed-Head Day?"

I went to the kids' rooms, yanked a couple of pairs of sweat pants out of the drawers, and shoved my squirming progeny into them. I wiped off their ketchup-smeared faces and dragged a comb through their matted heads of hair. I gave up on Ruby's curls, and just crammed the mass of red under a baseball cap. Then I went into the kitchen. I was suddenly famished. I riffled through the refrigerator and finally settled on some chocolate pudding packs I'd bought for lunchboxes.

"Sweetie?" Peter said.

"What?" I mumbled with my mouth full of pudding.

"Should you really be eating? If you're sick?"

"I'm starving."

"I don't think you should be eating that if you've got food poisoning or a stomach flu. How about some clear soup?"

Soup? Soup! "I'm *famished*," I insisted, and then we stared at each other.

"Oh my God," he said.

"No. It's not possible."

"You're throwing up. And you're hungry. At the same time."

"It's just not possible. It's the fish from last night. I'm sure Beverly Hills is lousy with vomiting studio executives this morning."

He shook his head. "But you're *hungry*."

"Look, I'm just not going there. It's impossible, and that's that," I said, and called out to the children to get in the car so that I could drive them to school.

"Hey! That's *lunch* pudding!" Isaac hollered when he came into the kitchen.

"Don't worry. I put some in your lunchbox," Peter said.

"But she's eating lunch pudding *now*! In the morning!" He stood, hands akimbo, exuding the indignation that had lately become his specialty.

"Don't be stupid, Isaac. It's dinner-for-breakfast, remember?" Ruby said, rolling her eyes in disgust. "He's so dumb!"

"Stop calling your brother names!" I scolded around my spoon. I stuck my finger in the plastic cup and scraped up the last of the pudding.

"But that's *lunch* pudding!" Isaac said again. "Not *dinner* pudding."

"Oh for God's sake," Peter snapped, and stomped off in the direction of the bedroom. I forget sometimes that he isn't familiar with our regular morning routine of aggressive bickering. By the afternoon, when school's over and I'm no longer trying to rush them out the door, they've usually mellowed into a somewhat more manageable whining squabble.

Ruby complained the whole way about a boy in her class, Jacob, who had been picking on the girls. She had me worked up into a fit of righteous maternal indignation, but when she described how Jacob had trained spiders to attack the girls, and one of them had bitten her friend Malika so badly that her eyeball had to be removed, the kid lost me.

"The thing about lying, honey, is that people stop trusting you," I said, trying to sound schoolmarmish rather than irritated.

"I'm not lying."

"C'mon Ruby."

"I'm not. I'm being *creative.*"

I snorted and was about to blast her when a thought occurred to me. Wasn't that basically what her father did for a living? Made stuff up? After a while I said, "Maybe you should just *warn* us when you're being creative." I looked in the mirror to find her rolling her eyes at her brother. He smiled at her. Isaac thinks Ruby is God. He believes everything she says, likes everything she likes, and does everything she tells him to do. A few months before, I had watched heartbroken as he valiantly gave up *Blue's Clues* when Ruby informed him it was a baby show. He would still snuggle his stuffed Blue, but only when the commander-in-chief was not around to sneer at him.

After I dropped the kids off, I headed down the highway to Al's garage, our business's temporary quarters that lately had begun to seem suspiciously permanent. I found Al sitting at his ancient metal desk, cleaning a gun. He had spread a pale pink dishtowel on the scratched and pitted surface of the desk and laid out an antique pistol. He was polishing the brass barrel and gazing at it lovingly, as though it were a picture of one of his daughters.

"Do you do that on purpose?" I asked.

"What?"

"Play with your guns when I'm coming over. I swear you only do it because you know I hate them."

"Ms. Applebaum," he hissed the "z" on Ms. with extra emphasis, "the world does not revolve around you. I'll have you know that I just got this in the mail. It's a nineteenth-century naval officer's flintlock boarding pistol. Look at this little bayonet that swings out from under the barrel."

"Cute," I said. "I bet it cost you plenty."

Al nodded conspiratorially and then glanced over his shoulder at the door leading to the house. "Keep your voice down. Jeanelle thinks it's a *reproduction*."

"I very much doubt that," I said, and as if on cue, Al's beautiful, sweet-tempered wife walked through the door, holding a platter of muffins.

"Hi, Juliet. I baked you two some muffins. Blueberry." She laid the plate down on the table and ruffled her husband's remaining strands of hair. Al and Jeanelle might seem to an outsider to be the world's unlikeliest couple. After all, how many members of a gun-toting, antigovernment militia are married to black women? Al claims his unit is not the only multiracial one in the country, but I have a hard time believing that. Al and Jeanelle have been married for close to forty years. They have two daughters, who get their looks from their mother and their politics from their father. One's an FBI agent and the other is in law school, hoping to become a prosecutor when she graduates.

"The new toy," Jeanelle said, picking up the pistol and looking admiringly at the engraved lock and wood handle. It was tough to read her expression.

"Yup. Reproduction."

"Uh-huh. Impeccable craftsmanship." She smiled at him and headed back up the two steps leading into the house. "Don't work too hard, you two."

"Fat lot of chance of that," Al grumbled. It had been a slow month for us. There was barely enough to keep Al busy, and I hadn't billed a client in over a week. If I didn't bill, then I didn't make any money, and I wasn't much thrilled by the idea of sitting around Al's garage in Westminister for no money.

"I might have some work for us," I said, and told Al about Lilly's offer.

"The Chloe Jones murder," he said, rubbing his hands together. "That's definitely high-profile. It would get us noticed. Generate some business."

"Lilly asked me to do it specifically because she thought we *wouldn't* be in it just for the notoriety. She thought we'd be committed to helping her brother, not to drumming up new business."

"We can help her brother and help ourselves at the same time," he replied.

"You don't think it's a conflict of interest? My friendship with Lilly?"

He scowled. "Look, let's let the client decide. We'll ask the kid if he minds; we'll ask the lawyer if he minds. If they both give the okay, we take the case."

I didn't reply. I was too busy running to the bathroom.

"You okay?" Al shouted at my back.

"Bad fish," I groaned, crashing through the kitchen and making it just in time.

Four

I still wasn't feeling one hundred percent better the next day, but Al had set up an appointment for us to visit Jupiter Jones at the county jail. One of Raoul Wasserman's associates would be meeting us. Wasserman had, as it turned out, been willing to let us join the investigative team. I suppose Lilly's phone call telling him that she'd fire him if he didn't agree might have had something to do with that.

Unfortunately, we were supposed to meet at the jail at nine in the morning, and I couldn't drop Isaac off at preschool until eight forty-five. I was almost fifteen minutes late, and decidedly frazzled, when I finally hustled into the jail. I found Al chatting up the attorney from Wasserman's office. Her elegant black suit revealed a long stretch of very thin, very sexy leg. She wore gorgeous, dainty, slingback heels and I had to stifle myself to keep from asking her where she bought them and how much they had cost. I love impractical, beautiful shoes. As the only part of my body I don't actively loathe, my feet deserve to be rewarded with a pair of Manolos or Jimmy Choos on a regular basis.

The young attorney looked at me appraisingly, and I self-consciously pulled at the hem of my sweater, tugging it over the waistband of the skirt that I'd had to pin closed because the button had popped off long ago. At least I was wearing a nice pair of Stuart Weizman spectator pumps. I maneuvered one foot forward to show them off.

"I'm Juliet Applebaum," I said, sticking out my hand.

"Valerie Sloan. You're late."

I forced a smile. "I don't think Jupiter's going to mind. It's not like he's going anywhere."

"I have another appointment at ten-thirty," she said.

Al discreetly put a warning hand on my arm. I shrugged him off and smiled grimly at the arrogant young attorney. "Well, then, we'd better hurry," I said.

Jupiter Jones looked much younger than his thirty years, and drooped over the table as if he were trying to make his lanky body as inconspicuous as possible. His lips were chapped and peeling and he picked absently at them, dropping tiny flakes of skin on the table. I felt the gorge rise in my throat, and I battled it down. The young attorney introduced him to us, and he nodded almost imperceptibly.

"I'm a friend of Lilly's," I said, and he finally raised his eyes to mine. "This is Al Hockey." Al nodded once as Jupiter flashed him a nervous glance. "Lilly wants us to help in your case, to work on your investigative team."

He mumbled something.

"Excuse me?" I asked.

"Can you get me out of here?" he said softly.

"Mr. Wasserman is doing what he can, Mr. Jones," Ms. Sloan said. "We're going to appeal the denial of bail. You know that. Mr. Wasserman told you that in the letter he sent you."

Jupiter nodded and ducked his head. I watched him peel another curlicue of skin off his lip. He licked nervously at the bright red dot of blood that appeared. I shot the attorney an irritated glance. Why is it that some lawyers never seem to learn how to talk to their clients? Is it that they are so full of their own importance, so confident that they know what's best, that they can't see the person for whom they work as anything other than an incompetent child, one who needs to be told what to do? I fear I had had something of that attitude myself, when I first started at the public defender's office. I was full of good intentions, excited about my role as advocate for the underprivileged. It was a bank robber named Malcolm Waterwright who taught me, finally, to see my clients as people, like myself. He was a middle-aged man with a drug habit. I'd negotiated his guilty plea, and basically forced him to accept it. Of course the choice was his, but I made it clear to him that I knew best, and that there wasn't really any other option. And truthfully, that was the case. There was a mountain of evidence against him, and we certainly would have lost at trial—pleading guilty reduced his sentence. We were preparing a letter for the judge, asking that he be sentenced on the low end of the applicable sentencing range, when Malcolm blew my complacency away. I asked him about his educational background, and he told me that he had a B.A. in English literature—from the same small New England college that I'd attended. I was stunned. Although I never would have admitted it, I had always felt that my clients were somehow a completely different breed of human than I. They were of a different class, a different society, had a different level of intelligence. I stared at Malcolm, overwhelmed by the realization that there but for the grace of God, and a drug habit, went I. I never treated another client the same after that, even the ones like Jupiter Jones who were accused of crimes that I found personally sickening.

"What's going on, Jupiter?" I asked. "Is someone hurting you?"

He didn't answer, just chewed on his lips. I could imagine what was happening to him. Rapists have a terrible time in jail. The only people who suffer more abuse are those accused of child molestation. The ones who, like Lilly's stepbrother, look weak and afraid are in particular danger.

"Jupiter, tell me what's going on. If you're in danger, Mr. Wasserman can make an emergency petition for bail. Or at least request that you be put in protective seclusion."

He shook his head quickly. "I don't want to go to the hole."

Inmates who are in danger and inmates who *are* a danger get the same treatment. They are put in the SHU—the Segregated Housing Unit—where they spend all but one hour of their day alone in a tiny cell. For that reason, more often than not, victims opt to stay in the general population and just deal with the harassment.

"I told you. Mr. Wasserman has already presented a bail application," Valerie said reprovingly.

Al and I looked at each other, and he made a couple of notes on the yellow pad he'd brought. One of our first jobs would be to find out exactly what it was that Wasserman was doing about getting Jupiter out of jail before he ended up dead, or worse.

I asked Jupiter to tell us what happened, reminding him that we, like his lawyers, were bound by the laws of attorney-client privilege. Everything he told us would be confidential.

"Why don't you start with the day Chloe died. Did you see her that day?"

Al and I had to lean over the table to hear Jupiter's low monotone as he described what he'd done the day his stepmother was murdered. It had been a day like most others. He'd slept late, until almost noon. No one was home when he awoke. His father was out, presumably at the CCU center in Pasadena, where he spent much of his time.

"Where is your room?" I asked.

"In the basement," he replied. "I have kind of an apartment down there, with a bathroom and sort of an office or game room. It's where I do my work."

"What kind of work do you do?"

He shrugged. "I design computer games. At least I'm trying to. I sold one game a few years ago, but it never really made it to the market. I'm working on another one. And I do a little writing. Mostly science fiction."

I nodded. "Okay, so you got up at around noon, and then what?"

"Ruth, that's the housekeeper, always saves breakfast for me. I got my plate and my coffee and went out to the pool."

"You ate by the pool?"

"Yeah."

"And then what did you do?"

"I don't know. I swam a couple of laps, I guess. Read the paper. Maybe took a nap."

"A nap? But you just woke up."

He shrugged again. "I was tired."

I could see Al's lips pulling into a disapproving line. I knew what he was thinking. What a slacker, lolling around in bed half the day. It was hard not to think that myself.

"And at some point Chloe came home?"

He nodded.

"Did she come out to the pool?"

He nodded again. "We hung out for a while. Got some sun. You know."

Not really. My skin has all the lovely sun-kissed glow of the underbelly of a scrod.

"And then?"

"Mr. Jones's semen was found in the victim's body. There was a DNA match," Valerie said in a voice much too loud for the small interview room. Jupiter and I both flinched. Al just kept jotting notes.

"Ah," I said. "Why don't you tell me a little bit about that?"

He didn't answer.

"Hey, Jupiter. I know this is hard. But we're going to have to talk about it," I said.

He ducked his head and shrugged.

"Did you have sexual relations with the victim on the day of her homicide?" This was the first question Al asked and he sounded exactly like the ex-cop he was. Al's career with the L.A.P.D. Hollywood Division had ended when a jacked-up meth freak, two hours out of county jail, had fired a 38mm in Al's general direction, and managed to hit him bang in the belly. Al always says he was happy to retire, and the shooting was just a convenient excuse to get out early with a full pension, but I know the injury must have been worse than he pretends. Only serious disability would have kept him from the job he loved.

Jupiter was curled up into as small a ball as he could be and still be sitting on the chair. He was gnawing on his lips like they were chewing gum, and his Adam's apple was working up and down. "Yeah," Jupiter whispered finally. All that effort for such a small word.

"We will be presenting a defense that the sex was consensual," Valerie said.

Would it have killed her to *pretend* that she believed him?

"Do you mind telling us where it was that you . . . er . . . had sex?" I asked, tamping down the feeling of discomfort that always comes over me when I have to talk to clients about that kind of thing. I once had a client who was a cross-dressing bank robber. I had been young and naïve enough to let that embarrass me. Now I wish I could send the guy a picture of Isaac in the pink tutu he liked to wear.

"In my room," Jupiter said.

"Was that the first time you and the victim engaged in sexual relations?" Al barked. I kicked him in the shins under the table. "What?" he said to me testily.

"Jupiter, were you and Chloe romantically involved?" I asked.

He nodded. "I knew her first. I introduced her to my father."

"Really?"

"Uh-huh." He seemed to unwind a bit, and sat up a little straighter. "We were in rehab together."

"You met Chloe in rehab?"

He nodded.

"What were you there for?" I asked, keeping my voice as gentle and nonjudgmental as I could. It wasn't difficult. I don't condemn people for using drugs. Addiction's a disease, not a moral failing, and I consider myself lucky not to suffer from it. And hell, if I were to condemn drug use, I'd have to start with my husband. He spent much of his teenage years stoned. What else could possibly have inspired his horror movies?

"Coke. Her too." I could barely hear his whisper.

"Where were you in rehab?"

"At the Ojai Rehabilitation and Self-Actualization Center."

I hadn't heard of it, but then the kinds of centers my clients frequented were the places that accepted Medicaid or didn't charge anything at all. I had a feeling that Jupiter Jones had experienced an entirely different kind of rehab.

"Chloe got me through, you know?" Jupiter said. His words came out in a rush, but he was talking to the table, tugging on his lips with his fingers. "We did it together. The steps. All of it. We helped each other. We were, like, partners."

"Did your relationship continue once you were released?" I asked.

"I thought it would. I got out two weeks before she did. I waited for her. I drove up to Ojai to pick her up. I even brought her back to my house. She didn't have anywhere else to go."

"And that's when she met your father?"

"Yeah." A tide of red crept over his face. For the first time he didn't look scared and beaten down. He looked angry. Very very angry.

"What happened?"

"What do you *think* happened? She took one look at the house, and the cars, and *him*. She knew what was what." With that, he tore another piece of skin off his lower lip, and the blood gushed. He looked down at his red-speckled fingers with surprise. I closed my eyes and swallowed, willing away the nausea. Al and Valerie were both staring at Jupiter—Al with a kind of sick fascination, and Valerie with a moue of disgust so prissy it was comical. I dug into my pocket and pulled out a packet of baby wipes. I freed one and handed it to Jupiter.

"Press hard," I said.

"Thanks," he whispered, and winced as he pushed the cold, damp cloth against his mouth.

"So Chloe broke up with you when she met your dad," I said.

"She didn't have to. I saw what was happening. I took off." He took the cloth away from his lips and looked at it. It was smeared with brownish blood. He looked around, as if searching for somewhere to put it. Then, he carefully folded it, and tucked it into the sleeve of his shirt.

"Where did you go?" I asked.

"I flew down to Mexico. For a couple of months. When I got back, they were married."

I nodded. Then I remembered how we'd started talking about this in the first place. "But you were still sleeping together at the time she was killed."

He smiled, a grim, tight smile. "My old man is, you know, old. And Chloe's not the kind of girl to do without, if you know what I mean." He puffed up a bit, as if the memory of his father's failures, and the contrast with his own presumed success, made him feel less vulnerable, stronger.

Valerie wrinkled her nose in obvious disgust. The truth was, I might have joined her, but I had better control. I'd spent plenty of time pretending not to be horrified and disgusted with my clients. Some of them had even done worse things than sleeping with their stepmothers.

"And what about you, Jupiter?" I asked. "Why were *you* doing it?"

He shrugged.

"Jupiter? Why did you keep sleeping with her, after she'd left you for your dad?"

He shook his head silently.

"Jupiter?"

"I don't know," he said. Then he looked me in the eye for the first time since he'd sat down at the table. "Love?" he said, his voice rising, as if asking *me* if that were the reason.

"Did you kill Chloe?" I asked softly.

"Don't answer that question!" Valerie nearly shouted. She glared at me. "We don't need to know the answer to that."

There are two breeds of criminal defense attorneys—one likes to know the truth and the other would just as soon stay in the dark about his or her client's actions. I'd been both types in my career. Sometimes, knowing your client is guilty can put a serious cramp in your style. An attorney is not allowed to suborn perjury. So, if I knew for sure a client had committed the crime with which he was charged, I couldn't allow him to take the stand and testify that he was innocent. I never asked those clients the ultimate question. I neither wanted them to lie to me, nor confess their guilt, and thus limit their own options. However, there had definitely been times, like this one, when I wanted to know the truth. Valerie was obviously of a different breed—she was a lawyer who was always convinced of her client's guilt, and thus never wanted to take the chance of hearing it spoken aloud.

"Walk away, Valerie," I said softly.

"Excuse me?" Her indignation was palpable.

"If you don't want to hear the answer to this question, just walk away."

"I will not! I'm going to call Mr. Wasserman as soon as I—"

"I didn't kill her," Jupiter interrupted, his voice firm and loud. "I loved her. I would never have hurt her."

The four of us sat silently for a moment, and then I leaned forward and put my hand on his arm. "I have just one more question, Jupiter. Did you and Chloe stay clean? Did you use again? Did she?"

He shot a quick glance at Valerie. "Yeah. Yeah, we stayed clean."

Jupiter Jones was a lousy liar.

Valerie and I didn't speak as we packed our bags, said goodbye to Jupiter, and waited for the guards to buzz us out of the visiting room. Al winked at me once, and I rolled my eyes in reply. Once we were finally out into the waiting area, I turned to Valerie to give her a piece of my mind, and the benefit of my greater experience, and found myself staring at her Dior-clad back as she raced to the bathroom. I followed her in—at least this way I could be sure she wouldn't be able to walk away from the dressing-down she was owed. I was just in time to hear her gagging in a stall. My own nausea hit me full force at that moment, and I banged open the door to the neighboring stall and leaned over the toilet, trying desperately to keep from actually touching anything while I lost what little remained in my stomach. God only knows what microbic horrors lurk in the bathroom in the county jail.

When I came out, I found her rinsing out her mouth with a travel-sized bottle of Scope. I blinked, impressed that there even existed a person who traveled so utterly prepared for such eventualities. She passed me the bottle, and I smiled, grateful for her unexpected generosity. And to think I'd been about to call her an insensitive fool.

"God, I hate this," she said.

"Me too. As my five-year-old would say, totally gross."

"So this isn't your first? I don't know why they call it morning sickness. It's more like all-day sickness. I'm only eight weeks pregnant and I swear I'm not going to make it. How far along are you?"

Pregnant? Was she crazy? I was most assuredly not pregnant. "I just ate some bad fish."

"Oh, sorry. I just assumed . . . not that you *look* pregnant or anything. I mean, you're not . . ." Her voice trailed off before she could say it. Fat.

I stared at myself in the mirror. I was a bit on the plump side, but surely I didn't look fat enough to be pregnant. Then, the question I'd been suppressing all day, the question I'd refused to allow Peter to ask, made its inevitable way to the front of my consciousness. Was I pregnant?

I wracked my brain, trying to remember the last time Peter and I had made love. With two kids, Peter's demanding job, and my pathetic attempts to build a career out of the rubble of carpool and playdates, our sex life wasn't as, well, vigorous as it used to be. Don't get me wrong, we still managed to find time to be together, it just wasn't as often, or as memorable, as in our preparenting salad days. Suddenly, I recalled a dinner at our favorite local Italian, a bottle of Chianti, and an empty package of condoms. "Congratulations," I said.

Valerie smiled and pressed a hand to her belly. "Thanks. I hope you feel better."

"I hope so, too," I said, and looked at myself in the mirror. Did my face look fleshier? Was I breaking out? Was my waist thicker? I surreptitiously pressed a hand against my breasts. Were they tender? I winced. Yes, they were. I felt my stomach seize up again, but this time not from nausea.

Five

"WE need a bigger house," I told Peter. We were in the kitchen, putting away the groceries.

"Why? The kids don't seem to mind sharing a room. *Eight* boxes of macaroni and cheese?"

I made a face. "I *hate* shopping with them. I always end up with a cart full of ridiculous junk." I brandished a bag of veggie chips. "You should see the crap I *refused* to buy."

"Worse than this?" Peter held up a package of Mango Mania yogurts, each equipped with a foil pack of orange and black Halloween sprinkles. "Just because it's yogurt doesn't mean it's healthy."

I threw a roll of paper towels at his head. "Give it a rest. If you don't like what I buy, you can do the shopping. And then *you* can try to convince the kids that carob-covered raisins count as a treat."

He smiled, but I wasn't having any of it.

"We need a bigger house," I said again, and left him with the rest of the unpacking. I went into the living room, where the kids were staring, slack-jawed, at the TV set, pulled Isaac onto my lap, and nuzzled his neck. He gave me an absent-minded kiss and dug his little feet into my thigh. I winced, and closed my eyes. I was just so tired. And I'd promised Al that we'd spend the afternoon interviewing witnesses on the Jones case. I'd bought the afternoon off from parenting duties by taking the kids with me on an early-morning grocery run, leaving Peter snoring under a mound of blankets. He didn't usually get to sleep late on Saturdays, so he owed me.

I dozed for a few moments, and then hoisted myself off the couch, tumbling Isaac onto the floor next to his sister.

"Mama?" he said.

"What, honey?"

"You're my best friend."

I tapped his behind with my toe. "Thanks, little guy. You're one of my three best friends, too."

"Me and Ruby and Daddy?"

"Ruby, Daddy, and *I*," his sister corrected him. My little grammarian. I once overheard her respond to a babysitter's request to take a nap, "I can *lie* down, but I can't *lay* down." I wonder why I could never get that sitter to come to our house again?

I shoved a notebook and a miniature tape recorder into my oversized, beat-up leather bag and slung it over my shoulder. "I'll be back before dinner," I called to Peter as I clomped down the stairs to my car.

"You forgot to buy coffee! Pick some up on your way home," he yelled after me and then, a moment later, "I love you!"

That's what it's like when you have two kids—the "I love yous" are all too often an afterthought. As I drove down the block, I punched my home number into the cell phone.

"Hey, honey?" I said when he answered.

"What?"

"Let's go on a date tonight. Can you call around and see if you can find a sitter?"

"Why? Is there something in particular you want to do?"

"Not really. I just want some one-on-one time with you. I miss you."

"I miss you, too. I'll get the sitter."

"I love you, Peter."

"I love you, too, babe."

Feeling like I'd done at least a little something to keep my marriage from turning into a business arrangement devoted solely to the raising of children, I headed across town to the freeway to Pasadena. Al and I had arranged to meet in front of Polaris Jones's house. Polaris had grudgingly agreed to talk to us, but only on Saturday, the one day he was neither working at the CCU offices nor preaching before the television cameras. The CCU had its own cable network, and they shot a week's worth of sermons every Sunday.

Miraculously, I'd left the house a little early, so I had enough time to pull into a Coffee Bean and Tea Leaf and pick up a pound of Peter's favorite Fair Trade Organic Blend. As I was heading back to my car, I passed a pharmacy, and paused. Was indulging my neurotic anxieties sufficient justification for wasting twenty bucks? I stood in the street and stared at the window display of a woman's slender thigh. The money would surely be better spent on magical cellulite disappearing cream. And why were they so expensive anyway? Because the world is full of apprehensive women like myself, who are willing to spend the money to assuage their nerves. Finally, I went inside and bought the pregnancy test I still couldn't quite believe I needed. Figuring that this probably wasn't going to be the last month in my life I would let myself be tortured by a false alarm, I bought the double pack.

I drove through San Marino's winding streets, flanked by high fences and intricate entrance gates, and wondered if every person who lived in this expensive and exclusive neighborhood had an income higher than the gross national product of most Central American nations. I found Al parked in front of Polaris's pale pink mound of a Mediterranean villa. He was leaning against the side of his four-door gas guzzler and staring up at the house. He'd slicked back his hair with the pomade he used on special occasions, and for special clients. The tracks of the comb were visible from where I sat in my car. I could swear I could already smell the cloying citrusy perfume. If he'd slathered on his usual Brut, I was definitely not going to be able to make it through the interview without losing my lunch.

"Is it a wedding cake, or is it a house?" I said when I'd parked my car and joined him. I inhaled, tentatively, and breathed a sigh of relief. Lemon hair gel, yes, but thankfully no miasma of cheap cologne.

"What do you figure? Three, four million? More?" Al said.

I shrugged. "I haven't any idea. The real estate market depresses the hell out of me."

"Why? You two buying a house?"

"Someday." We were going to have to if I really was pregnant. There was no way five of us could squeeze into our duplex apartment. But that was the last thing I wanted to tell Al. I wasn't even pulling my weight in our business now. I couldn't imagine what a terrible partner I'd make with a brand-new baby. I pushed the thought out of my mind. I wasn't pregnant. I couldn't be. I simply did not have the time.

We strolled to the front door along a path that meandered through what looked to be an acre or so of Japanese rock garden. Someone had raked swirling designs into the fine, white sand. I resisted the urge to trace my initials in between the stones.

Polaris Jones had, as Al later put it, lawyered up. In a big way. One of his blue-suited representatives greeted us at the door, and there were two more waiting for us in the solarium where the Very Reverend received us.

The sun poured through the walls of windows in the long, narrow room. Large, brightly painted Umbrian pots planted with ferns graced the four corners of the room, and rows of tubular and vaguely erotic orchids drooped along one wall. The man himself sat in a tall, white, wicker chair, wearing a caftan. It was long, white, and elaborately embroidered with sparkly blue thread. I'd never seen Polaris, either in the flesh or on television, but his picture regularly adorned the ubiquitous CCU billboards, and from what I could tell, the Jesus robes were a standard uniform. He had a high forehead with long, thinning hair, and his thick, black eyebrows looked like they should have met in the middle over his beak of a nose. I was sure he plucked them. He wore white leather Birkenstock sandals, and his long, manicured toenails were buffed to a shine. There were gold bands inset with tiny diamonds on the second toe of each foot. I had a hard time wrenching my eyes away from those pampered feet—the sight of the talon-nails was making me sick all over again. I just can't stand long toenails. Never have been able to. Polish them all you want, a long toenail is still a claw at the end of a calloused and horny foot.

In addition to the three lawyers he'd seen fit to have present at our interview, there were also two other men in the room, both of whom wore simpler versions of Polaris's robes. One had a groomed snow-white goatee, and the other was smooth-shaven. By the set of Al's jaw, I could tell that he was doing his damnedest not to smile.

We were offered drinks and I sipped gratefully at the sparkling water into which I'd squeezed a healthy squirt of lime. The tang of the fruit kept my nausea at bay. Al flipped open his notebook and nodded at me. I opened my mouth to ask Polaris how it was that he came to be married to his son's girlfriend, and suddenly I had an overwhelming need to pee. I excused myself, much to Al's disgust and the others' confusion, and headed out to the front hall. One of the caftan-clad assistants pointed me toward a small bathroom. I shut the door behind me and spun around, confused. There was a pedestal sink with gold fixtures and a white and gold armchair, but no toilet. After a few befuddled moments, I realized that the seat of the armchair cleverly concealed a commode. I unbuckled my pants and then glanced at my purse. It wouldn't take more than a minute, I convinced myself.

It took more flexibility than I had to keep from sprinkling all over my hand. There was just something strange about the angle of that throne toilet, and the ridiculous foot pedestal didn't help. It was absolutely not my fault that I ended up dropping the plastic wand into the toilet. So much for saving the second test for another month. This time I kept a viselike grip on the handle. A few minutes later, I was enthroned on the armchair, willing one of the two pink lines to disappear. How had this happened? Peter was so overworked and exhausted he could barely remember my name. How had he managed to knock me up?

Finally, I shook myself and got up. I couldn't spend the day in Polaris's bathroom, pondering my unplanned pregnancy. And I was pretty sure that if there were a private eye's handbook, it would strictly prohibit leaving intensely personal items strewn about an interviewee's bathroom. I had to get the pregnancy test out of the toilet. I'd become something of an expert in toilet extraction during Isaac's flushing phase. After successfully removing from my own toilet a plastic fire engine, my toothbrush, countless Barbie doll heads, a pair of socks, half an apple, six two-inch hussars in full battle dress, a Gundum, a spatula, a length of Hot Wheels track, and other things too numerous either to mention or recall, one wouldn't have thought that rolling up my sleeves and fishing around in Polaris's would have made me quite so sick.

I was a bit distracted, to say the least, when I returned to the solarium. I smiled apologetically at Al, and took my little tape recorder out of my bag.

"Lovely bathroom," I said. "You don't mind if I tape-record this, do you? I have the world's worst memory. Two kids." Three. Three kids, God help me.

One of the attorneys put a warning hand on Polaris's shoulder. "We'd prefer just to have a conversation at this point. Should we feel a more formal interview is in our client's interest, we will arrange that. With Mr. Wasserman, of course."

Of course. Not with us lowly investigators. I sighed and put the recorder away. I hoped Al could take better notes than I.

"I'd like to thank you, Mr. Jones—" I began.

"Very Reverend," the smooth-shaven CCU aide interrupted. I turned to look at him and he bobbled his head up and down. Then he beamed an unctuous smile at his boss.

"The proper title is 'Very Reverend,'" he said. Polaris inclined his head in a gracious nod. Proper? Why wasn't I surprised that these men in their bathrobes had an elaborate etiquette with which they expected us to comply?

"Right. Reverend Jones."

"Polaris," the aide said, his moon-face still creased in the beatific smile.

"Excuse me?"

"*Very* Reverend *Polaris*," he said.

"Oh, okay." I could hear the snort of disgust that Al was having a hard time suppressing. "Thank you, Very Reverend Polaris, for taking the time to speak to us. We'd like to extend our sympathies to you, both for your wife's tragic murder, and for your son's status as a suspect in the case." Polaris nodded regally. He had yet to say a word. "As your attorneys no doubt advised you, we have been engaged by your son's attorney, Raoul Wasserman, to investigate the case, and Jupiter's life, to determine if there are any factors in his situation, his background, that might mitigate against the imposition of the death penalty." I guess I tend to become a bit stiff when confronted with priests in toe rings and bathrobes. While I explained our job to the man, I tried to get a read on him. He sat very still, gazing at a point somewhere above my head, as though his concerns lay on a more ethereal plane. Or perhaps I was being ungenerous. He had, after all, lost his wife and, effectively, his son in a particularly horrific and gruesome manner. "Do I understand correctly that you have not yet decided whether you will support the imposition of the death penalty in the event that your son is found guilty of the crime?" I asked.

Polaris wrenched his eyes away from the ceiling as though the effort was almost too much for him. "My son is most assuredly guilty of murdering my wife," he said sternly and sonorously. I couldn't help but stare at him, startled. His tone of voice may have rung of a very reverend something or other, but his pronunciation was pure Brighton Beach. I hadn't heard a Brooklyn accent that thick since the afternoon bridge game at my Bubbe's retirement home. "As far as the death penalty goes . . ." His voice trailed off, and he shrugged his shoulders.

I waited for him to continue, trying to assimilate the idea of a Brooklyn-born leader of a New Age religious cult, but the moon-faced minion spoke up instead. "It is not the role of terrestrial beings to determine when another's time on this plane shall pass; only our astral guides may decide such things," he said, and then grew silent under Polaris's glance.

The other robed aide took over for his less circumspect colleague. "But clearly there are extenuating circumstances here."

The attorneys, obviously not eager to have Al and me witness the rift in the CCU leadership, requested that I limit my questions to Jupiter's life and relationship with his father. That was fine with me. I didn't really care whether or not the CCU opposed or supported the death penalty. My only concern was with acquiring enough information of Jupiter's background, life, and personality to allow Wasserman to make an effective mitigation argument. I decided to save my questions about the love triangle between Jupiter, his father, and Chloe for later, and asked Polaris to talk to me about Jupiter's childhood.

"If you seek to comprehend the path my son chose, and the reasons for his personal catastrophes and for the horror he has inflicted on me, you need look no further than his mother," Polaris said, the formality of his diction contrasting oddly with his Brooklyn accent. His voice was Harvard and Yale, filtered through Flatbush Yeshiva. And yet, strangely, there was something soothing about it—it was neither harsh nor discordant.

Jupiter's mother was, according to Polaris, responsible for her son's behavior, his drug use, for everything up to and including the murder of his stepmother. "I should have sought refuge from that wretched woman the first time I found her sleeping on the floor of my house in Topanga," he said.

"Topanga?"

He shrugged his shoulders. "My search for enlightenment

took me many places." Topanga Canyon is a strip of road that winds through the Santa Monica mountains from the Valley, and spills out to the Pacific a little north of Malibu. During the 1960s and into the seventies, Topanga was a psychedelic paradise. Women, naked under flimsy gauze gowns, nursed infants in the parking lot of the grocery store; bearded men directed traffic according to a soundtrack playing in their own heads; and communes raised marijuana as a cash crop, although most tended to smoke up any profits before they were realized.

"What were you doing there?" I asked.

"Very Reverend Polaris's activities are hardly relevant to your inquiries regarding his son," one of the lawyers said.

I could have argued that they were, in fact, very relevant, but we all knew that Al and I were there on sufferance—Polaris wasn't required to talk to us at all. If he wasn't willing to answer questions about his life, there wasn't anything I could do to make him.

"Was Jupiter born while you and his mother were living in Topanga?" I asked.

Polaris turned to look directly at me, for what I suddenly realized was the first time. His eyes were dark and piercing. He merely nodded his head, but under his gaze, I began to grow conscious of a subtle force to his personality. Even in the face of his incongruous accent and the robes, toe rings, and vaguely astrological trappings of his cult, Polaris had a kind of magnetism. When he looked at me, I had the eerie but not entirely unpleasant feeling that he was looking inside me. That he could *see* inside me. I'd never felt anything quite like it before. I not only felt like I was the absolute focus of his attention, but I felt compelled to make him the focus of my own.

I shook off the sensation, reminding myself that I was here to do an investigation, not be converted to a crackpot religion, and continued with my questions. "What was it about his mother that explains his . . . his actions? Was she unusual in some way?"

"Unusual?" He smiled thinly, and looked back up at the

ceiling. I was relieved to be out from under his stare. "It isn't particularly unusual, but Roberta was an acid freak of the highest order. In fact, it was as close as she came to a vocation." Given the formality of his normal speech, his use of slang was jarring, an effect that was not, I thought, unintentional. But whatever his purpose, he had given us useful information. If Jupiter had any lingering effects of his mother's drug use, we might be able to argue that he was as much a victim as a victimizer, and deserved some kind of leniency.

I glanced over at Al, who was scribbling away in his notebook, his mouth a thin line. My partner does not approve of drug use of any kind, other than alcohol. He considers it a sign of weakness. In fact, "pothead" has always been one of his favorite insults. On the other hand, he is violently opposed to the criminalization of drugs. Al's a staunch libertarian, and can't abide anything that smacks of big government trying to tell people what to do with their lives. He feels nothing but disgust for politicians, the media, and folks that don't get that a gun is man's best friend, and that people have a right to be as ignorant and stupid as they want to be. He manages to overcome his abhorrence when it comes to me, though. Don't get me wrong, he doesn't hide his contempt for my lily-livered liberalism—he just likes me anyway. Maybe he figures that he'll convert me, and one day I, too, will end up a pistol-packing libertarian.

"Was Jupiter ever evaluated for brain damage or anything else stemming from his mother's drug use?" I asked.

Polaris held me once more in the beams of his altogether too acute eyes. It was downright disconcerting. "My son is a remarkably intelligent young man. A genius, if you will. His Stanford-Binet score is well over 170. It's his soul that's damaged, not his brain."

So much for that. I made a note to myself to do some research on the effects of prenatal drug exposure on emotional development. Maybe I'd find something useful. It wouldn't hurt to have Jupiter evaluated in any case.

"Do I understand that you were never married to Jupiter's mother?" I asked Polaris.

He laughed, and it was strictly Brooklyn. A loud bray of mirth. "Hell no," he said, and his robed attendants winced.

"But you had a child together?"

He nodded and flicked a finger at the pious attendant, who rushed off. I raised my eyebrows at his departing back, but no one bothered to tell me where he'd gone. "Roberta and I had a brief fling, and Jupiter was the outcome. I probably wouldn't even remember the woman's name if it hadn't been for the fact that she gave birth to Jupiter nine months after we had sex."

I didn't know how to phrase this delicately, so I decided not to bother trying. "Are you sure that Jupiter is your son?"

He nodded, and sighed. "I took a paternity test when the boy was a baby, and then again in the late 1970s when they invented the white blood cell antigen test. It was state of the art, back then. They both came out positive. I wanted to check again about fifteen years ago, when they began using the DNA test, just to be sure, but Jupiter would have none of it. He was over eighteen by then, and I couldn't force him. Perhaps," Polaris said, turning to his lawyers, "we can resolve that issue now, while he's in custody."

"If you like, I can speak to the prosecutor about it," the older attorney responded, and then glanced meaningfully in my direction. "I think we should discuss this later, in private."

Polaris nodded. "Let's."

"I understand that Jupiter grew up with you," I said.

At that moment, the man who had left the room at Polaris's signal came rushing back. He carried a small wooden tray with an iron teapot and a single miniature, black teacup.

"Thank you, Aldebaran," Polaris said. The assistant poured a cup of tea and handed it to Polaris.

"Do you drink green tea?" the Very Reverend asked me.

"Sometimes," I said. My old trainer Bobby Katz had been a big green tea drinker.

"It's a tonic with remarkable curative powers; brought to us from the heavens. Studies have found it to be effective at reducing incidences of cancers. It's also quite soothing. I recommend it."

I could certainly stand a little soothing, although I'd always thought that tea grew on bushes, rather than dropping from the sky. "I'll give it a try," I said. "We were talking about Jupiter, how he grew up with you, rather than with his mother."

"Roberta abandoned the boy. That and her weak genetic legacy are surely what have made him what he is. She left for India when my son was an infant. Some kind of pilgrimage, she said, although I imagine she was seeking mind alteration rather than transcendence. She never returned. Or perhaps she did, but not to her child. I remember someone saying that she became the third or fourth wife of a Saudi Arabian oil sheik, but that might just be a rumor." He sipped his tea and frowned. "Aldebaran, if the tea steeps for any more than forty-five seconds, it takes on a rather unpleasant, bitter flavor, as you know."

"I'm so sorry, Very Reverend Polaris. Shall I make you a new pot?" Aldebaran asked, his lips pursed in concern.

"It's fine. I'll drink this. Just remember next time." Polaris smiled gently at the man, who blushed, and then slowly smiled back, his face transformed with something that looked almost like rapture.

"Of course, of course I will." If he had bowed and scraped any lower, he would have gotten rug burn on his chin.

"So Jupiter lived with you?" I continued.

"Yes."

"And where was this? In Topanga?"

"In the commune in Topanga for a while. And then in Mexico."

"Mexico?" I said, pretending I knew nothing about their time there.

"Yes. After Roberta made her great escape, I met a girl at the commune. A very lovely girl." His voice grew soft and I could swear his eyes were misty. "*This* girl I married—as soon as she would have me. We moved together to Mexico."

"Why did you move to Mexico?"

He laughed. "Why not? We were free spirits. We went where the wind blew us. A group of people were heading down to San Miguel de Allende and we decided to join them."

"And you took Jupiter?"

"Of course. And Trudy-Ann's little girl, Lilly."

"The four of you moved down to Mexico," I prodded him.

"Yes. San Miguel is a remarkable place. A true spiritual nexus." He seemed to enjoy his recollections, was almost lost in them. "We lived in a massive old colonial mansion that we rented for no more than a hundred dollars a month. You know, *Chloe* would have loved it. I've never really thought of that before. She was a true aficionado of Mexican art and furniture. She was a woman with brilliant taste, was my young wife." He waved his hand around the room. "She designed this room herself."

I glanced at the sun-filled room and murmured appreciatively. I admire anyone who can keep a single houseplant green, not to mention an entire solarium. I can't even keep a dozen roses alive long enough to get to a vase.

"Yes, Chloe would certainly have adored San Miguel," he said. "Those days of youthful freedom, of exploration and irresponsibility." He smiled at the robed assistant with the beard. The man smiled back and raised his eyebrows.

Polaris turned back to me. "We were very young, Trudy-Ann and I. We lived on the occasional check from our parents, and that was enough to meet our simple needs and pay our bar tab at La Cucaracha, the local bar. Don Chucho, the owner of the bar, was the first person to know when the checks from home made it to the post office. It was quite a scene in those days. Everyone made it to San Miguel, and to the Cuc, sooner or later."

"Everyone?" I said.

He looked at me, and for some reason I blushed. I had no idea why. What *was* it about this man? "Everyone. The Beats were regulars. Neal Cassady died there after a particularly inebriated night. Back in 1968, before we arrived, the entire cast of the musical *Hair* had their heads shaved by the local police. I'm not sure why, but the story was famous."

"And Jupiter? What did he and his stepsister . . ." I made a show of looking through my notes for her name. ". . . Lilly, do in San Miguel? Did they go to school?"

He shrugged. "The children were too young for school. Jupiter wasn't more than two when we got down there, and Lilly was perhaps a couple of years older. They amused themselves at the house. It was, I think, rather a bucolic life."

I tried to imagine my kids, Ruby and Isaac, having fun hanging out with a bunch of random grown-ups while Peter and I drank with Neal Cassady and the cast of *Hair*. I couldn't. And I couldn't imagine Jupiter and Lilly as children enjoying themselves, either. I've always found children to be somewhat less liberal in their views than your basic snake-handling Baptist minister. Children like order. They like routines. They like to be and do exactly what everyone else is and does, and they expect their parents to live up to some imagined ideal of domesticated mundanity. Every once in a while, when I manage to put on a skirt instead of my usual jeans, you should see Ruby's face. She smiles so hard it hurts my own cheeks to look at her, and she employs positive reinforcement. It's really quite humiliating. "Look at how nicely you're dressed, Mama. You look lovely." Once, she even told me that I looked like "a real woman." According to my three-and-a-half-foot-tall arbiter of gender classification, a pair of overalls does not a female make.

"When did you return to the States?" I asked.

"We stayed just a little over a year. Jupiter must have been about three or four when we returned."

"And why did you come back?" I asked. At that moment the rustling of the bearded assistant's robes caught my eye. I glanced over at him. He was sitting quite still, his face wiped clear of any expression.

Polaris looked down at his hands and carefully adjusted his thick gold ring so that its flashy diamond rested in the dead center of his finger. "We came home after Trudy-Ann transitioned," he said, his voice much softer than it had been before.

"Transitioned?"

"Died," the bearded assistant interrupted.

"How did she die?" Al asked. It was the first time he'd opened his mouth in quite a while and everyone in the room turned to look at him. He looked up from his notebook and raised his eyebrows, waiting for a response.

"There was an accident," Polaris said.

"What kind of an accident? A car accident?" I said.

He didn't answer for a moment. Then he said, "Something like that." He glanced over at the sundial in the middle of the room. I knew he couldn't possibly have read it. "It's getting late," he said. "I'm afraid I've got things I must get done today." He looked over at his lawyers, and they jumped to attention.

"We've barely touched on Jupiter's life," I said before they could end the interview. "I'm going to need information about his medical history, his psychological history. How he did in school. What problems, if any, he had before this unfortunate event. I'm going to want to talk about his drug use, his recovery. And of course, we need to discuss his and your relationships with Chloe. All that information is critical to preparing for the penalty phase of Jupiter's trial."

Polaris shot a glance in the direction of his lawyers. The one who had spoken up earlier said, "I'll prepare a list of physicians, therapists, teachers, and friends for you. You can contact those individuals, and after you've done so, if you feel another meeting is necessary, we can consider the possibility."

"No one knows Jupiter as well as his father," I said. "The Reverend is likely to have all sorts of information that those other individuals do not."

The attorney snapped his briefcase shut and rose to his feet. "Then you can put your questions in writing, and submit them to me. I'll communicate the *Very* Reverend Polaris's responses to you. Good day."

With that, Aldebaran and the other robed man began hustling Al and me out the door. I shook my arm free and extended my hand to Polaris. "I'm very sorry for your loss, Very Reverend Polaris. I hope we haven't offended you in any way. You understand that our job is to help your son, don't you?"

He stared at me for a moment, and then smiled bitterly. "You'll forgive me if I don't wish you success in your endeavors," he said.

six

"'SOMETHING like that'? What kind of an answer is that? Either she died in a car accident or she didn't," I said.

"Yup," Al said. He was sitting in the driver's seat of his car, drumming his fingertips against the steering wheel. I stood outside his window, and peered up into his face. Al's Suburban sported oversized truck wheels, and since I'm about five feet tall, my head barely grazed the bottom of the window.

"What do you think?" I said.

"I think we'd better find out how ol' Trudy-Ann kicked."

"Al," I said. "Jesus. Lilly's my *friend*, remember? You're talking about her dead mother."

"Yeah, well, I'd like to know how her mother got that way."

"Any ideas how to investigate a death that happened thirty years ago, in Mexico?"

He shrugged. "Hell if I know."

"I'll talk to Lilly. See what she knows."

"Good idea. What's with you and the Rev, by the way?"

"What?"

"Five more minutes in that house and you would have been getting fitted for your own white robe."

"What are you talking about?" I said, feigning an anger I knew was unreasonable. There was just something about Polaris.

"You couldn't keep your eyes off the funny-looking little guy."

"That's ridiculous!"

"Is it?"

I opened my mouth to insist on my innocence, but then sighed. "Didn't you feel it? He's . . . I don't know . . . compelling."

Al shrugged. "I'm pretty immune to that kind of thing. Maybe it's because I'm a man."

I frowned. "No, it's not sexual. At all. He's just . . . he's just hard not to look at. When he looks at you, that is." I shook my head, frustrated at my inability to pinpoint the exact nature of the man's appeal. "Anyway. I'm thinking our next step needs to be the rehab center. We'll get information on Jupiter's drug habit. How hard he worked to kick it. That kind of thing. I'll bet there's at least one shrink at the center who can testify on his behalf."

"Yeah, that's what I was thinking," Al said. "When can you head up to the Ojai Self-Absorption Center? Monday?"

"The Ojai Rehabilitation and Self-Actualization Center. Yeah, Monday, I guess. I'll leave a message for the director letting him know we're coming. We can get on the road as soon as I drop off the kids."

Suddenly, I remembered what I'd found out sitting on Polaris's throne. I didn't say anything, though. I wasn't ready to believe it myself, let alone tell my partner. I could only imagine what a pregnancy was going to do to my productivity, such as it was. And when the baby came, well, I'd be completely useless to Al. It was just so frustrating. Here I was, beginning to get something of a life back for myself, and this happened.

After Al left, I sat behind the wheel of my car for a few moments, debating whether I wanted to take the coward's way out and tell my husband over the telephone, or if I should go home and make my announcement in person. I felt the saliva gather in the corners of my mouth. I opened the car door, leaned out, and threw up on the elegantly appointed streets of San Marino. Nice. First I had to go up to my elbow in Polaris's toilet; now I was either going to have to find a hose somewhere, or leave a delightful little calling card on his curb. My cell phone rang as I was wiping the sweat from my forehead.

"Don't come home!" Peter said as soon as I answered the phone.

"Why not?"

"Because I found a babysitter, but her mother won't let her stay out past eight. Meet me at Off Vine in half an hour."

"Who's the sitter?"

"Bethany, from next door."

"Peter! Bethany's like twelve years old!"

"No she's not. She just turned fourteen. And you should see her—she's grown up a *lot* in the past couple of months. She looks like Pamela Anderson."

Was *that* what he was doing while I was driving carpool? Scoping out the local teenage girls? "I missed the section in T. Berry Brazelton where he says that you should judge a babysitter by her breast size."

"Juliet, give me a break. She's *fine*. Her mom is right next door. Just get your butt over to the restaurant. We haven't had an evening without the kids in I don't know *how* long. Let's have some fun, dammit."

Oh well. A cute little restaurant in a renovated cottage in Hollywood was as good a place as any to tell my husband that our lives were in for a drastic upheaval. Again. I slammed my car door, determinedly not looking at the mess I'd made in front of Polaris's house. It's biodegradable, after all.

On my way across town, I called Lilly. Her assistant patched me through to her cell phone.

"Hi, Juliet!" she shouted over the sound of traffic. Her freeway was moving faster than mine.

"Hi. Listen. I hate to ask you this over the telephone, but do you mind telling me how your mother died?" There was only the sound of cars on her end, the hiss of a cellular connection. "Lilly? Are you still on the line?"

"Yes," she said. "There was an accident."

We already knew that. Why, I wondered, had Lilly used precisely the same inexact words to describe her mother's death as had her stepfather? "What *kind* of an accident?" Again the only sound in my ear was the hum of traffic. "Lilly?"

"I'm still here. Juliet, I'm sorry. I can't talk to you about this. It's too . . . too traumatic."

"But—"

"No. No, I can't." And she hung up.

As I drove the rest of the way to the restaurant, I pondered Lilly and Polaris's unwillingness to talk about Lilly's mother's death. Something had happened in Mexico, but what? And could it possibly have anything to do with Chloe Jones's murder? But I had my own problems to worry about, and I pushed thoughts of Lilly's mother out of my mind. I made it to Off Vine before Peter, and sat down at a table on the front porch under the heat lamps, nervously eating my weight in bread. I smeared inch-thick layers of butter on the crusty rolls—For the calcium! Really!—and looked around the empty restaurant. Apparently, Peter and I were the only two people in Los Angeles uncool enough to be dining out at 5:30 P.M. I glumly counted off how many years it would be before we didn't have to rely on a babysitter to go out for the evening. By then we'd be old enough to qualify for the early-bird special, and would still be eating dinner while it was light out.

When I saw Peter's vintage orange BMW 2002 pull up to the valet stand, I took the pregnancy test out of my purse and put in on his plate.

He bounded up the stairs and gave me a kiss. "Date night!" he said happily, and squeezed me around the middle. I smiled despite my trepidation and squeezed him back. He plopped down in his seat and reached for his glass of water. The smile disappeared from his face when he glanced down at his plate.

"Surprise," I said softly, trying to smile. I couldn't read the expression in his gray eyes. He didn't speak.

"Kind of a shock, huh?" I asked.

He nodded slightly and gingerly picked up the pregnancy test. "On my plate?"

"Excuse me?"

"You put it on my plate." He handed it to me. "It's, like, full of pee."

"Eew. Right. Sorry," I said, and stuck the test back in my purse.

"You're going to save it?" he said.

"I saved both of the others."

"Huh."

"What does that mean? Huh?"

"Nothing. Just huh."

My eyes got hot and prickly, and I could tell I was about to cry. "So I take it this isn't good news."

"No, no. It's not that. It's just . . . it's just a surprise." He rubbed at his jaw and exhaled loudly.

"No kidding." I tore off another hunk of roll and spread the butter with short, angry jerks of my knife.

"It's just that I kind of thought you had to have sex to get pregnant," he said.

I glared at him. "What's that supposed to mean?"

He smiled weakly. "Nothing, I mean, we're not exactly doing it all the time."

"Yeah, well, we're obviously doing it enough." I snatched up my menu and pretended to read it.

"C'mon, sweetie," he said.

I ignored him and studied my menu. "What the hell is a cardoon? And why is it on every damn menu in the city?"

"Juliet. Honey. Look at me."

I didn't.

Suddenly, he got up and walked around the table. He

kneeled down next to my seat and took me into his arms. I stiffened, not yet ready to forgive him for feeling the same ambivalence I did. But after a moment, I leaned into his chest and buried my face in the folds of the old flannel shirt he hadn't bothered to change out of. Then I started to cry.

"Aren't you happy?" he said. "I'm happy. Let's be happy about this, okay?"

"You are *not* happy," I wailed. If there had been another living soul in the restaurant, they would have stared at me.

Peter smoothed my hair out of my streaming eyes and kissed me. "I am. Really. It was just kind of a shock. But I'm happy. Definitely. Are you happy?"

"I don't know," I said, wiping my nose on his shoulder. "Didn't you sleep in this shirt?"

Peter and I agreed to wait until we were sure the pregnancy was going to stick before we told the kids. He tried to convince me that the secret should be kept from everyone else, too, but he knew that was a lost cause even as he made the argument. I'm just not constitutionally capable of keeping my mouth shut about something like that. I'm fully aware of the ludicrous irony of a private investigator who can't keep a secret. But to give myself a little credit, I've never violated a client's confidence. It's really only the intimate details of my own life about which I'm embarrassingly indiscreet. My poor long-suffering husband found out about my little problem the hard way. We had been dating only a few weeks when Stacy came to New York on business. One of her clients was performing in a spectacularly bad play off Broadway (Models turned actresses should never, I mean *never*, attempt Strindberg. I think that's actually a federal law, and if it's not, it should be.), and Stacy had begged us to come to a performance. She took us out for dinner afterwards to thank us for being the only people in the theater who hadn't rushed the exits at the intermission. Over dessert she congratulated Peter on his sexual prowess. I believe her exact words were, "Juliet says you're the best lover she's ever had." First he turned red, and then green, and then kicked me under the table.

"Oh, honey," Stacy had said to my blushing boyfriend, "get used to it. Juliet and I tell each other everything. And I mean, everything."

I think for a while Peter deluded himself into thinking that it was just Stacy, my best friend, who was privy to all my most intimate secrets, but when he came upon me comparing severity of menstrual cramps with a woman standing in front of me in line at the health food store (she introduced me to red raspberry leaf tea, a truly miraculous substance), he had finally to confront the ugly truth. I can't keep my mouth shut. He knew before he even suggested the opposite that I was going to tell all my girlfriends, and my mother, that I was pregnant.

"But what if you have a miscarriage? Are you really going to want to have to call everyone and tell them that you're not pregnant after all?"

"How long have you known me?" I asked my husband. "If I have a miscarriage, I'm going to be on the phone crying to every single one of my friends anyway. You can't get emotional support unless you let people into your life."

He raised his hands in a gesture of defeat. "But not Ruby or Isaac, right?"

"Of course not," I said, and wondered exactly how long it was going to be before I slipped up and mentioned it in front of them. Wasn't Ruby bound to ask why it was that I was spending so much time in the bathroom, throwing up?

Seven

THE next morning, Al and I met in the parking lot of Isaac's preschool. We were heading almost two hours north of the city, to Ojai, and I was running late. When Al pulled up, I was still trying to wrestle my son's shoes onto his feet.

"Problem?" Al asked, jumping down from his truck.

"No," I said, gritting my teeth and shoving a squirming foot into a Hot Wheels sneaker.

"Wrong foot, Juliet," Al said.

I shook my head and scowled at him. "I know that." I crammed the foot into the shoe and tugged the Velcro strap tight.

"It hurts!" bellowed my son.

"Well, of course it hurts," Al said. "It's the wrong foot."

I grabbed Isaac's Barbie lunchbox, a hand-me-down from his sister that he, for some reason, adored, and opened my arms to my son. "Jump up, buddy," I said.

"The kid's shoes are on the wrong feet, Juliet," Al insisted again.

I held up Isaac's legs and waggled them at Al. "No, only one of them is. He's wearing two left shoes."

Al laughed and shook his head in disgust. "You let your kid out of the house with two left shoes?"

I made a face. "No, of course not. I told him to go get sneakers. And he did. He got one Hot Wheels sneaker and one Thomas the Tank Engine sneaker. Left ones."

"And you didn't *notice*?" I knew what he was thinking. *Jeanelle* would never have made such a mistake. When his girls were small, Jeanelle always made sure that they had the right shoes, and the right clothes, and the right weaponry for any situation.

I shrugged. "Ruby was having a freak-out about her hair. I braided it *wrong*. Again. Because, apparently, I am the worst mother in the kindergarten. Or maybe in the history of kindergartens altogether. Anyway, by the time she stopped screaming, I was grateful just to get out the door. I didn't notice his shoes until just this minute."

"I don't *want* to wear two left shoes," Isaac wailed. I kissed his round cheek, the only part of him that still retained that baby softness.

"Stop crying, honey. We'll check and see if the teachers have a pair of shoes you can borrow for the day."

By the time I got back from signing Isaac in, putting his lunch in his cubby, and helping him put on a pair of chartreuse Chinese sandals embroidered with lotuses, Al was back in his car with the engine running.

"Let's get a move on," he said, "or we won't have time to hit La Superica in Santa Barbara for tacos after we finish interviewing the docs."

One of my favorite things about Al is his encyclopedic knowledge of every taco stand, noodle shop, mom-and-pop burger joint, and date shake shack in Southern California. The man lives and dies for junk food, but only of the most obscure kind. If there are absolutely no other options, he'll make do with an In-n-Out Double Double, animal-style, but he's only truly happy standing at the counter of a Vietnamese dive in a strip mall in East L.A., say, slurping Pho out of a plastic bowl. When we had worked together at the Federal Public Defenders Office, we had always planned our field investigations around lunch. We'd take pictures of the interior of the bank our client was accused of robbing, interview a teller or two, and then drive back to the office, our chins shiny with the grease of a Cuban *medianoche.* I should have known Al would have planned to hit the best taco stand in Southern California. Too bad it was a cool hour out of our way.

On our way we discussed Lilly's reaction to my question about her mother's death.

"Definitely strange," he said. "But can it possibly be related to the murder?" Then he yelled an obscenity at a passing car. "Did you see that idiot?"

"Who? The eighty-year-old woman in the diesel Mercedes? Yeah, I saw her."

"The old bat's going to kill someone, creeping along like that in the fast line!"

"She was doing the speed limit, Al. Maybe Lilly's mother's death has nothing to do with anything, but you're the one who always says there is no such thing as coincidences in criminal investigations. We've got a murder, and another suspicious death thirty years ago. It's certainly possible that they're related, don't you think?"

He shook his fist at another car, and then said, "How did you go from an accident that Lilly doesn't want to talk about to a suspicious death?"

"It's suspicious that no one wants to talk about it. And will you please *stop* giving people the finger! Haven't you ever heard of highway shootings? Are you trying to get me killed here?"

He rolled his eyes. "Let's worry first about what we're being paid to worry about, okay? We'll work on gathering the mitigation evidence. Then, if we've got time, we'll follow up on the Mexico thing."

I acquiesced, albeit a bit unwillingly, and sank down in my seat so that I could not be visible to enraged drivers responding to Al's vigorously expressive highway maneuvers.

The Ojai Rehabilitation and Self-Actualization Center was located in the hills above the town for which it was named, a farming community that had over the years become something of an artists' colony. Al and I wound our way through the little streets, passing signs for open studios and gallery openings, and fresh farmer's cheese. Much to Al's chagrin, I broke the hermetic seal of his air-conditioned SUV and rolled down my window as we drove up a long road through rolling hills of brown grasses and scrub oaks. I took a deep breath, inhaling air redolent with dried brush, cow manure, and surprisingly, given how far inland we were, the faint tang of salt and sea.

A wooden sign so discreet that we almost missed it pointed us to an electronic gate that guarded the entrance to the center. Al pulled up to the gate and leaned precariously out of his window to reach the microphone.

"Lucky you've got that gut to provide ballast," I told my partner. "Otherwise you'd fall head first out the window."

He grunted and hauled himself back in the car. "Very funny. The director's waiting for us in the main building."

The gate slid silently open. We drove through and continued for another half a mile or so along a road of crushed gravel, bright white, shaded on either side with feathery cottonwood trees. Beyond the trees, paths wound through gardens planted with cacti and succulents. The grounds were dotted with people sitting on redwood benches, faces raised to the sun. One woman swung lazily on a wooden swing that dangled from the limb of a tall oak. The road ended in a circular driveway, before a ranch house, its thick stucco walls painted terracotta, with brilliant purple and red bougainvillea spilling down from its roof. Huge pots of brightly colored Mexican pottery bursting with geraniums and nasturtiums flanked the massive oak doors, which were propped open to catch the breeze. An orange cat lay in the doorway in a patch of sun.

"Nice place," Al said as he pulled into a parking space next to the building.

"It's a long way from the crack house," I said. I couldn't help thinking of all the drug rehab centers where I'd visited clients over the years, of the grimness of those facilities, made even more apparent by their pitiable attempts at cheerfulness—barred windows hidden behind bright polyester curtains, narrow cots covered with children's bedspreads that might once have been cute but had long since grown pilly and faded from years of institutional laundries. Their grounds, if they had any, weren't rolling meadows sprinkled with swings and benches, but cracked asphalt yards, with patches of garden tended by the patients themselves, one of the many chores they were required to do. Although all that gardening and cleaning was supposed to be therapeutic, I could never discount the suspicion that it had more to do with limited maintenance budgets. I jumped down from the truck and looked around, squinting against the glare of the sun reflected off the glistening white gravel.

"Why do I think it might be a lot easier to kick a drug habit here, than in one of the county-run dumps our clients always ended up in?" Al said.

"I don't know," I said. "I mean, what happens if you get clean and sober? They make you go home! I'd keep shooting up, just to stay here for as long as possible."

Inside, the building was delightfully cool. The walls were decorated with imitation Gaughins and Diego Riveras. At least I *hoped* they were fakes. I peered at the lower corner of a portrait of a bare-breasted woman in a grass skirt. There was no signature that I could see, and I breathed a sigh of relief. That really would have been too much.

"May I help you?" a soft voice said, and I turned to find a young woman standing next to Al. She had long blond hair tucked behind ears that stood straight out from her head. She was standing with her back to the sun, and it shone through her ears, lighting them up like little pink lanterns—almost the same pink as her cashmere sweater. She smiled pleasantly.

"We have an appointment with Dr. Blackmore," Al said.

"Of course. Mr. Hockey and Ms. Applebaum?" We nodded. "I'm Dr. Blackmore's assistant, Molly Weston." We shook hands. "He's waiting for you out on the terrace."

We followed her through the lobby, kind of a mock living room with overstuffed chairs, built-in bookshelves overflowing with fat paperbacks, and a massive stone fireplace. There was a teenage boy sprawled on the rug in front of the fireplace, his head pillowed on a book, and a number of other people sitting in small groups around the room, chatting or reading. They all looked vaguely disheveled, as if they had just woken from a nap, or hadn't taken the time to look in the mirror when they got dressed. They seemed either too thin, gaunt and twitchy, or like they'd grown fat on a diet of donuts and French fries. A few glanced up as we passed, and I smiled a greeting. Only one person smiled back, a man of about thirty, with long tangled hair and a patchy beard. He looked familiar to me, and I wondered if we'd gone to college together. It was a moment before I remembered where I'd seen his face—on the cover of a CD Peter had played incessantly for a month or two a couple of years ago. My expression must have betrayed my dawning recognition, because he winked and shrugged ruefully before turning back to his book.

Reese Blackmore was sitting at a wrought iron table on a flagstone terrace that overlooked a swimming pool. He had the most beautiful hair that I'd ever seen, chalk-white, worn long, brushing his collar. It shone in the sunlight, and his skin glowed with the kind of even, honey-brown suntan acquired only under the blue lights of a tanning booth.

"Can I offer you something to drink?" the doctor asked once we'd joined him at the table. "Some tea? A soymilk chai latte?"

"I'll have a coffee. Black," Al said.

"Ms. Applebaum?" Molly invited.

"I'll try the chai latte. But do you have milk milk? Cow milk?"

"Nonfat?"

Was that a comment on the baby fat I was already packing on?

"That would be fine. Dr. Blackmore," I began.

"Please. Reese," he said, his voice as smooth and even as his skin.

"Reese. Did you receive Jupiter Jones's waiver of confidentiality that I faxed this morning?" We had asked Jupiter to sign a paper indicating that his doctors had permission to speak to us, as members of his defense team, about his medical history. Otherwise, doctor-patient confidentiality would have precluded any conversation.

"Yes. Yes I did. How is Jupiter? I've been *sick* at the thought of him in jail. He's not the kind of person who can defend himself very well."

I nodded. "He's having a hard time. But his attorney is doing what he can to get him out." I explained our role to the doctor, and asked him if he could begin by telling us a little bit about his facility, and how Jupiter had come to be a patient there.

"First of all, we don't call them patients. They are residents, or clients. While the center is, of course, a medical facility in that its mission is to treat the disease of addiction, we like to view this as more of a retreat, a place for wounded individuals to come, rest, and do their work of healing surrounded by others engaged in the same endeavor. Our system is based on group therapy, group motivation. Every resident is both a patient working on his or her own disease and, in a very real sense, a therapist helping the other residents in their struggles."

I delicately and gently stomped on Al's foot to stifle the groan of disgust I knew the doctor's speech would produce in my partner. Al doesn't have a lot of patience with "wounded individuals" unless those wounds bleed and can be bandaged with actual gauze.

"The center is lovely," I said.

"Being surrounded by natural beauty helps our residents. At first many of them don't even notice the surroundings. And then, after a while, their work progresses, and they become able to focus on something other than their desperate need to alter their consciousnesses. That's when they begin to take note of the environment, to allow its beauty to give them pleasure, even a kind of natural high of its own."

"Swell," Al said, and I hoped I could hear the disdain in his voice only because I knew him so well, not because it was so obvious. I didn't share it. Sure, the doctor was slick enough to have spilled from the hold of the *Exxon Valdez,* but what he was saying made sense to me. When I was a public defender, almost all of my clients had been drug users. Their entire lives were structured around the next high—where they were going to get it, how they would come up with the money. They didn't commit crimes under the influence of drugs; they committed crimes in order to *get* under the influence. I had often wondered what would have happened if we just gave all the junkies their drugs. They wouldn't have to steal to support their habits, and if they knew where their next fix was coming from, they would suddenly have all this time to think about something else, like what had become of their lives. I bet at least some of them might have time to *develop* lives that would one day become reasons to get off drugs entirely.

Anyway, I certainly believed that when they first showed up at the Ojai center, the residents were not able even to see the gorgeousness of its setting. And it made sense to me that once they could no longer spend all their time and energy trying to get high, the beauty they hadn't before noticed might begin to creep into their consciousness, and even give them a reason to be happy.

"How much does it cost to come here?" Al asked.

"Quite a bit, I'm afraid," the doctor said, with a smile that had the tiniest hint of smugness. "Generally around seven thousand dollars a week." Al whistled through his teeth. "Yes, I know," Blackmore continued. "It sounds like a lot, but I promise you we don't make much of a profit. The program costs a fortune to run, and the grounds"—he waved around him—"well, the upkeep is just astonishing. But we do our best not to be just a clinic for the very wealthy. In cases where we feel that the individual would benefit from our program, but can't afford it, we try to make special arrangements. And because I believe all of us in the therapeutic community have a civic responsibility, we always take a certain number of state-sponsored individuals, primarily referred through the drug courts. By and large, however, our residents are very successful individuals, many of whom are in the public eye. We provide a supportive and anonymous environment that doesn't force them to sacrifice the comforts they are accustomed to."

I looked across the terrace and down at the pool. It was irregularly shaped and its water was dark, almost like a pond or small lake. A waterfall bubbled over rocks and plants at one end, and at the other, steam rose from a small area separated by a low wall of rocks. One or two people soaked in the hot tub, and a few others lay on wooden chaise lounges under striped umbrellas. A dark-skinned man in a white T-shirt and shorts distributed tall glasses of water and towels to the sunbathers. Nope. Nobody at the center was sacrificing any of the comforts of home.

"When was Jupiter Jones here?" I asked.

"Jupiter joined us almost exactly four years ago. He checked in for a ninety-day residency to help him end his dependence on cocaine. He completed the program and participated in our outpatient program in Santa Monica for another few months."

"You have an outpatient program?"

"Yes. Most of our clients are from the Los Angeles area. We run a program of group and individual therapy to help our clients manage the transition back into their regular lives. That is a very dangerous time for a drug-dependent individual. It is significantly easier to stay sober surrounded by others doing the same thing, in a place where drugs are hard to find. Most find it much more of a challenge when they return home, to the same environment, family, and friends, where they acquired their self-destructive habits to begin with. We aid them in finding social and living situations that don't encourage their return to drug use."

"And Jupiter participated in that?"

"Yes, for a few months."

"Is that a normal amount of time?"

"What do you mean?"

"Is three months the amount of time you expect people to stay in the outpatient program?"

"We have no expectations. Different people use it for different amounts of time. It depends on the individual."

"What's the average?"

He looked uncomfortable. "Well, perhaps a little longer. More like six months or a year. But each client is different."

Al grunted, and this time I agreed with what it was that he wasn't saying. I was willing to bet that Jupiter Jones hadn't quit the program because he was so well on the road to recovery that further treatment had become superfluous.

We had intended to ask Dr. Blackmore to testify on Jupiter's behalf at the penalty phase of the trial. His job would be to describe for the jury Jupiter's battles with drug addiction. But if Jupiter had dropped out early, then I wasn't sure that the doctor's testimony wouldn't do more harm than good. Even if that weren't the case, Dr. Blackmore was the kind of witness designed to grate on a jury. The slick suntan, the carefully tended hair, the New Age speak. All that was sure to turn the jury off in a big way. Worse, if the prosecutor decided that in order to prepare for his cross-examination of the doctor, he had to send a detective up to visit the center, we would be in serious trouble. I was sure that a jury would not be inclined to sympathize with someone whose rehab experience included being waited on by uniformed pool boys.

I made a notation to discuss the pros and cons of Blackmore's testimony with Wasserman, and then said, "Jupiter told us that he met his stepmother here, and that in fact he was the one who introduced her to his father."

The doctor looked at me sternly, as if I were a patient who had spoken out of turn. "Our rules of confidentiality don't allow me to discuss anyone other than Jupiter with you." He looked at his watch. "Oh, my goodness. I have a session with a patient that I absolutely must prepare for." He rose to his feet. "Molly!" he called, "Please see Mr. Hockey and Ms. Applebaum out." Molly rushed out to the terrace and stood awkwardly next to the table, as if awaiting instructions.

"Chloe Jones is dead," Al said, his gruff voice making the doctor wince just the tiniest bit. "What possible reason could you have for protecting her confidences at this point?" I was surprised. Al wasn't usually so ham-fisted in his approach to witnesses, and he never let them get to him. The good doctor must have really rubbed him the wrong way.

"There are many people here whose heirs would expect us to honor our commitment to secrecy even after they died, Mr. Hockey," the doctor said.

"Of course, we understand that," I said, trying to soothe him. Bad cop was one thing, but antagonizing a potential witness was never a good idea. "Anonymity is critical to the success of your program."

"Exactly, and now, if you'll excuse me," Reese Blackmore said, and began to walk away.

"Dr. Blackmore," I called, but he ignored me.

"We can get a court order," Al said. The doctor stiffened and turned back to us. His mouth twitched slightly, and I could see that it was costing him something to retain his smooth demeanor. I nodded at Al and put my good cop hat firmly on my head.

"Al! We're not going to need to do that," I said. "Dr. Blackmore, my partner just means that we can get a subpoena for any and all records that might assist in preparing a defense. Of course we don't want to do that any more than you want us to. I mean, the last thing I'm interested in doing is spending days or even weeks in Ojai, sifting through your patient files, billing records, even personal papers. Can you imagine what a huge task that would be?" Even the good cop can be scary, sometimes. The doctor blanched the color of his snowy hair. I smiled sweetly and continued. "It's just that we have an ethical obligation to Jupiter Jones that's every bit as legally binding as your doctor-patient privilege, as I'm sure you're aware. If you could just tell us a little bit about his relationship with Chloe, we can avoid all that messy legal stuff."

Looking at his watch, he lowered himself back into his chair. "I can give you two more minutes," he said.

"That's wonderful. Thanks so much, Dr. Blackmore. So we were talking about how Jupiter and Chloe met. They were here at the same time?"

"Yes."

"What was Chloe in for?"

"She was also struggling with cocaine addiction, as I recall. I'd have to check the records to be sure. Cocaine, and maybe heroin as well."

"You can call me with that information once you check your records," I said. "Do you know how it was that Chloe could afford treatment? Who paid for it?"

He glanced at Molly. She said, "She was part of our special residency program. There are donors who provide sort of like scholarships for people who would benefit from our program but would not otherwise be able to afford it."

How come none of my homeless, smack-addicted clients had ever heard of that program? "How was it that she got a special residency? Did she submit some kind of application?" I asked.

"One of our donors must have recommended her for the program. I can check her file, if you like," Molly said, and winced under the frown that Dr. Blackmore shot her way. "Um, actually that information is confidential," she said.

"We understand that Chloe and Jupiter were very close friends. Perhaps even *more* than friends," I said.

The doctor shook his head vigorously. "If you are implying that they had a sexual relationship, then I can assure you that that is not possible. The work residents undertake at this center involves delving into their pasts, uncovering the trauma that led to their addiction. This exploration makes them fragile and vulnerable. It would be far too emotionally dangerous for them to enter into any kind of physical relationship. I expressly forbid that type of behavior."

And my mother expressly forbade me from making out in the back of parked cars. "Perhaps they broke the rules," I said.

He sputtered, "Impossible. Now, I think this conversation has gone on long enough. I am eager to help Jupiter, but not at the cost of divulging confidential information about other clients. I invite you to try to get your court order if you want any more information about Chloe Jones, or any resident other than Jupiter." He spun on his heel and walked away across the terrace.

I raised my eyebrows at Al, who winked slowly at me. I turned back to Molly. She was nervously tucking her hair behind her jutting ears. "I guess I ticked him off," I said.

She frowned. "I'm afraid Reese hasn't taken this whole thing very well. I think he's afraid that it will reflect badly on the center. Maybe even give people second thoughts about coming here."

"Do you think it will?" I asked.

She shrugged. "I don't know. I mean, I'm sure that what happened had nothing to do with the center. But I guess I think it's troubling that they were both residents at one time, and had successfully completed the program. Especially since they were using again when this happened."

Al looked up from his notes and I raised my eyebrows. "They were using again?" I asked.

Molly flushed and glanced quickly around as if to make sure that there was no one nearby who could report her indiscretion back to Dr. Blackmore. Then she leaned closer to me. In a low, rapid voice, she said, "I don't actually know about Jupiter. Not firsthand, that is. Chloe had started doing cocaine again. Or maybe she never stopped. Anyway, she was here for some intensive therapy not that long before she was killed, and she was definitely wired when she showed up."

"High on drugs?" Al asked.

Molly nodded. "Coked up."

"Are you sure?" I said.

"Sure? No, but I'm usually pretty good at figuring out when someone's high."

"I imagine that's a skill you develop around here."

She smiled ruefully. "Yes."

"When was it that Chloe checked back in?"

She leaned back in her chair, more relaxed now. "I'm not exactly sure. A couple of months before she died."

"And what did you mean by intensive therapy?"

"Sometimes clients don't have time for the ninety-day program, or even the twenty-eight. Reese is so generous with his time. He'll occasionally do a few days of intensive therapy with individual clients, if they've slipped, or are in danger of slipping."

"How long did Chloe check back in for?"

"Just a couple of days. She told me that she'd told everyone other than her husband that she was going to Big Sur on a yoga retreat. It would have been pretty awful if the CCU folks had found out she was using again. Their church is violently opposed to drugs, as I'm sure you know. One of their basic tenets is that the CCU cures its members of the need to do drugs. I guess it would have caused a public relations nightmare if it had gotten out. That's what happened with poor Jupiter. Everyone at the CCU was freaking out when they found out about his cocaine addiction. You know, like if the Reverend can't keep his own kid off drugs, how can he help anyone else."

Was I imagining it, or did I detect a hint of a sneer in her voice when she talked about the CCU? "What do you make of the CCU's claims? Can they really cure drug addiction?"

She snorted, and then covered her mouth with her hand. "They are very good clients of ours."

"That doesn't exactly answer my question."

She glanced around again, and then shook her head. "Look, if they could cure drug addiction with their astrological stuff, why would they need us? We have an arrangement with the CCU to provide care for their parishioners who need drug treatment. A full third of our patients at any given time are CCU members. Reese is the one curing them, not Polaris Jones."

I nodded. "Reese, and the rest of you." No harm in giving the woman a little stroking. "But Chloe didn't want the CCU to know that she was back. So she checked in anonymously, right?"

"Everyone is here anonymously. But yeah, she asked us to keep it hush-hush."

"And she finished her intensive therapy uneventfully?"

Molly shook her head. "*That* time, she did."

"What do you mean that time? As opposed to her first residency?'

Molly bit her lip. "Look, I'm only telling you this because she's dead, and because I want to help Jupiter. I can't believe he killed her. I mean, I know he did, I read about the DNA evidence. But I just know there must have been a really good reason."

"Excuse me?" I asked.

"Chloe was a nightmare. A complete bitch. And the most manipulative woman I've ever met in my life. She came to the center in the first place because she convinced some guy to give her a free ride. That's what she does; she gets men to pay her way. And then as soon as she got here and met Jupiter, and figured out who he was, she decided she had to have him. He had really been progressing before she showed up, and she just destroyed all the work he was doing. He'd been processing his relationship with his dad, his mom's legacy of drug use. When Chloe dug her little claws into him, it was all over. He's never been the same since. Never. Poor Jupiter."

Molly's eyes had filled with tears, and she dashed them away.

"You were close to Jupiter, back when he was here?"

She nodded. "I was his counselor. Everyone here gets assigned a counselor, like a sponsor. Someone who's been through the program, and through the staff training. I was Jupiter's."

"You've been through the program?" She seemed so sensible, so reasonable, so healthy. It was hard to believe she'd ever been a drug addict.

"Yeah. I first came here about seven years ago." She looked around the terrace, her brow wrinkled. It was almost as if she were surprised to find herself still there, all those years later. Then she turned back to me and shrugged. "Heroin."

"Heroin?" That shocked me. The heroin addicts I knew were emaciated and hollow-eyed. They didn't have glossy blond hair and an athlete's body. They also didn't wear pink cashmere.

She flashed her rueful smile. "Yeah, I know. I don't look like a junkie, do I? Neither did anyone else in my sorority. We were all using. We didn't shoot up, though. That was too gross for us. We snorted it. We thought that was safe, but we were wrong. I ended up getting sick. Turns out you can pass Hepatitis C through a nasal tube. After I got out of the hospital, my parents checked me in here. I never left. I started out as a resident, then a counselor. I got my master's, and now I'm Reese's research assistant." There was more than a hint of pride in her voice.

"You seem to be doing really well," I said.

She smiled. "Reese has designed a brilliant program. It works, if you use it like you're supposed to." The warmth and affection in her voice when she said her boss's name were unmistakable.

"You were telling us about Chloe?" Al said in a gentler voice than I would have expected, given his feelings about drug users, even recovered ones.

Molly inhaled deeply, and shook her head. "Chloe pretty much took Jupiter over. He spent all his time with her. They were sleeping together. Rules or no rules. I had hoped that once he left, that would be the end of it, but of course it wasn't. He even came up to get her, on her last day. Did you know that?" I nodded my head. "He picked her up and took her home with him. And the next thing we knew, the *L.A. Times* was reporting Polaris Jones's wedding to Chloe Pakulski at the Hollywood Bowl. Ten thousand CCU members were there, and the mayor officiated, along with two CCU ministers. I felt so bad for Jupiter. He loved her so much. She didn't deserve it for a minute, but he loved her."

I wondered if Molly might have felt for Jupiter the same emotion he had wasted on Chloe.

"Was Jupiter the only person Chloe was sleeping with?" I asked.

Molly looked shocked. "Of course he was. Wasn't that bad enough?" Then she looked at her watch and frowned. "I think I'd better see you out. I've got to get back to work."

I fished around in my purse and found a card for her. "Call me if you remember anything, okay?" I said, giving her a meaningful look.

She nodded briskly, shoved the card into her pocket, and strode away across the patio, leaving us to follow her out.

Eight

MUCH to our mutual disappointment, Al and I didn't have time to make it all the way up to La Superica in Santa Barbara. We grabbed a couple of inferior turkey sandwiches from an organic deli in Ojai and sped down the highway in a doomed attempt to make it back to Isaac's preschool in time to pick him up. I did my best to keep nausea at bay with an extra-large bag of blue corn tortilla chips.

"Are you all right?" Al said.

"Mmm?" I mumbled, my mouth full of food.

"You're looking a little green around the gills."

I blushed. "I'm okay. I just need to eat something." I put another handful of chips in my mouth.

He tossed his unfinished sandwich on the dashboard. "Eat? I would have thought eating this crap would make you feel worse."

I took a long gulp of milk to wash down the chips.

"And what's with the milk?"

I blushed again. "Nothing. Calcium. Every woman needs calcium. I don't want to end up hunchbacked."

He raised his eyebrows at me. He slowed down as the traffic thickened, and I felt my stomach rebel at the change in speed. I gobbled up another handful of chips.

"You do *not* look good. Are you sure you're okay?" he asked.

"Of course I'm okay. I'm fine," I snapped.

He raised one hand in surrender. "Bite my head off, why don't you."

"Sorry. I'm fine. Really. Why wouldn't I be?"

"Don't ask *me*. You want me to pull over or something?"

"No, I do *not* want you to pull over. It's just the traffic. All this stopping and starting is making me carsick. Your truck doesn't have the smoothest ride in the world."

"So it's my fault?"

I laughed. "Yeah. It's your fault, Al. Everything is your fault. Anyway, what did you make of all that back at the center?"

He shook his head. "That Molly had the hots for Jupiter, that's for sure."

I nodded. "Yup. Do you think she and Jupiter were sleeping together before Chloe showed up?"

Al wrinkled his brow and thought for a moment. Then he said slowly, "I don't think so. She doesn't seem like someone who would break the rules."

"Maybe not. Except she broke the rule on confidentiality."

He nodded. "Yeah, I guess so. But the girl's dead."

"True. So we don't think Molly was sleeping with Jupiter. Can we agree that she was in love with him?"

He nodded. "Looks that way. And maybe a little in love with her boss."

I wrinkled my brow. "Maybe," I said doubtfully. "Or maybe she just admires him. How much weight do we give to her opinion of Chloe?"

Al frowned. "I believe her. That Chloe seems like a bad apple. Marrying her boyfriend's father? Maybe we should use Molly as a character witness? In favor of Jupiter, and maybe even against Chloe if Wasserman can figure out a way to get that in without an objection from the prosecution."

"I don't know. I mean, she'd probably make a good witness. Juries like blondes. But I'm not sure she wouldn't do more damage than good."

"Why?"

"She cares for Jupiter, and she hates Chloe, that's obvious. So she might seem biased in his favor. But even worse, she knows just how messed up Chloe made Jupiter. She told us that Chloe had really interfered with his therapy, that he'd loved her, and that he'd been utterly devastated when she'd married his dad. That plays right into the prosecution's theory of motive."

"Good point. Well, what about the doctor?"

I shrugged. "I don't know how he'll play. He'd have to give testimony about Jupiter bailing out on the program. And a jury might have a problem with the clinic. It's pretty posh."

"Disgusting. They should be sweating it out in jail, not in a hot tub," Al said.

"Al, for God's sake. Addiction is a disease."

"Yeah, right. Show me a cancer ward that looks like that."

We argued all the way back to Los Angeles and until Al dropped me off at the front gate of Isaac's nursery school. I'd called when it became clear that we weren't going to make it in time, and begged the school to allow Isaac to stay in the afterschool program until I showed up. I'd also called Peter, who had agreed to leave a meeting at the studio early to pick up Ruby. I found Isaac sitting at a table, gluing macaroni to a piece of construction paper and chatting with two other little boys.

"Mama!" He stood up, his hands on his hips. "You're late! All the other one-ers went home and I had to stay with the three-ers. But I'm *not* a three-er."

"I know, honey. I'm sorry." I took him in my arms. "Did you mind being a three-er just for today?"

He kissed me on the cheek and rubbed his nose on mine. "It's okay, Mommy. Except they only had apples for snack. And that's not really a good enough snack. So I'll need a cookie. Or some ice cream."

"We'll see, buddy." I squeezed him tight. There was only the barest hint of baby left in him, around his soft full cheeks and tender-skinned neck. The rest of him was pure little boy—all pipestem legs, sharp elbows, and bony knees. The dimples were disappearing from his knuckles, and his sweet baby fragrance had been almost entirely replaced by a little-boy smell vaguely reminiscent of puppies, sand, and the contents of his pockets. In a few months this little boy would be my baby no more. He would stumble off into the world, pushed out of the way by another round, soft bundle. I wished I could keep him with me for just a little longer. As I clung to my son, and he clung to me, I rebelled against the end that I knew was coming. Someday, Isaac was going to stop wrapping his arms and legs around my body, stop hugging and kissing me. He was going to grow too big, too self-conscious to express his love with such utter abandon. I anticipated his abdication with dread. The tragedy of parenting is that if you do your job well, your love is doomed to become an unrequited passion. I would always remain as obsessed with Isaac as I was at that moment, but his job would be to find other objects for his adoration. I thought of my own mother, and how, while I loved her and my father, the real core of my life, the sun of my solar system, had become my own small family. Ruby, Isaac, and Peter. Someday, Isaac would feel the same. He would still love me and his father, but his focus would be his own partner and children. I held him closer, and tried to memorize the feel of his body in my arms. I inhaled the smell of his hair, buried my mouth in the silken skin of his neck, and willed myself to record the essence of Isaac for the day when it would no longer be mine in any way other than memory.

The next morning I called my doctor to make my first prenatal appointment. Miraculously, they had had a last-minute cancellation, and could fit me in that morning. If I timed everything perfectly, I would be able to drive east to Los Feliz to take Isaac to preschool, dropping off Ruby at her school on the way, go back west to the doctor's office near Cedar's Sinai, and make it back downtown in time to meet

Al at the county jail for another interview with Jupiter. I'd have to traverse the city three times, but if the traffic cooperated, I'd be fine. Ask a Los Angelino how long it takes to get somewhere and you're guaranteed to get the response "twenty minutes." By some magical arrangement of denial and automotive optimism, all points in the city are exactly twenty minutes away from all others. Except when there's traffic. Then multiply that twenty minutes by a factor of ten, and you'll still be sitting on the road, engaged in the eternal debate: Should you risk getting off the freeway and trying the surface streets?

I had my routes down pat. I whipped down side streets, using the speed bumps as launching pads, and was on my back, knees up and feet in the stirrups, before my hair was dry from my morning shower. The doctor confirmed what I already knew. I was pregnant. Seven weeks and eleven pounds along. Well on the way to whale-dom.

At the receptionist's desk, I made a trimester's worth of appointments, and received a goodie bag full of prenatal vitamins, coupons for hand lotion, and pamphlets from infant formula companies instructing me that while breast was *of course* best, they were ready and waiting to make my life easier with a steady supply of chemically and nutritionally perfect milk for my new baby. I hefted the bag in my hand, wondering if I should toss it in the trashcan behind the counter, or wait to throw it out until it had rolled around in my car for a few months.

"First baby?" a voice said. I turned to find another pregnant woman standing behind me. She was tall, with one of those bullet-shaped bellies very thin pregnant women manage to acquire.

I shook my head. "Third," I said.

Her eyes widened and her smile grew stiff. "My goodness," she said, and backed away from me as if my fecundity were contagious. Hers was the first of what was to become an all-too-familiar reaction. Being pregnant with your first baby is, in the eyes of the world, cute. Your second is less interesting, but still acceptable. By the time you've imposed your genetic material on the universe for the third time, people are much less inclined to approve of you. Reactions range from shock to disapproval, even occasionally to disgust. Every so often another mother of three or more greets you with a sympathetic smile. I find those the most terrifying, frankly. It is a moment of kinship like that shared between strangers who realize that their jobs force them to wear the same unflattering uniform or that they are suffering from the same disfiguring disease. Rueful recognition of mutual doom. That's what you get from those other mothers smiling down from their cereal-encrusted minivans.

I drove back across town, imagining myself chasing three kids, juggling three sets of activities, doing three children's worth of laundry. A nanny. I was definitely going to need a nanny. I was pretty well freaked out by the time I got to the county jail. I had planned to break the news of my pregnancy to Al, but I couldn't seem to find the right moment. It wasn't the kind of thing I could say while we were going through the rigmarole of metal detectors, identification inspections, and bag searches necessary to enter the jail's visiting room. I almost said something while we were killing time, waiting for them to bring Jupiter down, but Al was on one of his tears about the conspiracy to silence libertarian voices of dissent, and I couldn't get a word in edgewise.

"Do you really think it's an accident that websites critical of the liberal media's hegemony are so much slower to load?" he said as he pulled his notebook out of his pocket. "It's all about AOL/Time Warner. They control the Internet. They decide what speed everything runs on. They're counting on everyone getting restless, waiting for the truth to appear on their screens. They're figuring Americans are so damn impatient that they'd rather click over to a website that serves up nothing but bogus half-truths than wait for a minute. And they're right. The herd would rather slurp at CNN's trough of lies than take a minute to learn the truth. But not me, girlie. Not me. I'm a patient man. I'll wait until kingdom come before I get my information from a media conglomerate."

"Maybe you should get a DSL line," I said.

He looked at me, obviously pitying my inability to recognize the reality of my own victimization, and opened his mouth to launch into another explanation of why the threat of global terrorism was really a media-created stunt to increase revenues, when Jupiter finally arrived. He greeted us with a nod of his head and sat down at the table. He looked less agitated. He'd stopped chewing on his lips, and he wasn't fidgeting quite so much.

"How are you doing?" I asked.

He shrugged. "Better, I guess. I'm working. In the laundry. It's pretty awful work—it's a furnace in there, and you're on your feet, bending over and picking up these huge, stinking piles of filthy sheets and clothes and stuff. But I don't mind it. At least I'm somewhere away from everyone. I don't just sit there in my house waiting for someone to jump me."

I've never gotten used to hearing inmates refer to their cells as houses. There is something so sad about it—the very attempt to replicate normality serves only to highlight how truly constricted their world is. It was probably a good sign that Jupiter was getting more comfortable with jailhouse lingo, though. It meant he was getting accustomed to his situation; that he was figuring out how to swim in the admittedly poisonous waters. It was better than drowning.

"Jupiter, I want to ask you something. Do you remember what happened to Lilly's mother? How she died, I mean?"

Jupiter looked up at me blankly. "What do you mean?"

"I know that she died in Mexico, and your father said something about an accident. I was wondering if you remember what happened."

He shrugged his shoulders and looked down at his hands. "I was really young."

I leaned forward, ready to press him. "About two or three, right?"

He shrugged again and began chewing his lip. "Yeah."

I thought of my Isaac. He was more or less the same age as Jupiter had been back then. I had a hard time believing that if something happened to me, he wouldn't remember it.

Jupiter remembered. I knew he did. Why wasn't he willing to talk about it? Why wouldn't anyone tell us anything about Lilly's mother's death?

"Come on, Jupiter," I said, letting my impatience show. "We can't help you unless you're straight with us. What happened in Mexico?"

He glanced up at me anxiously, his face pinched and his teeth once again clawing at his lips. "Did Lilly tell you anything?" he asked.

"What happened in Mexico? I asked again.

"I don't know," he said, his voice the nervous whine of a young child.

I wasn't getting anywhere by confronting him. Maybe it made more sense to pretend to believe him. "You never talked about it with your father?" I said gently.

He shook his head. "My father and I never talked about anything. Except what a lousy son I was."

None of us spoke for a minute, and then Al said, "Jupiter, we went up to Ojai. To the rehab center where you met Chloe."

Jupiter said, "How's Dr. Blackmore?"

I replied, "Fine. Molly sends you her regards." At the sound of her name, his face brightened. "She likes you," I continued.

"She's the best," he said. "If I'd listened to her four years ago, none of this would have happened."

"She doesn't seem to have been too fond of Chloe."

He smiled ruefully. "Molly saw right through her. She tried to warn me, but I didn't listen."

"Did you know that Chloe had checked back in to the center a couple of months ago?"

He nodded. "Yeah."

"Did your father know that she was using again?"

He nodded his head ruefully. "He caught her doing a line in her bathroom. I thought he was going to kill her."

The three of us stared at each other for a moment, as it dawned on us what he'd said.

"Did you mean that?" I asked him.

He paused for a moment, as if considering my question. "No. No, I don't think so. I mean, I don't think my father could have killed her. He loved Chloe. He really did. I can't believe he'd go that far."

"How far *did* he go? Was he angry?"

He grunted. "You could say that. He busted open her lip. That counts as angry, doesn't it?"

"He hit her?"

Jupiter nodded. "Yeah."

"Was that the first time?"

"I dunno," he said. "Maybe. Maybe not. He's that kind of guy, you know?" Was he? Was that remarkably magnetic man really violent?

"Did he ever hit you?"

He rolled his eyes. "All the time, man. All the time."

Evidence of child abuse is terrifically useful in a mitigation case. It doesn't work unless the jury is already predisposed to give the guy life instead of death, but if they want to save him, it can be the hook on which to hang their hats.

"Did you ever go to the hospital?" I asked, holding my breath and hoping for medical records.

He shook his head, and I sighed in disappointment. I looked at him intently. Was this just a convenient story, made up to shift the blame to his father, or was it the truth? I couldn't tell.

"What happened after he hit Chloe?" I asked.

"He threw her out. That's when she went back to the center."

"Was that a typical response for him? Throwing her out like that?"

"Yeah. You should have seen how he lost it way back when he found out I was using. And then the rest of them were freaking out, too."

"The rest of them?"

"The CCU ministers. They had this huge powwow to figure out what to do with me. I mean, can you imagine? The Very Reverend's son, a cokehead? They never could have lived that down."

"Why not? I mean, I understand that the CCU is opposed to drug use, but wouldn't your father's parishioners have understood? Maybe it would have made him more human to them."

"They don't want him to be human. He's supposed to be closer to God than they are. It's not just that the CCU is against drugs. My father is supposed to be a healer. He cures people of drug addiction. And homosexuality. And depression, and just about anything else. You pay for the program, and you're cured. They guarantee it. If Polaris couldn't heal his own kid, then why should other people pay him to heal them?"

"I don't get it. How can the CCU possibly guarantee a cure?"

He shrugged. "If you fail, then it's your fault. You weren't pure enough. You weren't committed enough. God saw through your pretense. Work a little harder. Take a few more classes. Pay some more money. You'll be cured in time."

"Did the congregation ever find out about you?"

"Only once I got clean. Then my dad and the other ministers billed it as a CCU success story. My recovery was attributed to CCU, not to three months of rehab."

"And Chloe?"

"Same thing. Chloe was the poster girl. Polaris laid his hands on her, brought her to God, and she was transformed."

"So it would have looked terrible if it had gotten out that her cure didn't last."

"Right."

"So he kept it a secret from the CCU?"

"Yeah."

"Here's something I don't understand. Why did he take her back? Was it just to hide what happened from the CCU?"

He shook his head. "I don't know why. I mean, I never thought he would. When he threw her out, he sounded like he hated her. But she was back a few days later. And she was the same old Chloe."

"What do you mean? Was she using?"

He nodded. "More than ever."

"What about you, Jupiter? Were you using again?" I said.

He began chewing on his lip again. Then he nodded, almost imperceptibly.

"Cocaine?"

"Yeah," he whispered.

"For how long?"

He shrugged.

"How long?" I repeated.

"I never really stopped," he said. "Neither of us did."

I stared at him. "Never?"

He shook his head.

"You were using as soon as you got out?"

"Almost. I was sober while I was waiting for Chloe, all the way to the day I picked her up from the hospital."

"The day you picked her up?"

He shrugged.

I leaned back in my chair and raised my hands up. "Wait a second. Are you telling me that Chloe started using again on the very day she got out of rehab?"

Jupiter shrugged. "It's not really that uncommon, you know?"

He explained that Chloe had instructed him to have a line of cocaine waiting for her in the car on the day he picked her up in Ojai. He'd cut it on the dashboard, and the two of them had snorted and buzzed their way down to San Marino. Their relationship, defined as it was by a shared addiction, and sex, had taken a brief hiatus while he was in Mexico, recovering from Chloe's transfer of her affections to his father. It picked up again when he came home. This time, however, there was a twist. Jupiter satisfied the craving for the drugs that Chloe's position as Polaris's wife and partner in his ministry made it difficult for her to acquire on her own. In return, she satisfied his craving—for her. Sex for drugs. So it went, for almost four years. And then one day Chloe was dead and Jupiter was folding laundry at the L.A. county jail.

I looked over at Al, whose lip was curled in a disgusted sneer. Jupiter had just confirmed all his worst expectations of drug users. I knew Al had figured this guy for a liar and a weakling from the moment we first met him. I had felt sorry for Jupiter; I still did. I didn't think he was weak, just not as strong as his disease. However, I'd forgotten that trusting someone in his situation wasn't wise. I was going to have to remember that, from now on.

Nine

"WHAT are the odds of the prosecutor finding out the gory details about our client and his stepmother?" Al asked. I handed him a napkin, and he mopped up the grease on his chin. He took another huge bite of his French dip and mumbled something.

"I can't understand a word you're saying," I said, trying to keep from looking as nauseated as I felt. I picked at my own soggy roll. This pregnancy was really going to be a bummer if it made me lose my appetite for Philippe's. We'd stopped at the downtown culinary institution for a late lunch after our meeting with Jupiter. Al and I are in full agreement that the only way to get the stink of jail out of our clothes and hair is to cover it with something even smellier. Like the odor of roast beef *au jus*.

"I said, are you going to eat your macaroni salad?"

I pushed it across the narrow, scarred, wooden table. Al shoved a heaping forkful in his mouth and followed that with beet-red, pickled egg. I stared for a minute at his grinding jaws and then leapt to my feet and ran as fast as I could across the sawdust-strewn floor, dodging through the crowd of municipal employees in ill-fitting suits, construction workers in dirty overalls, and the occasional nattily dressed politician. I made it around the model train exhibit to the ladies' room just in the nick of time. Lucky for me there was no line. There rarely was. Male customers outnumbered female by about four to one at Philippe's. On occasion, I'd found myself to be the only woman in the place, other than the waitresses in their starched uniforms and little white caps.

After I lost what little of my French dip that I'd managed to swallow, I stood in line for a baked apple. As I put my money down onto the metal tray the waitress extended—the woman who makes your sandwich at Philippe's never lets her hands touch the contaminated surface of your dollar bills—I I felt her eyes appraising me.

"How far along are you?" she asked. She looked, like all the other women behind the counter, like a refugee from the 1950s. Her faintly blue hair was rolled into a bun and tucked up under the white frilly cap that perched on the top of her head. Her lipstick was drawn on just a bit larger than her actual mouth and her eye shadow was a shade of sea-green that I'd begun seeing on the teenagers who shopped on Melrose Avenue. I didn't think the waitress was expressing the same ironic retro-chic as the kids who shared her taste in makeup.

"Seven weeks," I said. "How did you know I was pregnant?"

"I saw you running for the bathroom. It'll pass in a few weeks."

"Let's hope so." I took my apple and went back to Al.

"What's with you?" he said.

"I'm pregnant."

He paused with the remains of his sandwich halfway to his lips. "Really?"

"Yup."

He crammed the sandwich into his mouth, chewed twice, and swallowed. "Congratulations," he said.

We sat for a moment in silence, while I took a few bites

that seemed more sugar and melted butter than fruit. I handed the rest to Al, and he made short work of it.

"What's your plan?" he asked.

"What do you mean?"

"How long are you planning on working?"

"As long as I can, I guess."

He nodded, looking a little troubled.

I rested my head in my hands. "I'm so sorry, Al. Really I am. I know I've been a lousy partner. I'm always late. I don't even make it to work half the time. I can't imagine how I'm going to manage with a new baby in addition to everything else. I completely understand if you want to fire me. Really, it's okay."

He shook his head. "I can't fire you."

I raised my face. "What?"

"You don't work *for* me; we're partners. I can't fire you."

"Oh. Well, I understand if you don't want to be my partner anymore."

He sighed and popped another crimson egg in his mouth. Whole. He chewed noisily, and then swallowed with an audible gulp. I willed my stomach to settle.

"I'm not worried about *that*," he said.

"What?" I asked, confused.

"I'm not bothered by your schedule. In case you haven't noticed, we have barely enough work to keep us both working part-time. Once you have the baby, you'll do stuff at home for a while. On the computer. Whatever. I'm not worried about it. We'll work it out."

Relief flooded me. I had been so sure that Al would dump me and find someone whose workday wasn't dictated by the exigencies of carpools and playdates. Truth be told, I couldn't really understand why he hadn't. Whatever he said, I knew it couldn't be easy dealing with me and my schedule. But I wasn't going to press him too hard. I loved this job. I made a vow to myself to be better organized, to be a better partner, to somehow limit the wrench a baby was going to throw into the already shaky works of my burgeoning career as a private investigator. "Thank you so much, Al. I promise I'll figure it out. Like you said, I'll work from home or something. And we've got over six months before I'm going to need to worry about any of this. I'm going to put in six really good months."

"Now, *that's* what I'm worried about," he said, interrupting me.

"What?"

"Look, Juliet, I don't want to have any repetition of what happened when you were pregnant with Isaac."

I assured him that I had no intention of getting shot again—recovering once from a C-section and a bullet wound at the same time was once too often even for me. He replied with a grunt.

"No, really. I'll be careful."

He shook his head. "I'll believe *that* when I see it."

Rather than argue with him, I decided to answer the question he'd asked before I'd made my elegant sprint across the room. "If Jupiter doesn't tell the prosecutor about his little sex-for-drugs arrangement with Chloe, I don't honestly see how it can come out at trial."

"Unless she told someone else."

"True."

"You think he did it?" Al asked.

"What, the murder?"

Al nodded.

For all that Jupiter had lied to us about his drug use, I still had an oddly unshaken belief in his innocence. Maybe it was because of Lilly, maybe because of my own stubbornness. It's not like I have an infallible instinct for evaluating the truth. I just didn't think he could have done it. "Jupiter says he didn't kill her. And given what he told us about Polaris, I'd put my money on the father, rather than the son, wouldn't you?"

Al shrugged. "That's if the son is telling the truth."

It wasn't unusual in our partnership for Al and me to wait this long to have a conversation about our client's guilt or innocence. When we'd worked together at the federal public defender's office, we'd learned to avoid the subject altogether.

The few times it had come up, Al had quickly grown disgusted with my willingness to consider the possibility that the guys we were defending hadn't committed the crime of which they were accused. Al was wrong—I wasn't naïve. I knew as well as he that our clients were, by and large, guilty. I simply believed that as the one person in the system whose job it was to be on their side, I owed it to them to have some faith. So if my client told me he thought he was delivering a pound of flour wrapped in a black plastic bag to a one-eyed Hell's Angel named Snake, rather than the half a kilo of premium-quality Afghani heroin the cops found on him, then that's what I believed. Or at least, that's all I would admit to believing. I just wasn't cynical enough to present a defense to a jury in the morning, and then denounce it to my colleagues as nonsense in the afternoon.

"You met Polaris. Don't you think he seems like a more likely suspect?" I said.

Al raised his eyebrows. "I'm not the one who thought he was . . . what did you call him? Compelling?"

I blushed. "I never said I thought he was a good guy, or anything. He's just got some . . . I don't know. Power or something. That doesn't make him more likely to be innocent, or Jupiter to be guilty."

Al snorted. "What about Jupiter's positive DNA test?"

"Consensual sex."

Al shook his head. "Anyway, it's hardly relevant. We're not gathering evidence for the guilt phase. Just the penalty phase. Next step?"

"Don't we have to report in to Wasserman's office at some point?"

"That, my dear, is a job for you," he said, getting to his feet.

"For me? Why?"

"Because you're the lawyer. You know how to talk lawyer-talk. I'm going to go back to the office." He ignored my smirk at this glorified description of his garage. "I'm sure I can find something else to keep me busy. Your friend Lilly may be rolling in dough, but I doubt she'll stand for us double-billing her forever."

"You're probably right," I said. "Lilly watches her money, and this isn't a two-person job."

Ten

"I don't like clothes shopping with you. I like shopping with Daddy," Ruby said as I disentangled a sweatshirt with a sequined collar from her copper curls.

"What's wrong with shopping with me?" I made my voice sound nonchalant, but really my feelings were hurt. This was our special time. The time I'd set aside just for Ruby, per the instructions in every parenting manual I'd ever read. She was supposed to treasure these moments of my undivided attention. I'd been promised by those pediatricians and psychologists who seemed to be primarily in the business of inducing feelings of guilt and failure in overextended mothers like me that special time was the glue that would hold the rest of our lives together.

"Because Daddy never looks at the price tags."

No wonder we never managed to save enough in our house fund actually to buy a house. My darling husband was spending his entire income on miniature flared jeans with unicorns embroidered on the seat, and pastel-colored, high-heeled sneakers. "You know, Ruby, it can be *fun* to look at the price. Isn't it neat when we get a bargain?"

Ruby looked at me with a combination of disgust and pity, and flicked disdainfully at the pile of fleece sweatshirts and miniskirts I'd plucked from the sale rack.

"These are *preschool* clothes. In kindergarten we have to wear jeans. And belly shirts like this one." She held up a metallic green scrap of fabric that she'd somehow managed to smuggle into the dressing room with us.

"Belly shirts?"

"You know, the ones that show off your belly button." Were the other kindergarten mothers really letting their daughters go to school looking like lip-synching nymphets from a Destiny's Child video?

I looked at the price tag and gasped. "I'm not spending forty dollars on half a shirt."

"That's okay. Daddy will."

"No he will *not*." Special time. What a delight. "I have an idea," I said, faking a smile. "How about we get some lunch?"

By the time we'd finished eating, Ruby and I were friends again. Maybe it was because I made no objection to her chosen meal of French fries and a chocolate milkshake. *Au contraire*—I shared it with her. In my first trimester, I try to consume as much sugar and fat as possible. They're the only things that don't make me feel like vomiting.

Ruby had no school because of one of the many in-service, out-service, parent-teacher, teacher-teacher conference-meeting-seminar days that her school instituted specifically to destroy any hope I had of getting in a decent day's work. I could afford to blow my morning on outfitting a miniature Las Vegas street walker, but I'd received a summons to appear that afternoon before Raoul Wasserman himself to update him on the status of our investigation, and so some arrangements had to be made. I'd never managed to find a decent babysitter after one disastrous early attempt, so I'd tried to prevail upon Peter to reschedule his own afternoon meeting. He had reminded me that studio executives don't take kindly to last-minute cancellations, and my suggestion that he take

Ruby along had been greeted with a gasp of horror. He had asked me if I really thought he should remind the money men that he was old enough to have a kid her age. Peter harbors a neurotic fear that there are hordes of postadolescent screenwriters yapping at his heels, eager to steal his ideas and take his assignments. Given the glorification of youth culture endemic in Hollywood, where nineteen-year-old film school dropouts get million-dollar multipicture deals while middle-aged Oscar winners can't get a job lettering cue cards, his paranoia may not be that unreasonable.

Al was working a fraud investigation for a new client, a courier company convinced that its employees who were out on disability and workers' comp were actually shirkers. He was due to spend the next few days following burly men and women around with a camera, waiting for someone to pick up a heavy box, or go windsurfing, or do cartwheels on the front lawn. Meeting with Wasserman was my responsibility, anyway. It was the least I could do, since in about seven months I was going to be even more nonexistent a partner than I already was.

So Ruby came with me. I packed a bag with gel pens and black paper, a Walkman with two hours' worth of story tapes, and enough gummy worms to choke a flock of robins. I ignored the glare of the receptionist, and cleared a few glossy magazines off the coffee table in the waiting area outside Wasserman's office. I laid out Ruby's supplies and poked the straw into her juice box.

"Okay, honey," I said. "I'll be back in half an hour. When the big hand is on the six." I pointed to the ornate clock hanging on the wall over the receptionist's head.

"What if I have to go to the bathroom?"

"Just ask the nice lady. She'll tell you where to go." I smiled at the receptionist, a sour-faced young woman with short, spiky hair dyed platinum blond. A silver chain dangling across one of her eyes connected the ring in her nose to the one through her eyebrow. Ignoring me, she flicked open a compact and examined her goth makeup in the mirror. She pushed aside the chain and scraped an invisible trace of kohl out of the corner of her eye with a long pinkie nail polished in black with a tiny, silver death's head appliqué.

"You don't mind showing my daughter the way to the ladies' room if she needs it, do you?" I asked her. The receptionist shrugged and murmured into her headset.

"Mr. Wasserman will see you now," she said.

"Okay, Rubes. I'll be right back. You behave yourself."

Rubes nodded and put her headphones on. She pulled out a piece of black paper and began drawing with her fluorescent pens. Crossing my fingers and hoping for the best, I followed the receptionist's pointed finger down a long hall.

Raoul Wasserman's office contrasted sharply in its Spartan décor with the oriental carpets and faux antique furniture of his waiting room. His desk was a vast expanse of burnished steel. It was empty except for something that looked like the controls of a jumbo jet, but might have been only a telephone. He directed me to a couch with a steel back and armrests, and I breathed a sigh of relief that I'd left Ruby with the pierced young thing out in the waiting area. I could only imagine the short work she and her pens would have made of the white leather seat.

I sat down and Wasserman joined me, folding his lanky body into something that looked more like a metal mesh basket than a chair. His knees poked up on either side of him, and when he leaned forward, they were about level with his shoulders. It couldn't possibly have been comfortable, but his athletic grace made it seem the most natural of seating positions.

"So, Ms. Applebaum, you are a friend of Lilly Green's," he said.

"I am."

He leaned back in his chair, resting his large hands on his jutting knees. "I don't normally allow my clients to tell me which investigator to hire."

I felt a tiny bead of sweat forming on my brow. What had I expected? Of course the man was going to resent having been forced to hire me. "I can understand why Lilly's request might have bothered you. After all, you surely have investigators you normally use."

He raised his eyebrows. "I have three investigators whom I employ on a full-time basis."

This *was* a big firm. Normally, criminal defense attorneys hire independent private investigators on a case-by-case basis. But I shouldn't have been surprised. Wasserman was the most important criminal lawyer in the city, maybe even the state. Of course he had enough investigative work to keep three people busy full time.

"Mr. Wasserman, let me assure you, my partner and I understand that we work for you. My friendship with Lilly is the reason she feels comfortable having me here working on her brother's behalf, but it will have nothing to do with how I do my job. Our role in this case is to gather information for the penalty phase of the trial, if there is one. That's what we plan to do."

He looked at me appraisingly, and I got the sense that he appreciated my deference. "Thank you, Ms. Applebaum. I appreciate that."

"Please, call me Juliet."

He smiled for the first time, and it was a broad, friendly smile. Suddenly, he looked more like the amiable basketball player he must have been, and less like the superstar lawyer by whom, I'll admit, I was pretty intimidated. "The truth is," he continued, "we have a number of cases that are keeping this office quite busy. I'm happy to have the help. My investigative team has been preparing for trial, but they had not yet begun the mitigation work when Lilly made her wishes known. Your presence frees them up to work on other things."

I leaned back in my seat and felt myself relax. I hadn't even realized I'd been so tense.

"I understand from my associate that you were once an attorney," he said.

Once? Wasn't I still? I always thought that once you passed the bar, you were a lawyer until your dying day. It was like being Jewish. Or Catholic. You might convert, practice another religion or profession, but in some inner core of your being, you remained a member of the tribe. "I was with the federal public defender's office."

"The practice of law didn't agree with you?"

"No, it wasn't that. I left work when my daughter was a baby."

"Ah," he said, and nodded with a kind of condescension I recognized so well—it had been a constant theme of the movie industry parties that had come to make life on the fringes of Hollywood so unbearable to me. Before I'd quit my job, I had enjoyed regaling people with my tales of life among the bank robbers and gang bangers. The studio executives and agents had no stories to compare with those, and even the directors and writers were interested—more than one had tried to pick my brain for ideas for a movie. I would still find myself talking to empty air if even a minor television actress walked into the room, but at least among the hangers-on I could hold my own. Once I traded in courtrooms for changing tables, however, I became a pariah. The low moment came when a supercilious female producer who was compelled to chat with me only because of her desire to hire Peter for a project said, "Oh, you're a mommy! How sweet. I just wish I weren't so ambitious and successful. It would be so nice to be able to be satisfied with spending the day just playing with my kids." I stared at her, mouth agape, trying to think of a biting rejoinder, but managed only to come up with, "It's not all fun and games." She smiled patronizingly, as if to let me know that although whiling away the hours with a pack of children would be a waste of the abilities and talents of someone like her, she was sure it was a fine life for someone like me. It added insult to injury that I could have worn her black miniskirt as a leg warmer.

Wasserman's smile inspired in me the usual rush of humiliation, and I winced at the thought of the blush that was surely creeping up my neck and face. When was I going to stop being so defensive about staying home with my kids? Why wasn't it enough for *me* to know that I was a competent, educated person who had made a reasonable, even worthy, decision? Why did I feel like I needed to prove that to everyone else? The insecurity that now seemed a defining feature of my personality hadn't been so obvious before I quit my job, when I was getting daily validation of my professional skills and intelligence. Once I became a stay-at-home mother, I lost whatever self-assurance I'd had. Maybe it was because I had serious doubts about my own competence as a full-time mother and had never had any about my abilities as a lawyer.

I reminded myself that I was a fine attorney and an able investigator and mustered up some confidence. I launched into a description of the course of our investigation into Jupiter Jones's life. I had rushed the kids to bed the night before so that I would have time to type up my notes on my conversations with Polaris, Dr. Blackmore, and Molly Weston. I briefly told Wasserman what we'd accomplished thus far and handed him a stack of impressive reports. He skimmed through them, and as he turned the last page, I saw a little round circle stuck to the back of the document. A *Cheerio.* So much for any appearance of professionalism I might have managed to fake. I reached over and, excusing myself, peeled the remnants of Isaac's breakfast off the page. Wasserman frowned, and I muttered, "Cheerio," holding it up for him to see. Then, not seeing anywhere to throw it away, I raised it to my lips. He frowned, and blushing again, I put it in my pocket.

We talked for a few minutes about the investigation, and I managed to redeem myself by providing a cogent assessment of each potential mitigation witness I'd interviewed. Then I asked, "Do you have a trial date?"

"I think we'll go in about two months. *If* we go."

"If? Is Jupiter considering a plea?"

The lawyer leaned back as much as his basket-chair would allow. "It's always a possibility."

Jupiter had insistently proclaimed his innocence to me, but I knew that it was possible that he would, nonetheless, plead guilty. Virtually everyone pleads guilty, especially if the prosecution has amassed significant physical evidence. The fact that Jupiter insisted he hadn't committed the murder didn't mean he'd necessarily be willing to risk a trial, especially one which could result in him getting the death penalty.

"Have you talked to the prosecutor about a plea?"

He shook his head. "I don't ever approach them. I let them come to me." He never approached them? I couldn't help but think of all the times I'd groveled before the Assistant United States Attorneys, begging for a plea agreement that would spare my clients at least a couple of years. What would have happened if I'd adopted his approach and never went to them on bended knee? Would my clients have fared as well as his did? Or would the prosecutors have thrown the book at them, not even granting the minuscule adjustments that were the usual results of my suppliant beseeching?

"In this case, even if the prosecutors do come to you, they're not likely to do more than take death off the table. If they're willing to consider a plea at all," I said, probably more because I wanted him to know that I knew what I was talking about than because I thought he really cared about my opinions on his chances for a plea bargain.

"Perhaps. It depends on the strength of our case." He leaned back in his basket.

"Has something come up?" I asked, hoping to hear that there was some exonerating evidence.

"The judge granted our discovery motion, and yesterday we received the victim's financial information, including bank statements."

"And?"

"And there are some curious entries."

"Curious? How?"

"Chloe made a series of large cash deposits during the few months before her death."

"How large?"

"Two deposits of fifty thousand dollars apiece."

I whistled. That was large.

"Who were the checks from?"

"They were banker's drafts drawn from a numbered account in a Latvian bank."

"Latvian?"

"It's the latest thing in offshore banking. We might be able to trace the account holder, but it will be a challenge."

"Is there any indication of who the money came from?"

"Not so far. In his witness statement, Polaris Jones denies any knowledge of the deposits. One of my investigators is working on the case, but it would be helpful if, as you interview witnesses, you asked them about the deposits. You may be able to turn up something."

"No problem," I said, glad he felt comfortable giving me an assignment. Perhaps Al and I would do such a great job on this case that we'd impress Wasserman. Maybe he'd hire us again, maybe even recommend us to other lawyers. Then we'd really be in business! I put the brakes on my overactive imagination, and said, "Polaris may know more about the deposits than he admits. We've heard some stories about him." I told Wasserman what Jupiter had said about Polaris's abusive behavior.

"My client could be lying," the lawyer said.

"Maybe," I said doubtfully.

"Let me know what you find out." He put his hands on his knees, readying himself to rise.

"What about the issue of bail?" I asked.

He paused and looked at me, frowning. "What about it?"

"Jupiter is having a difficult time in jail, as I'm sure you know. I was wondering whether you'd planned on submitting another bail application?"

Wasserman's jaw tightened, and I had the sinking feeling that I'd squandered the goodwill I'd managed to acquire over the course of our meeting. "Our bail application was denied, as was our appeal. Frankly, I didn't expect it to be granted. Jupiter has a history of drug use, and of residence in foreign countries. He has no home and no source of income other than his father. His ties to the community are tenuous at best."

I nodded and almost left it at that. Then I remembered Jupiter's bitten nails and torn lips. "What about an inpatient drug treatment facility? Couldn't you arrange to have him released to rehab?"

Wasserman frowned again. "I'll look into it." He looked pointedly at his watch.

"There's just one more thing." I told him about the death of Lilly's mother. "She died in an accident of some kind. Polaris refused to provide details of it, but I'm going to try to find out what happened."

Wasserman shook his head. "Don't bother. An accident thirty years ago doesn't have anything to do with this case."

"It might," I insisted. "Maybe it wasn't an accident. Maybe she was murdered."

He shrugged. "Even so. Jupiter was a child when that happened. Chloe wasn't even born yet. It's irrelevant. Don't waste your time, or our client's money." I began to protest, but he silenced me with a raised hand. "It's a waste of time, Ms. Applebaum."

"But it might shed some light on the motive for Chloe's murder!"

"I doubt it. Now, if that's all, I have a court appearance that I must prepare for."

He hoisted himself up out of his basket chair, making the awkward maneuver look easy, and waited for me to follow. I gathered my things together, fuming over his refusal to consider the possibility that there might be something worth looking into in Mexico. Suddenly, it dawned on me why he didn't care: He was convinced of his client's guilt. He was looking only for evidence, like the bank deposits, that would muddy the waters. If he could find enough dirt on Chloe to make the prosecutor worry that a jury would find her unsympathetic, Wasserman would be able to convince them to offer Jupiter a plea. Jupiter would plead guilty, he'd get a sentence of something less than death, and Wasserman would be seen as the white knight who plucked victory from the jaws of defeat.

And it was entirely possible that that *was* the best outcome for Jupiter. Unless it was true that he hadn't harmed his stepmother. If he was really innocent, then any sentence was too long. I realized at that moment that I might be the only person who was willing to believe Jupiter's protestations of innocence. Unless, of course, Lilly believed him, too. I hoped she did, since she was the one signing the checks.

Wasserman opened the door of his office for me, and as I followed him out to the reception area, he said, "I'll have my associate Valerie show you the bank records . . ." His voice trailed off when he saw Ruby lying on the couch with her head hanging over the side, her tongue lolling out of her mouth. It might have been his own receptionist who was the cause of his consternation, however. She was similarly draped over her desk, mouth agape. Her tongue had a grommet through it. She stood up when she saw us, which involved rolling off the desk and landing with a thud that made Ruby burst into gales of laughter.

"I had some childcare problems," I said.

Wasserman shocked me by smiling warmly at my daughter. "Don't worry about it. I have four of my own."

"Four?"

"Four-year-old twins, and two daughters about your age."

"I'm betting you never have to bring them to work."

He laughed. "Only my oldest." He pointed to the sign over the receptionist's desk. I read the words WASSERMAN, HARRIS, ROTHMAN & WASSERMAN. The first name was about twice the size of the other three. "Susan is a partner in the firm."

My age and already a partner. In her father's firm—but still.

Ruby was perfectly content to amuse herself with the receptionist, who turned out to possess the unlikely name of Tiffany. Being saddled with that *Dynasty*-vintage name was surely what had inspired her adoption of the skateboard punk aesthetic. As I made my way to Valerie's office, I thought about Ruby all grown up. Would she set off metal detectors? Or did something worse await me? I tried to imagine a fashion less appealing than staples through your tongue. Chopping off parts of your body in a kind of voluntary amputation like a Western Yakuza? I shuddered at the thought.

Valerie was busy at her computer when I knocked on her door. She waved me in without looking up. I leaned against the door jam to wait for her to finish typing and tried not to be too obvious as I looked her up and down. I was impressed by her carefully tousled hair. I'd once attempted a haircut like that, sure that it was the answer to my blow-dryer phobia and morning time-crunch. It turns out, however, that it takes hours to achieve that precise level of nonchalance. I was lucky if had time to put pants on in the morning, let alone painstakingly put my hair into precise disarray.

Finally, Valerie looked up and caught me peeking at her shoes. "Please have a seat," she said coldly, and I jerked my head up from where I had bent it, trying to see under her desk. Whatever warmth had been engendered by our shared experience in the jailhouse bathroom had dissipated. Conscious that I was doing so just to crack the young woman's frosty veneer, I smiled brightly and said, "So, it turns out that I'm pregnant after all!"

Her face lit up instantly. "Really?" Her voice was suddenly warm and welcoming. "How far along are you?"

"Almost eight weeks. How about you?"

"Nine. We're so close!"

"But you don't look like you've even gained an ounce." It wasn't *merely* a venal compliment designed to soften her up.

"Thanks. I'm really working on it. I'm going to the gym every morning, and I'm following a strict high-protein diet." She tried, unsuccessfully, to keep her eyes from glancing at my obvious belly. That morning I'd pushed every piece of clothing that buttoned or snapped to the back of my closet. I was already deep into elastic waist territory.

"I should try that," I said. "But French fries and ice cream seem to be the only things that keep me from throwing up."

She sighed sympathetically. "Isn't it awful? My doctor says he can prescribe something for it, but I'm afraid to take anything that might hurt the baby. I don't even drink coffee."

I thought guiltily of the glass of red wine I'd allowed myself at dinner the evening before. Maybe I should cut that out. But coffee. How could I live without coffee?

"Raoul asked me to show you the Jones discovery," Valerie

continued, pushing a thick stack of papers across the table. "It's mostly nothing, but there are a few curious things. Did he tell you about the bank deposits?"

I nodded and leafed through the first couple of pages.

"I had my secretary make you copies," she said.

I put the papers into my bag.

"I'm glad you're pregnant," she said. "I don't really know anyone else who is. I'm the first one of all my girlfriends. It's nice to have someone to talk to about it." She blushed then, as if she were surprised at herself for confiding in me.

"It's nice for me, too. It's always fun to complain to someone who can really sympathize," I said, and I meant it. I love talking to other pregnant women, or women with kids. If I ever stopped to consider that I was actively enjoying an entirely unironic conversation about the relative merits of Huggies versus Pampers, I might have bemoaned my lost intellectual life, but honestly, who has the energy for that kind of self-analysis? I'm too busy swapping intimate details about my weight, sex life, and my children's bowel movements with total strangers I meet in the playground. It's one of the beauties of being female. The only damper on all this confidence sharing is the sport of competitive mothering in which all too many women engage. Nothing can ruin a good hen party like hearing about someone's recipe for sugar-free spelt cookies shaped like letters of the alphabet.

Eleven

LILLY lived in Benedict Canyon, the site of the most notorious of the Manson murders. Driving up the winding road through the lush trees and beautiful villas always sent a shiver up my spine, as though the evil that had momentarily ruined the peace of the bucolic canyon had left behind a trace that was almost, but not quite, palpable.

Like most movie stars famous enough to have their own corps of fans and stalkers, Lilly lived behind a massive, electronic gate. Because we weren't expected, it took her people a while to let Ruby and me in. When the gates finally rolled silently open, I drove up the long driveway and up to the house, a Craftsman bungalow modeled on the Greene & Greene houses sprinkled throughout California. The house was massive, with huge, exposed oak rafters, wide eaves, and a low-pitched roof. It managed, despite its size, to look welcoming, probably because of the kids' paraphernalia jumbled on the square-columned porch running the length of the front of the house. Ruby had fallen asleep in the car, so I hoisted her into my arms and carried her up the steps of the porch, picking my way carefully over the bicycles, roller blades, scooters, piles of sand toys, and miniature rakes and shovels. The door was flung open by one of Lilly's twins.

"Hey, Amber," I said.

"I'm Jade," she replied. "Is Ruby sleeping?"

"No. She's been put under a spell by a wicked witch."

The eight-year-old rolled her eyes to let me know that she was much too mature for that kind of silliness. "Call me when she wakes up." She hollered over her shoulder, "Mom! Juliet and Ruby are here. But Ruby's sleeping. I'm going for a scooter ride." She picked up a bicycle helmet, strapped it under her chin, and zipped off across the porch on her scooter.

"Where's Amber?" I called after her.

"On a time-out," she yelled, and humped the scooter down the steps.

The twins had their father's thick black hair and dark eyes and their mother's lanky body. They should have been beautiful; both Lilly and Archer were. But somehow when their parents' features were put into the genetic slot machine, the girls had pulled the levers at all the wrong places. The pointed nose that contributed to Lilly's gamine beauty looked ratlike when combined with Archer's slightly weak chin. Worst of all, they'd missed out on both their father's thickly lashed black eyes and their mother's luminous blue. Theirs were a less spectacular hazel.

But they were sweet girls, lively and friendly like their mother. They had always been nice to Ruby, including her in their games even though she was a couple of years younger. They'd even invited her to join their club—they called themselves the Jewels, and Ruby fit right in.

I walked through the front door and found Lilly sitting in the inglenook by the fire blazing in the imposing fieldstone fireplace. My greeting froze in my throat when I saw Archer sitting on the seat across from her. Lilly and Archer had had an ugly divorce; one that had been played out more in the tabloids and on entertainment news television than in the courtroom. Lilly had spent hours raging to me about her incompetent lawyers who were unable to circumvent the community property laws that gave Archer half of the money she'd earned on her films. For a while she and Archer hadn't even spoken, using assistants and drivers to transfer the girls from house to house.

"Hi, Juliet," Archer said.

"Uh, hi," I replied articulately.

"Nice to see you, Juliet," Lilly said. "Do you want to put Ruby to bed in the girls' room?"

"No, I'll dump her on the couch. I'd just as soon she woke up. Otherwise she'll be up all night."

"Amber will be done with her time-out in about three minutes," she said, looking at her watch. "I'm sure she'll be happy to wake Ruby up for you."

I plopped Ruby down on the overstuffed, slip-covered couch, and she grumbled and buried her head in one of the many pillows.

"What's going on?" Lilly asked, obviously surprised to see me. We were friends, and I'd been to her house countless times, but I'd never before dropped by unannounced. "Is everything okay? Did something happen to Jupiter?"

"No, no. He's fine," I said, looking over at Archer.

"I know what's going on. Lilly's told me everything," Archer said.

I looked back at Lilly and she nodded. What was going on here? Why was Lilly's ex-husband sitting so comfortably in her living room, and why had she confided in him the details of Jupiter's case? I stifled my curiosity and said, "It's not Jupiter. Although it does have to do with his case. Wasserman found some bank statements of Chloe's. She deposited a hundred thousand dollars into her bank account over the course of the few months before she died."

I couldn't swear it, but I thought I caught Lilly giving Archer a meaningful look.

"That's a lot of money," he said, his voice neutral.

"The checks were drawn off an anonymous offshore account," I said.

"Do they have any idea whose account it was?" Lilly asked.

"Not yet." I paused. "Do you know anything about it?"

"Of course not," she said quickly. "I'm sure it's just some CCU thing. I wouldn't be surprised if they have secret bank accounts all over the world. The whole thing is just a huge scam. I'm sure Polaris is worth hundreds of millions of dollars."

"To them a hundred thousand is nothing," Archer agreed. "It's probably just Chloe's pin money."

Why were the two of them working so hard to convince me not to be concerned about the money? What did they know? I looked at Lilly, trying to figure out what was going on behind those clear blue eyes. But the woman is a brilliant actress, and all I saw was bland unconcern. "I'm sure Wasserman will check back and see if the deposits were unique or if Chloe regularly got large sums from those accounts," I said. Then I pressed her. "Are you sure you don't know anything about it?"

"Of course not," Lilly said firmly.

"How is the rest of the investigation going?" Archer asked. I had the distinct impression that he was trying to change the subject.

"It's moving along. We've interviewed Jupiter and had an initial meeting with his father."

"Have you guys found what you need to keep Jupiter off death row?" he asked.

"It's not really a question of finding something in particular. It's about amassing information so that we can present the jury with a sympathetic picture of a whole person, someone they can identify with in some way. We want them to get to know Jupiter, because if they do, it will be harder for them to kill him. We want every juror to think that but for the grace of circumstance, a difficult childhood, personal tragedy, Jupiter could be his son." When I said the final word, my voice trailed off. I couldn't help but think of that man whose son Jupiter was, who nonetheless seemed to want him dead.

"What?" Lilly said. I looked up quickly. "What's wrong?" she said.

"Nothing, nothing. I was just thinking about something . . . it's nothing."

She leaned forward, resting her elbows on her knees. Her shorn hair was beginning to grow in, and the blond caught the light of the fire and glowed. "Is it Polaris?"

"I can't really talk about the specifics of the case with you. I'm bound by attorney-client privilege," I said. "Because I work for Wasserman, the privilege extends to me, too."

"It's Polaris, isn't it? He won't help you." Her voice was flat, and the muscles in her jaw twitched.

"Not exactly," I said. "He talked to us, but he hasn't decided what position to take on the imposition of the death penalty."

She shook her head. "The man of God." She bit the words off and spat them out.

"Does it matter?" Archer asked.

I nodded. "The victim statement matters. It matters to the prosecutor—sometimes they won't go for the death penalty if the family is opposed. It definitely makes an impression on a jury. I don't know how Polaris will come down on this. His aides at the CCU seem to be looking for some consistency with their public position of opposition to the death penalty. At least one of them is."

Lilly buried her head in her hands, and Archer walked behind her chair and rested his hands lightly on her shoulders. She leaned against his arm for a moment and then turned her face up to his.

"Thanks," she said, her voice warm and low.

He squeezed her shoulders. I felt like I was eavesdropping on a moment too intimate to be shared, and I fixed my eyes on the dancing flames in the fireplace.

Just then, a young woman, dressed in khaki pants and a denim shirt, the casual livery worn by Lilly's household staff in place of black polyester dresses with starched aprons, walked into the living room. "Lilly, can I tell Amber her time-out is up?" she said.

"Sure," said Archer. "Tell her to come down and say goodbye to Daddy." He squeezed Lilly's shoulders one more time and walked back to his seat. He picked up the soft suede jacket that was crumpled next to where he'd been sitting and shrugged it on over his shoulders.

"You're going?" Lilly asked him.

"I promised my mother I'd take her to a movie tonight," he said apologetically. "Do you want me to cancel and have dinner with you and the girls?"

"No, no. That's okay. I'll let Phoebe and Stephanie feed them and put them to sleep. I plan to have a bath and a massage, and be in bed by eight. I'll see you when I bring them over on Saturday."

"Let's have brunch, all of us together."

"I'd like that." She lifted up her face to him and he kissed her on the lips. It was a quick kiss, but it certainly seemed like more than a friendly buss.

By the time Archer had said goodbye to his daughters and left, Ruby was awake. Her sleep-creased face crumpled when she found herself on a strange couch, but before she could begin to cry, Amber and Jade hustled her off to their playroom to play with their Habitrail full of gerbils. Lilly and I sat quietly for a moment after they'd left. I wanted to ask her more about the money. Her answers had made sense, but they'd felt too glib. First, though, I had to find out what the heck was going on with her ex-husband. "Are you planning on telling me what that was all about?" I said.

She smiled faintly and tucked her knees up under her chin. Her feet were crossed at the ankles and her long delicate toes dug into the fabric of her bench. Everything about Lilly was lovely, even her feet. I wriggled my own unmanicured toes in my shoes and sighed. "Well?" I said.

"What do you mean?" Lilly asked, coyly catching one edge of her pale lip in between her teeth.

I rolled my eyes. "Archer? You? Brunch?"

She smiled the same small, private smile. "I wish I knew."

I raised an eyebrow.

She hugged her knees to her chest. "Things have been really great between us lately. I can't explain it. We went for nearly a year almost without seeing each other at all. And then one day, about four months ago, he dropped the kids off himself, instead of sending one of the nannies to do it. We ended up talking for hours. Since then we've been spending time together. We do stuff with the twins. Lately we've even started going out alone."

"You're dating Archer?"

She laughed. "I guess so."

I bit back the words that leapt to my mouth. Words like, "Are you out of your mind?" Words like "Don't forget this is the guy who tried to take all your money." Words like "Archer's a poisonous cretin who's only nice to his own mother because he stands to inherit money from her."

"That's nice," I said. "Listen, Lilly, about the bank deposits . . ."

"Bank deposits?" she said, picking a piece of chipped polish off her baby toe.

"The deposits to Chloe's bank account."

"Hm. What about them?"

I leaned forward, pushing myself into the line of sight that seemed altogether too focused on her pedicure. "Are you sure you don't know anything about them?"

"Of course not," she said, sitting up and glaring at me. "What are you getting at, Juliet? Are you trying to imply that I had something to do with those deposits?"

Maybe. "No, no. Of course not," I said.

"Good, because I'd hate to think you were suspicious of me. I mean, I hired you because you're my friend. Because I knew I could trust you." Her eyes were wide, and her gamine face looked hurt, but there was a hint of iron in her voice.

I decided to forgo reminding her once again how my ethical obligation was to her brother, not to her, no matter who paid my bills. Instead I broached another subject guaranteed to bother her. "You can trust me. Of course you can. Can you tell me a little more about your mother's death? What else you remember?"

"I can't talk about it, Juliet. It's too painful for me to talk about."

I sighed. "Are you sure? I mean, it would help me set this

all in context. It has to have been a pretty traumatic memory for Jupiter, too. It might be something we can use in our mitigation argument."

She shook her head. "I can't. I just can't."

I gave up. We ended up having a desultory conversation about schools—how the twins liked their exclusive private school where members of the Hollywood elite mollified their liberal guilt by supporting a wonderfully generous scholarship program that resulted in a student body evenly divided between fabulously wealthy white children and black and Latino children from backgrounds of varying deprivation. Ruby went to a magnet public school not too far from where we lived. It was a sweet little school with nice teachers. It only went up to fifth grade, however, and I was pretty sure private school was in our future after that. She probably wouldn't be able to get into the twins' school, though. We were neither sufficiently famous, nor sufficiently bereft.

After a little while, one of the attractive, khaki-clad nannies brought the girls down for dinner. I refused Ruby's entreaties to stay and eat with the twins—"but their cook made chocolate cake for dessert!"—and bundled her into the car for the twenty-minute trip home.

Ruby was still whining when I pulled into our block. I had already given her one time-out—hardly an effective tool in the car—and was ready to put her to bed for the rest of the night. As I was about to swing into our driveway, I briefly turned my head to tell her once and for all to be quiet. I turned back around, and gasped. I slammed on my brakes and just missed hitting the low black car that was right in front of me, parked at an angle in front of our house, blocking the driveway. The webbing of my seat belt bit into my neck and chest, and I exhaled with a loud grunt.

"Are you okay, honey?" I shouted, jerking the car into park. I unsnapped my seat belt, turned around, and reached into the backseat to touch Ruby to make sure with my own hands that she was okay.

"My seat belt squeezed me!" she said indignantly.

"What hurts?" I said, frantically groping her arms and shoulders. "Your neck? Your arm?"

"Nothing *hurts*. I just don't like being squeezed."

I patted her once more, reassuring myself that she was really okay, and then said, "You wait here." I jumped out of my car and stormed over to the parked car to see just who it was who had blocked my driveway. Our block wasn't one where you'd normally find a Jaguar, let alone an illegally parked one. As I was bending over to jot down the license plate number to report to the cops, one of the car's windows glided down, surprising the hell out of me.

Lilly's ex-husband leaned out of the window, resting an elbow on the frame. "Hi." His voice was so soft it was almost a purr.

"Archer, are you crazy? Why are you parked across my driveway? I almost plowed into you!"

"I just wanted to talk."

He smiled, and the hairs on the back of my neck rose just the slightest bit. Suddenly, he opened his door. I stepped back and bumped into the grill of my car.

"I've got Ruby in the backseat," I said unnecessarily. He knew she was there.

"We need to talk." Archer came up beside me and pressed his hand on my shoulder. I sat down on the hood of my car. He took his hand away and sat down next to me. I swallowed.

"Why don't you come inside?" I said, making my voice bright and friendly. I glanced back at Ruby, willing her to sit quietly in her car seat.

"Let's talk here." His tone was even and bland, and for some reason that scared me more than if he'd been shouting. I didn't know Archer well. Peter had gone to a couple of ball games with him, but I had always spent time with Lilly alone, or with Lilly and the girls. I couldn't honestly think of a time I had socialized with Archer and Lilly as a couple, other than the few times he'd joined her at some party or other. Their marriage had been on the rocks almost from the first time we'd met Lilly, although it had taken them a while to call it quits. Still, he'd never been anything but perfectly pleasant to me, and of all the complaints Lilly had about him, she'd never accused him of being violent. So why was he making me so nervous?

"It's getting dark early nowadays," Archer said, tilting his face up and leaning his body back on his elbows.

I looked at him. Was I supposed to sit on the hood of my car making small talk? "What do you want, Archer? Why are you here?"

He didn't turn to me, just continued to look up at the night sky. "Your job is to keep Jupiter off death row, right?" he said.

"Right."

"You find witnesses who can testify about what a hard childhood he had, what a nice guy he is, that kind of thing."

"More or less. Why are you asking me this? We talked all about it at Lilly's house no more than an hour ago."

He smiled at me, and now there was just the barest hint of menace in his face. "I think you should just do your job."

"Excuse me?" I said, leaning away and looking at him.

"Just do your job. Talk to people about Jupiter. About what a hard life he's had. About how his mother abandoned him. That kind of thing."

"That's what I'm doing, Archer." I began to get down off the car, but he reached out a hand to stop me.

"Yup. You should just do your job. Leave the rest of it alone." His fingers pressed ever so gently into my arm. I shook him off and stood up.

"The rest of it?" I said as I opened the door of my car.

"Just leave Lilly out of it."

That stopped me. I stood with the door half open and stared at him. "What?"

"You heard me. Just leave Lilly out of it. The bank accounts, all that stuff."

"Lilly hired me to investigate. That's what I'm doing—investigating."

"Lilly's your friend. You know she's not involved in any of this. You don't need to investigate her."

"I'm not investigating her. I'm investigating the case."

He smiled at me. "Well, great. Then we're both on the same page. You're not going to investigate her. Or bother her with this anymore."

"Bother her?"

"Lilly and Jupiter were really close when they were kids, and this is all very difficult for her. Did you know that she's been so freaked out that she got her doctor to prescribe antidepressants for her?" I shook my head. "She's taking Zoloft, and sleeping pills, because she's had a terrible time sleeping since this happened. I don't want you to upset her more than she already is. You need to just back off, do your job, and leave her alone."

I closed the door again, to keep Ruby from hearing any more of the conversation. "What exactly are you saying, Archer? It sounds like you've got something to hide. It sounds like you're threatening me."

He jumped down off the car. "Of course I'm not. Why would you say that? I'm not hiding anything, and I didn't threaten you. I would *never* threaten you. I'm just letting you know how painful this is for your friend." He opened his car door and got in. Then he leaned his head out the window again. "I know you'd never hurt Lilly. I trust you. Give Peter my regards." With that, he took off down the street. I stood staring after him for a moment, then shivered and got into my car.

"Why was Amber and Jade's daddy parked in front of our house?" Ruby asked.

"He just came by to say hi," I said, and pulled my car into the driveway and around back to the garage. I got out of the car and unbuckled Ruby from her car seat. Then I grabbed her and hugged her, hard. She wriggled in my arms. "Don't be afraid," I said.

She tipped her head back and scowled at me. "I'm not afraid!" she said disgustedly. I hugged her again. She might not be, but I sure was.

I had a hard time explaining to Peter why Archer had unnerved me so much. While he agreed that it was weird for him to have shown up at the house, he told me that I was jumping to conclusions by assuming that Archer was trying to warn me off the case.

"He's probably just worried about Lilly. She's clearly taking this incredibly hard, and he doesn't want her more upset," Peter said. We were sitting on the couch, enjoying a few minutes together after we'd put the kids to bed and before he went to work.

"Lilly's not some delicate creature who needs to be protected. Anyway, Archer certainly never bothered to take care of her in the past. More like the other way around. She was always the one worrying about him."

Peter shrugged.

"What?" I said.

"I don't know that she ever really worried *about* him. More like worried about what he was *up* to."

I nodded. "I guess so. But still. How do we get from that to him lurking in front of our house like some extra from *The Sopranos*?"

Peter shook his head.

"What?" I said again, irritated now.

"Maybe he's changed. You said yourself they seem to be having some kind of reconciliation. Maybe he's trying to do more for her."

"Like terrorize her friends?"

Peter poked me in the side with his toe. "You were hardly terrorized. Don't be so melodramatic."

I pushed his feet off my lap. "He was waiting in front of the house in the dark. He told me to back off my investigation. It sure seemed to me like he was trying to scare me. And guess what? It worked. I'm scared."

Peter leaned over and hugged me. "Don't be scared," he murmured into my hair, except he said it in a Bugs Bunny accent, and then he giggled.

I shook him off and jerked to my feet. "I can't believe you. What, are you and Archer in some kind of husband brotherhood? Why doesn't this bother you?" I'm afraid my voice was a little shriller than I would have liked.

Peter sat back and shook his head. "I'm sorry, honey. It's

just that I know Archer a little better than you do. He's just trying to impress Lilly by playing the macho husband."

I stomped off into the kitchen to call Al, sure that he would find Archer's behavior as suspicious as I did. I'd forgotten about his crippling sexism.

"What do my hormones have to do with anything?" I shouted.

"They're all out of whack. It makes you overreact."

"Overreact? Overreact? I don't get this. You and Peter are always on me to be more careful, to take more precautions. Hell, you even want me to carry a gun! And now you're saying I'm overreacting? I'll give you overreacting!" I clapped the phone down in his ear.

It rang a moment later. "Sorry," I said into the receiver.

"That's okay," Al said. "Like I said. Hormones."

I gritted my teeth and didn't reply.

"Tell you what, how about I get one of my buddies to put him through the computer, check on any priors. Would that make you feel better?"

"I guess so." Was I overreacting? I didn't usually scare easily. That was actually one of my problems—sometimes I didn't scare easily enough.

"Why don't you try a bath?" Al said.

"What?"

"That's what Jeanelle always does when she's upset." The condescension in his voice was palpable, and it was all I could do to keep from hanging up on him again. "Anyway, if you're really worried, you should call your friend Lilly and ask her what's up with her ex."

That wasn't a bad idea. I decided to do that first thing in the morning. I did end up taking a bath, but not because Al told me to. The idea had been in the back of my mind ever since Lilly had announced her plans to have one. I only wished that I also had someone on staff to give me a massage. If I was substantially more serene when I got out of the tub, that certainly wasn't something I was ever going to admit to Al.

My calm lasted through the next morning. I woke up early,

feeling peculiar. I jumped out of bed, got dressed in the dark, and went out to enjoy a solitary cup of coffee before waking the kids. Then I had an inspiration that might have been motherly, but probably had more to do with my own cravings. It was while I was painstakingly pouring out the pancake batter into Mickey Mouse ears, and placing the chocolate chip eyes just so, that I identified the strange sensation that had come over me. It wasn't anything I was feeling—it was what I wasn't feeling. I wasn't exhausted. For the first time in weeks, I actually felt rested. I smiled in surprise. I'd better enjoy it—it wasn't going to last. Pretty soon I'd be spending my nights waddling off to the bathroom every fifteen minutes. Then, when the baby came, I'd be even worse off. If the new one was anything like the others, I was doomed to become a test case for a sleep deprivation study.

For once the kids didn't give me a hard time about getting dressed and ready for school. They were like little hound dogs, with the scent of pancakes in their noses. They whipped on their clothes, snapped the Velcro on their sneakers, and were sitting at the kitchen table, faces covered in syrup, in no time.

Isaac gobbled his Mickey Mouse as fast as he could, and then came around the table to bury his face in my stomach. "Mama?" he said.

"What honey?"

"You look pretty in those pajamas."

I looked down at my T-shirt and red Capri pants. "These aren't pajamas, sweetie. These are clothes."

He looked at me critically. "Well, you're pretty, anyway."

I kissed the top of his head. Ninety-nine mornings out of a hundred, the kids do nothing but bicker and drive one another and me crazy. And then, every so often, generally when I'm just about at the end of my rope, one of them fills my tank, recharges my batteries, and gives me the energy to keep driving through my days.

"You're not bad yourself," I said.

Once I had the kids fed and settled in front of morning television, I picked up the phone. It took a while for Lilly's assistant to clear me, but I finally heard my friend's voice. When I told her what had happened the night before with Archer, there was silence on the other end of the line. "Lilly," I said. "Are you still there?"

"Yeah. Yeah, I'm here. Listen, I'm sorry. Archer's just worried about me. I don't need to tell you how freaked out this whole thing has made me. He was just overreacting. I'm sorry."

"You don't need to apologize. It's just . . ." My voice trailed off.

"What?" she said.

How did I go about telling her that I thought her ex-husband was a scary creep and that I wished she'd cut him loose once and for all? "He just doesn't seem like the most stable guy in the world," I said lamely.

She sighed. "I've got to go, Juliet. I've got *In Style* magazine showing up in fifteen minutes and I've got to go get made up."

After I made the school rounds, I drove out to Pasadena, to the CCU campus. I didn't know if I'd get in to see Polaris without an appointment, but even if I wasn't admitted to the inner sanctum, it wouldn't hurt to nose around a bit.

I got off the mobbed freeway as fast as I could and made my way on surface streets through the less attractive parts of Pasadena. There are vast stretches of Los Angeles that look the same—interchangeable districts of long, straight avenues with strip malls on either side. The stores are a hodgepodge of Vietnamese donut shops, Guatemalan mail centers, Mexican travel agencies. The telephone poles and streetlights are festooned with campaign posters: ERNESTO ACOSTA FOR SUPERIOR COURT JUDGE, RUTH TAGANES FOR CITY COUNSEL, VOTE NO ON 6, YES ON 113. I love these ugly parts of the city as much or more than the neighborhoods of ostentatious homes with Astroturf green lawns, or the winding canyons where the houses cling precariously to the hillsides, raising a defiant fist to the god of earthquakes and landslides. This schizophrenia of gracious elegance and decaying tackiness, of natural beauty and urban blight, is the essence of Los Angeles. It's what makes those of us who love the city defend it against its many and vocal detractors. In all cities poverty exists side by side with wealth, but here we don't pretend otherwise.

The CCU campus was set on a broad boulevard of palatial homes, behind a high iron fence. I pulled off to the side of the road so I could take a minute to figure out how I was going to weasel the guard in the gatehouse into just letting me onto the grounds. As I sat there, a black BMW SUV came tearing down the driveway from inside the compound. The driver paused only long enough for the guard to begin to lift the barrier arm that blocked the exit. I heard a squeal of metal as the car jerked forward, driving through the gate before the bar was fully raised. The bar smacked against the roof of the car, and the guard leapt out of his box, arms raised in astonishment and anger, shouting after the car as it sped away. The Beemer tore off down the block, and without thinking clearly about what I was doing, I set off in pursuit. I had managed to catch a glimpse of the driver, her face red and twisted in a tortured scowl. It was Lilly.

Lilly made it easy for me. She stopped at the first café we passed. I followed her into the parking lot and pulled into a spot at the far end. I slouched down in my seat and angled my rearview mirror so that I had a clear view of her. After a moment, the driver's side door opened. Lilly got out, looking pale and wan, and walked into the café. I sat up and tapped my fingers on my steering wheel, trying to figure out what to do. I was horribly torn. I wanted to jump out of my car and comfort my friend, to help her with whatever it was that was causing her so much pain. At the same time, however, a worm of suspicion wriggled its way through my concern, and I couldn't help but wonder why Lilly had gone to see Polaris, why she was so upset, and what any of this had to do with the murder of Chloe Jones. Finally, I followed her. When I entered the café, I saw her standing at the far end of the counter, waiting for her coffee. When she saw me, her face grew even paler.

"Hi," I said, walking over.

"Uh, hi."

"Let's sit down and talk, okay?"

She nodded and walked across the room to a small table tucked behind a row of tall plants.

I placed my order and waited a few moments for my own latte.

"That'll be seven seventy-five," said the young woman behind the counter as she handed me two mugs.

I stared at her. "For a cup of coffee?"

She rolled her eyes. "Two decaf lattes. Yours and your friend's." Lilly had stuck me with the check. Again. I invariably ended up paying when Lilly and I went out. It's not that she was cheap, exactly. The basket of muffins, cheeses, and wine she sent us every Christmas probably cost as much as a month of Isaac's preschool. I think it's that Lilly, like all movie stars, never had to deal with the minutiae of life, like paying the bills. There was always someone else around to take care of that kind of stuff—a studio executive, a talent manager, a personal assistant. A short, chubby friend.

Once I'd sugared up my latte and sprinkled on enough powdered chocolate to compensate for the lack of caffeine, I joined Lilly at the secluded table she'd chosen.

"How'd you find me?" she asked as I sat down and handed her her coffee. "Are you following me?" I didn't think she sounded angry, merely resigned.

"Sort of. Not really. I was just pulling up to the CCU campus when I saw you tear out of there. Then I followed you."

She nodded and sighed. Her shoulders shook slightly.

"What's going on, Lilly? What were you doing there?"

"I went to see him."

"What for?"

She took a trembling sip of her drink and darted her tongue out to lick the foam off her lips. "To convince him to help Jupiter."

"What did he say?"

"He threw me out. Well, *he* didn't, the coward. He had those bathrobe-wearing goons do it for him." Her voice held just the barest hint of the girlish spunk that was her stock-in-trade.

"How did you even get in there in the first place? Didn't the guard stop you?"

"He asked for my autograph." She didn't seem pleased with the ease of access her fame had bought her—on the contrary. She appeared disgusted—with the guard, but perhaps most of all with herself, for taking advantage of it.

"What did you think you could tell Polaris that would change his mind?"

"I could tell him *why* Jupiter killed his wife."

I had just taken a sip of my drink and I froze, the coffee scalding the inside of my mouth. I swallowed, and carefully put the mug on the table. "What are you talking about?" I said.

Whatever spirit she had managed to muster dissolved, and her face collapsed. "I'm the reason Jupiter did it. It's my fault. He's going to die, and it's all my fault." She began to cry—dry soundless sobs that shook her whole body. I'd watched her blue eyes fill with tears time and time again on the screen and always envied her ability to weep so prettily. It turned out that in real life Lilly Green, like me and like everyone else, looked haggard, blotchy, and ugly when she cried. She put her head down in her arms. I reached across the table and laid my hand on her shorn head. I stroked her stubbly hair for a moment and then, when she didn't move, brought my chair around the table and put my arm around her. She leaned heavily against me, and continued to cry. I was grateful for the plants that screened us from the view of the other people in the café. The last thing she needed was to see an item in *Movieline* detailing Lilly Green's breakdown in a Pasadena coffee bar.

Finally, she raised her head, sniffed loudly, and wiped her nose on her hand. "I'm okay," she said.

I nodded. "I think it's time for you to tell me what's going on."

Lilly inhaled with a shudder. "Jupiter killed Chloe to protect me," she said.

"To protect *you*?"

She nodded. "*I'm* the one who wrote Chloe those checks. She was blackmailing me."

Even though somewhere in the back of my mind I'd feared this very thing, even expected it, it still took me by surprise. I sat back heavily in my chair and stared at my friend. "Why? Why was she blackmailing you?"

Lilly laughed bitterly. "Why? Because she was a vile little bitch, that's why."

"That's not what I meant."

"I know," she said.

"What was she blackmailing you with, Lilly?" I said, my voice no more than a whisper.

Lilly's eyes filled with tears again, and she took a deep breath. "She told me that if I didn't pay her, she would go to the newspapers and tell them that I killed my mother."

Twelve

FOR once, Peter didn't object when I called to tell him he was going to have to pick up the kids at school. He must have heard something in my voice—the distant echo, I suppose, of a shot fired in San Miguel de Allende thirty years before.

Her head bent over, her eyes on the table top, and her hands wrapped around her mug as if trying to squeeze some warmth from the cooling coffee, Lilly told me that when she was five, she had found a gun in her mother's bedroom.

"My memories are very vague, almost wispy," she said. "I can remember playing with Jupiter out in the courtyard of our house in San Miguel. There was this fountain, and Jupiter and I were dropping leaves into it. He was too small to really reach over the side, so I would pick him up under the arms and kind of haul him up high enough to toss his leaves in and look at them floating in the water. I remember we were pretending that they were boats. We put ants on the leaves—they were supposed to be the sailors. But we couldn't pick the ants up without killing them." She smiled faintly. "We ended up floating these leaves dotted with dead, smushed ants around the fountain." She shook her head, as if to remind herself that this childhood memory had no place in the story she was recounting. "Anyway, for years all I could remember was the leaves and the fountain, and then the screaming. I don't know who was screaming. Probably one of the maids. Or maybe me. To this day those are my clearest memories. For a long time I didn't remember going into her room, or picking up the gun, or firing it. I completely repressed all that. I just remembered the leaves, and the fountain, and her . . . her . . ."

"Her body?" I whispered.

"Not even really clearly her body. Just her dress. She was wearing a long white dress. Like maybe a nightgown? Or one of those peasant dresses?" Lilly's voice had a dreamy quality and her eyes were vague and unfocused. "I remember the white of the dress. And red. Red everywhere." She shuddered. "The fountain, and then her white dress covered with blood. Those are still the clearest memories I have."

"You repressed the rest?" I said.

She nodded. "It took years and years of therapy just to begin to remember what went on in that room."

"Because of the trauma?" I said.

She leaned slightly against me. "For a little while after it happened I got sort of catatonic, or something. Overwhelmed by the guilt. I wouldn't talk, would barely eat. After a while I got better, but it was as if I had just erased everything that happened from my mind. But I was lucky. I had a very good therapist. Over the years he helped me to remember most of what happened. With his help I recovered the memories of playing with the gun, and how it went off. And how she died." Her voice trembled.

"And Chloe?" I asked. "What does she have to do with all of this?"

"About four months ago, she called. I'd never met her before, but she called my private line and told my assistant she was my stepfather's wife. I happened to be around, so I got on the phone. She just said it flat out. She said she knew

I'd shot my mother, and that if I didn't want everyone in the world to know, too, I'd have to hand over some serious change. That's what she said, 'some serious change.' "

This explained why Archer had been so protective of Lilly. He had been trying to keep me from discovering that she had a motive for killing Chloe Jones.

"How did Chloe find out about what happened to your mother?"

"I don't know. Jupiter swears it wasn't him. I was sure it was Polaris. I mean, who else could it be? I went there today to tell him that what happened was his fault. If he hadn't told her, she wouldn't have blackmailed me, and I wouldn't have gone to Jupiter for help. And then Chloe wouldn't have died."

"You paid Chloe off, right?"

"Yeah."

"But *why*, Lilly? Why did you care if anyone found out? I mean, it was an *accident*. You were practically a baby. No one would blame you."

She shook her head. "I'd be a freak. The actress who killed her mother. Anytime anybody saw me, that's what they'd see. It's hard enough to get cast in this goddamn town when you're a woman who's over thirty. Do you really think a director is going to want to deal with all that? There are two hundred other actresses he could use instead—actresses who don't come with the same horrible baggage."

"But you won an Oscar!"

"Two women win Oscars every year. Two a year, Juliet. At least six more are nominated every year. And not a single one of those killed her mother."

It was hard to argue with that. I knew how hard Lilly had worked to break out of the B movies that had launched her career. I knew, too, how ambitious she was. It was one of the things that had always impressed me the most about her. "How did you get the money without anyone finding out?" I asked. "I mean, don't you have financial advisors, managers, that kind of thing? Didn't they notice that the money was gone?"

"My business manager would definitely have noticed. I had to tell her."

"You told her?"

"Sort of. I mean, I told her that I was being blackmailed, but I didn't tell her what about. I just said that I had to pay the person off, and that I wasn't going to go to the police. She wasn't happy, but she got the money for me." Lilly smiled bitterly. "I think she figured it was some creepy sex thing."

"What happened after you gave Chloe the money?"

"She asked for another hundred thousand, and I couldn't do it. I mean, I could afford it, but I just realized that it was never going to end, that she would milk me completely dry. So I refused."

"But she didn't go to the media?"

Lilly shook her head. "She didn't have time. When she called asking for more money, I called Jupiter and told him that Chloe had found out about my mother. I asked him if he told her. He swore that he hadn't."

"Jupiter knew about what happened?"

"Of course. He was there."

I wasn't surprised that he'd lied to me. Clients lied to me all the time, with even less justification. I did wonder, however, if Jupiter had lied to protect Lilly, or to protect himself.

"I begged Jupiter to help me," Lilly said. "I figured that since he knew Chloe so well, he might know something I could use, or be able to find something out. Then I could sort of . . . well . . . blackmail her back."

"And did he? Did he find out anything that could help you?"

"You could say that. He told me about their relationship. Jupiter said that if Polaris found out that she was sleeping with him, he would throw her out. And she certainly wouldn't want that. I could only give her so much. Polaris is worth tens of millions."

"So why was she blackmailing you to begin with? If he had so much money?"

"Jupiter said Polaris had her on a strict allowance. He

didn't give her that much more than he gave Jupiter. And that was barely anything."

"But if he divorced her, she'd get half. At least half of whatever he earned while they were together."

She shook her head. "His people had made her sign a prenup. Jupiter told me. She'd get basically nothing."

I nodded. That made sense. Then something occurred to me. "But what about Jupiter? Wouldn't Polaris have thrown him out, too?"

Lilly nodded, and the tears began streaming down her face again. "Yeah. But he said he didn't care. That he cared more about me. And I would have taken care of him if Polaris had thrown him out. He's my little brother—the only one I ever had. I would have taken care of him."

I patted her on the back, and she inhaled raggedly.

"So what happened? Did you confront her with the information Jupiter gave you?"

Lilly dashed her tears away with her fist. "No, *he* did. He was just supposed to talk to her. He was supposed to threaten her that he'd go to Polaris if she didn't lay off me. But I guess something went horribly wrong. The next thing I knew, she was dead."

"Did he kill her?"

She shrugged. "He must have. I would never have thought he could do something like that. I still can't believe it. The only thing I can think of was that he was trying to convince her to stop blackmailing me, and she wouldn't, and then somehow it got violent. He'd never have planned to hurt her. He's just not that kind of person."

He hadn't seemed capable of premeditated murder to me either, but the truth was neither Lilly nor I really knew what kind of person Jupiter was.

Lilly drained the last of her coffee from her mug. I looked down at my own cup. I hadn't touched it. I took a tentative sip and grimaced at the tepid bitterness. At that moment, a shrill voice screeched in my ear.

"Ohmigod! It *is* her! It's Lilly Green!"

I looked over my shoulder and saw a small woman bearing

down on us. She dodged the bank of plants and flung herself at our table, calling out, "It's Lilly Green. It's Lilly Green!"

I looked at Lilly. She had carefully wiped her face of any expression. The woman skidded to a stop at our table. She was wearing a pair of turquoise hip-hugger jeans and a matching top that left her midriff bare. She was very thin, and the wrinkled skin around her pierced belly button betrayed her age.

Lilly assumed a facsimile of the wide, unpretentious smile for which she was famous, and said, "Hi."

"Ohmigod! Ohmigod. Your hair! What happened to your beautiful hair?" Lilly didn't answer, just raised her eyebrows. The woman didn't seem to notice. "I am such a fan, Lilly. I've seen all your movies. Every one. Even that weird foreign one."

"Thank you," Lilly said. "It's so nice to meet you. I wish we could stay, but I'm afraid my friend has to be somewhere." She gently kicked me under the table as she rose to her feet.

I leapt up, a forced smile plastered to my face, and said, "Right! We've got to go pick up the kids."

"Ohmigod!" the woman said. "You *do* drive carpool! Just like it said in *People* magazine! That's so great!"

We beat a hasty retreat to the parking lot. "Where's your car?" Lilly said.

I pointed to my squalid Bratmobile.

"Can you drive me?"

"Why? Your car's right there." I lifted my hand but she grabbed it before I could indicate her car.

"Don't. I don't want her to know which is mine. Let's just take your car, okay?"

"Okay." We walked quickly over to my station wagon, and I opened the door for her. I tried to sweep the passenger seat clean of debris, but she pushed me aside impatiently, got in, and slammed the door. I walked around the car, got inside, and closed my own door. I looked over at her. She was leaning back against the headrest, her eyes closed, and her face pale and drawn.

"Just drive," she said.

"Okay."

"I'm not being paranoid," she said. "It's just that if she saw my license plate, she could find out my address."

I pulled out of the parking lot and into the stream of traffic. "Lilly, I don't know if you've noticed, but there are guys on half the street corners in L.A. selling maps to the stars' homes."

She shrugged. "I just couldn't bear the idea of that woman knowing anything about me. Even what kind of car I drive."

"How will you get it home?"

"I'll have someone pick it up."

I sighed, trying to imagine a life in which there was someone available at your beck and call to pick up a car you left in a random strip mall out in Pasadena. But then, that was the same life that left you open to being accosted by strangers in cafés. I thought about the price my friend had paid for her privacy, and the price Jupiter might have to pay for it. I sighed deeply. There was nothing about poor Lilly's life to envy. Nothing at all.

"I talked to Archer," Lilly said suddenly.

"Oh?" I kept my voice purposefully neutral.

"At first he denied going to your house."

"What?" I sputtered.

"Don't worry, I told him I believed you," she said.

"You did?" I was somewhat mollified, but still irritated.

"Yeah. And he admitted it, but said it was because he was trying to protect me."

"Oh." I couldn't think of anything else to say.

She said, "I'm sorry, Juliet."

"That's okay."

We sat for a while in a silence that grew slowly thicker and more uncomfortable. Finally, more to make conversation than anything else, I asked, "So, how did you and your mother end up in Mexico?"

"Now that's a story," Lilly said. She pushed her shoes off and put her feet up, resting her chin on her knees.

Her mother and father grew up together in Lubbock,

Texas, where the soil was so arid that the flower of sixties activism withered and died before it had a chance to bloom into anything more than macramé and marijuana. When Trudy-Ann Nutt found herself pregnant at age eighteen, her boyfriend agreed to stay with her on one condition—that they exchange the passions of drag racing and high school football for VW buses and communal hot tubs. They hitched their way to L.A., and Lilly was born in a commune in Topanga Canyon, the same commune where Artie Jones had been living with his girlfriend, who would later give birth to Jupiter and abandon him to his father's dubious care.

"I have so few memories of that time in Topanga. I was only five when my mom and I cut out. My dad was in charge of one small corner of the garden—that I remember. He used to grow these tall bushy plants." She laughed grimly. "Pot, I'm sure. I remember sleeping on a mattress on the floor with my mother. But not with my dad. I guess old Raymond found other places to sleep. It was like that. People kind of fell into bed with whoever was around. You know, that whole sixties free love kind of thing." Lilly's face grew thoughtful and she frowned slightly. "I don't think my mother liked it, though. I can remember her crying at night, sometimes."

I remembered something I'd seen in a gossip column recently. The teaser was "When the cat's away," and the bit had mentioned a sighting of Raymond dining with a very young TV actress at a chi chi restaurant popular with the junior Hollywood set. Lilly's stepmother Beverly had been on a political junket to Honduras, I believe. It didn't look like Raymond had changed his ways much.

"Is that why she and Polaris got together? Because your father was sleeping around?" I asked.

She nodded. "I suppose so. At some point my father just kind of drifted away. I don't know what happened; I just don't have any more memories of him from that time."

"What about your stepmother? Was she around back then?"

Lilly smiled. "I'm not sure exactly when she and my dad got together, but it was probably around that time, or soon after. I think they might have met in the commune, too. I don't really know; at the time I was a lot closer to my mother—my biological mother—than to my dad."

"But you and your stepmother are close now, aren't you?"

Lilly nodded. "Very. I think of her as my mother. I mean, you know that. Most people don't even know that she's not my biological mother."

"And Polaris? How did he come into the picture, do you know?"

Lilly grimaced. "All I really remember is that he started sleeping in the same room as my real mother and me, and then a whole bunch of us moved down to Mexico."

"Who moved there with you?"

She wrinkled her brow. "My mother and Polaris. Of course, he was Artie back then. And at least a few other people. I don't really remember the grown-ups. They weren't around very much. I do remember one night, though." She paused and seemed to be straining to grasp a faint wisp of memory. "They were all sitting around a table with a white tablecloth. The room was really dark, but I remember the tablecloth sort of glowing blue. That's weird. How could a tablecloth glow?"

"Maybe it was under a black light?"

She smiled at me. "That must have been it! And there was a shoebox on the table. I remember that, too. I wasn't allowed to touch it, though. I remember Artie saying that. He said that there were mushrooms in the box, but that Jupiter and I weren't allowed to touch them, because they were special magic mushrooms."

I laughed. "Psychedelic mushrooms?"

She nodded. "I think so. And you wonder why I'm such a neurotic mess. My parents sat around tripping on mushrooms while I played under the table . . ." Her voice trailed off as she remembered that other source for her neurosis.

"I don't think you're a mess, Lilly. You've never seemed like a mess to me. On the contrary. You've always seemed absolutely sane, and incredibly sweet. Considering what you've gone through in your life, you're a paragon of mental health."

Tears puddled in her eyes and clung to the thick, sooty eyelashes that contrasted so sharply with her fuzz of blond hair. "I'm an actress, Juliet. It's all an act. I'm just a really good actress."

Thirteen

IT would be difficult to imagine an upbringing more different from Lilly's than my own. My parents had waited until they were in their forties to have their family. Lilly's had been teenagers when she was born. Lilly's childhood was spent frolicking with bands of half-naked children in communes in Topanga Canyon and Mexico. And mine? Watching *Brady Bunch* episodes in a split-level in Fair Lawn, New Jersey. Our parents' political sensibilities may well have been more alike than different, however. Mine had made the uneasy transition from socialism to the Democratic Party back in the fifties, and had always been the most active of pacifists. They might have met Raymond and Trudy Ann at an antiwar rally, although my mother's appearance would surely have caused Lilly's some consternation. Her look has always been solidly Jewish Grandmother—permed hair, cardigan sweater with a wad of tissue peeping out the sleeve, and in the crook of her arm, a public television tote bag stuffed with knitting, boxes of raisins, and old copies of *Dissent* and *Commentary*.

I couldn't imagine having a parent who, like Lilly's, practiced free love and did drugs. Until my mother instructed me to smoke pot, that is.

"What did you say?" I said, sure that I'd misheard.

"I've been doing research on this, and I have every confidence it will help."

"Ma. Let me get this straight. You want me to take an illegal drug for my morning sickness?"

"Oh please. Don't be so dramatic. It's not a drug, it's medicine. That's why they call it medical marijuana."

I took the phone over to the couch and plopped heavily onto the cushions. I was going to need to sit down for this conversation. I'd woken up at dawn the day after my morning with Lilly and had spent a long half-hour in what had become an all-too-familiar position, on my knees in the bathroom. It was way too early in the morning to bother any of my friends, so I'd called my mother two time zones away to whine about how lousy I felt.

"It's illegal," I said.

"It is not. Not with a doctor's note. Remember Marcia Feinman's aunt, the one who lives in San Francisco?"

I didn't—it would take a government research grant to plot the tangled network of my mother's friends and relatives, and all their ailments. "Sure," I said.

"Well, she has cancer. Poor thing. The woman is a mass of tumors. They're chewing through her internal organs one at a time." I winced. When it comes to diseases, Margie Applebaum has always had a way with words. "The chemo was making her so nauseated, poor thing, that she couldn't keep a single thing down. The starvation was going to kill her before the cancer could. Her doctor wrote her a prescription for marijuana. It's totally changed her life. I mean, the poor thing is still going to die, but at least now she can eat! She's a member of a club. She goes there, she eats a brownie, and she feels a thousand times better."

"Mmm. A brownie." I considered making a batch, but decided that just looking at a raw egg would make me throw up. "You know, call me crazy, Mom, but when they passed the medical marijuana law, I don't think California's voters envisioned pregnant women smoking pot."

"Well, why *not*?" She bristled. "It's one of the most benign substances known to medicine! Chinese midwives have used it for centuries!"

"Mom, how do you know this stuff?"

"Oh for heaven's sake. You think I'm an idiot? The Internet!"

I laughed. "Of course, I don't think you're an idiot, and I am grateful to you for surfing the web on my behalf, but I'm not going to smoke pot. Honestly, Mom, you should hear the grief I get for drinking *coffee*. Do you really think my OB is going to let me toke up?"

"Listen, little miss smarty pants. You know how many people die from taking Tylenol every year?" She didn't wait for my answer, not that I could have given her one. "Over *two thousand*. You know how many people have ever died from using marijuana? None. Zip. Zero. But you do what you want. Spend the next nine months throwing up if you want. Just don't come complaining to me."

"I won't," I said, my voice rising in response to hers. I bet she'd tell you that I started the fight. It was always like that.

"Kiss my grandchildren for me," she said, still yelling.

"I will," I shouted back.

"Call me tomorrow."

"Fine!" I slammed down the phone.

"Who was that?" a little voice said. I turned to find Isaac standing in the doorway. His face was swollen with sleep, and one leg of his Batman pajamas was hitched up above his knee. The Velcro cape had become detached from his shoulders and restuck itself on his tush.

"Hey, you!" I said. "Come on up here."

He jumped up on the couch and burrowed into my side. I winced as his little toes dug into my belly. I moved his cape to its proper position and kissed the top of his head.

"Who was that, Mama?"

"Grandma."

"How come you always yell at Grandma?"

"I do not always yell at her!"

"Yes you do."

I considered this for a moment. "Well, because she always yells at me."

"You should use your words, Mama."

"Okay, buddy. From now on, I'll use my words." He snuggled in closer to me and I moved back a bit. "Careful of my tummy, honey," I said.

"Because of the baby?" he said. I sat up and stared at him.

"How do you know about the baby?"

"Ruby told me."

"How does Ruby know?"

He shrugged. As far as he was concerned, Ruby knew everything. I picked him up and carried him into his sister's bedroom. I dumped him on her bed and shook her awake.

"Ruby, wake up," I said. She pulled her pillow over her head. "Wake up, Rubes. It's time for school." She sat up, rubbing her eyes. When I finally got her alert enough to answer a question, I said, "How did you know I was going to have a baby?"

"Because you're fat, and you keep throwing up."

"But how did you know what that meant?"

She shrugged and rubbed the sleep from her eyes. "That's what happened when Isaac was in your tummy."

"You remember that? How can you possibly remember that? You were only two years old!"

She shrugged. "I remember everything, Mama."

I sat down on the bed next to her and pulled a kid close to me with each arm. "Well, guys, how do you feel about having a new baby?"

Isaac looked over at his older sister, as if looking for instructions on what emotion she would permit him under these circumstances. Ruby wrinkled her eyebrows and thought for a moment. "We're okay with it," she said. Isaac nodded.

I breathed a sigh of relief and squeezed them close. I couldn't help at that moment to compare my daughter to Lilly. Was Ruby's memory unusually precise? Lilly's was so foggy—although that surely was a result of the horrors she'd experienced. Still, memory was a strange thing. Would Ruby's remain as acute, or would the memories that were so clear to her now fade with time? Then I had a truly horrible and self-indulgent thought. If I died now, would Ruby remember more of me than what dress I was wearing.

Fourteen

AL was coming up from Westminister for a meeting with the courier company that had retained him to investigate its employees. We had arranged to meet for breakfast after I dropped the kids off at school. I'd promised to give him a mini-lesson on the intricacies of workers' compensation law and had done an hour or so of research the night before. People think that being a lawyer means that you have a wealth of laws, rules, and cases filed away in your memory. That's a myth. The most important thing, really the only thing, that law school teaches you is where to look to find the answer to a legal question. That's enough, frankly. A good lawyer doesn't necessarily know anything at all—she's just adept at research.

Al and I made our discussion of insurers' assumption of liability, wrongful termination, ERISA, and other scintillating topics more palatable with biscuits and sausage gravy. Then, as we sopped up the last of our meal, I told him about Lilly and her mother. When I was done, Al leaned heavily back in his chair, cupping his hands around his mug of coffee.

He shook his head and said, "You going to Wasserman?"

That was, of course, the ten-thousand-dollar question. Should I give this information to Jupiter's defense attorney? I knew exactly what I would have done with Lilly's story if I were the one representing Jupiter at trial. I would have used it to deflect attention away from my client. I would have argued that there was one person in Chloe's life with a motive to kill her, one person whose future depended on her perpetual silence: Lilly Green. I would have subpoenaed the movie star and convinced the jury that hers was the finger that pulled the trigger. Not even the fact that Lilly was one of my very good friends would have dissuaded me.

"I've got to tell him," I said.

Al nodded.

"I sure as hell don't want to, though."

He nodded again, and said, "What do you make of it? Do you think she did it?"

I pushed my plate away, suddenly not feeling hungry anymore. "I honestly can't imagine her doing it. I can't imagine her killing anyone."

"So, who then?"

"Lilly thinks that when Jupiter confronted Chloe about the blackmail, something happened. Somehow things got out of control, and he ended up killing her."

Al shrugged. "I guess it's possible." He raised a hand and waved at the waitress. We sat silently while she filled our cups. I moved mine aside, having drunk my allotted single cup of coffee.

Once she'd gone out of earshot, I said, "It's certainly no more unlikely than Lilly killing her. Lilly's not a murderer. She's ambitious, she's strong willed, but she's also unpretentious, and thoughtful. She's got an amazing sense of humor. She's not a killer."

"But she is."

"Excuse me?"

"She *is* a killer, isn't she? She killed her mother."

"A gun went off accidentally when she was five years old. That hardly makes her a killer."

He raised his eyebrows.

"What?" I said. "You don't believe any more than I do that a five-year-old is responsible for a gun accident. If anything, it was her parents' fault for leaving the gun around."

"Maybe it wasn't an accident."

"What?" I said.

"Maybe it wasn't an accident. Maybe she shot her mother on purpose. Maybe that's why she's so afraid of the story getting out."

I reached across the table and snatched the cup of coffee I had just pushed aside. I took a gulp. When I was sure that I was calmed sufficiently that I wasn't going to bite my partner's head off, I said, "No five-year-old shoots her mother on purpose. She wouldn't have known how to do it, for one thing. And even if the gun didn't just go off, even if she meant to pull the trigger, a child that age doesn't understand what she's doing. She has nothing even remotely like the *mens rea*, the state of mind, necessary to make her guilty of murder. A kid that age doesn't even know what death means."

"I'm not saying she would have been convicted in court, or even that she would have understood what she did. I'm just saying, maybe she wasn't just playing around, and the gun went off. Maybe she meant for it to go off, and that's what she's afraid Chloe would tell people."

I shook my head firmly. "I still can't imagine Lilly killing anyone. I mean, honestly, can you?"

"Sure."

"Sure?"

"Yeah, sure. People are capable of pretty much anything to protect themselves. Lilly Green is no exception."

Is that what being a cop does to you? For a moment, I felt sorry for Al. I felt bad that his years on the job had made him so cynical, had made him so willing to believe all people capable of that kind of violent self-interest. Then I shivered as a thought occurred to me. Maybe Al's experiences had served not to blind him, but to open his eyes to a fundamental truth: that all people possess the germ of violence.

Perhaps I was the one with the twisted perception. Perhaps my belief that most of us are simply incapable of murder was just naïve.

I forced myself to consider the possibility that Lilly had murdered Chloe. I tried to imagine the scene. But I couldn't. It just felt wrong.

"Even if that's true, even if Lilly is capable of murder, she wouldn't have done it herself. She would have hired someone to do it for her," I said. We looked at each other for a moment as we considered that possibility.

"So, you think she hired someone?" Al said.

"No! That's not what I said. I just said that if she *did* want Chloe dead, she's more likely to have hired someone. I didn't mean that that's what she actually did."

"It's possible, though, isn't it?"

I didn't answer. I didn't need to.

Then I had an idea. "It could have been Archer!" I said.

Al nodded. "Maybe. He's clean, by the way."

"Really?" I was terribly disappointed. It would have been so convenient if he'd had a criminal record.

"So you're going to Wasserman," Al said.

"Yeah. But not just yet. I'm going to poke around a little more, see what I find out. Maybe I won't *have* to tell him, after all." Both Al and I knew just how unlikely that was, however. If there was even a shade of a chance that Lilly had committed the murder, either by doing it herself, or by hiring someone to do it for her, I had to alert Jupiter's attorney. Even if everything happened just as Lilly said—if she had asked Jupiter for help, and he had killed Chloe only to protect her—I still owed it to Jupiter to make Wasserman aware of all the facts. Jupiter's relationship with Lilly, his actions on her behalf, would be important to the defense's theory of the case. A jury might be less likely to recommend the death penalty for a murder motivated by chivalry. The fact that he had had sex with the victim before killing her made Jupiter seem less of a white knight perhaps, and more of a knave, but figuring out how to present that to the jury was Wasserman's problem, not mine.

"Poke around a little more where?" Al asked.

"Around Polaris, I guess. And Jupiter. I've still got to continue with the regular investigation, too. Follow up on the child abuse allegation, talk to his teachers from elementary school. Old friends. It wouldn't hurt to talk to people who knew Chloe, too. You never know what I might turn up."

Al got to his feet with an old man's creaking groan. "Lucky you. I'm off to sit on my butt growing piles in the course of what promises to be a very long and tedious surveillance." He sucked loudly on his teeth and shook his head. "Maybe we should rethink our policy about divorce cases. They've got to be more interesting than this worker fraud crap."

I smiled. "More dangerous, too. Aren't you the one who told me that the most dangerous calls for police officers are the ones for domestic disturbances?" I said.

He grunted. "True. It's like I always say, nobody hates you like the people who are supposed to love you."

On that cheerful note, Al grabbed the check and headed off to the cash register, pushing away my hand as I tried to give him some money for my meal.

Fifteen

I didn't have it in me that morning to face the county jail. I just couldn't handle the smell of that place. Even in the visiting room there's a faint odor of disinfectant overlying something dank and horrible—sweat, or worse. My stomach roiled at the thought. I decided to save Jupiter for another day and called Polaris's office instead. I got stuck at the receptionist. Or maybe at the receptionist's receptionist. At any rate, I didn't get close to reaching Polaris Jones on the telephone. Finally, after a frustrating twenty minutes of talking to cheerfully unhelpful assistant after cheerfully unhelpful assistant, all of whom seemed incredulous at my assumption that I was good enough to engage in a conversation with the Very Reverend himself, I lost my temper.

"Listen," I said to the most recent of minions who had refused my request to speak to the man. "You tell the Very Reverend that I very much want to talk to him about Trudy-Ann's very fatal shooting."

"The Very Reverend's transitioned wife was named Chloe."

There was that word again. Transitioned from what to

what? I was pretty sure they didn't mean from flesh to worm-riddled dust. "You just pass that message on exactly as I gave it to you." I gave her my cell phone number. I said I was pretty sure her boss would want to get back to me immediately upon hearing the message. Then, while I waited, I stopped in at Whole Foods and loaded up my basket with every item that I'd ever heard could alleviate nausea, including gingersnaps, Japanese pickled ginger, lemons, citrus lozenges, herbal Dramamine, watermelon, lemonade, potato chips, and a pair of wristbands that were supposed to help with seasickness. I was snapping the wristbands in place, sniffing the lemon, and sucking on the candy, when my cell phone rang.

"This is Hyades Goldblum," the caller said.

"Excuse me?"

"Reverend Hyades, of the Church of Cosmological Unity. We met when you interviewed the Very Reverend Polaris."

The bearded, less agitated assistant. "Of course. I've been trying to reach Polaris . . . er, the Very Reverend Polaris."

"He is unavailable at present," Hyades said, his voice so smooth it was almost oily. "But I may be able to assist you. I understand you have some questions regarding the first Mrs. Jones?"

"Yes. I'd like to talk to him about how she died."

"Ah. I believe I might be able to spare a few moments for you, Ms. Applebaum."

"You? Do you know anything about her death?"

"Of course. I knew Trudy-Ann quite well. I was, in fact, living in the house in San Miguel when she transitioned to the next astral plane."

THE underground parking lot of the CCU campus had an entrance so discreet that it was virtually invisible from the street, and was crammed with some of the most expensive cars I'd ever seen. I slotted my beater between a gold Bentley and some silver thing with wings that looked like *it* had undergone the transition to the next astral plane. I banged my rather corpulent behind on the door of the silver car while I was trying to squeeze out, and had to rush out of the lot to the tone of a wailing alarm that sounded less like a siren and more like an aging soprano's rendition of "Dido's Lament."

An elevator took me directly from the parking lot into the main building, and when I walked out of the elevator, it was hard to believe I was in the same antebellum mansion I'd seen from the outside. The interior of the building had been wiped clean of any trace of Tara. Instead of the elaborate moldings and the sweeping wooden staircase that must have once graced the entry hall, I found myself facing a huge, almost empty space that looked like a set from *Star Trek*—the later series, when the production values were better. The room had been painted a kind of silvery white, and the walls seemed to sparkle. The floor was white marble, polished to an intense shine. Instead of a staircase, there were two escalators leading to the second floor. The ceiling was dark blue, and sprinkled with luminous stars, and a massive silver model of the solar system dwarfed the hall. As I watched, it rotated, each orb spinning at a different speed. Some of the smaller moons were moving so fast they were almost a blur. At the far end of the hall, three young women in white robes sat talking into telephone headsets behind a long metal counter that seemed to hover in midair. As I peered at the counter, I realized that the effect was created by a clear, glass base.

I skirted the orbiting planets and went up to the counter. I stood in front of one of the women, waiting for her to finish her telephone conversation. She smiled at me and held up a finger, indicating that she'd be done in a minute. Her nails were polished in gleaming silver. I looked over at the other two receptionists. They all wore the same shining nail polish. Their hair was tucked up into silver mesh snoods and they were wearing makeup with a touch of glitter.

"Welcome to the Church of Cosmological Unity. May I help you?" the young woman asked, her smile wide and gracious.

"I'm here to see Hyades Goldblum," I said.

"Of course. Ms. Applebaum. *Reverend* Hyades is expecting you." Her voice held just the slightest hint of rebuke at my failure to include the honorific. "His assistant will meet you on the second floor." She pointed to the escalator. Another young woman in an identical white robe and silver snood was waiting for me at the top. I followed her down another gleaming marble-floored hallway, past closed doors, all of which were painted glossy blue. The walls were painted the same silvery white as the downstairs entryway, and again the hallway ceiling was covered in thousands upon thousands of twinkling lights. The shimmering light reflecting off all the brilliant surfaces was beautiful, but it was starting to give me a headache, and I wondered how the CCU staff could stand it.

The windows in Hyades's office were covered with linen draperies, the lights were dim, and the walls were paneled in deep brown mahogany. I sat, as instructed by the assistant, in a plain oak Morris chair in front of a massive oak desk. Hyades's Arts and Crafts furniture couldn't have been more different from the space-age décor outside the closed office door. I wondered if it was designed to be a statement, or if he just shared my discomfort with the constant sparkle of the outer rooms and halls.

The assistant stood at attention next to the desk, and we waited in silence. Within a moment or two, a door to the left of the desk opened, and the man I remembered from my initial meeting with Polaris walked in. He was slightly taller than average, with close-cropped gray hair that contrasted with his pure white beard, and a sharp-pointed nose. His eyes were gray, and in his white robe he looked like a black-and-white photograph of himself. He was wiping his hands on a small yellow towel, which stood out against his white-clad body like a splotch of sunlight. He handed the towel to the assistant, and she carried it reverently out of the room, as though it were made of porcelain rather than terry cloth. He lowered himself into a tall leather and wood executive chair, leaned his elbows on its arms, and tented his fingers in front of his chest.

"Tell me, Ms. Applebaum, what is it that you'd like to know about Trudy-Ann?"

I looked at him appraisingly, wondering whether he knew as much as I about the circumstances of her death. Rather than give anything away, I merely sat down opposite him and said, "I'm exploring the possibility that her death might shed some light on the recent tragic events."

"Ah." He tapped his lips with the tent he'd made of his fingers. "Why? If I might ask? What would a death that happened nearly thirty years ago have to do with . . . what did you call it? The 'recent tragic events'?" The quotation marks were audible. Did he not consider Chloe's death tragic?

"I don't know. I was hoping that Very Reverend Jones could help me figure that out."

"The Very Reverend is far too distraught about the violent death of *this* wife to bring his thoughts to bear on that of the previous one."

I was puzzled for a moment, trying to figure out just how much more he knew, and how to get him to talk to me about it. I decided to play dumb. "How did Trudy-Ann die?" I asked.

"Don't you know?" He stretched his thin lips into a smile.

I said nothing, just looked blandly back at him.

"Yes, of course you do," he said. "She was shot by her little girl, Lilly. You know Lilly Green, of course. She is, after all, paying your bill. Curious, that. Don't you think? That the famous Lilly Green is paying for the defense of the murderer Jupiter Jones? Of course you're good friends with Lilly, aren't you? Through your husband, isn't it? Peter Wyeth. He wrote that appalling cannibal movie Lilly starred in. Dreadful stuff your husband writes. Although I suppose it pays for your children's education."

It wouldn't have been that hard to find any of it out. The press kits for Peter's movies listed his marriage to me. Lilly's past as a B-movie actress was obviously well known. It would have taken only a bit of research to put it all together. As for the fact that Lilly was paying for Jupiter's attorneys, well, I didn't know how he knew that. Maybe Lilly herself had said something when she'd come to see Polaris. Maybe Hyades had just put two and two together. He knew Jupiter had no money of his own, and he knew Wasserman didn't come cheap. One thing was certain—the reason he'd made me aware of the breadth of his knowledge was in order to intimidate me. And I suppose if I were honest with myself, I would admit that it had worked. But if I have one great gift, it's for denial.

"What were you doing in San Miguel back in the sixties, Mr. Goldblum?" I asked.

"Please, Hyades. Or Reverend Hyades, if you will. What were *any* of us doing in the sixties? Psychedelics, I suppose." He paused, as if waiting for me to appreciate his joke. I said nothing. "San Miguel was full of young American seekers, back then. Nowadays, I understand it's full of elderly American retirees. Seeking what, I wonder? Anyway, a group of us came down to Mexico from Topanga Canyon. But then Polaris told you that."

"And were you there when Trudy-Ann died?"

His supercilious smile faded just the tiniest bit. "Yes," he said.

"What can you tell me about her death?"

"Little more than you know already. The little girl was playing in Trudy-Ann and Polaris's room. She found the gun, and when her mother came in, she accidentally shot her. Trudy-Ann died instantly."

"Why was there a gun in Trudy-Ann and Polaris's room?"

He leaned back in his chair and shook his head slightly. "Texans," he said ruefully.

"Excuse me?"

"Trudy-Ann was a down-home girl, and when her daddy found out she was in the lawless land of Mexico, he did what any Texas daddy would do. He sent her a handgun."

"What happened after Trudy-Ann died? Did the police investigate the shooting?"

"They asked a few questions. They spoke to the maids, and to Polaris. I think they might have talked to a few of the other people living in the house, but I'm not sure. They certainly never interviewed me, and I'm fairly confident they never talked to Lilly. Not that they would have gotten very far if they had. She became virtually catatonic almost immediately. She didn't speak for weeks." He paused and stroked his lip with his finger. "As I recall, the police didn't even take the body. The mortuary people picked her up. Trudy-Ann is buried there, in San Miguel, you know. On the first *Dia de los Muertes* after she died, we visited her in the cemetery. We brought food, and flowers, and had a party on her grave. That's the custom in Mexico. Her first death day party was, alas, also her last. It was something of a last hurrah for the commune. Most people had already gone back home by then. The rest of us left soon after."

"Why?"

"Why did we leave?"

I nodded.

"Trudy-Ann's death put a damper on the fun, I suppose."

I blinked at the sarcasm in his tone. The violent death of a wife and mother hardly seemed something someone should joke about, especially if that someone was supposed to be a man of God. "How did Polaris react to the death of his wife?" I asked.

Hyades rocked forward in his chair and leaned his arms on his desk. "He was devastated, of course, and he was also very worried about the little girl. I remember him holding Lilly in his arms at the funeral. She looked so odd. Pale and silent. Stunned. He just held her close to him. I think that's when I realized that there was something special about him. That he was spiritually different from other men. There, in the midst of his own grief, he focused on this needy child."

I wondered what kind of man this Hyades was if he thought it so unusual that Polaris would have comforted his wife's child during her funeral. Isn't that what a parent is supposed to do? It's certainly what any *woman* would do. "What happened to her, to Lilly?" I asked.

"Like I said, she seemed to slip into a catatonic state. She stopped speaking, stopped eating. Polaris sat by her bed for days, feeding her by hand, changing her clothes when she soiled them. He was absolutely devoted to that child. We had a few house meetings to decide what to do, how to help her. Some of us tried to convince Polaris to pretend to her that it hadn't happened. To tell her a different story about how Trudy-Ann died. After all, it seemed pretty clear that the girl remembered nothing. At one point I think he even considered it. One of the girls had a father who was a psychologist back in the States. Polaris called him, to ask what to do with Lilly, how to help her. The doctor said that lying to her wouldn't do her any good. Even if we could all convince her that she hadn't killed her mother, that Trudy-Ann had died in some other kind of accident, somewhere in Lilly's mind she would always know the truth. That truth would torment her. The trauma would express itself in some other way."

"So what did Polaris do?"

"It became clear that Lilly wasn't going to get any better in San Miguel. She needed intensive therapy, and there wasn't any to be had there. At the time it was nothing more than a primitive little city in the Northern Highlands of Mexico. Polaris sent Lilly back to the States to live with her father. You must understand, this was a very traumatic decision for him. He was much more than the girl's stepfather. When Polaris and Trudy-Ann got together, he stepped into a void in Lilly's life. Raymond hadn't paid any attention to her since she was a baby. Polaris became her father in every way. Sending her away was absolutely devastating for him. He made Raymond promise that he'd get therapy for the girl. I think Polaris even paid for it himself. Not that he had two dimes to rub together back then. But whatever he did have, he sent to Raymond, to pay for Lilly's treatment. It was clearly the right decision. She ended up coming out of her catatonic state. And the rest, of course, is history. Oscar-winning history."

"If he was so attached to her, why didn't he have more of a relationship with her after he returned to the States?"

"He tried. He always kept up with her, through Raymond. When he came home, he visited her. He brought Jupiter to see her—the two children were very close. But it soon became clear that his presence served only to remind her of the trauma she'd experienced. Raymond and Beverly were married by then, and they asked Polaris to stay away, for Lilly's sake. He did, by and large. I think he and Jupiter would come to see her every once in a while, but not often. Losing his place in the child's life was a tremendous sacrifice for Polaris. But he did it for her; to keep her mind from breaking again."

I tried to imagine that pompous oddity enthroned on his wicker chair with his robes and ringed toes and his history of smacking people around as the devoted father Hyades described. It was hard, but not impossible. Even the most peculiar, the most self-absorbed, the most abusive people can love their children, especially when those children are small. When they are young, vulnerable, and utterly dependent on you for their very existence, it is so easy to be devoted to them. As they grow older and begin the work of separating from you, that's when loving them becomes much more of a challenge.

"Of course, by then, Polaris had much more important work to do," Hyades said. "He had an entire flock to care for, not just a single little girl."

"How did that happen?" I asked. "How did the CCU start?"

Hyades smiled. "You mean, how did we go from a commune in San Miguel to all this?" He waved around the room, symbolically taking in all the CCU campus and its various holdings.

"Exactly."

"It began soon after Trudy-Ann and Lilly were gone. Polaris was deeply moved by the Mexican funeral rites, by the celebrations of the day of the dead. The Mexicans understand death to be a part of life. It is simply another passage, a transition, that each of us must experience. He began to study the Aztec and Mayan civilizations, and found inspiration in their shamans' teachings about the spirit world. Birth is the emergence from the world of the spirit. Death is simply the return back home to the spirit realm. Then, as Polaris immersed himself in these teachings, he had a transformative moment of epiphany."

I could tell that Hyades had told the story of the CCU's origins many times—that it was something of a ritual. His voice had become sonorous almost in imitation of his boss, although without the Brooklyn accent. He stared up at the ceiling, his palms open on the tabletop.

"One night, Polaris climbed to the top of a hill outside San Miguel. He lay on his back and stared at the night sky. Suddenly, a silvery beam of light shone from the stars, directly into his eyes. It was the gaze of our fathers in the spirit realms of the planetary heavens." I stared at him, wondering how a man who seemed perfectly intelligent, and not a little cynical, could believe what sounded to me like such utter nonsense. He face betrayed no skepticism, and yet I wasn't convinced. Was there something a tiny bit ironic about his tone?

Hyades continued. "The fathers looked down to this world and saw below them on that hillside a pure and true guide. They found, after millennia of searching, the man who could bring the truth to this world. The beam of light transferred teachings directly from the heavens into Polaris's very mind. In an instant, the wisdom of the ages was given to him. And the Church of Cosmological Unity was born."

Either Hyades genuinely believed in the spiritual nonsense that had made them all so tremendously wealthy, or he was a remarkably adept faker. I decided to bring the conversation back to the terrestrial plane.

"Do you know if Chloe knew about Trudy-Ann's death? About Lilly's involvement in it? Would Polaris have told her about it?"

Hyades shook his head firmly. "No. I know for certain that he would never have told Chloe anything. We all swore a blood oath to keep what happened an absolute secret. Polaris cut his own palm and pressed it to the open wound of everyone who lived in that house at the time. He would never have violated his vow, even within the bonds of marriage."

I blinked at the minister. "I'm not sure I understand. If

you took a vow, why did you tell me everything just now?"

He shrugged and leaned back in his chair. "You knew the bare bones of the story already. It was important for you to understand that truth."

I nodded. There was only one other question I had. "Reverend Hyades, is it true that Polaris has a history of violent behavior? I've been told that he was aggressive with Jupiter, and that he hit his wife at least once."

Hyades shook his head. "That is the most ridiculous allegation I've ever heard. Nonviolence is one of the major tenets of the CCU. If there's nothing else . . ." He rang a bell on his desk, and his devoted acolyte came to escort me back to my car.

Sixteen

THE next morning I got a welcome phone call from Wasserman. The judge had agreed to an inpatient placement for Jupiter. He could get out of jail, as long as he checked into a rehab facility approved by the court.

"It was really your insistence that inspired me to press for his release," Wasserman said to me. "Why don't you tell him the good news."

I rushed down to the jail as soon as I dumped the kids at school. Despite all my pleading, and my threats to get sick right on the desk to prove to them how much I needed it, I could not get the marshals to allow me to take my Ziploc baggy with half a lemon in it into the visiting room. I was about to give up and deposit the lemon in the locker that already held my cell phone, purse, and shopping bag full of nausea-abatement snacks when a female guard approached the front desk.

"What's up?" she asked. She looked familiar; then I recalled that she'd been working at the jail back when I was at the federal defender. In those days, even though I'd spent most of my time at the federal lock-up, I'd still gone to county often enough to know most of the guards. I knew which ones would keep me waiting in between the security doors for no reason other than that they just didn't like defense lawyers. I knew which ones would cinch my client's handcuffs just tight enough to hurt. And I knew which ones would wish me a pleasant day, or take an extra moment to allow an inmate a lingering goodbye with a wife or child. She was, I remembered, one of the good ones.

"This lady's trying to bring food into the visiting room," said the guard who'd been giving me a hard time, holding up my lemon in its plastic bag.

The female guard was small, not much taller than I, and round. Her uniform strained over the shelf of her breasts, and her hair was ironed into a precise bob. Her skin was nut brown, and she had a pleasant smile that she shone my way. "Morning sickness?" she said.

I nodded.

"I read about that lemon trick in one of my pregnancy books," she said. "Never did much for me."

"I thought the lemon might help with the smell in there," I said. "It's just awful when you're pregnant."

"Don't I know it. I've got five kids, and I was sick as a dog with every single one of them. You think the smell in the visiting room is bad, you should try it up in the SHU, when the inmates plug up their toilets and they overflow into the halls. It's enough to make you want to die."

I groaned. "You know what? I think I'll give that a miss."

"You can keep that lemon," she said. "It's not going to do you a bit of good, but go ahead and bring it on in with you."

She was right, of course. The lemon didn't do a bit of good. I kept myself from throwing up only by stuffing my mouth full of Spicee Hot, the ginger-flavored chewing gum Peter had found for me in a Chinese grocery store.

Jupiter mustered a smile when he saw me waiting for him, and I saw a flash of the charming boy that lurked under the miserable inmate he'd become. I smiled back, and said, "I've got really good news."

His eyes widened and his lip began to tremble. "Bail?" he whispered.

"Yup," I said. His eyes filled with tears and he laughed. "Wait," I continued. "Before you get too excited, you're going to have to go into an inpatient drug treatment facility."

"That's fine," he said. "I mean, it's better. I want to be in rehab. Can I go back to Ojai? Would that be okay?"

I shook my head. "I don't know. I mean, the court might decide it's too far away. You need to be back in Pasadena for your court appearances."

"That wouldn't be a problem. At least I don't think it will."

He grabbed my hand and squeezed it. I jumped a little. This was the first time he'd touched me other than to shake my hand. I patted him on the wrist and said, "I'll talk to Wasserman about it. Maybe. We'll see, okay? Now it will take some time to engineer the release; to get the rehab center approved, and all that."

His face fell and he dropped my hand. "How long?"

"Maybe a week," I said.

He sighed. "Okay. I can handle that. A week."

"But now we've got work to do," I said. Jupiter and I made a list of every teacher he'd ever had who thought he was a decent student, every person he'd been close to who thought he was a decent human being. We carefully listed every job he'd ever worked, from his stint as an usher in a movie theater in high school to the Mexican surf shack he worked in during his escapes to Baja, to the computer game companies that had expressed interest in his designs. Finally, when I was confident that I had the names of absolutely everyone who would have a remotely kind word to say about him, I stacked up my papers and buckled them up in my briefcase. Jupiter began to rise from his seat, but I put out a restraining hand.

"There's something else we need to talk about," I said.

He sat back down and looked at me, his eyebrows slightly raised.

"Lilly told me about what Chloe was doing to her. About

the blackmail. And she told me that she asked you for help." Jupiter grew very still, except for his fingers, which were spread out on the tabletop. They trembled, tapping the Formica. Suddenly, he clenched his fists and shoved his hands into his lap.

"You don't need to tell me anything," I said. "I'm a part of your defense team, and what you say to me is confidential, but at the same time, I have certain obligations. I'm sure Wasserman told you this, but I'll say it again. A defense attorney is an officer of the court. As such, we aren't allowed to put testimony that we know is perjured on the stand. Let me explain what that means. If you tell me something, like, for instance, if you tell me that you killed Chloe . . ." He opened his mouth to object, but I raised my hand. "This is purely hypothetical. If you admit something like that to me, then your options will become limited. If you choose to take the stand, Wasserman will not be allowed to have you testify that you were innocent of the crime. A lawyer can present testimony that he doesn't personally believe, but he's forbidden to present testimony that he knows for certain is a lie. So if you tell him, or me, that you did it, you won't be able to testify that you didn't. Do you understand?"

He nodded.

"Understanding what I just explained to you, is there anything you want to tell me about what happened between you and Chloe?"

He chewed his lip. "I didn't kill her. I'm going to tell that to the jury. I didn't kill her." He looked up at me. "I'm not just saying that because of what you told me. It's true. I didn't kill her." He stared into my eyes unflinchingly.

"Was she blackmailing Lilly?"

"Yes. I mean, that's what Lilly told me, and I'm sure it's true. She wouldn't lie."

"Why did you tell me that you didn't know how Trudy-Ann died?"

He blushed. "Because . . . you know. For Lilly."

"But you do know, of course."

He nodded.

"Did you see it? Did you see Lilly shoot her mother?"

"No. I was looking for Lilly, I think. I was in the hallway when everything started happening. I remember seeing some stuff, mostly just the blood, I guess. And the sound of everybody screaming." His voice faded away.

"Do you remember anything else?"

"No, not really. I was really little. I don't remember very much from Mexico at all. I remember Lilly, though. I loved her so much."

"Do you still?"

He nodded. "She's my sister, you know? Even if our parents were only married when we were little kids. She's my sister. She'll always be my sister."

"Did you confront Chloe about what she was doing to your sister?"

"I tried to. When we were lying out at the pool together. I told her she had to stop blackmailing Lilly, but she just told me that I was in over my head, and then she laughed at me."

"And then what happened?"

He paused, and a dull red flush crept up his neck. "Then she . . . she got up and went into my bedroom."

"And you followed her?"

He nodded.

"To have sex?"

He nodded again.

"Did you talk any more about Lilly when you were . . . done?"

He shook his head. "No. It felt, I don't know, wrong or something, to keep talking about it. You know, while we were in bed. I knew I had to talk to her. I mean, I promised Lilly I would get her to stop. But I couldn't bring myself to do it there, in bed. I guess I figured I'd talk to her about it later."

"And did you talk to her about it later?"

He shook his head. "There wasn't any later. She was killed before I had a chance to see her again."

I believed him.

I didn't want to. I wanted to believe that Jupiter had killed Chloe in a fit of rage after she'd refused to stop blackmailing Lilly. I wanted the murder to have taken place like that, because then Wasserman could argue that it was an unpremeditated homicide, carried out under the influence of emotion or provocation. Premeditation is a necessary part of first-degree murder. Without it, the murder is at worst second degree, and not subject to the death penalty. Presenting the argument would also allow the defense to introduce evidence of Chloe's scheming behavior, her flouting of the law, her lack of anything resembling a sense of moral decency. I wanted Jupiter not to be innocent, but to be guilty of that lesser crime, because the other possibility was intolerable to me. The idea that my friend Lilly was guilty of murder was unacceptable. But I believed him. God help me, I believed that Jupiter Jones was innocent.

Seventeen

WHEN I got home that afternoon, I found Lilly sitting at my kitchen table and my husband lying on the floor at her feet.

"Am I interrupting something?" I asked, trying to pretend a nonchalance I didn't feel.

"I found him like this," Lilly said, and laughed.

I looked at her closely. Was she a murderer? I shook myself. Of course she wasn't. She was my friend. I would know if she were capable of murder. Wouldn't I?

I crouched down next to Peter. "Are you okay, honey?"

"My back gave out," he whined.

"Where are the kids?" I asked.

"I brought Patrick, one of my nannies," Lilly said. "He took all the kids to a café on La Brea to get steamed milks."

"Oh. Great." I smoothed Peter's hair away from his forehead, and he winced. "Do you need anything?"

He moaned.

"Peter told me about the baby," Lilly said. "Congratulations."

I resisted the urge to kick my prone husband while he was down. I was the one who got to tell my friends about the pregnancy. And even if Lilly counted as one of *his* friends, she was still my client. "Thanks," I said.

"I was just saying how much I admire you guys, going for three," she said. "I could never handle it."

"Neither can we," Peter said, and moaned again. This time I did kick him, but softly and just with the toe of my shoe. He howled.

"We'll be fine," I said.

"How do you know that?" he said, leaning up on his elbow. "I mean, we can't even handle the two we have. We've had like one night out alone in the past six months. We're always running from place to place, and half the time we end up not showing up on time. How many times have we been fined by the preschool for picking Isaac up late? And let's not even talk about the money. You're barely earning anything, and who knows if I'll get another movie after this one. We don't have enough time or money for the kids we have, let alone another one!" With that he sank back down onto the floor.

I stared at him and felt tears pricking at the back of my eyes. "Are you saying you want me to get rid of it? Have an abortion?" I whispered.

"No," he groaned. "I'm just freaking out. I'm allowed to freak out, aren't I?"

"I'm freaked out, too," I said. What I really wanted to tell him was that it was *my* career that was going to go down the toilet, *my* life that was going to be torn apart again. He'd pretty much go on as before, working, and spending time with the kids when he could. Sure, the financial burden rested on him, but every other part of it was squarely on my shoulders.

"I'm pretty freaked out, myself," Lilly said. "Not about your baby, obviously. But everything has just gotten too much for me. This whole thing."

I glanced down at Peter. She followed my gaze.

"I told Peter everything," she said.

I hoped he had done a good job of faking ignorance. I mean, Lilly probably knew I was confiding in him, but technically I was supposed to keep professional confidences even from my husband.

"I came by to cry on your shoulder, and Peter's been giving me some great advice on everything. On Archer, in particular."

"From down there?" I said, pointing at him.

"I have incredible clarity from this position," my husband said.

"Good to know," I said.

"Peter said I should take some time away from Archer, and from Jupiter and everything else. To kind of clear my head."

I nodded.

"I have an offer from an advertising agency in Japan. Peter says I should take it. Take the girls and get out of town for a couple of weeks."

Great. Now my husband was instructing suspects in my murder investigations to leave the country.

Lilly flung her feet off the table and stood up. "I'm going to go round up the kids and head home. I'll drop yours off on my way. Tomorrow, if I can put it together, I'm getting all of us on a plane." She bent down over Peter and planted a kiss on his cheek. "Thanks, buddy. You're a good friend."

He smiled, and then groaned again.

I walked Lilly to the door and came back into the kitchen. Peter was standing in front of the open refrigerator door, staring at the contents.

"How's your back?" I asked.

He placed his palms on the small of his back and leaned back. "Better. I got hungry."

I rolled my eyes. "You want to talk about this whole baby thing?" I asked.

He shook his head. "We'll work it out."

"Yeah," I said. But would we?

Eighteen

I spent the next two weeks overwhelmed with work, following up on the lists that Jupiter and I had made of people who knew him. I drove around the city, interviewing school teachers and Boy Scout troop leaders, neighbors and distant relatives. I talked to CCU members whose children Jupiter had babysat when he was a teenager, and even to two windblown surfers who had taken lessons from him down in Mexico. I interrogated his Narcotics Anonymous sponsor and his therapist. I concentrated on creating a dossier on Jupiter, and did my best to suppress my fears about Lilly. Thankfully, I didn't have to see my friend. She had left for Japan as promised, to shoot a series of commercials for Suntory beer.

Wasserman engineered Jupiter's release to the Ojai center, which made my life a lot easier. I could call Jupiter with questions and for follow-up information, and could relax a little, knowing he was being waited on by pool boys and not tortured by oversized inmates looking for a girlfriend.

Every few days, I prepared a thick packet of witness statements for Wasserman and dropped them off, along with the tapes I made of my interviews. I never saw the man himself. Valerie and I compared belly sizes and swollen ankles, and I ignored my responsibility to tell Jupiter's defense lawyers about what I'd discovered about Lilly. Finally, however, the guilt overwhelmed me.

I was in Valerie's office, listening to her describe, in excruciating detail, the size of the needle that had pierced her abdomen during her last obstetrical appointment, when Wasserman poked his head in her office door.

"Honestly, the thing was the size of a meat thermometer. Richard looked like he was going to faint. He was more afraid than I was," Valerie was saying.

"What are you ladies chatting about?" Wasserman asked.

"Uh, CVS," Valerie mumbled, a flush creeping up her neck. "It's a test for genetic problems. Like an amniocentesis, but you do it earlier."

"I'm having mine this afternoon," I explained, "and your associate was doing her best to terrify me in anticipation."

"Ah," he said, nodding. "Girl talk."

Valerie's face turned a mottled red, and I could imagine the calculation going on inside her head. Just how much extra work was she going to have to put in now, to remind her boss that she was a competent professional? Criminal defense is a brutally macho field of practice. It's where the most aggressive men end up, the ones with the most to prove. It's also a field with more than its share of dinosaurs—lawyers who much prefer to see a woman holding a stenographer's pad and not a litigation briefcase. A woman defense lawyer has to work double time to prove that she's as tough, as determined, and as ruthless as the men around her. Being pregnant adds an extra burden. It's hard to be one of the guys when your belly is sticking out two feet in front of you, your gums are bleeding, and your bra size is a letter in the second half of the alphabet.

"Actually, Valerie and I were just evaluating a new wrinkle in the Jones case," I said. She stifled an expression of surprise.

"New wrinkle?" Wasserman said, and walked into the

room. "What new wrinkle?" He sat down on the edge of her desk.

I took a deep breath and told him about Lilly. I reminded him of the death of Trudy-Ann, and although I refrained from saying anything about it, we both recalled the conversation in which he'd told me that a thirty-year-old homicide had nothing to do with the guilt or innocence of our client. He didn't speak as I described Chloe's blackmail, just motioned to Valerie, who had already begun taking notes on a yellow pad.

"Did you get all that?" he asked her when I was done.

"I think so," she said.

He began to pace back and forth in the small office. "We're going to have to be very careful with this information."

"We can use it to argue lack of premeditation," Valerie said. "He goes to talk to Chloe, to convince her to stop her blackmail. There's an argument, and he kills her."

Wasserman shrugged. "I liked the sex for that better, frankly. They make love, he begs her to leave his father, she refuses, he kills her. Crime of passion. With the blackmail, it's too easy for the prosecution to argue that he decided to murder her to help out his stepsister. And then the sex works against us. The jury's already predisposed to dislike a man who has sex with his victim before he kills her. If we're arguing that he loves her, and that her rejection caused him to have a sudden burst of anger, that's one thing. If we tell the jury that she's a blackmailer, and that first he had sex with her, and then he killed her while he was trying to convince her to leave his movie star sister alone . . ." Wasserman shook his head. "I don't like this. This doesn't help us."

"Well, it could," I said.

He looked at me and raised his eyebrows, waiting. I continued, "It could help, if what you're arguing for isn't just second-degree murder. You could use it to present a defense of innocence."

Wasserman stopped his pacing. "Innocence?" he said, as though the very idea that his client might not be guilty of the crime were anathema to him.

"Yes. Jupiter has said all along that he didn't commit the murder. These allegations of blackmail seem, to me at least, to lend credence to the idea that someone else killed her."

He stared at me incredulously. "Isn't Lilly Green a close friend of yours? Are you seriously suggesting that I mount a defense that she killed Chloe?"

"Yes, Lilly's my friend. And Jupiter is my client. I'm not suggesting that you pin the murder on Lilly, necessarily. Anyone who cares about Lilly might have done it. Her husband, her manager, her agent, her parents. Anyway, you don't necessarily need to pick a suspect. You could present the jury with a whole host of potential killers." I knew as well as Wasserman did that it is always better to give the jury a coherent and believable story, and that that generally requires a specific suspect. But I couldn't bring myself to suggest that he convince the jury that Lilly committed the murder. Something else occurred to me. "Maybe Lilly wasn't the only person Chloe was blackmailing. If she did it to Lilly, she may well have done it to other people. One of them might have killed her."

Wasserman sat back down on the edge of Valerie's desk. I could see that he wasn't convinced by any of my possible scenarios. He still believed Jupiter to be guilty, and if anything, the information I'd given him had served only to affirm that belief. At the same time, he was a good lawyer. He was responsible and thorough. He knew he couldn't just dismiss what I'd told him as at best unhelpful and at worst damaging, even if that was what he believed. His obligation to his client required more. "Are you willing to investigate this? Both Ms. Green's story, and the possibility of any other potential blackmail victims?" he asked me.

"Of course," I said.

He paused and looked at me.

"For free?" he said.

I swallowed. Al was going to kill me.

"We can't exactly expect your friend to pay us to explore

the possibility that she is a murderer," Wasserman continued.

He was right. It would be absolutely unethical to charge Lilly for this part of the investigation.

"For free," I agreed. And sighed.

Nineteen

I had to rush to make it to the obstetrician's office on time. When I'd been pregnant with Ruby, Peter had come to absolutely every OB appointment. He'd held my hand through pelvic exams and blood tests, gazed adoringly at the screen during the ultrasounds, taken copious notes during the labor and delivery classes. When I was pregnant the next time, with Isaac, he had been there for the ultrasound appointments, and even joined me at the midwife's office a few times, though he left his notebook behind. This time, I had a feeling that I was going to have to beg if I wanted him there at all. I called him from my cell phone on my way across town.

"Meet me at the OB's office in ten minutes," I said as soon as he picked up the phone.

"Is something wrong?" he asked, an edge of panic in his voice.

"No, no. I'm fine. I just want you to be there."

He groaned. "Oh, honey, do you mind if I give it a miss? I have a ton of work to do today."

"Yeah. I mind." I looked at my watch. Eleven forty-five. "You have to be there in fifteen minutes."

"Sweetie, you don't need me. You've done this a thousand times before."

"I have not." I punctuated my sentence with the gas pedal, and the car jerked forward. I hit the brakes, just missing rear-ending a cherry-red BMW that was stopped at a traffic light. "I'm having my CVS today. And they might have to stick this huge needle in me. I need you there."

"Okay. Okay. It might take me a little while, though. I'm not dressed." Of course he wasn't. I couldn't remember the last time Peter had managed to shed his bathrobe before noon. I knew the man wasn't lazy. He worked hard every night. He had for as long as I'd known him, but somehow the thought of him in his pajamas in the afternoon still gave me just the tiniest flash of irritation. Maybe it was because his schedule almost always gave him a full night's sleep, and mine almost never did. And my maternal state of perpetual sleep deprivation was only going to get worse when the new baby came.

It took Peter almost an hour to get to the doctor's office, but I was still sitting in the waiting room, quietly seething, when he rushed through the door. Before I had time to blast him for keeping me waiting, he scooped me up in a hug.

"Sorry, sorry, sorry," he said, bussing me on the cheek and collapsing in the seat next to me. "Mindy Maxx called right as I was heading out the door."

I stifled the flicker of jealousy I always felt at any mention of the beautiful blond producer who had once taken up so much of my husband's time and attention. "It's no big deal," I said, my tone belying my words. "They're behind. As usual." He kissed me again, and I smiled despite myself.

Much to my relief, the nurse came to call us before I had to sit through too much conversation about the fabulous project Marvelous Mindy was pitching to my husband, and how smart she was, etc. etc. We went to the back of the office to a room full of medical equipment. We weren't going to be seen by my normal physician because the procedure was so specialized that there was only one doctor in the practice who performed it. I followed the nurse's instructions to remove all my clothes and did my best to drape the tiny paper towel she gave me over my already protruding belly. The doctor walked in while I was still trying to decide which part of my body it was less embarrassing to expose. It was hard to believe the guy had been around long enough to have the opportunity to become an expert in any field other than, say, riding a bike without training wheels. If it weren't for his bald pate, I would have thought he was about nine years old. When exactly did I get old enough to have physicians who were younger than I?

"How far along are you?" the baby doctor said gruffly, flipping through my chart. "We don't really like to do this past thirteen weeks." Bedside manner was clearly *not* one of his specialties.

"I'm only ten and a half weeks pregnant," I said.

"Hmm," he murmured doubtfully, looking at the size of my belly.

"I'm just fat," I said.

"You're not fat; you're pregnant," Peter said. This was the first opportunity he'd had to say that in this pregnancy, but if my previous two were any indication, it was soon to become a mantra.

"Well, the ultrasound will tell us how old the baby is." The doctor pushed Peter out of the way and sat down on a stool next to the bed. He squirted some gel onto my stomach, and I leapt at the chill. "I'm not going to be able to do this if you keep jumping around," he said.

Peter opened his mouth to object to the doctor's obnoxiousness, but I silenced him with a glance. I did, however, make a mental note to let my own doctor know that I wasn't interested in having this rude kid present in the delivery room when I had my baby. I was about to ask the doctor to stop poking me so hard when he flipped around a monitor that was hanging on an arm along one side of the bed so it faced us.

"Here's your baby," he said.

Peter and I gaped at the screen. We'd seen each of our children on the ultrasound when they were *in utero*, but either the technology had changed or our memories had grown dim. We could see everything so clearly. The baby was tiny, curled up like a little shrimp, and its entire body was visible on the screen. Its forehead hadn't yet lost that early fetal bulbousness, but we could see eyes, a mouth, and a nose that I could swear possessed the trademark Wyeth hook. As we watched, it pushed one little arm up and kicked a leg. I looked over at my husband. His smile was as big as my own.

"Look," Peter said, "she's waving at us."

"She?" I asked.

"Yeah, it's a girl," Peter said.

"It's impossible to differentiate at this early stage," the doctor snapped, but we ignored him.

"Hi, little girl," I said, tears spilling down my cheeks. For the first time in weeks, Lilly and Jupiter were entirely out of my thoughts. There was room only for this beautiful new baby. And her father.

The doctor moved the ultrasound wand around, and the baby swam out of view. Peter and I looked at each other, and I could see that he was crying, too. He smiled at me and kissed my forehead.

"Your uterus isn't positioned for a transcervical procedure," the doctor said. "I'm going to have to punch through your abdomen."

That hurt every bit as much as it sounded like it would, and I spent the rest of the day recovering in bed. Peter was wonderful. He made me endless cups of tea, and when that proved insufficient to silence my whining, he took the kids out for an hour and returned, arms laden with Rocky Road, jars of hot fudge, and a can of whipped cream. I fell asleep that night with Ruby and Isaac curled up in bed next to me, our faces covered in chocolate, and our dreams full of babies waving hello.

Twenty

AFTER a day in bed, I got back to work, concentrating my investigation on Chloe. I decided to start with the person likely to know the most about her, the person who would, if my own were anything to go by, possess both a clear-eyed sense of her failings and an utterly disproportionate estimation of her talents—her mother. Chloe's mother lived in Laguna Beach, a small seaside town in Orange County, about an hour south of the city. I'm not sure what I was expecting from the mother of such an unsavory character, but it certainly wasn't the pleasant woman with graying blond hair who greeted me at the front door of a little blue cottage covered in bougainvillea and shaded by a massive avocado tree.

Wanda Pakulski was beautiful, with full lips and large blue eyes, and clear, pale skin entirely unsullied by makeup. She had a few laugh lines, but she hardly looked old enough to have a daughter in her late twenties. Her hands were broad and capable, with close-trimmed nails, and she answered her front door in her bare feet. Her hair was swept off her high forehead with the kind of turquoise hair clip that is sold in gift shops on Indian reservations. She was wearing faded blue jeans, and I found it difficult to keep from staring at the disconcertingly massive breasts straining at the buttons of her bright white men's Oxford cloth shirt. I forced myself to look around the room I had just walked into, taking in the vaguely Southwestern décor and the walls covered in small square paintings of flowers. The painter was clearly heavily influenced by Georgia O'Keeffe. "Are these yours?" I asked, pointing at the walls.

"Yup," she said. "I'm in a floral phase right now."

"They're lovely," I said, without lying. The paintings were pretty, the colors soft and pleasing, the flowers more than competently rendered.

"Too lovely," she said, looking critically at a small canvas. "They're a little bit Hallmark, don't you think?" She shrugged. "People seem to like them, though. They're selling like crazy. Come on in the kitchen. I've got coffee made."

"Please, don't go to any trouble," I said, following her through the living room into the small, bright kitchen. She bustled around the room, pouring coffee into cups and arranging a few muffins on a plate.

"It's no trouble at all," she said.

"I really appreciate your agreeing to talk to me. It's very generous of you, considering the fact that I'm working for Jupiter."

She paused and looked up at me. Her blue eyes were dry, but she looked incredibly sad. "You'll probably think I'm crazy for saying this, given everything that happened, but I always liked Jupiter. He was very sweet to Chloe. I felt so sorry for him when she married Polaris."

"But you must be very angry with him now."

She shrugged. "Yes, of course. But somehow I still can't help feeling sorry for him. Has he said anything? I mean, about why he did it?"

I weighed what my obligation to confidentiality would allow me to reveal. From the very beginning, Jupiter had publicly denied his guilt. That much I could tell her. "Jupiter says that he's innocent of her murder."

She sighed. "Yes. I read that in the papers. Is he, do you think? Is he innocent?"

"I think he is," I replied. "But then, he *is* my client."

She nodded. "I've had such a hard time believing it was him. I just don't think he could have hurt her. He always loved her. Always."

I didn't tell her what I knew to be true. Loving someone and hurting them are hardly mutually exclusive.

"If he didn't do it, then the person who murdered my daughter is still out there." Her voice quavered.

"Yes," I said gently.

"But the police aren't looking for him."

"No."

"Are you?"

That gave me pause. Was I looking for Chloe's murderer? If Jupiter was innocent, as he claimed, then the best way of proving that was to find the real killer. No matter who that was. I pushed the thought of my friend Lilly out of my mind. "I'm trying to help Jupiter. Any way that I can," I said.

Wanda nodded. "Let's go out into the yard."

She put the cups and plates on a tray and led me out the back door into a perfect, miniature garden. She balanced the tray on a tiny wrought iron table and motioned for me to sit down in one of the two chairs. There were flowers everywhere. Roses climbed the arbor underneath which we sat. The air was thick with the smell of honeysuckle, wisteria petals littered the brick patio like purple confetti, and the flowerbeds alongside the house were a jumble and tangle of pinks and blues, fuchsias and violets, as though someone had dumped bag after bag of wildflower seed. It was all utterly enchanting.

"Is this where Chloe grew up?" I asked, wondering how someone who came from such a beautiful place could have turned out so wrong.

Wanda smiled ruefully and shook her head. "Hardly. When Chloe was a girl, I could never have afforded this. I can't really afford it now. She helped me buy this place. Or rather, Polaris did. He was very generous with me."

"He bought you the house?"

"When he and Chloe were first married, he gave me the money for the down payment. Or rather, he gave it to her to give to me."

"Are you and Polaris close?"

She shook her head, and something about her expression made me feel that my next question would not come as too much of a shock.

"Do you know if Polaris was ever . . . well, abusive towards Chloe? Did he ever hit her?"

Wanda wrinkled her brow. "No. No, I don't think so. I mean, not that she ever told me. But then, she might not have, you know? Chloe often tried to protect me from the sad things in her life. Did you find something out? Did he hurt her?"

"Jupiter said he did."

Wanda smiled sadly. "But he might be lying, mightn't he. To protect himself?"

I nodded back, wondering if that were true.

Wanda pushed the plate full of muffins across the table. I took one. My teeth crunched through the sugary outer crust and into the soft, buttery inside. The tang of blueberries filled my mouth. "Oh my God, these are amazing," I said.

"I'm a woman of many talents," she said, the bite of sarcasm belied by the small smile of pride playing across her mouth. "Here, have another one."

I helped myself to more, and said, "Where did you live when Chloe was young?"

"All over, but mostly in L.A. I traveled a lot, for my work. When Chloe was little, she came along with me, but when she got old enough for school, I had to leave her behind. She usually stayed in L.A. while I was on the road."

"What did you do?"

"I was an exotic dancer. I went by the name of Cherrie Delight." Her voice was matter-of-fact, as though taking off your clothes for a living were no different from, say, being a flight attendant or a truck driver. And maybe it wasn't. Who was I to say? At any rate, that explained the size of her chest.

"You don't look old enough to be a mother of someone as old as Chloe."

"That's because I had her when I was sixteen. Chloe and I kind of grew up together." She swallowed hard and turned her head away from me. We sat in silence for a few moments while she gathered herself together. I liked Wanda Pakulski. She was open, and friendly, and not the least bit angry, which was remarkable given the fact that her only child had been murdered. She was, very simply, a nice woman. I didn't want to force her to talk about her daughter. I didn't want to make her sad, and I didn't want to ask the unpleasant questions that I knew I had to if I was going to find out if Chloe had been blackmailing anyone else.

"I was much too young to be a mother, and that's probably why she was such a complicated person," Wanda said.

"Complicated?" I asked.

"Chloe wasn't easy to get along with. I'm sure that's because she spent her childhood going from club to club with me, or living with relatives while I was on the road. Poor baby. I don't think she ever went to the same school for longer than a year, and then she ended up dropping out so early."

"I guess it couldn't have been easy. On either of you."

"No, but *I* was supposed to take care of *her*. I was supposed to keep her safe. Everything that happened is my fault." She said those words firmly, as if instructing me of a fact, not giving me a window into a private pain. But her eyes were moist, and her lip trembled.

"What is? What's your fault?"

"Everything that happened to her. How she dropped out of school. The drug use. And then what happened later. Her death. I know it's no excuse, but when she was a little girl, I honestly felt that I was doing the best I could. I was on welfare when she was born, but I hated that. And then when I started dancing, I was making so much more money than I could have made at any other job, I couldn't bring myself to stop. Don't get me wrong, I don't think there's anything morally wrong with the work. I never did anything I was ashamed of. It was just the travel, and having to leave her alone for such long periods of time. I kept promising myself that I'd dance just another year, but the money kept getting better and better. Once I started doing movies, then it really became impossible to walk away from it. Not that I had much to show for it." She shook her head, obviously disgusted with herself. "Most of what I earned disappeared right up my nose. Poor Chloe got that from me, too."

I didn't know whether Wanda was responsible for Chloe's failings. Had she grown up in a perfect two-parent home in a perfect small town, Chloe might have been an entirely different person. She might have finished high school, gone to college, volunteered in the Peace Corps, and gone on to a career as a neurosurgeon. Or she might have ended up dropping out of school and becoming a coke addict. Plenty of kids from all kinds of families do. We'd never really know if it was the circumstances of her childhood or something about her, something hardwired into her brain, that made her who she was. But one thing was for sure: Wanda would feel guilty for the rest of her life. Mothers do.

"Do you have kids, Ms. Applebaum?" Wanda asked.

"Call me Juliet, please. Yes, I've got two."

"Any pictures?"

I raised my eyebrows. "Do you really want to see them?"

"I'd love to."

I pulled a couple of snapshots of Ruby and Isaac out of my purse. "These are about a year old," I said. "I keep meaning to put some newer ones in my bag."

She looked at the photographs of Ruby astride a pony and of Isaac's face peeping out from under a crown of bubbles in the tub, and then traced a delicate finger across the children's faces. "They're precious," she said, her voice quavering just a bit.

"Thank you," I said.

She swallowed firmly, blinked back tears, and then said brightly, "Is this it for you? Are you going to have any more?"

"Well, at least one, that's for certain." I laid a hand on my stomach.

"You're pregnant! Congratulations!"

"Thanks. Thanks so much."

She handed me back the pictures. "Well, what else can I tell you about my Chloe?"

"Well, the most important thing, I suppose, is if there was anyone who might have wanted to hurt her, other than Jupiter. Did she have any enemies that you know of?"

Wanda closed her eyes for a moment. Then she said, "There were probably women—wives—who didn't like Chloe very much."

"Wives?"

"The wives of men Chloe was involved with. My daughter had a lot of boyfriends before she met Polaris. Mostly older men. She started dancing as soon as she was old enough. She knew all the managers of the better clubs, through me, so it was easy for her to get on the circuit. She called herself Little Cherrie."

So the minister's wife was a stripper. Why hadn't I heard that before? Polaris must have known. He was close enough to Wanda to have bought her a house, and she clearly didn't keep her own past a secret.

"Did Polaris know that Chloe was a . . . dancer?" I had been about to say stripper, but I stopped myself in time.

"Of course. They all did. That was part of the story. You know, loose woman saved from drugs and sexual perversity by God and the church. They loved that crap."

"What about you? Did they try to save you?"

She laughed. "I had already stopped dancing by then or I'm sure they would have tried."

"When did you stop?"

"Not long after Chloe started. We played the same club once, and that kind of ended it for me. When I saw her up on the stage, it made me question what I was doing. Not that I think there's anything wrong with exotic dancing," she said hurriedly. "There isn't. It's a great way for a girl to make a living. The money is amazing, and you're in total control of your own life. You are," she said at my dubious frown. "You dance when and where you want to. You decide how much you're going to do. Even with private dances, it's the girl who is in complete control. The guys aren't even allowed to touch us."

Wanda pushed the muffin plate toward me, and I shook my head. Then, reconsidering, I took another. She smiled briefly.

With my mouth full, I said, "If you liked dancing, and if you think it's a good way to make a living, then why did Chloe's dancing make you want to quit?"

"I guess I just felt embarrassed. Like if I had a daughter old enough to do it, then I shouldn't be doing it myself. And I had had enough of the life. I was ready to quit the travel. It can really wear you down. Once I stopped working, it was really easy to stop using drugs. It was like I didn't really need them anymore. I haven't had more than an occasional glass of wine since I retired."

"Did Chloe like dancing? Was she happy?"

A small sad smile flickered across Wanda's lips, and she shook her head. "My daughter had a real hard time being happy," she said. "She liked the money, I know that. I think she liked the attention. She was a beautiful girl, and she liked it that people noticed. That men noticed. I'm sure she liked the power."

"Power?"

"The power to make men want her, to want to do anything just to have her. Even to leave their wives for her."

"*Did* they leave their wives for her?"

"I don't know. Some probably did. And even if they didn't leave them, they certainly cheated on them."

"What made Chloe decide to stop dancing? Was it Polaris?"

Wanda shrugged. "I guess. One of her clients arranged for her to go to this fancy rehab center in Ojai. She met Jupiter there, and then he introduced her to Polaris. I don't know if she would have gone back into it if she hadn't married him. Probably. It's a hard life to walk away from. Where else can a girl with no education earn a couple of thousand bucks in a single night?"

"Do you know who was the client who paid for her to go into rehab?"

"No one paid. The doctor who ran the center let her in for free."

"Dr. Reese Blackmore let Chloe have a free ride? Why?"

"I told you. He was one of her clients. He must have fallen in love with her. Most of them did."

I stared at Wanda, stunned, my coffee cup halfway to my lips. Blackmore was sleeping with Chloe! Maybe something more was going on. Chloe had begun a relationship with Jupiter while she was at the clinic. Could that betrayal have made Reese angry enough to kill her? But then why would he have waited so long to exact retribution? I was obviously going to have to dig around the center a little more carefully. For the time being, though, I needed to take full advantage of Wanda's willingness to discuss her daughter's life with me.

"Do you mind telling me a little bit about Chloe's relationship with her husband? Was Polaris generous with her? Did she have as much money as she wanted?"

Wanda took a sip of coffee. "She certainly lived well. And he bought her stuff. Nice clothes, jewelry, a car. That kind of thing. All she had to do was ask, and he'd give her whatever it was she wanted. At the beginning, like I said, he even gave her money to give me."

"But did she have any money of her own? Did she have a regular source of income? Like an allowance? Or did she always have to ask him when she wanted something?"

"That's exactly what bothered Chloe. I don't think it was that she minded asking him for things. She probably would have asked for presents no matter how much money of her own she had. But she did want to have her own money. She told me that it drove her crazy that he knew how she spent every dime. And sometimes, well, when things weren't so great between them, it was harder for her to get what she wanted."

"What do you mean?" I leaned forward eagerly.

Wanda blushed, seeming to regret her words. "Nothing. I shouldn't have said anything."

"Please, Wanda," I said, extending my hand. "I need to know the truth, no matter how irrelevant it seems to you. It could help me understand what really happened to your daughter."

Wanda wrinkled her brow, and then nodded. "I'll tell you, but please, I don't want you to overinterpret this. Chloe and Polaris went through a rocky period. People do. Especially when there's an age difference. I think it's only natural."

"Sure," I said encouragingly.

"During those times, Polaris wasn't as generous with Chloe. She felt . . . strapped. You know. Because she didn't have a job or anything. It was hard for her."

"Do you think Chloe might have tried to get money some other way?"

"Like how?"

I paused. I didn't want to hurt Wanda's feelings by insulting her daughter. But there was no other way for me to get the information I needed. "Blackmail," I said. "Do you think it's possible that Chloe would have resorted to blackmailing people?"

Wanda didn't express any outrage at the suggestion. She just leaned back in her chair and looked up at the roses overhead, considering it. "She might have. I don't really know. Do *you* know if she was blackmailing someone? Is that why you asked the question?"

I didn't answer her directly. "Does it sound like something she might have done?"

Wanda replaced her cup in its saucer and sighed. "Maybe. Like I said, my daughter was a complicated person."

"Before she died, did she seem to have more money than usual?"

Wanda wrinkled her brow. "Actually, she did. I know because she gave me some. I hadn't asked her for it. She knew

I was saving money to buy into a gallery downtown. She showed up one day about three months before she died. She hadn't called or anything. She surprised me. I made her lunch, and she gave me a check for twenty-five thousand dollars. She told me to use it to buy a share of the gallery. And then a week later she called and told me I wasn't going to have to worry about my mortgage anymore. She was going to pay it off for me." For the first time since I'd arrived at her house, tears began to roll down Wanda's cheeks. "I just assumed she got the money from Polaris. But she was blackmailing someone? Oh that's just so like Chloe. To do something so awful, and then to do something so wonderful for me with the money. To be so bad and so sweet at the same time."

Twenty-one

WHAT I wanted to do the next morning was drive right up to Ojai and confront Blackmore about his relationship with Chloe. What I had to do instead was go see Lilly. One of her assistants called me at the crack of dawn to let me know that Lilly was home from Japan and could "fit me in" if I could make it to her house by ten. I dropped off the kids and made it in plenty of time. The assistant showed me into the breakfast room. The table was set for four, with pale blue crockery and crisp white napkins. A matching blue bowl held a stubby bouquet of fragrant peach-colored roses. A glass pitcher of fresh-squeezed orange juice sweated in the middle of the table, and steam rose from a carafe of coffee.

"Help yourself to juice and coffee. The cook will have breakfast up in just a minute," the assistant said. "As soon as Lilly and her mom are done with yoga." I certainly was getting fed well on this particular investigation. It made being a pregnant PI positively pleasant.

"Beverly's here?"

"She and Mr. Green came down from Sacramento a couple

of days ago. Their L.A. house is being renovated, so they're staying here."

I was about halfway through the *Los Angeles Times* when Lilly's father joined me. He clomped into the room awkwardly, wearing his biking shoes and clutching his helmet under his arm. His tight black bike shorts clung to his muscled behind, and his lycra bike shirt covered in French logos fit snugly over his chest and across his shoulders, revealing defined biceps and browned forearms. His hair was cropped so close to his skull that it was difficult to determine its color, and he had a small gold hoop in one ear. He was damp and sweaty, and looked young for his age, but there was something stiff and almost ironed about his face, and I couldn't help but wonder whether its smooth youthfulness was real.

He greeted me with a smile and said, "Good morning."

"Hi."

"I've got to drink something." He gulped down a huge glass of the orange juice and wiped the back of his hand across his mouth. "I remember you. We met at Lilly's divorce party." When her divorce was final, Lilly had thrown a huge party, to which she'd worn a nineteen-thousand-dollar Vera Wang wedding dress—dyed black. I wondered what she was going to do with the photos of that event if she really did get back together with Archer.

I said, "How are things in Sacramento? Is the state of California still solvent?"

He smiled. "That you'll have to ask my wife, I'm afraid. I try to pay as little attention to the politicians and pundits as possible."

"So you're retired now?" I asked, making small talk.

He nodded. "Yup."

"What was it you did?" I had a vague memory of Lilly telling me a couple of years before that her father had retired from some kind of political work. Given his past as a denizen of communes and marijuana farms, I could imagine what it was.

"I was a lobbyist for a few different environmental groups," he said. "Mostly community groups dealing with environmental racism."

"Oh, right," I said. Now I remembered reading about a campaign Raymond had spearheaded to force the government to pay for the cleanup of a public housing project full of toxic mold.

Raymond pulled out a chair and sat down. "Beverly's election kind of put the kibosh on my career. It's hard for the husband of the Speaker of the Assembly to be a lobbyist." Was I making assumptions, or did I detect the faintest hint of bitterness in his voice? "My last project was keeping a waste processing plant out of Richmond. We made the rich white lawyers and doctors in Walnut Creek smell the poop for once. And the rich white liberals in Berkeley, for that matter."

I felt a momentary surge of embarrassment. I was, after all, a white lawyer, and compared to the overwhelming working class and minority population of Richmond, a grim little city north of Oakland, I probably could be considered rich. But then, so could Raymond.

Lilly and her stepmother saved me from having to write a sizable check for a donation to assuage my liberal guilt. They came into the room, dressed in matching black, boot-cut, lycra yoga pants. Lilly's tank top was adorned with a picture of Ganesh, the elephant-headed Hindu god of India. Beverly's was more simple—black with a small embroidered OM in Sanskrit.

"How was Japan?" I asked after Lilly had greeted me with a hug, and her mother had shaken my hand firmly.

"Well, it was nice to be out of L.A. It was pretty exhausting, though," Lilly said. "Next time, I'm taking Saraswathi with me. There isn't a single decent yoga teacher in all of Tokyo."

"She's really quite wonderful," Beverly said, stretching her arms up over her head. "I don't know when I've had a workout like that. This is honestly the first time I haven't had a sore neck in ages." Beverly was small and stocky, with a helmet of evenly colored brown hair. Her shoulders were broad for her size, and her waist a bit thick. But she carried her weight well. She was a woman who had probably been pudgy and plain when she was younger, but middle age had leant her a kind of stout handsomeness. She looked strong and capable. And she was.

Raymond got up from his seat and squeezed his wife's shoulders. "She carries all her tension right here," he said. Beverly shook his hands away with a jerk. I looked at her, startled, and saw the ball of her jaw pulsing. She was gritting her teeth. Raymond sat back down in his chair heavily, the very faintest tinge of a blush creeping across his neck. Clearly, all was not happy in that marriage. Had they just had a fight, or was there something more serious happening? Then I recalled the bit in the papers about Raymond and his actress. Was that what she was making him pay for?

One of the denim-shirted maids came in just then, a huge tray loaded with food balanced on her shoulder. She unloaded platters of cut-up fruit, baskets of scones and muffins, and a covered baking dish. Lilly lifted the top off and announced, "Egg white frittata." We all waited for Lilly to fill her plate before we helped ourselves to the food. I was curious to see that even Lilly's parents treated her like a movie star, with a hint of deference that I imagined they would not have exhibited had she been, say, a cosmetologist.

Sipping coffee and munching on mango slices and cranberry pecan scones, it was difficult to remember that my suspicions of Lilly had been growing stronger. She was so quintessentially herself, cracking jokes, moaning in imitation of her yoga instructor (*"ooodianabanda, ooodianabanda"*), gently teasing her parents about their left-leaning politics. I just couldn't imagine her coolly shooting Chloe, or paying someone else to do it. But then, neither could I imagine any little girl shooting her mother, so perhaps my inability to conceive my friend guilty of murder had more to do with the failures of my own imagination than anything else.

About halfway through the meal, Raymond said, "So, Lilly. Have you given any more thought to that business plan

I showed you? That social justice venture capital fund is a great idea."

"Sorry, Dad. My money guys gave it the thumbs-down."

"But . . ."

"She said no, Raymond," Beverly said. "Leave it alone."

Her sharp tone cut through the companionable conversation and silenced us. Finally, Lilly broke the tension by telling us a story about Amber and Jade and their campaign for a pet snake. Relieved at the distraction, we all laughed far more hilariously than the actual tale warranted.

Finally, when breakfast had been reduced to a pile of crumbs and crumpled napkins, I steeled myself to broach the subject of Chloe's murder. Beverly beat me to it.

"Lilly tells us that you are helping Jupiter. Tell me what it is exactly that you're doing," she said. Beverly had a political reputation as a straight shooter, one of the few people in Sacramento who could be trusted to speak her mind and tell the truth. For that reason, and despite the fact that her politics were well to the left of center—to the left of left, in fact—she had allies and friends on both sides of the aisle. Even the Republicans trusted that, with Beverly Green, what they saw was what they got. If she made a promise, she'd follow through. If she reconsidered a position, she'd announce that she'd been wrong, publicly and honestly. Lilly had obviously learned her sense of humor at her stepmother's side. Beverly had a famously caustic wit, tempered by genuine warmth and concern for friends and strangers alike.

I briefly described the process of mitigation investigation to Lilly's parents, and then said, "While the victim's character isn't ordinarily relevant in the trial, in this particular circumstance . . ." My voice trailed off. I wasn't sure what they knew.

"You can talk freely, Juliet," Beverly said. "Lilly has told us everything."

I glanced at Lilly, and she nodded. I continued. "I think the fact that Chloe was blackmailing Lilly might prove valuable to the defense."

Lilly paused, her coffee cup halfway to her mouth. "Did you tell Wasserman?" she whispered.

"I'm sorry, Lilly. I had to."

Beverly reached an arm around her stepdaughter and hugged her reassuringly. "Does he plan to tell people about Lilly? About what happened in Mexico?" Beverly asked.

Lilly put her coffee cup down on the table with a trembling hand, and it rattled once in its saucer. Her father embraced her from the other side, and the three sat across from me, united.

"That's just not acceptable," Raymond said.

"There may never be a trial," I said, although I didn't really believe it. "It's possible that the prosecution might hear the story of the blackmail and decide to charge Jupiter with a lesser offense." I didn't believe that, either. If anything, they would probably view the blackmail as further evidence of motive for premeditated murder. It would be up to the defense to convince a jury that either Jupiter was innocent or he hadn't planned to kill anyone, but had rather been swept up in the heat of the moment.

"You don't believe that, do you? You think there's going to be a trial," Lilly said, her voice small and flat. The sparkle had drained from her eyes, and her skin had lost its luminous glow and was strained tight across her cheekbones. For the first time I wondered if she, like her father, had had surgical assistance in preserving her youth.

"I don't know, Lilly. There might be a trial, there might not be," I said.

"But if there is, then the whole story would come out. In court. And in the papers."

"Probably."

"That is simply unacceptable," Raymond said again, drawing his daughter closer. "You don't understand what Lilly has been through, how hard she's worked to overcome the horror of her mother's death. That would . . . that would devastate her."

Beverly turned to me. "Juliet, you're Lilly's friend. I expect you to do what you can to prevent her from being exposed. I can trust you, can't I?"

I wanted to say yes. I wanted to promise my allegiance. But I couldn't. "I'm a member of Jupiter's defense team," I said. "I have certain ethical obligations to him. But given that, I'll do whatever I can to protect Lilly."

Beverly nodded curtly. She knew that that was the best I could offer. She turned to Lilly. "Sweetie, I don't want this publicized any more than you do. Not after we've worked so hard to protect your privacy all these years. But you will not allow yourself to be devastated. It will be difficult. Your career will certainly suffer. But you're a strong woman. You've accomplished a tremendous amount in therapy. If for some reason we can't keep this out of the papers, you'll survive. We'll be here for you, and you'll survive."

"Yes, Mom," Lilly whispered.

"Jupiter says he's innocent," I said. "If that's the case, and if someone else murdered Chloe, then perhaps all this will become entirely irrelevant." I left unsaid the thought that had surely occurred to them. If Jupiter wasn't the murderer, and if Lilly had so much to lose, then it was inevitable that she be considered a suspect.

"If he didn't do it, then who did?" Raymond asked. "Who do you think might have killed her?"

"Maybe Lilly wasn't the only person Chloe was blackmailing. She may well have had a whole roster of victims. I'm doing what I can to find out more about her. I've spoken to her mother; I'm planning on tracking down her friends and acquaintances. If there's someone out there, I'll find him." I wasn't as cocksure as I pretended to be, but Lilly looked so fragile, so damaged. I couldn't resist the urge to reassure her.

Beverly squeezed Lilly's shoulder again, and then let her go. She poured herself a cup of coffee and looked at me. "So, Juliet. Tell us what we can do to help."

I smiled uncomfortably. "Well, just so we know that we've crossed all our *t*'s and dotted our *i*'s. Do you mind telling me what you were doing the day Chloe was murdered?"

Raymond began to sputter angrily.

Beverly interrupted his outburst. "What was the date?" she asked.

I told her.

"Give me a moment," she said. She got up from the table. She was back almost immediately, holding an electronic organizer. She tapped at it with the stylus a few times. Then she said, "I had a Northern California Democratic Women's luncheon at the Fairmont Hotel in San Francisco from noon to two. We left Sacramento at about ten-thirty, as I recall. After the luncheon I did a series of one-on-one meetings with party donors. Those lasted until around close to seven, and we were back in Sacramento by eight-thirty. We ate in the car."

"We?" I asked.

"My aides and I. They never left my side. Well, except for bathroom breaks. But much as I might have liked to do away with that horrible girl, I could not have flown from San Francisco to Los Angeles, murdered Chloe, and flown back while pretending to use the bathroom."

I jotted down the information and looked at Raymond. He shrugged his shoulders. "I haven't the faintest idea where I was. I mean, I was at the Sacramento house. And I probably went for a bike ride. That's what I usually do."

"Do you have a calendar you can check?"

He shook his head. "I don't really bother with that. Beverly keeps her calendar, and I have so few appointments that I can remember them without bothering to write them down."

We looked at each other uncomfortably. I'm sure they wished as much as I did that Raymond could have accounted for his time. I decided to move on. "One thing it's critical to find out is how Chloe knew about what happened in San Miguel. I think Polaris was probably the source of the information."

Beverly and Raymond looked at each other.

"Why do you think that?" she asked. "Have you heard something?"

I narrowed my eyes. Was there something she wasn't telling me? "No, but he seems the most likely possibility."

"I don't think he would have said anything," Beverly said.

"Why not?"

"Because he swore not to. He took an oath. Whatever we might think of the Church of Cosmological Unity, Polaris is a religious man. He would not have broken his pledge."

I raised a skeptical eyebrow, but refrained from telling her just how much I trust anybody's sworn oath. "Who else knew about the shooting?" I asked.

"You mean besides us and Polaris?" Raymond asked.

I nodded.

"The people living in the house at the time. Seth Goldblum, for one."

"Seth Goldblum? Do you mean Hyades? Polaris's assistant?"

Beverly rolled her eyes. "Those people and their names. Yes, Hyades. Back then he was Seth Goldblum from Parsippanny, New Jersey."

"Who else?"

"Kitty Forest and Angela Williams," Beverly said. "They were there. But it couldn't be them."

"Why not?"

"They're both dead. Kitty died of breast cancer about ten years ago, and Angela was killed in a car accident a few years after we came home from San Miguel. Angela's son was there, but he was only a few months old at the time of the accident, and only three or so when his mother died."

"Was anyone else living in the house?"

"No, not by then," Raymond said.

"That's not true," Lilly interrupted.

We all looked at her. It was the first thing she'd said in a long time.

"There were other people there," she said.

"Who?" Beverly asked, her worry apparent in her voice.

"The maids. The maids knew."

"Of course," Beverly said. "But they couldn't have told Chloe. Could they have?"

Lilly shrugged.

I turned over a fresh page on the pad on which I'd been taking notes. "What were their names?"

Lilly squinted and looked up at the ceiling as if the answer to my question might be scribbled next to the light fixture. "Um . . . Juana, I think," she said. "Yeah, Juana. That sounds right. She was the one who took care of Jupiter and me. There were a couple more. I remember that there was someone who came to cook, and a man who took care of the garden. But I can't remember any of their names. They weren't there that much."

I was disappointed, but at the same time I thought it was pretty unlikely that Chloe would have met a maid from San Miguel de Allende, Mexico, who happened to know a secret involving Chloe's husband. It was just too unlikely a coincidence.

"What about the police?" I asked.

Raymond nodded. "They knew, of course, but Polaris fixed it with them, somehow. I'm not sure how. Maybe he paid them off. I don't know. I know they tried to interview Lilly, but she couldn't speak to them. She didn't actually talk until she came up here to be with us."

"The therapist!" I said.

They looked at me, confused by my excitement.

"Lilly was in therapy, right?"

"For more years than I'd like to think about," Lilly said.

"Your therapist must have known about it, then."

Lilly nodded. "Of course he did. But he wouldn't have told her. It's confidential. Dr. Blackmore would never do anything like that."

I felt a surge of adrenaline, and my heart started beating faster. I tried to calm my voice so that it would not betray my astonishment. "Dr. Reese Blackmore?" I asked.

Lilly nodded. "Do you know him? He treated me from the time I was a little girl until just before I got married."

"Is this the same Reese Blackmore who runs the Ojai Rehabilitation and Self-Actualization Center?"

"Yes, that's him. He's a recovered memory specialist, one of the pioneers in the field. And he also does drug and alcohol treatment. He says the two are very interrelated. People who suffer from repressed memory often self-medicate."

I stared at Lilly. "How could you not have told me this?"

"What?" she asked, sounding confused.

"That your therapist knew Chloe."

She raised her eyebrows. "Didn't I? When we talked about Jupiter? Didn't I tell you that Jupiter and I had the same therapist? And of course Jupiter met Chloe in Ojai."

I narrowed my eyes at her and said flatly, "Blackmore was a client of Chloe's."

"A client?" Lilly said.

"She was a stripper, and probably a high-class hooker, too. He was a client. That's why he brought her to his clinic," I said.

"I don't believe it," Lilly said, her eyes flashing with anger.

"Chloe's mother told me."

Raymond said, "Are you serious? Chloe's mother told you that she was a hooker?"

I said, "An exotic dancer who had a few private clients."

Lilly moaned softly.

"He knew about you and your mother, and he had a relationship with Chloe," I said.

She moaned again.

"How did Jupiter end up at the clinic?" I said.

"I'm sure Polaris sent him," Beverly said. "We've all known each other for years. Reese was a member of that first Topanga Canyon commune. That's why we sent Lilly to him. Because he was our friend. She was one of his very first patients, and the reason he ever began work in recovered memory." Her voice was soft, and horrified.

"Was he in San Miguel with Polaris?"

Beverly shook her head. "No. He was in graduate school by the time the Topanga commune broke up. In clinical psychology."

Raymond interrupted. "I can't believe Reese would have said anything to Chloe. The man is a nationally recognized expert in the fields of drug treatment and recovered memory. He saved Lilly's life, for God's sake. He would never have betrayed her confidence."

"No. No he wouldn't," Lilly said, shaking her head. She

had gotten over her initial shock, and her voice was adamant. "Dad's right. Dr. Blackmore would never do anything like that. Never. She must have found out from someone else. Polaris must have told her. And I don't believe Dr. B would have slept with her. He's just not that kind of person."

Unlike Lilly, I wasn't suffering from transference. I was perfectly able to imagine her shrink sleeping with a prostitute, and then setting her up to blackmail one of his patients. My husband might spend his days dreaming up horror, but it was my job that required the ability to imagine the true evil of which human beings are capable.

"How do you know that Chloe's mother was telling you the truth? I mean, maybe she was lying. Or maybe you misunderstood," Lilly said.

I sighed inwardly, but said, "I'll verify the information before I act on it. Okay?"

Lilly nodded, relieved. I would do what I'd promised; I'd call Wanda again, to satisfy Lilly. But I was also determined to investigate Reese Blackmore further, however that made my friend feel.

"If you're right, and Dr. Blackmore wasn't the source of the information, then that brings us back to square one," I said. "I think we should make a list of everyone who knew about what happened in San Miguel." I flipped to a clean page in my notebook and started writing. "The three of you knew. And Dr. Blackmore. Polaris and Hyades. The maids, Juana and the others. Jupiter, of course. Can you think of anyone else? Did anyone else know?"

Lilly shook her head, and then stopped. "Well, not anyone who would have said anything," she murmured.

"Who?" I asked.

"He wouldn't have said anything," she said again, the slight tremble in her voice betraying her doubt.

"Who?" I asked again.

"Archer," she said. "Archer knew. He's always known."

I looked at Lilly and her parents. The blood had drained from Beverly's face. Raymond's jaw was set. He looked grim, and very angry.

We sat silently for a while, and I wondered if they were each thinking the same thing as I. Which of the people that Lilly trusted and loved had betrayed her? Was it her ex-husband, the father of her daughters, with whom she'd begun to achieve a rapprochement? Was it her therapist, who'd brought her back to life when she'd come to him, a broken and silent child? Was it her childhood companion, the closest thing to a brother that she had? I hoped, for her sake and despite their insistence to the contrary, that the source of the information was Polaris. I couldn't help but believe that even blood oaths have a way of disintegrating when a man is lying in bed with a girl half his age.

Finally when the silence had grown thick and uncomfortable, I said to Lilly, "Do you mind telling me a little bit more about what happened in Mexico? I know it's painful for you, and if you can't, I'll understand. It's just that I think that if I know more about it, it might help me."

Lilly dragged her hand through her hair distractedly. The hair had grown back quickly. It was about two inches long and curled softly over her scalp. Romantic tendrils traced the perfect curve of her shell-like ear. Even with cropped hair and a face ravaged by anxiety and sorrow, Lilly was ethereally lovely.

"I'll talk about it," she said. "The fact that I can at all is thanks to my therapy with Dr. Blackmore. Like I told you, I started seeing him as soon as I got home from Mexico."

I turned to Beverly and Raymond. "You sent Lilly to see Reese Blackmore because you knew him?"

Raymond said, "Polaris and I agreed that it would be best for Lilly if nobody else knew about what happened. We trusted Reese. He had lived with us in Topanga; he knew us and had known Trudy-Ann. He was the logical choice."

"And the only one we could afford," Beverly interjected.

"He was wonderful," Lilly said to her stepmother. "He saved my life."

"How long did it take before you started speaking again?" I asked.

Lilly shrugged. "A while. At I first we would just sit there quietly. I remember sometimes he would play games while I watched. You know, board games, or dolls. Something like that. He had a huge pile of Barbies."

Beverly shook her head. "I hated that," she said. "I never let Lilly play with Barbie dolls, and I tried to convince him to get rid of those. But he wouldn't."

I could sympathize with Beverly's dislike of the dolls. I hated them, too. For years I hadn't let Ruby play with them, and when I'd finally succumbed to her entreaties, I did my best to convince her that it was more fun to cut off their hair and draw tattoos all over their bodies with permanent marker than to play Barbie and Ken's wedding day.

"It was a good thing he didn't listen to you," Lilly said. "Those Barbies were what finally got through to me. After a couple of weeks of being home in L.A. with my parents, and of seeing Dr. Blackmore almost every day, I started speaking again. I didn't remember anything about what happened to my mother. I think I told you about that. How I had memories of playing in the fountain with Jupiter, and then of someone screaming. And the dress. The white dress . . ." Her voice trailed off.

"We talked about that. And about how you slowly began to remember more," I prompted her.

"Playing Barbies helped me to remember. It wasn't immediate, by any means. My memory came back slowly. Over the years. We'd play with the Barbie dolls, and we would act out what happened. There was one doll that we always used to represent my mother. A Malibu Barbie. I guess I thought she looked like her."

Raymond stifled a laugh and then looked contrite. "I'm sorry. It's just that Trudy-Ann did kind of look like Malibu Barbie. She was tall, and blond, and had a great tan."

Beverly said, "She was always lying out, working on her tan. The first time I saw her was on the roof of the trailer parked in the yard of the Topanga house. She'd climbed up the ladder and was lying up there, getting a tan."

I wondered if I would be able to recount recollections of Peter's previous girlfriends with such equanimity. Probably not. That might be one of the reasons I had never joined a commune and practiced peace, happiness, and free love.

A small smile played across Lilly's lips, alleviating for a moment the look of strain and anxiety. "My mother was Malibu Barbie, and I was Skipper." The smile slowly faded. "We'd act out the day that she died. At first I couldn't remember much. Just what I told you. Dr. Blackmore would ask me questions sometimes. Like 'Where were you standing?' or 'What was Mommy wearing?' It was funny, but when I wasn't paying attention, that's when I'd remember something. I'd be looking at one of the posters in his office, instead of at the dolls, and he'd ask me where I was standing, and I'd immediately know—in the corner between the bed and the wall. As the years passed, more and more details came out. Finally, when I was about twelve or so, it became as clear as it is now. I remember pretty much everything. I remember holding the gun and the noise of it going off. It was so loud. Louder than anything I'd ever heard. I remember the look on Mommy's face. Like she was surprised. And sad. The saddest look in the world. There was blood all over her white dress, and all over me. My hands were wet and sticky with her blood. I kept screaming at her. Begging her to wake up. But she wouldn't. She just lay there, without moving. And her blood was all over my hands."

We sat in stunned silence. Suddenly the maid bustled in with a pitcher of coffee. She stopped, looked at us, and blushed. Then she raised the pitcher in the air wordlessly. Lilly nodded, and the maid refilled our cups and rushed out the door. For a few moments the only sound was the tinkling of teaspoons in the delicate porcelain coffee cups. I stared at the streak of thick cream swirling in my cup and tried to wipe the picture of Lilly's dead mother from my mind. I couldn't. It was too powerful an image, made even more dreadful by the substitution my own imagination had wrought. Instead of Lilly's anguished face, I saw my own little girl's.

"You're a brave woman, Lilly," Beverly said, breaking the silence. "And you were a brave girl. You confronted that truth again and again. I'm proud of your courage. I always have been."

Lilly leaned her head on her stepmother's shoulder. "Thank

you, Mom," she said. Then she looked at me. "You haven't asked me about Archer."

I shook my head. "No."

"Don't you want to know what's going on with him?"

"Do you want to tell me?" I said with some trepidation, reminding myself what happens to people who badmouth their friends' lovers. They lose their friends.

"Peter was right," Lilly said. "As soon as I was away from all this, I instantly had clarity about it. I think I was hoping it would work, for the girls' sake, and mine, too, I suppose. But that thing he did at your house. And then lying about it. He's still the same guy he always was."

I nodded.

"I told him that we were over. We'll be friends, for Amber and Jade's sake, but we're not going to get back together."

"What did he say?"

She shrugged and passed a hand over her short hair. "He cried."

Raymond snorted in disgust, and I raised my eyebrows. "Really?"

Lilly smiled ruefully. "Archer's always been a good crier. The problem has always been figuring out whether the tears are real."

"And do you think they were?" I asked over Raymond's dismissive grunt.

Lilly shrugged again. "Who knows. It doesn't really matter, though, does it?"

"And you really don't think he could have been the source of Chloe's information?" I asked.

Lilly shook her head. "I know Archer, and I know what he's capable of."

When I left Lilly's house, I replayed in my mind the complicated and devastating story she'd told me. I also wondered at my own ability to compartmentalize. Lilly was a suspect in Chloe's murder. Perhaps the most obvious suspect. Yet there I was, carrying on as if my friend were absolutely innocent. I hoped she was. I wished fervently that the killer were someone else. Someone like Polaris. Or Archer. Anyone would be preferable to Lilly.

Twenty-two

THE mother half of my working mother identity took precedence the next day. Isaac had come home the day before with a note pinned to his backpack. In flowery script, complete with smiley faces and misspellings, his preschool teacher informed me that I was delinquent in my volunteer duties, and thus was expected in class the next morning. The note had the tone of a cheerful jury summons, and I experienced the same trepidation as I had in junior high school when being called into the principal's office. The summons further instructed me to be prepared to officiate at a lice check, but since I refused to believe this could be anything but a typo (Rice check? Mice check?), I was utterly unprepared when Ms. Morgenstern handed me a comb and a pair of latex gloves.

"You can usually find the nits in the hair over the ears or at the nape of the neck," she said with a cheerfully condescending smile.

I stared first at the picture of the terrified louse stenciled on the comb and then up at her face. "Nits?" I could hear the quaver in my own voice.

"Little baby lice," she said. "Look for eggs, or the little critters themselves. I'd start with Madison if I were you. And Colby. The two of them have been scratching all week."

Since when had lice become a routine part of the academic experience? When I was a kid, nobody had lice. Or at least kids growing up in the New Jersey suburbs certainly didn't. Maybe those New York children had heads full of creepy crawlies; those same children who were gnawed on by rats while they slept. But not us; not the kids who rode their Big Wheels down wide sidewalks past manicured lawns. And now, here I was, picking through the fragrant, shampooed locks of a class full of Travises, Hunters, Jacksons, Sadies, and Maxes, looking for insects. I couldn't help but wonder if Ms. Morgenstern drafted me specifically because she knew I spent my working hours searching out the human equivalent.

The return of my morning sickness at the very thought of vermin infesting the scalp of my cosseted little boy and his passel of overly indulged friends caused me to be more thorough than I might have been otherwise. I ran the comb through the kids' hair and diligently lifted up each and every strand, terrified I would actually see a louse laying its eggs and wriggling its little legs. I was undoing Fiona's braids when my cell phone rang.

"How close are you to a newsstand?" Al said as soon as I'd answered the phone.

"Oh no."

"Yeah," he said.

"How bad?"

"Bad."

"Read me the headline."

He cleared his throat. "LIKE BROTHER LIKE SISTER—" he began.

"Okay, I get it," I said. "I'll call you back." I was still holding on to Fiona's head. I let her go and walked over to Ms. Morgenstern. "I'm sorry," I told her, and handed her the combs. "I've got to go."

She opened her mouth in protest, but I shook my head. "It's an emergency."

She pursed her lips and then widened them into her ubiquitous smile. "We'll expect you back next month."

I nodded and found Isaac. He was in the playhouse, wearing a pair of purple high heels. And a set of Viking horns. I kissed him goodbye.

My cell phone rang again while I was standing in line at the Quikmart, paying for the tall stack of *Daily Enquirers* I'd pulled off the rack. It was Lilly. And she was hysterical.

"Did you see it?" she screamed. "They know everything. Everything!"

"I know," I murmured into the phone. I looked down at the cover photograph. It must have been taken right after Lilly had first shaved her head for her recent film, and her fragile skull filled almost the entire front page. They'd caught her without her usual wide and friendly grin; her mouth was twisted in an unfamiliar scowl. The newspaper had done its homework. The article contained a detailed description of Trudy-Ann's death, and Lilly's role in it. Everything was there—her mother's relationship with Polaris, their life at the Topanga commune and in Mexico. There was a photograph of Dr. Blackmore with his hand to his face, refusing to be interviewed, and a sidebar detailing his theory of recovered memory of childhood trauma. They'd even included descriptions of papers he'd published in which he analyzed the case of a patient he referred to as "Little Girl Q." Little Girl Q had accidentally caused the death of her mother and then repressed all memory of the event. Through intensive work with Dr. Blackmore, she had recovered her memories, and as a result become an emotionally whole individual who did not need the assistance of narcotics to handle her emotional pain. The newspaper left it up to the reader to assume who Little Girl Q really was.

There was also a full rehashing of the Chloe Jones murder, although the paper stopped just short of accusing Lilly of being involved. Nothing in the article was libelous as far as I could tell, but it certainly left the impression that Lilly's violent past and Chloe's violent end were not likely to be merely coincidental.

The descriptions of Lilly's history, life, and troubles were intimate and detailed—how could they not be? Archer had told the newspaper everything he knew.

"I'm going to kill him!" Lilly screamed.

"Please don't say that out loud, Lilly," I said. I tossed some money on the counter and ran out of the store. I got in my car and locked the doors. Once I was safely away from prying ears, I tried to hush her tears. "It's going to be okay."

"How? How is it going to be okay?" She was no longer shouting—her sobs strangled all the volume out of her voice.

"Remember what Beverly said," I murmured. "It will be hard, but you'll end up okay. You'll pull through. I promise."

Lilly just cried harder. I leafed through the rest of the magazine. It was liberally sprinkled with photographs of Archer looking handsome, concerned, put upon. The long-suffering husband of a violent, irrational woman. Near the back was a small photograph of Beverly, standing in front of the state house. I skimmed the paragraph under her picture while murmuring words of comfort to a sobbing Lilly. Beverly and Raymond had survived the debacle relatively unscathed. They were, according to the paper, supportive and nurturing parents who had taken in a damaged and aggressive child and done their best with her. At some point, I knew Lilly was going to be grateful that they had been spared.

"Do you want me to come over?" I asked.

Lilly hiccupped. "No. I want you to go talk to Archer. Find out how much they paid him for this. I want to know what selling me out was worth to that son of a bitch."

"Does that really matter?" I asked as gently as I could.

Her voice turned cold. "Yes. It matters. It matters to *me*. Can you do this one thing for me, Juliet? Can you?"

I tamped down my hurt feelings. Lilly was devastated, and enraged at Archer, at the newspaper, at the world. She didn't mean to lash out at me.

"Yes, of course I can," I said.

Twenty-three

AL met me at Archer's house, a hypermodern monstrosity looming over its neighbors in a somewhat seedy part of Beachwood Canyon. "This will be fun," Al said as we climbed the long flight of stairs to the front door. I couldn't tell whether or not he was being sarcastic.

To my surprise, Archer answered the door. "Well, what do you know," he said, flashing a tight, grim little smile. His dark hair flopped in his eyes, and a mottled flush crept from his neck up to his cheeks. He held the door halfway closed with his hand.

"Can we come in?" I asked pleasantly.

"No. I don't think so," he said.

Al stepped forward. "Sir, we'd like to just ask you a question or two, if you don't mind." He was using his cop voice, all professional courtesy and just barely contained menace.

Archer flushed a deeper red, and his fingers tightened on the door.

We stood like that, at a standoff, for another moment.

Then I said, "Lilly wants to know how much they paid you." I kept my voice benign—almost friendly.

He paused for a moment, and then shrugged. "I don't care if she knows. Five hundred thousand."

I raised my eyebrows. "Wow."

Archer smirked, no longer quite as embarrassed. It was as if the sheer quantity of cash had given him a kind of confidence. "That's not all," he said.

Al and I waited.

"I have a book deal." He paused, clearly for effect. "One point six million bucks. U.S. rights alone."

"You're going to write a book?" I said.

"About my life with Lilly. What it was like having to deal with someone like her. Someone with that kind of history."

Al stepped forward. "And you've cleared all this with your lawyers, have you?"

I nodded. "You'd better do that, Archer. Libel laws. You know."

"Go to hell," he said, and closed the door in our faces.

Al shrugged, turned around, and stomped back down the stairs. I followed.

"Her lawyers'll sue him. Try to get a restraining order," I said.

"Will they succeed?" Al asked.

I shook my head. "Probably not. He can write about his life with her. He can write about almost anything he wants, as long as he doesn't accuse her of something that isn't true. It's only libel if it isn't true."

"That's the question, isn't it?" Al said.

I nodded. Yes, that was the question. Archer was bound to at least insinuate that Lilly was responsible for Chloe's death. Would that be libel or wouldn't it?

I punched Lilly's number into my cell phone. The phone rang and rang, but no one picked up. She must have turned her machine off.

"The worst part of this is that it rules him out," I said.

"For the murder?"

"And the blackmail."

Al nodded. "He certainly wouldn't risk this kind of exposure if he had that to cover up."

"Nope," I agreed.

"So, where to now?" Al asked.

"Wasserman," I replied. "We don't have much choice, do we?"

We found the lawyer in his office, the *Daily Enquirer* spread out on his otherwise immaculate desk.

"Al Hockey, I presume," Wasserman said. Al's strong hand disappeared into the grip of Wasserman's oversized fingers.

"You saw it," I said, pointing at the papers.

He nodded. "It'll hit the mainstream press tomorrow. They'll be embarrassed about the *Enquirer* getting the jump on them, so they're liable to do longer, even more thorough, stories."

I sighed. "How are you going to use it?"

"Well, we can't pretend it didn't happen, that's for sure. And she's been painted in a pretty ugly light. The trick is going to be convincing the jury that she acted alone, that our client wasn't involved."

"So that's your defense? That it was Lilly?" I said, although I'd known for a while that it would have to be.

He nodded. "Means I can't keep taking her money, though, doesn't it?" He shook his head. "Just what my firm needs, another pro bono case. As for you two, you can't stay on. You can't accept money from her, either, and I'm pretty sure you don't want to work for free. Not to mention the little ethical dilemma."

I nodded. I'd known that, too. I could feel Al's sigh.

Wasserman rose to his feet. "Try to get me a final report as soon as you can."

Al and I left in matching glum moods. We stood in the parking lot, leaning on his car. "Another paying client bites the dust," Al said.

This time I did the sighing.

"Tell you what," Al said. "I'm going to get back to work on that workers' comp case. You go do what I know you're planning on doing."

"And what's that?" I asked.

"Finding another murder suspect. Someone other than Lilly Green."

He sure knew me, did Al. We said our goodbyes. I had just over an hour before school was over, not enough time to go see Lilly, or to go home. I drove to a café across the street from Isaac's school and found a seat among the thirty or forty young men and women clicking and clacking assiduously on their laptops. The cafés of the city of Los Angeles are always lousy with wannabe screenwriters working on the next *Chinatown* or *Citizen Kane.* Something told me most of them probably weren't trying to come up with something along the lines of Peter's masterpiece, *The Cannibal's Vacation.*

I made myself comfortable with a decaf, a piece of coffee cake the approximate size of my head, and my cell phone. I wasn't sure what I was going to do, other than sniff up every tree to try to find someone other than Lilly or Jupiter who might have been responsible for Chloe's murder. For lack of a better idea, I decided to make good on my promise to Lilly to follow up on Chloe's mother's story. Wanda Pakulski sounded a bit breathier on the phone than she had in real life, and I couldn't help but wonder if her career in adult entertainment had included phone sex.

"I hope I'm not disturbing you," I said.

"No, no. Not at all. I was just out in the garden planting a little Japanese maple tree. For Chloe. Once it gets big enough, I'll put a little bench under it. Won't that be pretty?"

Whatever the circumstances of her childhood, Chloe had had a mother who loved her, and who clearly missed her terribly now that she was gone.

"It sounds lovely," I said.

"What can I do for you, Juliet?"

"I just want to be absolutely sure, Wanda. You know for sure that Reese Blackmore was sleeping with Chloe, and he was the one who arranged for Chloe to go to the rehab center?"

"Yes, as far as I know. I mean, that's what Chloe told me.

He was her client, and he paid for her to check into the clinic. Everyone at that clinic was so nice to her. She made some really good friends there. And you know, I never would have thought Chloe would go into rehab."

"Why not?" I asked.

"Well, I guess mostly because before she checked in, she'd never even admitted she had a problem. Once I'd quit the business and stopped using, I tried to encourage her to lay off the cocaine and crank. But she wouldn't. She'd just tell me that I was being ridiculous, that she was only using a little, and that I should mind my own business. But then one day she called and told me that she was checking herself in."

"Did she tell you why?"

Wanda paused. "No. Not really. She just said that she had a plan to change her life, and that Ojai was the first step."

Had Chloe's life-altering intention been to be drug-free, or had she had some other goal in mind?

"Have you seen the papers, Wanda? The *Daily Enquirer?*"

She hadn't, and she was horrified at the story I told her. "That's who Chloe was blackmailing?" she said. "Lilly Green?"

"Yes."

"I wonder . . ." Her voice trailed off.

"What?" I said.

"It's just . . . I don't know. A little while before she died, when Chloe came to visit me? The time she gave me the money for the gallery? She said something . . ."

"What? What did she say?" I asked, barely containing my excitement.

"She said something about knowing things about people that even they didn't know. How exciting that was. I just assumed she was talking about Polaris. I mean, because they were married and everything. I told her I wouldn't know, really, because I never had a husband, but I could remember things about her childhood that I was sure she'd forgotten."

"And what did she say?" I tried to keep my voice calm, but it trembled despite my efforts.

Wanda sighed. "I don't really remember. She just laughed, I guess. I'm not sure. We started talking about my plans for the gallery. I was so excited about that."

I hung up the phone and absentmindedly nibbled on my coffeecake. Chloe must have been referring to Lilly. How *she* knew about what Lilly had done even though Lilly's own memories were vague. I reduced the cake to a mere memory and glanced at my watch. I still had almost an hour before I had to pick Isaac up from school and then drive crosstown to get Ruby in time for her piano lesson. I looked around the café and saw, in a corner, a sign that said INTERNET ACCESS, TEN DOLLARS PER HOUR. The perfect way to waste some time.

I gave one of the bored young women behind the counter ten dollars and logged on to the cute little orange I-Book perched on the corner table. I clicked over to Google and input the full name of the Ojai Rehabilitation and Self-Actualization Center. The first site to come up was the center's own, and it was beautiful. It offered a three-dimensional tour of the center, testimonials by satisfied clients, and a long essay by Dr. Blackmore himself explaining the link between repressed memory of traumatic events and self-medication. Blackmore's theory appealed to me. It certainly isn't a coincidence that drug users are generally, although certainly not always, people who've experienced some kind of personal trauma or pain. That was absolutely true of the many drug-using clients I'd represented. It made sense to me that a person might abuse drugs in order to achieve a release from the pain. The disease of drug addiction has always seemed to my uneducated mind to be one that combines physical symptoms with serious emotional problems. Dr. Blackmore's hypothesis that these problems might have as their root the repressed memory of trauma made as much sense to me as any other explanation I'd heard.

I spent the next hour winding my way through the web, reviewing every reference to either Dr. Blackmore or the center. Just as Lilly said, her doctor was nationally recognized as a leader in the field. He'd written more than thirty articles on the link between repressed memory and drug addiction, the most recent dozen of which he'd coauthored with his assistant, Molly Weston. Unlike the majority of theorists whose research concentrated on repressed memory of childhood sexual abuse, Blackmore's writings explored a wide range of trauma susceptible to repression, including the death or injury of a parent. I found the Little Girl Q articles and E-mailed them to myself so that I could read them at my leisure. Then I spent some time looking for the source of the center's funding. I knew from my visit to the center that the majority of clients paid their own way, or benefited from generous health insurance programs. However, I soon discovered that Dr. Blackmore treated enough indigent clients to allow the center to receive a hefty share of public funds. One of the most important things the web has given investigators is access to records to which the public is entitled, but whose request used to involve an elaborate series of forms, and infinite patience. Searching through the records of the California Budget Office, I found a number of references to the Ojai center, including a notation of the unanimous approval by the California Assembly of Speaker Beverly Green's inclusion of the center on a list of state and private agencies singled out as models of effective drug rehabilitation. This made the center eligible for special consideration in the allocation of state funding. Beverly had obviously been very grateful to Dr. Blackmore for the work he did with Lilly.

It took a while longer to find the other major source of the center's funding. Finally, a web page publicizing the recipients of private foundation grants linked me to a list of the CCU's philanthropic activities. In the twenty-five years that the Ojai center had been in operation, it had received almost ten million dollars from Polaris's church.

I sat back in my chair and blew out between my lips. Dr. Reese Blackmore's center was funded in large part by the CCU, and by the State of California. Both Polaris and Beverly had been remarkably generous to Reese Blackmore. Was it gratitude that inspired their benevolence? Or was there a more nefarious reason for it? Had he threatened to expose

Lilly, and thus their own roles in keeping her secret? Were they funneling money to the Ojai center to keep him doing work they admired, or to keep him quiet? And what, if anything, did all this have to do with the murder of Chloe Jones?

I clicked back through the web pages, looking for anything I might have missed. This time, something new caught my eye. I hadn't bothered going to this site initially because it was an individual's home page. The graphics were plain black and white, and the text was full of typos. The page was called Stephanie's Story, and it was written by her mother.

Stephanie, I read, had been a lovely little girl, but had become lost in adolescence. Stephanie's mother wrote that, despite her family's attention and concern, Stephanie became addicted to heroin. After an overdose that nearly killed her, the girl checked into the Ojai clinic for treatment. That was, according to her mother, when the worst began. Much of the webpage was a screed by Stephanie's mother, accusing Dr. Blackmore of implanting false memories of abuse in her daughter.

Dr. Blackmore had, the web page insisted, convinced Stephanie that her father had molested her when she was a child. In therapy, and out, she recounted specific acts of violence that horrified all who heard them. Ultimately, her father was prosecuted for multiple counts of rape and child sexual abuse stemming from her accusations. Stephanie's mother, sure of her own memories, and of her husband's innocence, stood by him, testifying in his favor at trial. He was acquitted, but the family was torn apart. Years later, much to the mother's relief, Stephanie had recanted her claim, calling herself a victim of False Memory Syndrome.

I did a quick search for False Memory Syndrome, and hit pay dirt. The World Wide Web had become the theater of war for a bitter conflict between proponents of recovered memory theory and those of False Memory Syndrome. Cases like Lilly's, where the traumatic memory was one of the death of a parent, seemed to be rare; the battle was being fought almost exclusively over the issue of memories of childhood sexual abuse.

The proponents of the existence of repressed memory, I learned, argue that children who suffer victimization at the hands of someone from whom they cannot physically escape often suffer a kind of selective amnesia in order to cope with the trauma. Later in life, when their psychological survival does not depend on the repression of the traumatic memories, they begin to recall the events. This psychological theory has spawned a cottage industry of therapists, support groups, and self-help books and has led to the prosecution of crimes as old as thirty or forty years. Inputting "Recovered Memory" into Google led me to sober articles—some by Nobel Prize–winning neuroscientists—that tracked memory repression using tried-and-true scientific method, and to websites that encouraged individuals suffering every kind of emotional ailment from anxiety to insomnia to attribute their distress to repressed memories of sexual abuse at the hands of their parents. There were even a disturbing number of sites devoted exclusively to the idea that there was a huge movement of Satanic worship in the United States that had as its focus the sexual abuse, torture, and murder of children.

When I input the term "False Memory Syndrome" into my search engine, I found a similar range of sites. Some described the work of memory theorists engaged in clinical studies in which they successfully implanted false memories using techniques such as hypnosis, drug therapy, guided imagery, journaling, and even mere repetition—the precise methods used by therapists to uncover repressed memories. The authors of the studies concluded that the very attempt to recover repressed memory itself caused the implantation of false memories. Once false memories are "recalled," they are indistinguishable from memories of actual events. The False Memory Syndrome camp listed its own support groups, offering succor to parents and families who felt they had been wrongly accused of sexual abuse as a result of a family member's false memories.

The whole area of sexual abuse is fraught with the potential for confusion and debate. On one hand, it necessarily involves a perpetrator, someone subject to criminal liability, with a tremendous interest in calling the memories into question. On the other, it's an accusation that is difficult if not impossible to disprove, especially if the abuse was supposed to have occurred in the distant past. But Lilly hadn't suffered sexual abuse. Her trauma was a different kind altogether. I wondered if repressed memory really existed in other kinds of situations, for other kinds of ongoing trauma. I input the words "holocaust survivor" and "repressed memory" into my search engine. I found hit after hit. There was an entire body of research into the phenomenon of repressed memory, particularly among children who had survived concentration camps. For many children, their horrific experiences were remembered not at all, or in fragments. Once they began to recall incidents they, like those who claim to have suffered sexual abuse, often suffered hyperrealistic memories complete with intensified emotional and even physical effects.

Next, I input some key terms used by False Memory theorists, along with Blackmore's name. He had become a major player, it turned out, in the debate over recovered and false memories, vigorously defending his theories in print. Nonetheless, once the concept of False Memory Syndrome was popularized, and victim recantation cases hit the media, people seemed to have lost interest in exploring repressed memories as a part of drug treatment. Allegations of implanted memories by his own patients also seemed to have done some damage to his business. I found articles describing the clinic's descent from one of the most popular in California to one with empty beds.

Finally I found a reference to a short article from the *Pasadena Union Tribune* reporting a press release by the CCU, announcing that it was terminating its relationship with the Ojai center and opening its own Cosmological Unity Rehabilitation Centers. But try as I might, I couldn't find any further references to any CCU rehab centers.

Suddenly, a voice woke me from my Internet trance. "Your time's up."

"Excuse me?" I said, startled. I looked up into the face of the young woman to whom I'd paid my ten dollars. She still looked bored, but now she'd complicated that expression with a frown of irritation.

"Your time's up. And we've got, like, a line."

"Oh, sorry," I said. I got to my feet and then a sickening realization hit me. "What time is it?" I asked her.

"Like, twenty after one," she said.

I was going to get fined. Again. I was a full half-hour and thirty dollars late by the time I screeched into the parking lot at Isaac's school. And you know what? It turns out that Ms. Morgenstern doesn't always smile, after all.

Thankfully, Isaac fell asleep in the car, giving me time to think about all that I'd discovered. The recovered memory proponents, especially those discussing the particular biology of memory, succeeded in convincing me that it was possible for a highly charged emotional memory to be stored in a different place in the brain than more neutral memories, and thus to be forgotten and recalled in a different manner. The Holocaust studies were absolutely convincing, as were those cases of adults recovering memories of sexual abuse where there was corroboration. At the same time, however, the False Memory Syndrome folks had also found in me a supporter—other cases of recovered memory seemed to me to be more false than real. In particular, I simply wasn't able to swallow the notion that the countryside of Middle America was littered with the corpses of small children fallen prey to Satanic ritual, no matter how many individuals "remembered" this kind of abuse.

And what about Lilly's recovered memories of the killing that was now splashed all over the tabloids and would be in the international press as early as tomorrow? Lilly hadn't remembered shooting her mother until after she'd been in therapy for years, reenacting the gruesome killing with Barbie dolls. Everyone involved had attributed her failure to remember to the trauma of the event. But maybe there was something else going on. Maybe little Lilly couldn't remember killing her mother *because she hadn't done it*. Maybe someone else had murdered her mother and then had convinced them all that Lilly was responsible, leaving her to spend her entire life tormented by guilt for something she hadn't done.

As soon as I got home, I tossed Isaac in front of a video and called Lilly again. I wanted to talk to her about her memories, to explore the possibility that she was suffering from False Memory Syndrome. Her assistant told me that Lilly was "unavailable" even to me. Despite my repeated messages, she didn't call me back at all that day.

I was close to pounding the phone with frustration when I felt Peter's hands kneading the back of my neck.

"Relax, sweetie," he said.

"As if," I snarled, and was immediately sorry.

"Whoa!" He raised his hands over his head. "What's up with you?"

"Sorry. Sorry. I'm just incredibly tense about all this." I waved at the newspapers.

"Will dinner help?" He slipped his hands around my waist and rested them lightly on my belly. "Gotta feed the succubus."

Peter always had such lovely nicknames for our kids. I leaned my cheek against his arm. "Yeah. Dinner would help."

"Anything special? Any cravings?"

What I was really craving was an uninterrupted hour of bouncing ideas off my husband's warped but brilliant brain, but I wasn't opposed to the idea of a Double Double, animal style, and an order of fries, well done.

We took our In 'n' Out burgers to go, and went to sit in the park across the street. The kids gobbled their food and went to play on the slide. Peter and I sat on the grass where we could see them, and talked.

"So, basically, what you're saying is that maybe Lilly's recovered memories are accurate, and maybe they're not."

I batted his hand away from my pile of French fries. "Hands off. I'm eating for two, remember?" I took a bite of burger and, with my mouth full, continued. "I guess so. I mean, it seems physically possible for a memory as traumatic as the death of your mother to be repressed. On the other hand, even if repressed memory exists, there seems to be something unique about memories of sexual abuse. I don't know why. Maybe because the abuse is ongoing and the child cannot escape from it."

I swallowed the last of my burger and looked over at his.

"Still hungry?" Peter asked. I thought I caught him glancing at my stomach.

"I'm pregnant," I said defensively.

He pushed the remains of the kids' burgers toward me. "And you should eat," he said. "So what kinds of memories can be repressed?"

"A memory that was subject to repression would have to be an emotionally traumatic memory whose recollection somehow endangered the child, so that repression would be a survival mechanism. It seems like there has to be some kind of ongoing abuse, from which physical escape is impossible. That's why the child escapes psychologically."

"Do you think Lilly's recovered memory of killing her mother qualifies as that kind of memory?"

I shrugged. "I don't know. The death of her mother was certainly emotionally traumatic, but there wasn't any ongoing abuse. Unless, of course, being deprived of your mother counts as an ongoing trauma. It could, I guess."

"Is there some test she can take to figure out if it's an implanted false memory or if it really happened?"

"No. That's the thing about false memories. Once they're implanted, they function like real memories. They become indistinguishable."

"So how do you plan to figure out if she really did kill her mother or if she remembered something that didn't happen?"

"I guess it comes down to corroboration. Can someone somewhere independently corroborate the version of events that Lilly recalls? She was supposed to have been alone in the room with her mother, so it might not be possible to find the kind of confirmation I'd need to convince me that she really did it. But it's certainly worth a try."

At that moment we heard a shriek of purest horror. We ran into the playground and found Ruby, one hand over her mouth, pointing a trembling finger at her brother, who was squatting in a corner, a look of intense concentration on his face.

"He's pooping!" she whispered. "He's pooping in his pants!"

Isaac looked vaguely embarrassed.

"Oh God, Isaac. Are you really pooping?" I said.

He shook his head. "No," he said calmly.

"Thank God," I said.

"Not anymore. I'm all done."

"Oh honey! *Why?* You're a big boy! Why didn't you ask me or daddy to take you to the bathroom?" I picked him up and was hit with a truly noxious odor.

"I was too busy," he said.

"Too busy doing what?"

"Pooping."

"Yuck!" Ruby wailed. "Yuck yuck yuck!"

Maybe my indignant daughter would repress the horrifying memory of her brother's pooping in his pants in a public playground. I know that I'd love to forget what it was like to clean up the mess.

Twenty-four

As expected, the story broke in all the major newspapers the next day. Lilly still wouldn't take my calls, and frustrated, I decided to go to Ojai. My obligation to tell Jupiter that we were officially off the case would provide convenient cover for a much-needed conversation with Dr. Blackmore.

For once traffic cooperated with me, and I soon found myself driving up the Pacific Coast Highway with the window rolled down and the salt air tickling my nose. I was making such good time that I gave in to a craving and stopped at a date shake shack. This Southern California delicacy is just what it sounds like—a smoothie made out of sweet, ripe dates. I lingered for a few moments sipping my sweet frozen drink and watching the surfers lying on their boards, bobbing in the waves like seals sunning themselves on shiny white slabs of rock. Out in the distance, a swell threatened to turn into an actual wave. The surfers began paddling furiously, and as the wave caught them, they jumped to their feet, skidding and sliding along the white frosted edge. One by one they crashed into the foam until finally only one was left.

The lone surfer twisted and glided, riding the wave onto the shore with a casual grace. The dark wetsuit couldn't disguise the swell of the surfer's hips and breasts as she danced into the shallow water and scooped up the board with a practiced flip of her foot and a toss of her long blond hair. Every once in a while it becomes absolutely clear to me why I live in California.

I tossed my cup into a trashcan and got behind the wheel of my car. Just then, my cell phone rang. It was Peter.

"Juliet! There was a message from the doctor's office on the machine when I woke up," he said.

It had been two weeks since my CVS. I had been so busy with the case, I hadn't even noticed the time passing. "Oh my God. What did they say?"

"Wait. I'll play it for you." The phone buzzed hollowly in my ear for a moment, and then I heard the shrill beep of the answering machine. A nasal and rather formal voice said, "This is Santa Monica Obstetrics and Gynecology. The result of your genetic test came back normal." There was a pause. Then the voice became suddenly human and warm. "Congratulations!"

Peter got back on the phone. "She's fine!" he said.

"How do you know she's a she?"

"I just know."

"I want to know for sure. Call right now."

"Will they tell me? Or do you have to call yourself?"

After much incompetent fumbling, we managed to figure out how to use our three-way calling function. The receptionist at the doctor's office switched us over to a nurse, who cheerfully agreed to dig out our file. While we waited, Peter repeated over and over again that it was a girl, and I reminded him that we didn't care what sex it was, so long as it was healthy. Finally the nurse came back on the line. "Are you sure you want to know?" she asked.

"Yes!" we shouted in unison.

"It's a little girl!" she said.

Honestly, I hadn't cared whether it was a boy or a girl. Either would have been wonderful. But to be able, suddenly, to imagine the little daughter growing in my body filled me with an unexpected bliss. I suppose I can understand the desire not to find out your child's sex; the thrill of surprise, the romance of the unknown. But I've always loved knowing beforehand. It says something about the importance of gender, I suppose, that it is only once I have this information that I can really begin to imagine the baby as something other than a vague, fantasy infant. Now I saw a red-headed creature, pink and white and delicious, with my green eyes, and her father's bee-stung lips. And please God, without her big sister's temper.

The nurse congratulated us again and hung up the phone, disconnecting us. I immediately called Peter back.

"See, I told you," he said.

"I love you," I replied.

"Me too. Come home soon, okay?"

That brought home to me again what I was doing, and while my joy didn't evaporate, it did move to some other corner of my mind, one that wasn't occupied with death and tragedy. I suppose that's what life is like for most people—the constant give and take of birth and death, bliss and despair. My two occupations, mother and investigator, certainly made that dichotomy stark.

I almost didn't make it onto the grounds of the center. The entrance was blocked by trucks with satellite antennae on the roofs, and reporters milled around, drinking coffee and making periodic attempts to breach the gate. They were kept at bay by a sheriff's cruiser and two irritated Ventura County cops. It took a good twenty minutes of convincing to get the cops to call the center with my name, and another five for them to agree to admit me. Dr. Blackmore was not there, however. He had, according to Molly, sought refuge at a friend's house in Malibu and left her to mind the store. I'd probably passed him on the Pacific Coast Highway.

I was determined to make the best of it. I probably couldn't have gotten him to talk, but I was pretty confident that I could worm something out of his assistant.

Molly served me tea on the terrace.

"What a nightmare," she said as she passed me a cup. "Poor Jupiter. He's doing his best to continue his recovery work, but you can imagine—this is an awful distraction."

"I'll bet," I said. "Was it a terrible shock for you all? I mean, did you know Lilly?"

Molly shook her head. "I didn't really know her. I mean, of course I knew about her case. Because of my work with Reese. We work so closely together."

I nodded.

"It's terrible for her that all this has come out."

"And bad for the center, too, I imagine," I said.

She frowned. "Why would you say that? I mean if anything it's more evidence of the fundamental truth of our theories. Repressed memory causes terrible emotional and psychological stress. Lilly's case highlights the importance of recovering memory."

I wrinkled my brow. "Perhaps." Except for the fact that her memories provided an all-too-compelling motive for murdering Chloe Jones.

"I'm leaving," she said. "In a few months. Before the fall semester begins."

"Really?" I said, surprised. "Was that sudden? I remember you told me that you'd been here a long time."

She nodded. "Seven years. I've never been sober anywhere else."

I smiled encouragingly at her. "Well, I'm sure you'll do fine."

She nodded again. "I'm feeling pretty confident."

"What are you going to do?"

She shrugged. "Reese has arranged for me to teach at Santa Anita Community College. In the Psychology Department. Introduction to Psychology, and a seminar on recovered memory and addiction. They wanted him, but he convinced them that I'm the best person for the job."

"Wow, that sounds great," I said. "Dr. Blackmore must have a lot of confidence in you."

"He's a wonderful man. He really is. You know he gave me joint author credit on thirteen of his articles? Do you know how rare that is? He could have just thanked me in the acknowledgments or something. It's going to be very difficult for both of us with me gone. I'm just grateful we'll be able to continue to work on scholarship together." She seemed suddenly to remember the reason for my visit. "Jupiter will be out of group in about half an hour," she said.

"Great. I'm looking forward to seeing him."

"I suppose these revelations about Lilly have complicated the case against him."

I nodded. "Things have certainly taken some interesting turns. Molly, I wonder if you'd be willing to tell me a little bit about Dr. Blackmore and Chloe."

She bit her lip nervously. "What do you mean?"

"Do you know what their relationship was? Do you know, for example, if he was the person who made it possible for Chloe to enroll at the center?"

"Why would you think that?"

"Chloe's mother told me that Chloe didn't have to pay for her treatment here. I was wondering if you knew anything about why that was." I wasn't ready to tell Molly any more than that. Yet.

"Her mother told you that?"

I nodded.

"How is she?"

"Chloe's mother? She's okay, considering everything that's happened. They were very close. It's going to be hard for Wanda without her."

Molly shook her head ruefully. "I feel just awful. I never thought of Chloe even *having* parents, although of course she did. I should have sent a condolence card, or something. Whatever I thought of Chloe, her parents must still be grieving terribly."

"There's just her mom, and it's not too late," I said. "I'm sure Wanda would appreciate hearing from you. I know she misses Chloe terribly."

Molly looked at me eagerly. "Do you think so?"

"Definitely. Can you tell me how come Chloe never had to pay for her treatment?"

Molly sat quietly for a moment, and then she said, "I'm sorry. I really shouldn't talk about any of this."

I leaned forward and said intently, "Look, Molly. It's all going to come out sooner or later. The worst thing to do would be to force Jupiter's lawyers to get a court order. They'll get access to the files, they'll compel depositions of all of you. If you talk to me, we might be able just to leave it at that. And you'll be helping Jupiter."

She knotted her hands in her lap nervously. "I want to do what I can for him. Really, I do. But I want you to understand—Reese is an incredible man. I was a junkie when I came here, and I'm completely sober now. I owe him a lot."

"You owe *yourself* a lot. You're the one who did the work."

"But without his help I wouldn't have been able to do it. He taught me so much. He helped me to realize why I was drawn to the heroin. He helped me to remember what my father did to me when I was a little girl."

I wasn't going to touch that with a ten-foot pole. And I needed to stop her before she decided that she owed the doctor unmitigated loyalty.

"So Dr. Blackmore was the one who paid for Chloe's treatment?"

"Not exactly. I mean, I'm not sure how the billing went, but I don't think anyone paid for it. She showed up one day, and Reese told me to check her in as a special resident and not bother with a billing form."

"So she came for free?"

"Yes."

"What did Dr. Blackmore tell you about their relationship?"

"Nothing," she said softly. There wasn't any surprise in her voice, though, at the necessary implication of my question.

"Did you have any suspicions about them? Did you think they might have been, er, romantically involved?" I couldn't quite bring myself to suggest to the young woman that her idolized therapist and boss paid young women to have sex with him.

"That's a ridiculous suggestion. Look, Chloe might have acted like they were. I practically had to pry her off him to take her to her room. But first of all, Reese would never do anything like that. And second of all, it became very clear that that was just Chloe's way."

"What do you mean?"

"What happened with Jupiter, of course."

"You mean their relationship?" I said.

"Within a day or two it was clear that something was going on between Jupiter and Chloe. They did everything together. They ate together, they hung out together. One day in group she was even massaging his feet. It was pretty gross." She frowned with a vehemence that betrayed, once again, her feelings for the young man.

"Did you tell Dr. Blackmore about it?"

"You bet I did. I told him that if they weren't sleeping together now, they were going to be soon. Jupiter just wasn't ready for that kind of intimacy. It was distracting him from his recovery work. It was getting in the way of his therapy. And it was *supposed* to be against the rules."

"Did Dr. Blackmore force them to break it off?"

She snorted. "He tried to. He called them into his office, and I guess they said they'd stop. At first I thought they had. And anyway, Jupiter finished the program, and I figured that was that."

"But it wasn't."

"Obviously not."

The son of Polaris Jones, the extravagantly wealthy religious leader, would have seemed like a terrific catch for a stripper with a drug habit. I could see why Chloe would have gotten involved with Jupiter, and I could certainly imagine why, once she realized the extent of his dependence on his father and the limitation of his own resources, she'd set her sights on the real cash-cow, Polaris. But whatever his assistant believed, I was certain Chloe already had Dr. Blackmore, a wildly successful doctor who was clearly crazy about her. Why would she have needed to look any farther afield?

"Is the clinic in financial trouble?" I asked.

Molly glanced at me, surprised. "No, we're doing fine."

"Not even with the debate over False Memory Syndrome?"

She sighed. "That. Yes, well, of course that hurt us, for a while. Memory therapy is an integral part of the recovery process here at the center. We even have a saying: 'There is no recovery without the recovery of memory.' "

"Did people stop coming to the clinic because they objected to the theory?"

She nodded. "For a little while. You have to understand. There's a lot of resistance to recovered memory. People repress memories for one reason and one reason only, because they're traumatic. Recovering them, and facing the trauma, is incredibly painful. A person only becomes ready to face that pain when the alternative is worse."

"Worse how?"

"Well, like, for example, when their addiction is about to kill them, and they can't kick the drugs because the drugs are only a symptom of the problem, not the real issue."

"And the center felt the effects of the False Memory Syndrome movement?"

"We did, for a brief while. But that was a long time ago."

"But don't you have a lot of CCU clients? I read that the CCU threatened to pull its parishioners and its funding."

She frowned. "That's ridiculous. I mean I think they once floated the idea of opening their own clinic, and that might have hurt us. But our work here is unparalleled. I'm sure all it took was a brief examination to figure out what a huge undertaking it would be for them to try to provide similar services."

My web research had indicated more than just an idea being "floated." There had, it seemed, been a firm plan to open up a CCU clinic. The CCU's discomfort with the recovered memory movement had come at a time when Dr. Blackmore had been losing many of his clients to the same suspicions. What if Chloe hadn't betrayed her benefactor after all? What if her relationship with the son of the CCU's spiritual leader had been entirely Blackmore's idea? He had introduced her to Jupiter at a time when the future of his clinic seemed in doubt. She had gone on to marry Polaris, and Blackmore's relationship with the CCU had been sealed. Was it Chloe who had convinced Polaris to continue his support of Reese's clinic?

Even if all that were true, I still couldn't figure out what any of this had to do with Chloe's blackmailing of Lilly. And I still had no idea who killed her.

Molly left me to my musing and went to let Jupiter know I was waiting for him. It was hard to believe that the man who sauntered up to me on the terrace was the same person who I'd last seen cowering at a table in the visiting room of the county jail. Unwound from his defensive crouch, he looked at least six inches taller. His skin had lost its jailhouse pallor and glowed with the kind of golden tan I'd always coveted. His hair was clean and parted neatly in the middle.

He sat down, leaned back, and smiled at me. I smiled back.

"Happy to be out?" I asked.

He nodded. "Oh yeah. It was in the nick of time. Just. Another week and I might have . . . I don't know. Done something."

I frowned. I knew Jupiter understood that if he was convicted, he would have to go back there, and on to prison. Obviously, however, his relief at being freed, even into the somewhat constricting arms of the Ojai center, was so profound that it transcended worry about what the future might hold.

"It sucks about Lilly," he said. "The papers and everything."

I nodded. "It does."

"She didn't kill Chloe," he said. "I know she didn't."

"I know," I said, wishing I could be as sure as he was.

"This is my fault. I brought this on everyone. She was a horrible person, Chloe was. She was poison. I poisoned everyone when I let her into our lives."

There wasn't anything I could say to comfort him. Instead, I took a deep breath, and said, "Jupiter, Al and I are not going to be able to stay on your case. It wouldn't be ethical for us to continue taking Lilly's money, now that she's become a suspect."

"Wasserman said he'd continue representing me for free," Jupiter said.

"I know. I wish we could do that. But it's more than just a financial issue." I explained to Jupiter how my friendship with Lilly compromised my representation of him, since it was entirely possible that their interests would conflict now that she was a likely target both for the defense's theory of the case and for the prosecution's. As I spoke, I realized that I should have pulled out long before, when I had first had an inkling that Lilly might somehow be involved. All that was in the past, however. Right now I needed to do the correct thing.

Jupiter wasn't happy, but ultimately he told me he understood. I held my hand out to him, and he shook it firmly. He gripped my palm in his and said, "Lilly didn't kill Chloe. You should help her prove that."

I only wished I could.

Twenty-five

I had to see Lilly. I called again and told her assistant that I was going to take the kids to a beach in Malibu that I knew Lilly liked, and that I hoped she'd join me there. I bundled Ruby and Isaac into the car and packed a bag with sand toys, towels, and extra clothes. The fog lay in a thick mantle along the shore, wreathing the beach in icy tendrils and hiding the ocean almost entirely from view. I wrapped myself up in a sweater and a warm hat as I waited for Lilly to arrive, but Ruby and Isaac were impervious to the chill. They kicked off their shoes and socks, rolled up their jeans, and danced in and out of the surf, squealing whenever the water hit their ankles.

Just when I was about to give up on Lilly, Amber and Jade tore across the sand, screaming Ruby's name and ululating like a couple of banshees. Lilly plopped down next to me on the ratty cotton bedspread I'd laid out on the sand. She was traveling incognito, a baseball cap pulled low over her forehead and huge, round sunglasses hiding her famous azure eyes.

"Hey," she said.

"Hey, yourself."

She pointed at a young man who had followed her twins down to the water. "I brought Patrick with me. He'll watch the kids so we can talk."

The nanny was crouched down next to Isaac, ruffling his hair. As we watched, he reached into the teal blue backpack slung over his shoulder and pulled out a frisbee. Within moments he had all four kids standing in a circle, flinging the disk in the vague direction of one another. I could get used to this kind of parenting. It was a lot easier to enjoy being with your kids if someone else was actually playing the games with them. I wondered, in Lilly's position would I feel guilty? Would I feel like I should be the one running around on the sand with my children, instead of the cheerful young nanny? Perhaps. But perhaps not. After all, it wasn't like I'd been doing a whole lot of playing before Lilly and her brood showed up. I'd been huddled on the sand, watching Ruby and Isaac entertain themselves, and not for a minute feeling like I was neglecting them. Anyway, chances were I was never going to have to debate the pros and cons of too much child-care. I couldn't afford it, and even if Peter's screenwriting career really took off and pushed us into a different economic bracket, chances were I'd be too disorganized and busy to get around to hiring my own team of nannies.

Lilly and I watched the kids in silence for a while. I kicked off my shoes and scooted down to the edge of the bedspread. I dug my toes into the cold sand. Lilly followed me and kicked sand over my feet, burying them.

"Oooh," I said, wriggling my feet. "Popsicle toes."

"How are you feeling?" she asked.

"Better."

"That's good."

"And you?"

"Better," she said, and smiled.

I smiled back. "Good. Hey, guess what? I'm having a girl."

She smiled at me. "Congratulations. Girls are great."

"Yeah, they are." We sat in silence for a little while, watching our girls romp in the sand.

"Are you really okay, Lilly?"

She nodded, and then shook her head. "I don't know. I mean, I guess so. Beverly says just to lie low and wait for it to blow over."

"That's probably all you can do. Did the prosecutor ask for an interview?"

She nodded. "My lawyers gave them a statement. You know, I didn't do anything to Chloe, that kind of thing. I'll let them figure out how much to tell the DA, and when. It's not like there's any evidence linking me to the crime, or anything."

"Of course not," I said. Although of course there was. The money paid to Chloe's account. The request to Jupiter that he talk to Chloe. All that could be used as circumstantial evidence against Lilly.

"And your parents?" I asked. "Are they doing okay? I mean, I noticed some tension when I saw them."

Lilly snorted. " 'Tension.' That's one word for it."

I raised my eyebrows.

She shrugged. "The added pressure isn't doing them any good, but things haven't been great with them for quite a while. Ever since my dad was forced to retire after my mom was appointed Speaker. I think he just doesn't know what to do with himself, and when my dad's bored . . ." Her voice trailed off.

"What? What does he do when he's bored?"

She shook her head. "He tries to find something to entertain himself. Something young, and pretty."

"He's having an affair?"

She laughed bitterly. "*An* affair? Probably more like ten. Or fifteen. My dad's always been like that. I told you about the Topanga commune."

"Have you always known about his affairs?"

"We both knew. Both me and my mom. I mean, Beverly. Although of course my real mother knew, too. It was even more out in the open back then. They're children of the sixties, don't forget. Free love and all that crap. I guess my dad figured that if he told us everything, then he wasn't doing anything wrong."

"Does Beverly have affairs?"

"My mom? No. Never. She's not like that. She loves my dad, and that's it. Or that was it."

"What do you mean?"

"She's finally getting sick of it, I guess. I mean, now that it's becoming a political embarrassment for her. She's humiliated, and I'm worried that she's going to decide she's not willing to put up with him anymore."

"Do you think they might get divorced?"

Lilly heaved a sigh. "God, I hope not. But I don't know. After his most recent fling, she told him he had one last chance. We'll see what happens. He'll probably screw it up. He always does." She twisted her mouth into a rueful frown. "I can't talk about this anymore. It makes me too depressed. Tell me what's happening with the case. That ought to cheer me right up."

I kicked my feet loose and said, "The case. Yeah. Well, you'll probably understand why we can't continue to work for Jupiter."

She nodded. "I figured as much."

"But there is something I want to talk to you about. I've been doing a little research on repressed memory."

Her smile faded. "Really?"

I nodded. "Have you ever heard of False Memory Syndrome?"

She didn't answer. I waited. Finally, after a few moments she said, "I talked to Dr. Blackmore about that a few years ago. I read an article about it in the *L.A. Times.* You can imagine how I felt. I called him right away, and we had an emergency session. A few sessions."

"What did he say?"

"He told me that the research on false memories is really spotty. Nobody's proved that they even exist."

I refrained from pointing out to her that the same was essentially true for the theory of recovered memory.

"He's very sure that my memories are accurate," she continued.

"Are *you* sure?" I asked.

She didn't answer.

"Lilly, are you *sure* that you killed your mother?"

Her shoulders began to shake. I thought for a moment that she must be crying, but her eyes were dry. She was trembling, as if the cool sea breeze had grown to a frigid gale. I reached an arm around her and hugged her close. Her shoulder blades were as sharp as a bird's, and I felt them poking into the skin of my inner arm.

"Lilly?"

"I've been sure. I've known that I did this for so long. My entire life. I'm the girl who shot her mother, and who managed with years of therapy to salvage a life for herself. It's who I am. Little Girl Q. That's what Dr. Blackmore called me, did you know that? He wrote about my case in psychology journals."

"I know. I read some of the articles."

"When I read about false memories, I panicked. I know it sounds crazy, but I was reassured when Dr. Blackmore told me that it really had happened. That I really *had* killed her. Everything I've done in my life, everything I am, is to make up for this horrible thing that I did when I was five years old. What would it *mean* if it weren't true? Who would I *be?*"

I clasped her bony frame closer. I understood that it was terrifying for Lilly to imagine that the truth on which she'd based her life, the trauma from which she'd always tried to recover, had never really happened. But was that really worse than living forever with the guilt? Wouldn't bringing an end to the guilt also liberate her from the trauma?

Except, of course, that if the memories were wrong, if she hadn't done it, there would be a whole other kind of horror to imagine. Lilly had been silent after her mother's death. She had not assumed responsibility for the terrible crime. Another person had implicated her, had blamed her: Polaris Jones. The man who sat at her bedside, hovered over her, cared for her. Had he struggled to end her catatonia, or had he been responsible for it? The chilling image of a stepfather whispering lies of her guilt into the ear of a devastated and silent girl filled me with a cold, sick horror.

There was, of course, only one reason why Polaris would have blamed Lilly for Trudy-Ann's death: to deflect suspicion away from himself.

Lilly straightened up and rubbed her eyes with the heels of her hands. I smoothed the short, tangled curls away from her forehead. "As terrifying as it is to imagine that you've spent your life living this lie, isn't it worse to continue to believe it if it isn't true?" I said gently.

She inhaled deeply and then, with a movement so small as to be almost unnoticeable, she nodded.

"I think we need to find out what really happened in Mexico," I said.

"But how?"

Suddenly, I knew what I had to do. "What if I went down there? I could check the police records, track down anyone who might have information. I could talk to the detectives who investigated the death, to anybody who might have worked in the house. You know, maids, gardeners, whatever."

She looked at me, her eyes wet with tears. "You'd do that for me?"

"Of course," I said.

"And you don't have any suspicions . . ." Her voice trailed off.

I kicked sand over her feet. "No, I don't."

"You don't think I killed Chloe?"

I shook my head. "No. I know you didn't." I was naïve, and I was loyal, and I didn't believe my friend was a murderer.

Twenty-six

It was surprisingly easy to tell my husband that I'd be abandoning him with the kids, the carpools, and the playdates, and heading to Mexico for a few days. The only problem was that he decided to join me.

"Who's paying for this trip?"

"Um. We are. I can't take money from Lilly. It wouldn't be ethical."

He nodded. "When's the last time we had a vacation together without the children?" he said.

"Never," I replied.

We were lying together on the couch, having gotten the kids to bed early for once. A day at the beach always makes them sun-stunned and tractable. Isaac had actually fallen asleep at the dinner table, his face pressed into his plate of plain, buttered spaghetti. I'd wiped him clean and tucked him into bed, kissing the grooves the noodles had left in his plump cheeks. And after protesting mightily that she wasn't in the least bit tired, Ruby had fallen asleep by six-thirty.

"Exactly!" he said. "Never. And it's not like it's going to

get any easier when this one comes along." He lay his hand against the bulge of my belly, feeling for the kicks that wouldn't be apparent for another few weeks. "Hell, if I'm paying for it, I'm coming. It'll be great. Just the two of us. Off on our own. Think how romantic it will be!"

I wrinkled my brow dubiously. "I'm not going on vacation, Peter. I'm going to be looking through police archives, talking to witnesses. That kind of thing. I won't have time for romance."

He leaned over and kissed me lightly on the lips. "There's always time for romance," he said.

Having a husband who finds pregnant women intensely attractive is wonderful, except for the fact that in the first few months of pregnancy the absolute last thing I'm ever in the mood for is sex. I seemed, finally, to have survived the morning sickness part of my pregnancy, and I no longer felt like napping at the drop of a hat, but I hadn't quite begun to experience the renewed surge of energy and libido that heralded the second, more enjoyable trimester. And anyway, I had to work.

I sighed. "I'll call my mom. Maybe she'll be willing to fly out and take care of the kids."

And she was, although it was touch and go for a couple of days. She had tickets to a lecture on the history of Yiddish theater at the 92nd Street Y in New York City, and it took her a little while to decide what she'd rather do, see her only grandchildren or listen to a panel full of ancient Jewish thespians reminisce about the good old days on Second Avenue. We won, but only because she managed to browbeat the box office into letting her trade her tickets in for a lecture the following month on Third Wave Jewish Feminism.

A week after my conversation on the beach with Lilly, Peter and I were standing in the courtyard of Casa Luna, an inn in the heart of San Miguel de Allende, Mexico.

"I told you it would be romantic," Peter said.

The walls around the stone courtyard were draped with tumbling purple bougainvillea. Brightly painted pots of even more resplendent flowers flanked the wrought iron doors to our room, where we'd dumped our bags on a four-poster bed hung with white gauze. The innkeeper, a smiling American woman named Diane who'd come to San Miguel on vacation twenty years before and never left, had greeted us with chilled margaritas and a basket of homemade tortilla chips accompanied by a vivid green salsa so hot it made the inside of my mouth feel like it had undergone a chemical peel. A furry dog lolled next to the stone bench on which we were sitting, its wagging tail thumping rhythmically against the little table that held our late-afternoon snack.

"It's lovely," I said. "But remember, we're not here to enjoy ourselves. We're here to work."

Peter heaped salsa on a chip and popped it in his mouth. His eyes began watering and he gulped at his frozen drink. Once he recovered he said, "We're not going to be able to accomplish anything tonight. It's almost dark. Let's relax, wander around the city, find someplace nice for dinner. I promise you we'll stop having fun first thing tomorrow morning."

I reluctantly agreed, and armed with a map and guidebook supplied by our cheerful host, we set out to explore.

San Miguel is a Colonial city that looks much like it must have a hundred years ago, if you ignore the streets clogged with cars, the tangles of telephone and electrical wires hammered directly into the walls of the stone houses, and the cell phones pressed against the ears of the passing crowds. We walked along the high, narrow sidewalks flanking the cobblestone streets, passing by houses concealed behind high walls and elaborately carved wooden doors. The only sign of life in those old houses was the barking of the occasional dog.

At the corner of a busy street, we stopped and waited for a break in the traffic. An ancient man in a red embroidered vest walked by, leading a donkey that was pulling a rickety wooden cart. He was followed by a brightly painted bus festooned with lights and garlands of tinsel. A Chevy Suburban with Texas license plates ground to a halt in front of us, allowing us to jog quickly across the street. I waved my thanks at the blond woman driving the truck, and saw that the rear seats of her car were full of towheaded children, none of whom seemed to be buckled into their seat belts, let alone into car seats.

The light was fading, and the stone walls along the streets glowed pink and orange as the sunset turned the sky into a watercolor. It was ridiculously pretty, like a postcard or a painting on the wall of a shopping mall art gallery.

We found ourselves standing in a large square, the *Jardin*, around which Diane had promised us we'd find any number of restaurants. We sat down on a bench next to the gazebo in the heart of the square, and watched the people passing by. Venders hawked their wares—newspapers, sodas, balloons, and odd little metal toys that looked to be cut out of Coke cans. A small grimy boy dragging a wooden case offered Peter a shoe shine. I pointed out my husband's sneakers, but handed the boy a coin. When he smiled his thanks, I caught a glimpse of blackened teeth. There was a sudden clanging, and Peter and I looked across the square at the huge imposing stone church. The church bells bonged and jangled for a moment or two, and then tolled six o'clock.

I leaned my head against Peter's shoulder.

"It's easy to see why they came," he replied.

We looked at the passing crowd, many of whom were older North Americans wearing tennis shoes and carrying English newspapers and novels. There were a couple of ponytailed men and women in gauze skirts who looked like they might have been holdovers from San Miguel's incarnation as a hippie destination. Most of the *gringos*, however, looked like they would have been more at home in Leisure World than at Woodstock.

We ate enchiladas and drank beer in a cozy little restaurant, and wandered back to our hotel in the dark. It had grown cold, and once we got to our room, we got right into bed and burrowed under the pile of down comforters. We slept tangled in each other's arms and legs, oblivious to the peals of church bells that interrupted the otherwise still night. The crowing of a rooster woke us up at dawn.

The groggy night watchman informed us that Diane wasn't serving breakfast for a good three hours, so we decided to head over to the cemetery, where I had decided to begin my investigation. We walked through the dusty streets in the half-light of the dawn, marveling at the silence. The dogs that had howled and barked throughout the night seemed to have exhausted themselves. The streets were empty of cars, and the heavy smog that had thickened the air with the smell of exhaust and made us wrinkle our noses and cough the evening before was gone, blown away by the cool, crisp breeze. Every once in a while we had to step carefully around someone huddled under a bright, woven blanket in a doorway. As we passed what appeared to be the cable TV store, my eye was caught by a small, brown face peeping out of a bundle of blankets. I bent down and two eyes as big and round as chocolate coins stared up at me. The baby was lying tucked up against the sleeping forms of his parents. His cheeks were red and chapped from the cold and air, and his small mouth was pursed and pouched, as though he was pretending to nurse. He was wide awake, but completely silent. I had a sudden, irrational desire to slip the tiny bundle out of his mother's grasp and take him with me, away from this beautiful Colonial city where Indians, gaunt with hunger and exhaustion, spent their nights sleeping in the streets and their days hawking hand-sewn dolls to wealthy American tourists. Peter bent down and tucked a thick wad of bills into the fold of blankets under the baby's chin. The child mewed softly, and a woman's arm reached out from the roll of blankets and tucked him deeper into the nest. He closed his eyes, and we continued on our way.

We walked through the white arches of the cemetery and stood in the entry, staring at the tumble of crosses, angels, crypts, graves, and markers that lay like a crazy quilt as far as we could see. There was no grass to speak of. Rows upon rows of graves lay jammed tightly against one another. Many had simple crosses for markers, but others were decorated with tall angels, obelisks, and elaborately carved tombs. Some looked almost like little houses, with box-like tombstones and neat wrought iron fences.

"We're never going to find her grave," Peter said.

I didn't answer, just set off down the long path leading from the entry gates deep into the heart of the cemetery. We walked silently for a while, reading the names off the graves as we passed them. Suddenly, I was brought up short. Propped carefully in front of a cross, lying inside a grave surrounded by a white metal fence, was a plastic skull with wilted carnations poked through each eye socket.

"What the heck . . ." I murmured as I leaned closer to see.

"What?" Peter said. I pointed to the skull.

"Wow." He bent down and read from the marker. " 'Descansa en Paz, Lucia Mendiola.' She was nineteen. And look. Here's her baby."

I wiped the tears from my eyes, and we continued down the row until we reached a wall of what looked like the cubbies in Isaac's preschool classroom. Except instead of Teletubby lunchboxes, extra underwear, and hardened, cracked paintings labeled MY MOM AND ME and A T-REX EATING A STEGOSAURUS, this bank of cubbies held little piles of dried, twig-like bones.

I cringed at what seemed, to my American sensibilities, to be nothing short of gruesome, but then remembered what Hyades had told me about the tradition of celebration of death and the dead in Mexico. If death was not the end, but merely another step in the cycle of life, then skulls and bones and other reminders were not macabre symbols of horror, but simply fragments of the corporeal life, left behind by loved ones who no longer needed them.

We wandered for close to two hours, and finally, just when we were about to give up, we came upon a portion of the cemetery back near the entry that was walled off from the rest and closed behind a locked gate. Over the wall we could see a much more orderly graveyard. The markers were less elaborate than their native fellows. There were crosses, and even a few stars of David, but there were fewer weeping angels, and no statues of Christ with beseeching arms spread wide. Peering at a small square tombstone close to the wall, we could just make out the name IRVING SILVERMAN. Mr. Silverman had begun his life in Poland on July 18, 1914, and ended it here, in San Miguel, in the winter of 1977.

Peter and I looked at each other, and then, without a word, he made a stirrup with his hands. I put my foot into it, and he hoisted me up and over the wall. He clambered over after me, and we continued our wanderings through what was clearly the *gringo* section of the cemetery.

We found what we were looking for almost immediately.

Trudy-Ann's tombstone was simple and spare. A block of stone, roughened by the passage of time, it was etched with her name and the dates of her life. The stone was soft, and the words had begun to blur. There was no fence demarcating her grave, nor was there any decoration. It looked like what it was—the forgotten grave of a woman whose husband and child had left her long ago.

We stared at the marker for a few moments, without speaking. Then I crouched down and scrabbled through the dusty earth until I found a smooth, round stone. I brushed it clean against the side of my pants, and placed it carefully on top of the gravestone. I closed my eyes and dredged my memory for the words of the *Kaddish*, the Hebrew prayer for the dead. I recited them silently, skipping the parts I couldn't remember. Then we climbed back over the wall, leaving the remains of Lilly's mother alone again.

After breakfast, Peter and I made our way to the police station across the square from the church. The officer guarding the front door looked like he couldn't possibly be any older than twelve. He was too busy struggling to stay upright under the weight of a rifle almost as long as he was tall to ask us our business or block our entrance. There was a long counter against one wall of the entry hall, with just a single person behind it—a surly policewoman with purple lipstick and a mole on her cheek in a rather alarmingly similar shade.

In my best Spanish, rolling my *R*'s and coughing my *J*'s, I explained my business. I'd spent two months in an intensive Spanish language program in Guatemala before I'd gone to law school. My vocabulary of the names of baked goods was particularly excellent, since my tutor and I had spent every afternoon in a local café, eating cake and conjugating verbs. I was fluent enough to say that I was a private investigator from the United States and was seeking information about the death of an American woman in San Miguel thirty years before. The clerk stared at me balefully and wordlessly. Suddenly, she grunted, turned around, and walked through a doorway behind the counter. I turned to Peter and raised my eyebrows.

"Helpful," he said.

"Very."

"Now what?"

"God only knows."

We waited for a while, and finally, just when I was about to give up and tell Peter we could spend the rest of the day eating tacos and visiting churches and art galleries, the policewoman came back through the door, accompanied by a uniformed man who was about twenty years older and six inches shorter than she was. He sported a bushy mustache and a scowl. He turned to Peter, and in perfectly grammatical, if heavily accented English, he said, "I am the captain of this station house. I understand that you are a private detective working on a case. How may I be of assistance to you?"

I interrupted. "I'm afraid I'm the one who is the private investigator." I stuck out my hand for him to shake. "Juliet Appelbaum. And this is my husband, Peter Wyeth. He's assisting me."

The captain's eyes widened, but I ignored his aghast expression and explained once again that I was investigating a murder in Los Angeles, and had reason to believe that there might be a connection to an accidental death that had occurred in San Miguel in 1972. I refrained from mentioning that I no longer had a client, and when I'd had, he'd been the accused murderer. I was pretty sure that in Mexico, as in the United States, police officers had little time to spare for criminal defendants and their representatives. To my relief, the officer didn't ask who I was representing.

"Ah," he said. "Nineteen seventy-two. That is unfortunate."

"Excuse me? Unfortunate?" I said.

"Yes. Because of the fire."

"The fire," I repeated, my hopes sinking.

"The fire in this station. In 1979. Everything was destroyed. Files. Papers. All our records. Nothing remains."

"Nothing?" I said plaintively.

"Alas, nothing."

"Perhaps you remember the incident?" I asked. "A young North American woman was shot in her home?"

"Yes, of course. I was a young man. A very young man. New to the department. But I remember when the *gring* . . . the North American woman was shot by her own daughter. It was a tragedy. A great tragedy. But of course, it was not surprising."

"Not surprising?" I was beginning to sound like a parrot.

"Of course not. Those oppies. They were capable of anything. Anything at all. We were not at all surprised that they gave their children weapons."

"Oppies?" I said.

Peter murmured in my ear. "He means hippies."

"Oh, right. Hippies."

"That is what I said," the captain bristled. "Ippies. North American, drug-using ippies."

"Do you by any chance remember who was the investigating officer on the case?"

"Of course."

I waited.

He said nothing.

"Do you mind telling me?" I said.

He blew a puff of air through his mustache and the stiff hairs waggled for an instant. Then he said, "What do you intend to do with this information?"

"I'd just like to speak to him, to see if he can remember anything that might be helpful to me. It's been a long time, I know. But he may remember something."

"Ah."

"I just want to ask him a few questions. See if he might be able to shed some light on the events."

"I don't think he will be able to help you."

"Perhaps not, it's been a long time. But I'd like to try."

"Perhaps the man is busy. You know, his time is quite valuable."

Now I was beginning to understand. "Of course," I said. "Of course it is. And I'd be happy to compensate him for it."

"The others who came, they paid for *my* time, as well."

"The others?"

"From the newspapers."

I wasn't surprised that the papers had been there before me. I didn't know whether to be disturbed or grateful that the articles had included no great revelation from their Mexican investigation. On the one hand, I was relieved for the sake of Lilly's privacy. On the other, I had hopes of finding something new, something that would exonerate Lilly. If they'd been here before me and found nothing, that didn't bode well for my chances.

The captain stared at me blandly, waiting.

"Of course, I'll be happy to compensate you, as well." I reached into my wallet but the man held up his hand.

He shot a furtive glance at his colleague. She was staring off into space, giving a near perfect simulacrum of someone not paying attention to the goings-on around her. After reassuring himself of her silence, the captain said, "A fee of one hundred dollars is customary in these situations."

"Of course, how utterly reasonable," I said, smiling falsely, and handed him the money.

He returned my grin with one equally genuine, "The man you seek is Eduardo Cordoba. I will give you his address and notify him that you seek an audience."

Seek an audience?

"Thank you so much," I said. "What is your name, sir? So that I can tell him who sent me?"

"Captain Eduardo Cordoba."

"No, *your* name."

"That is my name. The man you seek is my father."

Twenty-seven

EDUARDO Cordoba, Senior, sat in an old, faded armchair in his garden. He was a big man, with a vast expanse of belly against which the suspenders holding up his pants strained like guy wires keeping a basket attached to a hot-air balloon. He wore a stained and frayed Panama hat, and had the same mustache as his son's, although his was yellowish white and stained with the coffee he was drinking when we arrived.

"Sit, my friends," he said, indicating a pair of wooden chairs pushed against the pale pink adobe wall of the house. We hauled the chairs over to him and sat down. We'd been greeted at the door by an overweight young woman in a faded cotton dress and a food-spotted apron who had led us through the large house, past rooms full of ornate wooden furniture, and out to the garden. She had vanished as soon as we sat down, but soon returned, bearing a blue glass pitcher. She poured us each a tall glass of cold lemonade. She blushed at our thanks, and scuffed her way back into the house. Her feet were stuffed into ancient men's bedroom slippers with broken backs that revealed the cracked skin of her heels. We sipped greedily at our drinks. It was cool in San Miguel, but the air was very dry and dusty.

The older Cordoba did not have the same facility with English as his son, so I conducted our conversation in Spanish. "We are interested, sir, in anything you remember about the death of the American woman, Trudy-Ann Nutt."

He nodded, but didn't reply.

I waited for a minute, and then I recognized his bland smile. It was identical to that of his son. I reached into my bag, pulled out my wallet, and removed one of the crisp one-hundred-dollar bills I'd withdrawn from the bank before we left Los Angeles. I handed it to the old man, who studied the bill, turning it over and holding it up to the light.

Finally, he nodded approvingly and said, "I'll tell you what I told the other North Americans—the ones from the newspapers. The woman was killed by her daughter. A terrible accident."

"What kind of an accident?"

"Shot. By her own daughter."

"You were the investigating officer?" I asked.

He grunted, and took off his hat, fanning himself with the crumpled brim.

"Can you remember what you saw when you got there?"

"El Señor was sitting out in the courtyard on the stone bench. He had the little girl in his lap. He told us what happened."

"In front of her?"

"Of course. She was in his lap." He seemed impatient with my interruption. "The girl had her arms wrapped around El Señor's neck. We could not pry her away. So we tried to talk to her there. I asked her questions, but nothing. No answer. She refused to speak. She never spoke, not once during the entire investigation. Not long after the shooting, they sent the girl home to North America. So we couldn't ask her any more questions."

"Did the Señor send her without your permission?" I asked.

He shrugged. "Permission? He didn't need permission.

The girl wasn't under arrest. One day she was gone, and that was the end of that."

I asked him questions about the scene, the location of the body, other witnesses. But he could remember nothing more, or at least would admit to no further memories.

Finally, I said, "Señor Cordoba, do you think it would have been possible for someone else to have committed the crime, and then blamed it on the little girl?"

"No," he said firmly, waving away the very idea with his hand.

All in all, the man told me no more than I already knew. One thing seemed very clear. The investigation had been shoddy, at best. The police had spent a day or two cursorily interviewing the residents of the house and then closed the case, deeming it an accident.

As we prepared to leave, I asked the elder Cordoba one final thing: the names of the Mexican employees at the house. He looked positively bewildered at the query, and wrinkled his brow and stuck his lower lip out. Finally, after much thought, he said, "I think it was Felipe Acosta's girl, Juana, who worked for them then. If there were others, I can't remember."

"Do you know where I can find Juana Acosta?" I asked.

He shrugged and shook his head. Then he rose creakily from his chair and walked across the courtyard. He disappeared into a door at the far end. Our hundred dollars' worth of conversation was up.

"Juana has a store in the market," a soft voice said in Spanish.

I turned to find the young woman who'd let us into the house.

"You know her?" I asked.

"She sells dresses in the central market. Confirmation dresses. *Quinceñeros* gowns. That kind of thing. She's in the market. Most days. You'll see the booth. It's the biggest one."

I smiled at her. Then I thought of something. "Did you tell this to the other North Americans who came here? The reporters?"

She shook her head. "They didn't ask about her."

I reached into my purse and pulled out another hundred-dollar bill. I pressed it into the woman's hand, and she stared at it, her face flushed pink. "Mother of God," she murmured, and then grabbed my hand and brought it to her lips. Mr. Cordoba obviously didn't pay her very well.

"So, what happened in there?" Peter said, once we were standing back out on the street. His Spanish is limited; unless you're talking guacamole and tortillas, he's clueless. So I summarized my conversation with Cordoba.

"Not very helpful," Peter said.

"Nope. But I did get the name of the maid who was there at the time."

We decided to head right over to the market. We only had another day in San Miguel and couldn't afford to waste time.

In the taxi, I turned to Peter. "Did that strike you as a rather fancy house for a police officer?" We'd walked through at least five rooms in the pink Colonial house, and there were many more than that. Each room had been bursting with furniture, none of which looked particularly inexpensive.

"I was looking through the open door facing out to the garden while you were talking, and I think I saw a big-screen TV in one room. But maybe he's got a wealthy family or something," Peter said.

"This is an intensely class-conscious society. I don't think someone whose family had enough money for a home like that would be a cop."

"Maybe he was well paid."

I shook my head. "I doubt it. I bet mine wasn't the first hundred-dollar bill he pocketed during the course of his career. Who knows, maybe he got a pile of them from Polaris Jones."

Just then we arrived at the central market. I paid the driver and we picked our way past the outspread blankets of vendors whose wares consisted of various tourist kitsch—little dolls wearing traditional indigenous clothing, ashtrays and pots painted in vivid colors, beaded earrings and necklaces. I stopped at one blanket and crouched down to look at the rows of little green wooden turtles with bobbling heads. I couldn't resist. I bought Ruby and Isaac each a handful of the tiny creatures.

We wandered deep into the market, past stall after stall of knock-off jeans and T-shirts, pens and flashlights, bright woven shopping bags with pictures of burros and the Virgin of Guadalupe. Tucked in between these stalls we found one that was unlike its neighbors. It was about twice the size of the others, and its wares weren't hung over bars or heaped on tables like the rest. Racks of pastel dresses dripping in tulle, beading, and sequins were carefully arrayed in cabinets behind glass doors. The counters were glass boxes, revealing rows of white gloves, hair ribbons, and fluffy hats decorated with fabric flowers and beads. I fingered the white gown that hung on a headless mannequin in a corner of the store. The nylon was shiny and stiff. I'd be willing to bet there wasn't a natural fiber in the place.

"Can I help you?" a voice said in thickly accented English.

A small woman stepped from behind the counter. In stark contrast to the dresses hanging around her, she wore a simple black skirt and a white blouse with just a touch of lace on her collar. A measuring tape hung around her neck, and a pencil poked out of the roll of black hair bobbing precariously at the top of her head. Her eyes were crinkled at the corners, as if she'd done a lot of smiling in her fifty-odd years. She was smiling at us now.

"You speak English?" I asked.

"Yes, of course," she said. "Do you buy for yourself, or perhaps for your daughter?"

I looked again at the rows of fluffy marshmallow dresses Ruby would have killed to own. "How much are the confirmation gowns?" I asked.

"For what size?"

"A six-year-old girl."

The woman pulled on the silver chain around her neck and a key ring appeared from deep in her cleavage. She unlocked one of the glass cases and pulled out four little piles of tulle and lace. One, in a white so creamy it looked almost peach-colored, had a bodice of pearls and little puffs for sleeves. It screamed Ruby Wyeth at the top of its lungs.

"This one," I said.

She checked a little white tag hanging from the sleeve and named a price in pesos that I was astonished to realize translated to less than forty dollars.

"We'll take it!" I said, and reached into my bag for the money. She carefully wrapped the dress in a black trash bag, flipping up the wire circles of the crinoline so that they lay flat. Then she took a pair of gloves and a tiara from behind the counter.

"These belongs to the dress," she said.

"Wow," Peter said. "Ruby is going to flip out."

"You have only one daughter?" the woman asked.

"And a son," I said.

"How old?"

"Almost four."

"One moment," she said. She ducked out of her stall, walked down the aisle, and turned into another stall at the end. In a moment, she was back, carrying another black garbage bag. She pulled out a miniature *mariachi* outfit, white with black piping. The sombrero was decorated with rows of pearls, similar to those on the dress.

"How much?" I asked.

"Same price."

"We'll take it."

I handed her the money, and as she was wrapping up Isaac's outfit, I said, "Is your name Juana Acosta?"

"De Suarez," she said.

"Excuse me?"

"Juana Acosta de Suarez. My husband was Angel Suarez. He is dead. Last year."

"I'm so sorry for your loss," I said.

She shrugged. "He is a good man, my Angel. But I give him no children, so now I am alone."

"I'm so sorry."

"This is life," she said. "Why you know my name?"

I took a deep breath. "I'm a friend of Lilly Green's. Do you remember her? From thirty years ago?"

Juana had been straightening the rows of gloves in her display case, but her hands froze. She stared at me and her face softened. "Lilly? Lilita? You know her?"

"Yes," I said.

"That is her, yes? The movie star? The one she has blond hair?"

"Yes, that's her."

"I *know* that that is Lilita. Not only because of the name. She looks the same. Just like when she was a little girl. *Mi pequenita Lilly. Ay yai yai.* Lilita. How is she? She remembers me?"

"She's good," I said. "She's all right."

"She sends you here to find me?"

"Not exactly. I got your name from Eduardo Cordoba."

Her eyes narrowed. "From the police?"

"The father, not the son," I said.

"Why he give you my name?"

"I asked him who was working in the house back then. Juana, I hope you can help me. Lilly might be in trouble. I'm trying to find out what happened to her mother. I think it could help her."

"Pobrecita. Pobre Señora Trudy," Juana whispered.

As soon as I'd mentioned Lilly's name, Peter had begun easing his way out of the booth. He knew that Juana was more likely to talk without him there. He caught my eye and raised his eyebrows, motioning over his shoulder. I nodded and he melted away, leaving us alone.

"Were you there when she was killed?" I asked.

Juana's chest rose as she heaved a sigh. She leaned on her elbows against the counter. "I am there, yes."

"Do you know what happened?"

"They say Lilita play with the gun and shoot her mother."

"And is that what happened?"

She frowned. "You try to help Lilita, yes?"

I nodded. "I'm her friend. Please tell me what happened. It's important. For Lilly's sake."

"It is long time ago. Many many years. Thirty years!"

"Juana," I said softly. "Lilly has spent her entire life believing that she killed her mother. Can you imagine what an awful thing that is to have to live with? Don't you believe she has a right to know if she didn't do it?"

Juana rubbed her forehead with one hand. She bobbed her head in a tiny nod. "Yes."

"What do you think happened in that room?"

"I don't know. All I know is this. Lilita could not kill Señora Trudy. She could not. I not believe it. I never believe it."

"Why not?"

"She is by the fountain, plays with the little boy. With Jupé." She pronounced it *Hoo-pay.* "I am washing clothes on the roof, and I hear their voices over the sound of the water. I hear them, right before I hear the gun. I hear Jupé say, 'Where you going?' and then I hear the gun."

Lilly herself had remembered playing with Jupiter in the fountain. "Are you sure? Are you sure she was still in the courtyard when you heard the shot?"

"Yes. I think so. Jupé say, 'Where you going?' and then maybe a few seconds more and I hear the gun. Only one minute. No time for her to go to the room, find the gun, kill her mama."

I leaned forward, excited. "Tell me everything that you remember from that day. Everything, no matter how small."

Juana's memory was as clear as could be expected, given the many years that had passed. She remembered little about the morning of the day that Trudy-Ann was killed. She did remember, though, fixing the children lunch and serving it to them out in the courtyard. She'd left them with their food and gone to do the washing.

"On the roof?" I asked.

"Yes. I do laundry on the roof. I have there a sink and strings for the clothes. I hear the children, and when I go to the side, I look into the courtyard and see them."

Juana had been scrubbing sheets and listening to the radio. She was sure she heard the children's voices beneath the sound of the music. She'd heard the sharp retort of the pistol and had dropped the sheet she was washing and run down the stairs. The courtyard was empty. She raced into the house, to Trudy-Ann's room.

"What did you see?"

Juana trembled and hugged her arms close to her chest. "Jupé in the hallway, crying. I run past him and through the door."

"Wait a second. Jupiter was there? Did he see what had happened?" Jupiter had claimed not to know how Trudy-Ann had died. Now, maybe that was true. Maybe he'd been too little to remember. But I doubted it. A memory like that seemed too traumatic to forget . . . unless it had been repressed. And you know what? I just wasn't buying that anymore.

"I think Jupé no see nothing. He crying from the noise. There's no time for him to see nothing."

Maybe. "What did you see when you got into the room?" I asked.

"Lilita. She screams, 'Mama, Mama.' Her hands, they are red. Red with blood."

"Who else was there?"

"Señor Artie, he there."

"He was in the room when you got there?"

She wrinkled her brow. "Yes," she said.

"What was he doing?"

"He holds her close to him. She is fighting him. Trying to get to her mama. She kick him, hit him. But he no let her go."

"Did you see the body?"

Juana was crying now, fat tears that left trails in the thick paste of her makeup. She rubbed a ribbon of mucus away from her nose with the back of her hand. "Half of Señora Trudy on the bed, half on the floor. Her white dress—red all over here." Juana motioned at her own chest. "So red. Her, what do you say, sleep dress? What she wears at night? It so wet with blood, I can see shape of her body, her breasts." She swallowed hard, and for a moment I was afraid she would be sick. But she just inhaled sharply and said, "I take the girl. Drag her from the room. I remember I am so angry. Her father he do nothing. Nothing."

"What do you mean? You said Artie was holding her."

"Not Señor Artie. I told you, he hold her back. Her father, Raymond. And his woman. They just stand, stare at us. They do nothing."

I felt like I'd been kicked in the stomach. "Raymond and Beverly were there?"

"Of course. They standing in the room when I get there."

"Raymond and Beverly were in *Mexico*, in the room when Trudy-Ann died?"

"Yes, of course," she said impatiently. "They come right before this. They say they all live together. All. But then after, they take Lilita and go back to *Estados Unidos*."

I tried to assimilate this information. Raymond and Beverly had said they were in Los Angeles at the time of Trudy-Ann's death. Hadn't they? I tried to remember. Had they ever specifically said they weren't in Mexico when Trudy-Ann was killed? I wasn't sure, but I did know that they had led me to believe they weren't in San Miguel. And what's worse, they had let Lilly believe the same. But why?

"Who killed Trudy-Ann, Juana? If Lilly didn't do it, who did? Could it have been Artie? Or Raymond? Or Beverly?"

She shook her head. "I do not know. I do not know who kill her. But I know it not my Lilita. She in the courtyard. With Jupé. I hear her when I do the washing."

"Would Raymond or Beverly have had a reason to hurt Trudy-Ann?"

"Señor Raymond, he would never hurt her. I think he loved her. I see how he look at her. Señora Trudy, she was very beautiful. I think he love her."

"Why? Why do you think that? They'd been together once, and then broken up, after Lilly was born. And she was with Artie, wasn't she? Was something going on between them?"

Juana's eyes narrowed. "I don't know nothing, but I think maybe yes. I see Señora Trudy when Señor Raymond comes.

She looks for him. She wears her white sleep dress when he is there. You can see her body under the dress, and I see that he is looking."

"Do you think they might have been having an affair?"

"In that house, they all do that. They sleep one night with this person, one night another. Señor Artie say to me that this is the right way. Everyone supposed to love each other. But I think he's no happy. I think he no want Señora Trudy be with Señor Raymond."

"But Trudy and Raymond were together?"

"Yes, I think so. I change the sheets, you know? And I think they are together. Señor Raymond, it his fault she die, anyway." She nodded her head emphatically.

"Why? Why was it his fault? If he didn't kill her?"

"He give her the gun. He bring it from her papa in Tejas."

"Wait. Raymond gave Trudy-Ann the gun? Why?"

She shrugged. "Señora Trudy, she tell me her papa give it to him for her. But Señor Raymond, he bring the gun into the house. So it is his fault the beautiful Señora is dead."

I nodded, not sure I bought the logic, but considering how I feel about guns, not willing to dismiss it altogether. "What about Beverly? Did Beverly mind that Raymond was sleeping with his ex-wife?"

"Señora Beverly, she says everything happy, good. But I hear her sometimes, with Señor Raymond. She scream at him. She no happy."

"Did she kill Trudy-Ann?"

She shrugged, lifting her shoulders almost to her ears. "I do not know. I know only one thing. Lilita, she in the courtyard."

"Did you tell anyone about this at the time?"

"Sí. I tell the policeman. I tell Eduardo Cordoba, 'Lilita not kill her mama.' He tell me I make a mistake. Lilita is, how you say, *culpable*."

"Guilty."

"Yes, guilty."

"And he never even investigated? Never tried to find out if you were right?"

She tossed her head. "Eduardo Cordoba is Eduardo Cordoba."

"What do you mean?"

She leaned her head close to mine. "I mean, he has very much money, Señor Cordoba. For a policeman."

"Yes," I whispered back.

"He does what he is paid to do."

"Do you think he was paid to say that Lilly killed her mother?"

She shrugged. "I know nothing. I know only that Lilita in the courtyard, she play with the water in the fountain. I know only this."

Suddenly, she pounded her fist on the counter. I jumped. "Who I am to say this?" she said bitterly. "Who I am to say Eduardo Cordoba he is a bad man?"

I frowned, not understanding what she was saying.

"Where I get the money for this *tienda*? Thirty years ago, Señor Artie gives me money when he goes away. He says for all my help. He gives me two thousand dollars. This very much money here in Mexico. I open this *tienda*, and I have very nice life. From his money, I have very good life."

The same could be said, I thought, for a number of other people.

Twenty-eight

PETER was disappointed when I insisted that we catch an earlier flight home, but he understood my sense of urgency. Beverly and Raymond's presence in Mexico at the time of Trudy-Ann's murder changed everything. I wasn't sure what it meant exactly, but I needed to get home and find out.

I called my mother from Dallas, when we changed planes, and she agreed to meet us at the airport in L.A. She sounded thrilled at the prospect of our premature return.

What does it say about me that I didn't start missing my kids until we were on the last leg of our return flight? I had barely thought about them for the two days we were in Mexico. I'd been too distracted by the case to worry about the children—even Isaac, who had never before been without his mother for longer than an afternoon. It was probably feelings of guilt over my maternal negligence, but by the time the plane taxied into the gate at LAX, I was bouncing up and down in my seat.

I ignored the flight attendants' warnings and unbuckled my seat belt long before we had come to a complete stop at the gate. By the time the hatch was opened, I had our flight bags slung over my shoulders and had poked and prodded Peter into the aisle. Unfortunately, an unacceptably slow woman in the row in front of us was impeding our progress out of the plane. I groaned in frustration and whispered in Peter's ear, "Just pass her, for heaven's sake. She'll move over."

"Juliet, the woman is on crutches. Will you chill out?"

I rolled my eyes and fidgeted from one foot to the other. When we finally made it through the hatch, I grabbed Peter's hand and dragged him past the woman with the crutches—it was taking her forever to lower herself into her wheelchair. We raced down the gangway and out into the terminal. We were, of course, at the very farthest gate, so it took us what felt like hours to make it to the exit, and by the end I was flat out running. Standing in the very middle of the exit ramp, right in everyone's way, pushing and shoving each other into the people who passed by, were my kids. I shouted their names at the top of my lungs. They looked up from their squabbling, saw me running toward them, and burst through the crowd, tearing past the signs warning them not to dare enter on pain of prosecution. Alarms began blaring and National Guardsman with guns came running toward us. Ruby and Isaac flung themselves into my arms, and I buried my face in their soft, damp necks, inhaling deeply. They smelled like they always did. Like warm, wet puppies. Like my babies.

"I missed you so much!" I said. And it was true. For the last few hours, I *had* missed them terribly. So much that it was almost unbearable.

Isaac put both hands on either side of my face, kissed me gently on the lips, and then, in a voice dripping with love and longing, said, "Mama?"

I smiled at my sweet little boy. "Yes, my darling?"

"What did you bring me?"

Twenty-nine

As desperate as I was to get to Lilly, to tell her what I'd found out in Mexico and to confront her parents, I couldn't leave my children that day. They spent the rest of the afternoon and evening pressed up against me, as if they couldn't bear not to be touching me. They immediately put on their Mexican finery and looked like a couple of grandees from the days when Alta California was just another Mexican territory. It took us hours to get them to bed, and we succeeded only by promising that neither of them would have to go to school the next day. It was an easy promise. The next day was Sunday.

Despite the hour, I called Al and filled him in on my trip. "She didn't do it," I said to him, gripping the phone under my chin as I pulled clothes out of my bag, checked for obvious stains, and hung them in the closet.

"But she *remembers* doing it," he said.

"Have you not been listening to me? False memories! The memories were all implanted!"

"Okay. Okay, I'll buy that. So who did? The reverend? The father?"

"Or the stepmother."

"Maybe," he said, his voice betraying his doubt.

"Why not her?" I said, sniffing the armpits of a shirt I couldn't remember if I'd worn. I winced and threw it in the hamper.

"Shooting. It's a man's crime."

I didn't even argue with him. The man's sexism was irritatingly ingrained, but neither did I feel like defending a woman's right to shoot. "Do you want to come with me to talk to Lilly?" I asked.

"Better not," he said. "But don't you go confronting Polaris without me. Or the parents. I don't want you taking any risks, in your condition."

I sighed, but didn't bother arguing with him. I hung up the phone and shoved my now empty suitcase into the closet.

"How's Al doing?" my mother asked. She was stretched out on my bed, propped up on one bony elbow, watching me unpack. My mother is one of those tiny, rail-thin women who get more and more minuscule as they age. By the time she hits her nineties, she'll probably be visible only with an electron microscope. This trait causes me no small amount of resentment. I've been putting on and taking off the same ten or fifteen pounds my entire life, and my mother has to carry Hershey bars in her purse to help keep her weight up. I've always believed that she burned calories through sheer busyness. The word "multitasking" was invented to describe my mother. When I was a kid, she used to cook dinner, vacuum the house, take dictation on the phone from her boss, and give me the third degree about where I'd been the night before, all at the same time. This might, in fact, have been the first time I'd ever seen her immobile in my entire life. The kids had definitely been harder on her than she'd been willing to admit.

"He's okay. He'd be happier if we had more paying work," I said.

"Do you want me to change my flight and go home early?"

"What? Of course not. Stay. I love having you here." I wasn't lying. For all that my mother and I can barely make it through a single conversation without it devolving into a bickering match, I always miss her terribly. I'd never imagined that I'd spend my life three thousand miles from my parents. And I know she hates being so far from her grandchildren.

"I organized your desk while you were gone."

"You what?"

"It was a mess."

"Mom! Those are my private files! You can't just go digging around in my stuff."

"Don't be ridiculous. I took care of your computer, too."

"What?" I shrieked.

"Your desktop was a disaster. I cleaned it up. And then I archived all your E-mails into subfolders."

I stared at her dumbly. "You read my E-mails?"

"Only enough to figure out what subfolder to put them in."

"I can't believe you. Did you go poking around Peter's office, too?"

"Of course not. Although, I did look over that contract he left out on the dining room table. You might want to take a glance at it yourself. I think he's getting a raw deal on the merchandising agreement."

My mouth dropped open.

"What?" she said. "I've been a legal secretary for forty years. You think I don't know my way around a contract?"

"You are so damn nosy, Mom."

She peered at me over the top of her glasses. "Where do you think you get it, darling?"

Thirty

THE next morning, when I told the kids that I had to go out, Isaac's lip began to tremble. With a howl of anguish, he leapt across the breakfast table, wrapped himself around my waist, and clung like a baby lemur.

"It'll just be for a little while, honey. I'll be back by lunchtime," I said, crossing my fingers and hoping that I wasn't lying.

Muffled sobs and trembling shoulders were his only reply.

"You've still got me, little man," Peter said. "How about I take you and Ruby to the Santa Monica Pier!"

Nothing.

I looked at Peter. He shrugged.

"Oh for heaven's sake," my mother said. "The way you indulge these children." She walked over to me and pried Isaac loose. "Enough of this silliness, Isaac. Your mother has to work."

"Mama's always working!" he wailed and clung to me all the more furiously. "She went away to work, and she doesn't even want to be with me now!"

I knew he was being manipulative. I knew that compared to mothers with real jobs, I spent *vast* quantities of time with my children. I knew that he didn't really believe that I loved my job more than I loved him. And I also knew that I was going to cave.

"All right, Isaac. You can come with me. You can play with Amber and Jade while I talk to their mother."

Ruby looked up from the cereal she was pushing around her bowl. "You're going to Amber and Jade's house? I want to come!"

"Hey, just a minute here," Peter said. "Doesn't anyone want to play with me?"

My mother, disgusted with our pathetic weakness in the face of our children's demands, stomped off, muttering something about children who rule the roost and parents who come to regret it. By dint of a series of bribes that began with the Santa Monica Pier and ended with a trip to the mall complete with promises of clothing purchases, Peter managed to convince Ruby to stay with him.

When we'd negotiated the gate and pulled up the long driveway to Lilly's house, Isaac and I found Amber and Jade riding scooters under the supervision of not one but two nannies. I left Isaac in their care, admonishing him to put on a helmet before he got within spitting distance of anything with wheels. Both my children have inherited my natural athletic grace, and by Isaac's third birthday we had already dealt with a fractured arm, two broken toes, and a split chin. I wasn't up to another trip to the emergency room.

I let myself in the front door of the house and called out Lilly's name.

"She's in the back, by the pool," a voice called back. I thanked the mystery servant and walked through the house and out the back door. Lilly was lying, wrapped in a Pashmina shawl, on a lounge chair by the pool. Steam rose from the heated water and shrouded her in wisps of fog. I steeled myself for the conversation to come, and made my way along the path of tiny, pale blue stones to the water's edge.

"Juliet!" she said when she saw me. "You're back? Did you

find out anything? What happened? Tell me!"

I sat down on the edge of the chaise next to hers and took her hand. "I found out a lot, Lilly. I found Juana, the woman who took care of you when you were a little girl."

"Juana," Lilly said softly, and her eyes clouded over. "I remember her, I think. She used to braid my hair with scraps of ribbon. And she had really rough hands, red and chapped."

"She told me about the day your mother died."

Lilly looked into my eyes with an expression at once eager and fearful. "What happened? Did she say what happened?"

"She didn't see the shooting,"

"Oh," Lilly said, her voice stretched thin with disappointment.

"But she heard everything. She was on the roof, doing wash, and she could hear you and Jupiter playing in the fountain. She could hear you when she heard the sound of the shot. You were still in the courtyard, playing with the water."

Lilly stared at me. "I was playing in the fountain." It wasn't a question.

"Juana ran down to your mother's room, but you got there before she did. She found you there, with Polaris. You'd run to your mother and tried to wake her up. That's how you got her blood on you. You shook her or grabbed her or something like that. Juana found Polaris trying to pull you away from your mother."

"Polaris? Did he do it? Did he kill my mother?" Lilly's breath came in ragged gulps.

I kept talking. "That's not all I found out, Lilly. I'm so sorry to have to tell you this. Raymond and Beverly were there. They were in the room when Juana got there."

Her face crumpled with incomprehension. "What? What? They were in San Miguel? In my mother's room?"

"Yes," a voice said over my shoulder. I spun around and looked up into Beverly's face. She stood, water streaming down her body, steam rising from her skin. Her voice was firm, but her legs were trembling. She took a towel from a pile at the end of the chaise lounge on which I was sitting and wrapped it around her body. She covered her head with another and draped a third over her shoulders. Only then did she continue. "Yes, it's true that we were there. We were in San Miguel when Trudy-Ann was killed." Beverly sat down on the end of Lilly's seat and put her hand on her leg. Lilly flinched and her stepmother lifted her hand back into her own lap. "Let me go get Raymond," she said. "And we'll tell you everything." She got up and walked to the house. Lilly closed her eyes and raised her hands to her face.

"I'm so sorry," I said, and then I thought of Beverly, in the house, finding Raymond, and coordinating her story with his. "I'll be right back," I said, and ran. I tore through the kitchen, making a beeline for the backstairs, and I almost tumbled over Isaac. He was sitting on the bottom step, crying while one of the nannies dabbed at his knee with hydrogen peroxide.

"Mama," he wailed. "I got hurt!"

I stared at him for a moment, desperate to follow Beverly up the stairs, to catch her before she got to Raymond. Then, with an inward groan, I sat down next to him on the step. "Let's see your boo-boo, sweetie."

"He skinned it pretty bad," the nanny said.

"You sure did." I took the cotton ball from her and finished cleaning the scrape. I carefully covered the wound with two of the Power Puff Girl Band-Aids she handed me. Then I kissed him on the cheek. "Are you going to be okay? Are you ready to go back out and play with the twins?"

He nodded. "But I get to ride the scooter. Because I'm injured."

I looked at the nanny and she nodded. "Okay. You ride the scooter. Just be careful, buddy. Okay?"

A sound in the kitchen caught my ear, and I looked up from my son just in time to see Beverly and Raymond walk out the back door. I caught up with them at the swimming pool. Beverly sat back down on the end of Lilly's chaise, and Raymond pulled the other one close to his wife and daughter. I stood on the other side of Lilly, awkwardly outside their tight little circle.

"I'm so sorry you had to find out like this, sweetie," Raymond said.

"What were you doing in Mexico?" I said, my voice sounding harsh and strident, even to my own ears.

Raymond ignored me. "Lilly, sweetie . . ."

"Answer her question, Dad," Lilly said. She jerked away from her stepmother. "Get off my chair."

Beverly rose quickly to her feet. I motioned to a table with four chairs on the other side of the pool. "Why don't we go sit there?" I asked.

"Fine," Lilly said. She heaved herself out of her chaise and strode over to the table. She yanked the closed umbrella out of its base in the middle of the table and sent it crashing to the ground behind the table. The sound of metal hitting tile reverberated through the air, as Beverly, Raymond, and I walked over and joined her.

The four of us sat down in the iron patio chairs, and I asked my question again, this time keeping my voice low and modulated. "What were you doing in Mexico?"

Raymond answered. "We'd come down a few months before. When the Topanga commune finally broke up. We didn't really have anywhere to go, and a bunch of folks had already gone down to San Miguel. Not just Trudy-Ann and Artie. A lot of different people had gone down there."

"Why didn't you ever tell Lilly that you were there when her mother was killed?"

"We never told anyone. We came back to the States right afterward."

"Why?" I asked.

"Almost everybody did," he said.

"We were scared," Beverly said calmly. "We were all very frightened. None of us knew what the Mexican police were capable of. We didn't know if they would hold us responsible for having kept the gun in the house. We were afraid we'd be arrested."

"Why did you bring her the gun, Raymond?" I asked.

He opened his mouth and stared at me.

"It was a gift from her father," Beverly said sharply.

"A gift?" I repeated.

"Raymond and Trudy-Ann were from Texas. Texans like guns," she said flatly.

Lilly interrupted. "What happened? What happened to my mother?"

Beverly leaned across the table and clasped one of Lilly's hands. This time, Lilly let her stepmother touch her. "Raymond and I were in our room, right across the hall from your mother's, when we heard the shot. We came running in and we found you there. Polaris was taking the gun out of your hands and trying to drag you away from her."

"That's not what the other witnesses say," I said firmly.

"What? What witnesses?" Raymond said.

"Juana," Lilly whispered. "Juana said I was in the courtyard, with Jupiter."

"You were, honey," Beverly answered, stroking Lilly's fingers. "And then you must have come inside. You were holding the gun when we got there."

I bit my lip. I knew she was lying, but all I had was Juana's word. Not enough.

"But you didn't see me do it," Lilly said. "Maybe it was Polaris. Maybe he did it. He was there when you got there, right? You said he was."

Beverly shook her head, gently. "I'm so sorry. I wish that were true. I wish it had been anyone but you. Polaris was taking the gun away from you when we got there. And you were . . . you were . . ."

"You were covered in her blood," Raymond said, the gentleness of his tone in stark contrast to the harshness of his words. "It was an accident, Lilly. You didn't mean to do it, but you shot your mother. Just like you remembered you did."

Lilly began to cry.

"Even if all that's true, that doesn't explain why you lied about being there," I said.

"I told you," Beverly said, to Lilly, not to me. "We were afraid. We came home to Los Angeles and got things ready for you. Polaris sent you home a little while later. You weren't speaking, and then, after Reese had worked with you for a while, it became clear that you didn't remember anything about what had happened. You didn't even remember that we'd been there. And somehow Reese didn't know that we'd been in Mexico. He'd left the Topanga commune before we had, and I guess he just assumed we'd been in Los Angeles the whole time. We let you both think that. We let everyone think that. And after a while the only people who knew otherwise were Artie and Seth. And we knew they wouldn't give us away. We were afraid. I'm so sorry, darling. But we were just so afraid."

I didn't believe a word of it. I didn't believe that Lilly had killed her mother, and I didn't believe that their fear of being held accountable for a crime they hadn't committed had inspired Beverly and Raymond to hold their silence all these years. But it was obvious that Lilly believed them. Maybe she loved them too much to think anything else. Maybe she was too frightened. For whatever reason, and despite what seemed to me to be a mounting pile of circumstantial evidence, Lilly had clearly decided that they were innocent. I stared at her as she clutched her stepmother's hand in one of hers, and her father's in the other.

"Did Chloe know about you?" Lilly asked.

"What?" Raymond said, leaning back a bit.

Lilly squeezed him closer. "Did she say anything when you gave her the money? Did she know that you were in Mexico when it happened?"

I could feel the blood rush out of my face. "What are you talking about?" I said.

Lilly turned to me. "Dad took the money to Chloe for me. I didn't want to meet her. And I certainly didn't want to send someone who works for me. Dad offered to do it."

"Why didn't you tell me that Raymond had made the money drop?" I said angrily.

Lilly shook her head. "I was afraid that if the whole story came out, the police would want to question Dad or something. I was worried about Mom's reelection. The Republican Party is really gunning for her. God knows what they're going to do with all this." She looked at me beseechingly. "Even if you have to tell Jupiter's lawyers, you won't tell them about Beverly and Raymond, will you? We just can't let people know they were involved. It's bad enough everybody knowing about me. If they think Beverly was there, if they suspect her of trying to cover it up, it'll destroy the election for her. It will."

I wasn't willing to promise anything of the kind. Whatever Lilly believed, I knew she hadn't killed her mother, and I also knew there was a chance that one of her parents had. I just shook my head.

Her face crumpled.

I turned to Raymond. "*Did* Chloe know that you were in Mexico when Trudy-Ann was killed?"

"Yes," Beverly interrupted. "She was blackmailing us, too."

"What?" Lilly and I said at the same time. I sounded shocked, and I was; Lilly sounded like she'd just found out that the people she loved most in the world had betrayed her, and they had.

"After your father gave her the money, he got a telephone call from her. She said she'd found out that we . . . that we . . ." Beverly stumbled over her words, uncharacteristically. She swallowed once, and seemed to steel herself. "That we were there when Trudy-Ann died. She said she'd expose us if we didn't pay her."

"And did you? Did you pay her?" I said.

Beverly's face was pale, almost gray. A lock of wet hair had escaped the towel and hung lankly over her eye. "Yes. Once. Like Lilly did."

"How much?"

"She asked for a hundred thousand dollars, but of course I couldn't raise that right away," Beverly said, grimacing. "Raymond went back to her. He gave her about five thousand and told her it would take some time to get the rest." Beverly twisted her mouth into a grimace. "She said five thousand was nothing. Walking around money. She told us we'd better come up with more, and fast. We were going to put the house on the market. That was the only way we could think of to come up with the cash."

"Oh, Mom!" Lilly said, hugging Beverly.

Her stepmother returned her embrace, patting her on the back. "It's okay, Lilly. It's all right," Beverly said firmly. Something about the way she said those words made me certain she'd repeated them many times during the course of their relationship.

I sat quietly, mulling over Beverly's story in my mind. Something about the timing bothered me. Chloe hadn't begun blackmailing Beverly and Raymond until after she'd received that first pile of money from Lilly. Why had she waited? What happened after her first successful attempt at extortion that led her to add new victims? Was it just the blush of success? Or had she only found out about them after she'd already begun blackmailing Lilly?

I looked across the table at Raymond, who was resting his head in his hands. And then it hit me. *Raymond* had happened. First Chloe threatened to expose Lilly's role in her mother's death. Then Lilly sent Raymond to deliver the money. And suddenly Chloe added another victim to her blackmail roster. Could it be a coincidence? Or might Raymond have had something to do with his wife's blackmail? Then I remembered what Chloe had told her mother. She'd been excited about knowing something about someone that that person didn't even know. I'd assumed she was talking about Lilly's fragmented memory of the killing. But what if what Chloe knew, what she'd found out halfway into her blackmailing scheme, was not that Lilly had killed her mother, but that she *hadn't*. I stared at Raymond, wishing I could tell the truth just by looking at him. Then I looked over at Beverly. Her expression was one of perfect concern for her daughter. She held Lilly's hand pressed up to her chest, close to her heart. Was *she* telling the truth, I wondered? What did Chloe know about Beverly? Was it simply, as the consummate politician had said, that Chloe threatened to tell the media that she'd been there in Mexico? Or was there something even worse? I looked from Raymond to Beverly, and back again. Had one of them committed murder?

Thirty-one

THERE was no room for me and my suspicions in that tight family circle. I took my leave, gathering up Isaac on my way out. In the car, I called Al and left a message on his voice mail. I told him what I suspected, and asked him to call me back as soon as he could. Then I went to see Wasserman. I hadn't been able to convince Lilly that her parents were implicated. Maybe I could convince Jupiter's lawyers that they had a defense available to them that didn't involve incriminating Lilly. Valerie greeted me in the reception area of the offices wearing the most beautiful maternity outfit I had ever seen. The pants were boot-cut and black, and showed off quite obviously the fact that her legs were still as long and slim as before she'd entered the realm of the hormonally challenged. She wore a matching black jacket cut with a little flare around her hips, and her vibrant, sapphire blue top looked like it had been spun from spiders' webs. It clung to her high, round breasts and the barely noticeable bulge of her belly. I gazed longingly at her black Prada boots, and then stared down at my own maternity outfit. I had on a pair of overalls and a white T-shirt. The overalls could no longer button on the sides, and the T-shirt rode up above my swollen belly. That morning, when I'd realized that you could see large swathes of unclothed skin through the gaping sides of my overalls, I'd pulled on a flannel shirt of Peter's and wore it open, like a jacket. I really had to go shopping.

Valerie gave me a pitying smile, which was at least better than the disdain with which she'd treated me when we first met. She waited while I set Isaac up with a pile of pens and paper, and then took me back to her office. She listened, mouth agape, to my update of the case.

"Holy shit," she said when I was finally done.

I smiled. I had actually broken through her composure. "Yup."

"We've got to talk to Wasserman."

The boss, it turned out, was skiing in Aspen. But he had his cell phone on him. As we talked, I imagined him schussing down the side of a mountain as he barked questions into his telephone headset.

"All this crap might have nothing to do with Chloe's murder," he said when we had finally tracked him down.

"I don't believe in coincidences," I informed him, giving him Al's pet theory. Al always says that if two things look related, then they are. There are no coincidences in criminal investigations. I'd come to believe that myself. "I mean, think about it. Chloe was murdered, and by the way she was blackmailing two or three different people? It's got to be connected."

"On your right!" he shouted suddenly.

"Excuse me?" I said.

"Nothing. Look, none of this proves your friend didn't commit the murder. Or that our client didn't, for that matter."

I shook my head in frustration. "Maybe not, but it sure complicates the prosecution's case, don't you think?"

"On your left!"

"What?"

"Nothing," he said. "Tell you what. You're back on the

payroll. Get me enough to ask for a continuance."

"You don't think you can get one based on what I've already uncovered?" I knew the answer to that. All I'd really managed to find out was that Chloe was a bad apple and that the case might or might not relate to a death in Mexico thirty years before. And that *that* death might or might not have been an accident. I had plenty of suspects but not enough hard evidence to convince the prosecutor to dump its bird in the hand to chase one of those winging around the bush.

Wasserman grunted. "Okay, that's better. Chair lift. Here's what I'm thinking. Maybe the Reverend's good for it."

"Exactly, Raoul. That's exactly what I was thinking," Valerie interrupted, leaning toward the speakerphone. She looked up at me in time to see my expression, and flushed just a tiny bit.

"It might be Polaris," I said. "But Beverly and Raymond have already lied about so much; why should we believe them when they say they didn't kill Trudy-Ann?"

"I'm putting my money on the Reverend," Wasserman said. "Go do some digging at the CCU. See what you uncover. I'll be home in two days. Get me enough for a continuance by then. And watch your hours; your money's coming out of my pocket now. Hey, Mike! How's it look on the black?" The phone went dead.

"Yes, sir," I muttered at the mute box of the speakerphone.

Thirty-two

THE Very Reverend was having his photograph taken against the backdrop of a wall of windows that overlooked the carefully tended lawns and low, shingled buildings of the CCU campus. Stars and planets embroidered in shiny gold thread decorated his dazzling white robes. He held his arms aloft, and his sleeves tumbled about his shoulders, revealing white forearms covered with wiry black hairs. He glanced once in our direction then glared at Hyades, who calmly ushered the photographer and her two assistants out of the room. He closed the door behind them and stood with his back to the door, watching me confront his boss.

Al and I had had surprisingly little difficulty convincing the Very Reverend's aide to arrange an audience for us. I'd called him on my way home from Wasserman's, and he'd instructed me to be at the campus the next day. When I'd finally reached Al and brought him up to date on the twists and turns of the case, and on our renewed status as paid investigators, he had insisted on joining me for the interview.

"What do you want?" Polaris barked, his thick Brooklyn accent sounding harsh to my ear.

"To ask a few questions about the death of Trudy-Ann Nutt," Al said in his politely intimidating cop's voice.

"I was under the impression that Lilly Green told you everything there is to know about that. What more can I possibly tell you?" In his anger, he had stripped his voice of the compelling smoothness that I'd found nearly spellbinding when I'd seen him for the first time.

I said, "You can tell us what you were doing in your wife's bedroom when the gun went off."

"What are you talking about? I wasn't in her room. I didn't get there until after she was shot."

"Where were you?"

He paused and looked at me, his eyes mistrustful slits. "In another room."

"I know that Lilly didn't kill her mother," I said.

"What are talking about? Of course she did."

"No. I have witness statements from individuals who will testify that she was playing in the courtyard and ran to her mother's room only when she heard the shot."

"Who? Who are your witnesses?"

I shrugged my shoulders.

A light seemed to dawn in his eyes. "No . . . no. They would never have talked to you." I was willing to bet every dime I had that the "they" in that sentence were Beverly and Raymond. And whatever his words, there was enough doubt in his voice to reveal that he was not at all sure of their silence.

"Who got there first, Artie?" I said. "Raymond and Beverly, or you?"

"Listen," he shouted. "I don't know what those sons of bitches told you, but I was the last person in that room. Lilly was there, and so were Beverly and Raymond." Suddenly, he spun around and yelped at Hyades. "Get them out of here. Now."

Hyades stepped away from the door and opened it.

"Right this way," he said. His face was blank, as though he found Polaris's rage unremarkable.

Al and I glanced at each other. Al shrugged, almost imperceptibly, and I nodded. We both understood that Polaris wasn't going to talk to us anymore. We'd gotten something, though—if only the unwitting acknowledgment that there was a secret being kept. We walked through the open door. Hyades followed.

"Let me escort you to your car," he said pleasantly.

None of us spoke until we were standing out in the parking lot, next to my car.

"So you know that Beverly and Raymond Green were in San Miguel," he said.

"You knew?" I said.

"Of course." Right. He'd been there, in the house, when Trudy-Ann was killed.

"Do you know who killed Trudy-Ann, Reverend Hyades?" Al asked.

"Lilly Green killed her mother," he said, a small smile playing across his lips.

I said, "You don't believe that."

"I believed that for many years."

"But you don't anymore."

He shrugged. "Do you know what I would do if I were representing Jupiter Jones?" he asked.

"What would you do?"

"I'd look at the money Polaris Jones spent on his wife." I noticed that he didn't use the honorific. Suddenly, Polaris wasn't the Very Reverend.

"What do you mean?" I asked.

"I'd look at how much money he gave her. And I'd ask the question, why so much more in the months before she died than ever before? What had she done to deserve it?"

"What *had* she done?" I wasn't enjoying this game of cat and mouse, but I had no choice but to play.

"Perhaps it's not what she did, but rather what she knew, that inspired such tangible devotion in her husband."

I've never been one to pussyfoot around. If I want to know

something, I ask it. So I did. "Did Polaris Jones kill Trudy-Ann? Did he kill Chloe?"

Once again Hyades replied with a languid shrug instead of an answer to my question. "You know what else I would do?" he said.

"What?"

"I'd review the support Polaris received from a certain well-placed politician. Why, you might wonder, has Beverly Green always been such an ardent champion of the CCU?"

"Why?"

Once again, the shrug.

"Why are you telling me this?" I asked.

He gazed across the parking lot, toward the buildings and gracious lawns. "This is a lovely place, don't you think?" he said.

"Yes."

"Suitable for a strong and important religion."

I didn't answer.

"One that exists independently of any single leader, don't you think?"

"Maybe," I said.

"Abraham never reached the Promised Land with the Children of Israel," Hyades said, looking over my head, into the sky. "New spiritual leaders were needed to guide the chosen people to their homeland."

"True," I said. "Look at Brigham Young."

"Exactly. I think each religion reaches a moment of transition. Polaris Jones is a prophet. But he is also a man. A complicated man, with a complicated past. It's time now for the CCU to enter into a new future."

"Guided by you," Al said.

"Perhaps," he smiled. "Or perhaps our cosmological arch-ancestors will make themselves known to someone else, and another prophet will emerge. Who can know?"

I raised my eyebrows. "Who indeed."

He extended a hand, shook mine, and then Al's. His grip was strong and confident. "Good luck with your investigations," he said, and with a rustle of robes, walked away across the parking lot.

Al nodded at the reverend's retreating back. "If we can find evidence of a payoff, that might do it," he said. If Hyades was telling the truth, and Polaris had paid for his wife's silence, and if we could prove it, then Wasserman would have the evidence he needed to get the prosecution to continue the case and take a closer look at Chloe's husband.

I nodded. "There's the money Chloe gave her mother to buy into the gallery. And the assemblywoman's support is all part of the public record. Remember, I found it online."

Al reached in the pocket of his red windbreaker and took out his keys. "Damn it," he said.

"What?"

"I'm supposed to finish the workers' comp stakeouts today. Can you get a start sniffing out this money trail on your own?"

"Sure." I looked at my watch and swore under my breath. "I've got to drive carpool, but I'll get on the phone to Wasserman's office as soon as I get home. See if there are any bank leads nobody's followed up on. And I'll call Chloe's mother, too."

Al sighed dramatically. "Carpool," he muttered, heading off to his car.

Thirty-three

As soon as I got in my car, I called Peter and told him what was going on.

"Wow. Pretty intense day," he said.

"No kidding. Listen, would you be willing to pick the kids up for me?"

"Um, I was about to head out for a meeting."

"What kind of meeting?"

"Um. Story conference."

"With whom?"

"Um, Sully?"

"Jeff Sullivan?" A fellow screenwriter, and a terrible influence on my husband. "A story conference, huh? Is that what they're calling spending the afternoon drinking beers and eating French fries at Swingers nowadays?"

"No, really. He says he's got a great idea for a movie we can write together."

I was about to tell my husband exactly what I thought of his alcoholic friends and their great ideas when my call-waiting beeped. "Wait a minute," I said and clicked over to the other line.

"Juliet?" It was Lilly. She was crying so hard that she was almost unintelligible.

"Lilly? Lilly? Slow down. I can't understand you. What's going on? What happened?"

There was silence on the line for a moment, and then another voice spoke. "Ms. Applebaum? This is Rochelle, Lilly's assistant. Can you come right over? Something terrible has happened."

"What? What happened?"

"Somebody killed Mr. Green."

"What? Raymond? Raymond is dead?"

"Please come, Ms. Applebaum. As fast as you can."

"I'll be there in twenty minutes."

I clicked back over to my husband and told him his afternoon plans were canceled.

I drove as fast as I could across town, pounding my steering wheel in frustration whenever the traffic ahead of me forced me to slow down. I dialed Al's number with one hand and cursed the vagaries of cell phone service that took him out of range when I knew he was no more than a few miles up the freeway from me.

The front gate to Lilly's house was ajar, and I tore through and up the driveway to the house. There were three police cars parked in front of the house. I pulled in behind them, slammed the car into park, and raced up the porch steps.

"Grandpa's dead," a small voice said, just as I was about to walk in the door. I turned toward the sound of the voice and saw two pairs of sneakered feet poking out from underneath the porch swing. I crouched down. Amber and Jade were huddled together in the shadows underneath the swing. They were each chewing on the end of a braid, and it took me a moment to realize that each twin had the other's hair in her mouth.

"Hi, Amber. Hi, Jade," I said.

"Hi," they whispered in unison.

"It's pretty scary in the house right now, isn't it?"

They nodded.

"And pretty sad, too, I'll bet."

"Yeah," one of them said.

"Would you guys like to go bike riding, or scootering? Do you think that might help you feel better?"

"No," they said, again as one.

"Can you think of something that would help you feel better right now? Maybe help you feel a little less scared?"

They looked at each other for a moment and then back to me.

"Maybe ice cream?" one said.

"Great idea. C'mon out."

They shook their heads again.

"Under here?"

"Yeah."

"Okay. I'm going to send one of the nannies out with some ice cream, okay?"

"Okay."

I hoisted myself up—it had already become something of an effort, even this early in my pregnancy—and went into the house. Everyone was in the huge front room. The first people I saw were the staff. They stood in a small huddle of identical khaki pants and denim shirts. A few of the girls were crying. I walked over and put my hand on the sleeve of Patrick, the young man who had watched the kids that day at the beach.

"Hi," I said. "Listen, Amber and Jade are hiding under the porch swing. I told them you'd bring them some ice cream."

He looked at me blankly.

I said, "I don't think they should be all alone out there. And they want ice cream."

He seemed to come to life all of a sudden. "Right, of course. Sorry." He took off in the direction of the kitchen.

"Maybe one of you can go sit with them while they're waiting for him."

One of the girls walked quickly out the front door to the porch. I turned back to the room in time to be greeted by a uniformed cop.

"Can I help you?" he said sternly.

"I'm Lilly's friend," I said. "She called me." I looked over his shoulder and saw Lilly for the first time. She was curled up on the bench in the inglenook, her face buried in her arms. Beverly sat across from her; her face faded to a sickly gray. Two police officers stood next to the women. Two other men, out of uniform but with the unmistakably officious manner of detectives, were also nearby. One of the detectives crouched on one knee, using his other as a table to support the notepad on which he was scribbling. The other, a middle-aged black man with a shaved head and a neck so thick that even his open shirt seemed to be straining to encircle it, sat at the edge of a leather chair he'd pulled up to the inglenook. A tiny gold cross dangled from one of his ears, and he leaned forward, talking in a low voice.

Ignoring the question of the police officer who had stopped me, I walked quickly over to Lilly. I squatted down next to her.

"Lilly, honey?"

She raised her ravaged face to me and grabbed my hands in both of hers. "Someone killed my father," she whispered.

"Excuse me, ma'am," a firm voice said. I turned to the seated detective.

"May I ask who you are?" he said blandly.

"She's a friend of Lilly's," Beverly said, sending me a clear message with her eyes.

"My name is Juliet Applebaum," I said.

"Detective Walter Stayner, Los Angeles Police Department. That's Detective Robbins." He didn't bother introducing the uniformed men.

"What happened?" I asked.

"That's what we're trying to determine," the detective said.

"They found Raymond's body in a rest stop on the 101," Beverly said. Her eyes were dry, but her hands were trembling violently.

"How did he die?" I asked.

"Gunshot wound," Detective Stayner said.

"Did you find the gun?"

He paused, looking at me appraisingly. "No," he said finally.

"So the killer is still armed."

"Presumably." He turned back to Beverly. "All right, ma'am, if you don't mind going over this one more time. What happened this morning?"

I considered for a moment stopping the questioning and telling Lilly to get a lawyer there immediately. I'm of the firm opinion that nobody—guilty or innocent—should ever talk to the police without the help of an attorney. There is just too much that can happen, too many things that can be said and misinterpreted. And goodness knows there was a hell of a lot more here than met the eye. I didn't want the detective stumbling on any of the story before Lilly had time to decide, with an attorney, how and when to disclose it all. On the other hand, I didn't want to make the detective think that Lilly might have anything to hide. I decided just to listen closely and put a halt to things if I felt they were treading on dangerous ground.

"We were having breakfast. He got a phone call and said he had to go meet someone," Beverly said.

"But he didn't say who it was that called him?" the detective asked.

She shook her head. "No. I mean, he said he needed to meet someone who had some information about a wetlands reclamation project he was involved in. He didn't say who."

My legs were beginning to ache, and I inched down to a sitting position. Lilly still held my hands in hers, but she'd lowered her head once more.

"What time did he leave?" the detective asked.

"I told you. I think around nine," Beverly said. "Lilly, it was about nine o'clock, right?" Lilly didn't reply. "I think it must have been around nine," Beverly said. "Because Saraswathi came at nine-thirty."

"And that's the yoga teacher?" the detective said.

"Yes," I said. He looked at me sharply, probably wondering why I knew so much about what was going on. I tried to smile reassuringly, but he wasn't buying any of it.

"She came at nine-thirty, we had a ninety-minute class, Lilly and I took showers, and then at about twelve we had lunch," Beverly said.

"You and Ms. Green?" the detective asked.

"And my staff." Beverly waved in the direction of a group of three young men and an even younger woman standing in a far corner of the living room. I hadn't noticed them before. They were all, every one of them, talking intently into their cell phones. "And Lilly's assistant."

"And after lunch?" the detective asked.

"I had work to do, so Lilly left us in the dining room."

"Did any of you leave the room at any time?"

"No. I don't think so. Someone may have gone to the bathroom. I don't really remember. But we were working until . . . until you came to tell us what happened." Beverly's voice caught in her throat.

Lilly lifted her head. "Don't you dare," she whispered.

We all stared at her.

"Don't you dare," she said again. "Don't you dare cry. Don't you dare pretend you care that he's dead."

"Be quiet, Lilly," Beverly said in a low, firm voice.

In the sudden silence, the only noise was the detective's pen scritch-scratching across his pad.

"Don't . . ." Lilly began again.

"Enough," Beverly said. Lilly's head sank back on her arms.

"And you, Ms. Green?" the detective said in the direction of Lilly's prone form. "What did you do after lunch today?"

She didn't answer, but I felt her hands grip mine more tightly.

The detective tried again. "Where did you spend the afternoon, Ms. Green?"

"She was with me," a voice said. We all turned and saw one of the uniformed assistants standing near us. "She was with me," she repeated.

"And you are?"

"Rochelle Abernathy. I work for Lilly. We were in her office. She had a stack of photos to personalize, and then we had a live online chat set up. That lasted about an hour."

"A chat?" the detective said, obviously puzzled.

"On the computer. Fans write in questions and Lilly answers them."

"And you were there together the entire time?"

"Yes."

"Are there other people who can verify that?"

"The nannies, I guess. And the rest of the staff. Oh, and a bunch of people called on the phone, too.

"Who?"

"Her agent. Her business manager—she called twice."

"Were you and Ms. Green together the entire afternoon?" the detective asked.

"Yes," Rochelle said. "Up until you got here."

Suddenly, Lilly sat up. "Juliet, I need to talk to you. Now. In my bedroom."

"I'm afraid I need to ask you a few more questions, Ms. Green," the detective said.

I stood up. "Come, Lilly, let's go to your room."

The detective put out his hand to stop me. "We're going to need to go over this one more time."

"Lilly, do you want to keep talking to this detective or would you like your lawyer to be present for any further discussion?"

She looked at me blankly for a moment and then seemed to understand what I was doing. "I want my lawyer," she said. "I'm not going to talk to you anymore without my lawyer."

Beverly stood up quickly. "Right. Right," she said.

"Are you asking for a lawyer, too?" the detective asked her.

Beverly seemed to consider this for a moment. One of her aides, a young man wearing jeans and a sweater who managed to look imposing despite his casual attire, walked quickly across the room, talking as he approached. "I think the Speaker has been very cooperative, Detective. But it's probably time now for the family to be left to their private sorrow."

The detective stood up. "I'm going to need interviews with everyone who was here today," he said.

"That's fine," the aide said. "Why don't we do that at our office downtown. Do you have any objection to that?"

The detective agreed, and then, with a troubled glance at us, pulled a card out of his pocket. "I'll just leave my number for you," he said. The aide plucked it from his hand and ushered him and the other police officers out the door.

Lilly grabbed my hand and dragged me down the hall and up the stairs. When we got to her room, she shut the door behind us and leaned against the closed door. I stood in the middle of the room, facing her.

"I remember," she whispered urgently. "I remember everything."

"What?"

"I remember what happened."

Suddenly, I realized what she was talking about. "To your mother? You remember what happened to Trudy-Ann?"

She nodded. Her eyes were glittering and her chest was rising and falling with her fast, sharp inhalations.

"It happened when I heard about Raymond. One of the maids came to get me. When I got out to the living room, Beverly was already talking to the police officers. I couldn't hear what they were saying as I walked across the room, but then I heard one of her assistants, the girl, cry out. She had her hands over her mouth. One of the men kept saying to the cop, 'Are you sure? Are you sure it's him?' I ran up. I think I was screaming, 'What happened, what happened?' The girl said, 'Somebody shot Raymond. Somebody shot Raymond.' And then I looked at my mother, at Beverly. She was standing absolutely still, and then she crumpled to the floor. She just collapsed, like her legs couldn't support her. That's when I saw it."

"What did you see?"

"Like a picture in my mind. Absolutely clear. I saw what happened to my mother—to my real mother." Lilly's breath was coming even faster than before. Her entire body was shaking so hard that it was thumping against the door. I grasped both her shoulders and led her over to the bed. She sat down and then toppled over to one side. She curled up into a tight ball. I sat down next to her and laid my hand on her still-quaking shoulder.

"What did you see, Lilly? What happened to Trudy-Ann?" I said urgently.

Her voice was soft, almost a monotone, and her eyes were squeezed tightly closed. "Jupiter and I were playing in the fountain. I remember he splashed me, and I was mad. I went inside. I was looking for my mother, to tell on him. I was in the hallway leading to her room, when I heard the shot. Like the loudest bang in the world. I was so scared of the noise. I ran the rest of the way to her room and saw her lying kind of half on, half off the bed. I reached out for her and put my hands on her chest. I thought there was a flower there. Like a red flower. Except it kept growing. And it was wet. I had my hands on her, and red just kept spreading and spreading all over her white nightgown."

"Who else was in the room, Lilly? Who was in the room when you got there?"

"They were," she whispered.

"Who?"

"Raymond was on the other side of the bed. I think . . . I think he was getting dressed. He was pulling on his pants. Beverly was in the middle of the room. I remember I had to push by her to get to my mother."

"What was Beverly doing?"

"She was standing there, with her arm stretched out, like this." Lilly flung one arm straight out, away from her body. "She had a gun in her hand."

"Be quiet, Lilly." Lilly and I both leapt at the sound of the voice. Beverly was standing in the doorway. Somehow she'd managed to open the door without us noticing. I had no idea how long she'd been standing there.

"I won't. I won't be quiet anymore," Lilly whispered.

"No one will believe you," Beverly said coldly.

Lilly sobbed. "Yes, yes they will," she said.

Beverly shook her head. "No they won't. Your memory is as changeable as the tide, you foolish girl."

I stepped toward her, but she held up a warning hand. "None of this matters," she said.

I shook my head at her. "I bet the cops will disagree. And the voters, too."

She snorted. "You really think the death of some drugged-out slut who slept with anyone who asked, some nasty little piece of work who couldn't keep her hands off other women's husbands, will make any difference at all to anyone?"

Her face was flushed now, and I stared at her. Thirty years later, she still hated the woman whom Raymond had been unable to resist.

She shook her head, as if shaking off her rage, and replaced it with a calm certainty that was all the more terrifying. "Anyway, whom do you think the police will believe? My stepdaughter with her history of mental illness, memory loss, and instability, or me? I'll tell the police that she's simply mistaken. That she's remembering it all wrong."

Lilly shook her head, but her eyes seemed to grow muddy and confused. "I remember . . . I do . . ." she said.

"How can you be sure?" Beverly asked, and laughed.

I put a protective arm around Lilly. "She's sure," I said.

"I am," Lilly said again, but this time it was a question.

"No you're not," Beverly said, and this time her voice was soft and almost wheedling.

"I remember," Lilly said, but all the certainty had drained from her voice. I had to put an end to it, before Beverly worked her malevolent magic on Lilly's memory . . . again. I leapt to my feet, grabbed Beverly's arm, and hauled her out of the room.

"Here's my professional advice, Speaker. Get a lawyer," I said.

She stared at me, and then turned and walked quickly down the hall.

I ran back into Lilly's bedroom. Once again she lay curled up on her bed. I sat down and began stroking her back, trying to figure out what the hell to do next. There wasn't a single doubt in my mind that the trauma of her father's murder had caused Lilly to recover her memory of her mother's death.

What she remembered was absolutely accurate—I was certain of it. Beverly had killed Trudy-Ann. But I would never be able to prove it.

I had watched Lilly's confidence in her own memory dissipate like vapor when confronted with her formidable stepmother. Beverly would blame someone else for the murder, perhaps Raymond, who was conveniently unable to defend himself. Had she killed *him*, too? Had she killed Chloe? Given that she had rock-solid alibis for both murders, had she paid someone to kill for her? I considered the possibility. She'd committed one murder thirty years ago; she was the obvious suspect for the later ones. A murder-for-hire was the neat and easy solution to this puzzle. So why didn't it seem like the right answer?

I wasn't having any doubts about Beverly's *emotional* capability to have paid someone to do her killing for her. Whatever moral compass she possessed quite obviously had profound self-interest as its true north. This was, after all, a woman who not only let a small child live a lifetime of crippling guilt, but also stepped into the shoes of the woman she'd murdered, even calling herself Lilly's mother. No, Beverly Green was not a woman who would balk at murder to keep her secret. But neither was she a woman who would take the risk of hiring some unknown person to do the deed for her.

It may be easy to find some lunatic to kill for you—*Soldier of Fortune* magazine is available online, after all. But Beverly would know that one's cyberfootsteps can be traced. She would understand that it was virtually impossible to hire a hit man without that person figuring out the identity of his employer. I couldn't believe that she would have been willing to risk placing her secret into unknown—and untrustworthy—hands.

That left the possibility that she'd convinced someone she knew to murder on her behalf. Perhaps. I considered the aides who hovered around her, running her office and doing her bidding. But keeping the Speaker of the Assembly's schedule was a far cry from helping her shoot her husband. No, I couldn't believe one of her employees would provide this service. A lover, maybe? Beverly was the least passionate, the coldest of women. Would she have a lover? None of this made any sense to me. But if it wasn't Beverly who killed Chloe and Raymond, then who was it?

I looked down at Lilly. To my astonishment, she seemed to have fallen into a deep sleep. I tiptoed out of the room and down the stairs. I found Rochelle sitting alone in the living room.

"Where is Beverly?" I asked.

"The Speaker and her assistants left."

I glanced around the silent, empty house, and raised my eyebrows.

"The kids are having dinner out in the pool house with the nannies," she said. She bit her lip. "I hope it's okay, but I called the bodyguards."

"Bodyguards?"

"Lilly sometimes uses this firm of bodyguards. You know, like when there's some weird fan parked outside the house or something? Anyway, I called them."

I sat down next to Rochelle and said, "Good idea."

At that moment the front doorbell rang. Rochelle ran to open it. She let in three burly men in plain blue suits. One was older, in his forties or even fifties. The other two were young men, probably no older than twenty-five. They all had identical cropped haircuts and expressionless faces.

"Thanks so much for getting here so fast, Dror," Rochelle said. "Juliet, this is Dror Amitav. He's the owner of the bodyguard agency."

"Personal protection," he corrected her in a thick Israeli accent, while looking me up and down suspiciously. "Who are you?" he asked.

"Juliet Applebaum," I said, extending my hand. "I'm glad to see you here." I pulled him aside and asked him to make sure that he let no one into the house, not even Beverly. Especially not Beverly. He didn't even blink, just nodded his head.

Dror sent one of the young men with me up to Lilly's

room. I peeked in and made sure she was still asleep. The bodyguard propped the door open about a foot and stood out in the hall in front of the open door, his feet planted hip distance apart, his hands hanging at his sides. He looked as if he was prepared to stand like that for the next ten or twenty hours.

I walked down the stairs and sat down in the living room, going over it all again in my mind. Was I too quickly dismissing the gun-for-hire scenario? At that moment, my purse, which I'd forgotten in the inglenook, began to beep. I scooped it out and pulled out my cell phone. I hit the "missed calls" button and my mother's number flashed on my screen. I resisted the urge to call her and get her advice or maybe just cry on her shoulder. Then I had a sudden epiphany.

I yelled Rochelle's name, and she ran into the hallway from the living room.

"Were you in the room when Raymond got the phone call at breakfast? The one right before he went out?"

She nodded.

"Did the call come in on one of Lilly's lines?"

She shook her head. "On Raymond's cell phone."

"Damn it!" I said, bringing my fist down on my thigh. I winced at the blow.

"Why?"

"Caller ID. I wanted to check the caller ID."

"Do you want to see his phone?" she asked.

"What? It's here? He didn't take it with him?"

"No. The battery ran out right after he got that call. I offered to charge it for him. We all use that same kind of Nokia phone."

I hustled her into the office. There, along a high shelf, was an entire row of telephone chargers, some empty, some holding cell phones. I snatched up the phone she pointed out to me and hit the "call history" button. I pushed the "incoming calls" button. There, at 9:11 A.M., was a call from a ten-digit number. I pressed the "callback" button and waited, holding my breath, while the connection was made. A moment later, the phone rang once. Then twice. Then someone picked it up.

"Hello?" a small voice said. It was a child. A very young child.

"Hello?" I replied tentatively. I didn't want this little person to hang up the phone. "Who is this?" I said in a gentle, friendly voice.

"Araceli," the little girl replied.

"Araceli, is your mommy there?"

"No. She's at home. But my daddy's inside."

"Inside where?"

"Inside the big store."

The big store? I listened closely and thought I could detect the sound of traffic. Was this a cell phone?

"Araceli, my name is Juliet," I said in Spanish.

"Hola!" she said brightly.

"Araceli, are you talking to me on your daddy's cell phone?"

"No. On the big store phone," she said. "It's a very, very big phone, and it rang!"

A pay phone!

"Are you standing outside a big store? Talking on the pay phone?"

"We're at Target!" she said. "And I'm waiting for my My Little Pony. Daddy's buying me a My Little Pony if I just sit here and wait."

"That's so neat! My daughter Ruby really wants a My Little Pony."

The voice on the other end suddenly grew doubtful and suspicious. "That's my toy. I'm not sharing it," she said.

"No! Of course you're not. Araceli, tell me, what is the name of the town you live in, do you know that?"

"Um . . . California?" she said.

"Right!" I answered. "But do you know the name of the place *in* California?"

"Um . . . Lincoln Street?"

I was beginning to lose hope. "Can you remember the name of the city, sweetie? Or the town?"

"Ventura!" she said.

"That's right!" I said. "Do you live in Ventura?"

"Yup!" she said.

"Who is this?" a gruff voice with a Mexican accent said suddenly.

"I'm so sorry," I said quickly. "Your daughter picked up the telephone. I'm just trying to figure out where this number is. I'm assuming it's a pay phone. Right?"

"Yeah," he said suspiciously.

"And are you in Ventura?"

"Yeah, so what?"

"Thank you. Thank you so much," I said, my voice not much more than a whisper. I hung up the phone and leaned back in my chair. Ventura, California. Nice enough town, I suppose, but not somewhere you'd ever bother to go. Unless, of course, you were on your way to Ojai. Thank God for neglectful fathers, and little girls who pick up pay phones when they ring. Otherwise I would never have been able to figure out who it was that had used a pay phone to place the call that lured Raymond to his death.

Dr. Reese Blackmore had worked a miracle cure on Lilly Green. He'd helped her recover her memory. He'd healed her. And he'd written article after article about his success. He had built his entire professional identity upon Little Girl Q's cure. If the truth became known, if the world discovered not that Lilly Green *was* a murderer, but that she *wasn't*, he would be ruined.

I looked at the phone again. The voice mail indicator was flashing. I punched the key and put the phone to my ear. Raymond had two new messages. They were from Beverly, asking him, in a voice so cold that it made me wish for a sweater, just where the hell he'd gone. I supposed it could have been a careful plant, but I tended to think it evidence of her innocence—of *his* murder, at least.

I clicked back over to the "call history" screen and pressed the "outgoing calls" button. There, at 7:42 A.M., was a call to the Ojai center. Raymond had called Blackmore. Blackmore had returned the call, careful to do so from a pay phone.

He'd somehow convinced Raymond to meet him, and then he'd shot him. Something Raymond said must have convinced Blackmore that he was too dangerous to let live. It couldn't have been difficult to persuade Raymond to meet him. He was running scared by then—scared he'd be implicated in the murder. Perhaps Raymond had gone to convince Blackmore that it was in both their interests to protect each other's confidences. I didn't know. We'd never know exactly how Blackmore had lured Raymond to his death, but I knew that he had.

I turned off the cell phone. Ignoring Rochelle's insistent questions, I picked up the office phone and called Al. Still out of range. Then I tried Valerie at Wasserman's office, nearly screaming in frustration when I found myself forced to leave a voice mail message. I told her that Jupiter Jones was innocent and that I knew who had murdered Chloe. At the sound of Blackmore's name, Rochelle gasped.

"Go tell the bodyguards not to let him into the house," I said to her.

"Are you going to call the police?"

Right. The police.

"Do you have that detective's card?" I asked her.

"No," she said.

I remembered that Beverly's aide had taken it. I dialed Information and got the general number for the Los Angeles Police Department. It took three different operators to be put through to someone who could take a message for Detective Staynor. I left my name and Lilly's number. I hung up the phone and only then realized that I hadn't called home in hours. I dialed my number and nearly threw the phone across the room when the answering machine picked up. I felt like I was having one of those dreams where you keep dialing and dialing but can't get through. I didn't bother to leave a message. Instead, I dialed my access code and listened to the messages on the machine. There was one from Al asking me where the hell I'd disappeared to. My jaw clenched in frustration. Then I heard Wanda's voice.

"Hi, Juliet. I got this number from the card you left me.

I hope it's okay that I'm calling you at home. I'm not sure why I'm calling, really. It's just that you said to call if anything came up. Anyway, I just got a call from the Ojai rehab center. Apparently there was some stuff of Chloe's that they want to return to me. They're sending someone down here to give me her things, and I thought there might be something you'd be interested in. For your case. For Jupiter. I mean, we all want to make sure he's really the one, right? Maybe there'll be something here to help you find out for sure . . ." There was a beep, and whatever else Wanda said was cut off. I stared at the phone in horror and then called Detective Staynor again. This time, I told the operator that it was an emergency and gave her my cell phone number. I hung up the phone and turned to Rochelle.

"If that cop calls, you tell him to call me immediately, okay?"

"Where are you going?" she said.

"Laguna Beach."

Thirty-four

BLACKMORE was on his way to Laguna Beach, and I had to get there first. I didn't buy that story about Chloe's personal belongings for a second. He'd killed Raymond, and he was on the way to do the same to Wanda. I snaked down Benedict Canyon with one eye on the road and one on my cell phone. Finally, Al answered his phone.

"Where are you?" I said.

"San Diego."

Damn. He was a full half hour farther from Laguna than I was. "What are you doing down there?"

"Followed one of the workers' comp slackers to a gun show," he said almost defensively. "Why? What's going on?"

I didn't bother to explain. I just told him to meet me at Wanda's in Laguna Beach. It tells you everything you need to know about Al that he didn't ask me a bunch of questions or badger me for more information. He just took down the address.

"Bring whatever you bought today with you," I said.

There was a beat before he replied. "Don't you go in there without me."

Before I could reply, the phone went dead. It flashed "out of range" the entire way down the 405.

By the time I got to Laguna Beach, it was dark. I pulled into Wanda's street and debated whether to cut my lights and engine and coast silently into her driveway. I could take Blackmore by surprise; ensure that he didn't run. On the other hand, what if he pulled the trigger during the few moments it took me to creep up to the house? I slammed my palm down on my car horn and squealed into Wanda's driveway. I ran up to the front door, tore it open, and then stopped, confused. Molly Weston, Blackmore's assistant, stood in the middle of the living room, partially obscured behind a large, plastic bag. Dr. Reese Blackmore was nowhere to be seen.

"Ms. Applebaum?" she said pleasantly. "It's so nice to see you. I'm just here to bring Wanda some of poor Chloe's clothes and things." She hefted the bag, but did not put it down.

I looked over at Wanda. She sat on the couch, her hands in her lap. She didn't rise to her feet, and neither did she greet me with the same friendly expression I'd been treated to the last time I'd visited her. She smiled, but it was a tight, nervous smile.

"Did Dr. Blackmore come down with you?" I asked Molly.

"Reese? No, of course not. He's too busy for this kind of errand, I'm afraid." She turned to Wanda. "He did say to tell you how very sorry he is."

I looked back at Wanda. Suddenly, I noticed her feet. They were bare, like they were the other time I'd been to the house, and she'd clamped her toes around the leg of the couch. I'd never seen white knuckles on toes before, but I knew what they meant. Wanda was terrified.

"Hey, Molly, why don't I help you with that bag?" I said, crossing quickly toward the young woman, my hands outstretched.

"No!" she said sharply, backing up. "No, no. I'm fine."

I noticed for the first time that one of her arms held the bag in place in front of her. The other hand was obscured from sight, tucked behind the bag.

"Juliet, I'm so sorry. It's really not a good time for me right now," Wanda said softly but firmly. "I need to . . . to have some private time with Molly. To . . . to go through Chloe's things." I wrinkled my brow and looked at her. What was she doing? "I'm sorry," she said. "We'll get together another time. You go and give those babies a kiss for me, okay?"

She was trying to save me. My children's faces flashed through my mind. I thought for a brief second about the one in my belly. I'd already been shot once while I was pregnant, and lived to give birth to my wonderful baby boy. Would I be so lucky again? I wondered how far away Al was. I wondered whether Detective Staynor had taken my message seriously. I considered leaving the house and calling the police. But you don't leave someone alone with a murderer. You just don't.

"I'm so sorry. I really should have called first. Of course you need time alone for this," I said brightly. "I'm just going to make myself a little cup of tea for the road, okay? Can I borrow a travel mug? Do you have one of those, Wanda?"

"In the cupboard by the sink." She began to rise, but I held out my hand. "No, no. I'll be fine. It'll just take a sec. Hope you don't mind, Molly. I'll be out of your hair in no time."

Molly shrugged. I walked behind her toward the kitchen, and she swung her shoulders around so that she was facing me. In that instant, I caught a glimpse of it. She'd shoved her hand deep into the soft bulk of the full plastic bag, almost entirely obscuring the gun. I saw only the butt, peeping from the bottom of her fist, but it was enough. She was pointing a gun at Wanda, and I knew what I needed to do.

I bustled around the kitchen, filling the tea kettle noisily, and lighting the burner. I smiled through the open door at Molly, who returned my grin with one equally false.

I dug around the cupboard. "Ooh, peppermint," I sang out. "I just love peppermint tea. No honey for me, though. I lose my taste for it when I'm knocked up." I wanted to make sure Molly knew about my condition, if she hadn't noticed it already. Nothing seems as benign as a pregnant woman.

"Can I make you two some tea before I go?" I called.

"No thanks," Molly said.

"How about for you, Wanda?"

"No."

They say a watched pot never boils—well, the same is true for a kettle being stared at by two terrified women and one murderer. It felt like hours before the shrill whistle of the steam made me jump.

I poured the boiling water into the oversized travel mug I found in the cupboard. Then I put the top on, making a great show of tightening it. As I walked out of the kitchen, I kept up a steady stream of patter. "Did you guys ever hear about that woman who sued McDonald's because her coffee was too hot? I mean, my God, too *hot*. Like, isn't coffee *supposed* to be hot, lady? People will sue over the most insane thing. Well, I'm on my way; this tea will keep me nice and toasty the whole way home." I walked in the wake of my own chatter to the front door, passing behind Molly. Once again she turned slightly to face me, still keeping the bag in front of her chest. When I was about an arm's length away from her, I jerked my hand out, and flung the cup I'd only pretended to close. The boiling water flew out of the cup and splashed her squarely in the face.

She screamed and fell to the floor, dropping the plastic bag. I stomped on her hand, sending the gun skittering across the floor. She scrabbled at her face with her nails, shrieking, and I sat down heavily on her chest.

"Get the gun, Wanda!" I shouted.

At that moment, the door burst open. Al leapt into the room, landing heavily on one knee, his gun drawn. "Not her!" I shrieked as he swung the gun in Wanda's direction. He paused and looked at me. I was sitting on Molly's chest, pinning her hands to the floor under mine. I looked down at her. Her face was scalded bright red, and as I watched, it faded to a sick, corpse-like gray. Then it began to swell. Blisters fat with liquid popped out across her eyelids and cheeks, and her lips inflated, growing five or six times their normal size. She moaned, and it was a horrible, afflicted sound, full of agony and fear and frustrated rage.

"Call 911," I said. Al had already reached for his phone.

I felt my stomach roil in the first wave of nausea I'd felt in over a week. I lurched to my feet and backed away from Molly's pustulating face. I had never hurt anyone like that before, and I was horrified at what I'd done. Suddenly, I felt a pair of arms encircle me from behind. A hand stroked my hair, and a soft voice whispered in my ear. "Thank you. Thank you for saving my life." I leaned back and rested my head against the comforting softness of Wanda Pakulski's silicone breasts.

When the paramedics had swathed Molly in soaking bandages and special blankets had rolled her away, and before the police began the interrogations of the three of us that would last well into the night, Wanda, Al, and I huddled in her kitchen. I gulped the water Wanda poured for me and tried to still my shaking.

"Nick of time, partner," Al said gruffly, leaning heavily against the counter.

"You sure were," I murmured.

He shook his head. "Not me. You."

Wanda nodded. "Another moment and she would have killed me, Juliet. Just like she killed my daughter, and just like she killed that poor man, Raymond Green."

I looked up at her. "Molly told you?" I asked.

She nodded again, and told us what had happened between her and the disturbed young woman. Molly had arrived with the bag of clothes, smiling and friendly. As soon as she was inside the house, and Wanda had closed the door behind her, she'd reached into the bag as though searching for something, and pulled out the gun.

"I froze at first, of course, but then I could see that her hands were trembling," Wanda said. "I started talking to her, like you would to a scared animal. And I started walking backward, trying to make it back to the front door. I thought if I could distract her with my voice, I might have time to wrench the door open and run. I'm not sure what I said. Something like, 'You don't want to kill me. I'm nothing to you.' Something like that. That's when she told me." Wanda's face crumpled, and for a moment I thought she might cry.

"Told you what?" a voice said. We all turned to see a fresh-faced, uniformed man standing in the doorway—one of the police officers who had arrived along with the paramedics.

Wanda swallowed hard, pulled herself together, and said, "She told me that she'd killed Chloe, and she'd killed Raymond Green, and she wasn't afraid to kill me, too."

The cop opened his mouth as if to ask another question, but Al laid a quieting hand on his shoulder. Something about my partner's demeanor, perhaps the authority he'd never lost even after he left the force, silenced the young man.

Wanda continued. "I think I started to cry then. I asked her why. Why she'd killed Chloe. And she said it was my baby's own fault. That if she'd done what Molly had told her to do, she would have been fine. That it was because she got greedy that she had to die. Molly said that Chloe was trying to destroy Dr. Blackmore, and that she, Molly, couldn't allow that. Except she didn't call him that. She called him 'my Reese.' She even said 'my sweet Reese.' She said she couldn't let Chloe hurt him, and she couldn't let Raymond hurt him. Do you know what she meant? Do you have any idea what was going on?"

I nodded, but before I could explain, a man in a crumpled blue suit pushed by the young police officer and walked into the kitchen, flashing his badge.

"Riley, get your butt back outside where it belongs," he said to the uniformed cop. Then he turned to us. "Which of you is going to tell me what happened here?"

Thirty-five

WHATEVER a family's tragedy, children demand to be cared for, fed, and played with. This is, I think, one of the great blessings they bring to our lives. Mourning must be filtered through the lens of their all-consuming needs, and their infinite capacity for joy. I found Lilly early the next day, sitting with her legs dangling in the heated water of her swimming pool. She was throwing brightly colored rings into the water for Amber and Jade to retrieve. The girls squealed as they hoisted themselves out of the pool into the chill of the cold morning air, and howled with victorious pleasure when they dove back in and returned to the surface, the red, purple, and blue rings stacked up on their skinny forearms.

Lilly raised a hand in a small wave. I called a greeting out to the girls, dragged a chair close to Lilly, and sat down, tucking my knees under the stretched-out fisherman's sweater I'd found in the bottom of Peter's dresser.

"How are you?" I asked gently.

She shrugged and spun the rings out over the water with a practiced snap of her wrist.

"Did you bring Ruby and Isaac?" Lilly said.

When I'd called the night before to tell Lilly about Molly Weston, she'd asked me to come by the next day, and to bring my children. "I can't bring myself to set up any playdates for the twins right now—I don't want strangers in my house. But they need to be distracted from all this," Lilly had said.

"Ruby and Isaac are around the front, playing on the scooters," I said.

"Thanks for bringing them."

"It's okay. They were glad to come. Should I go get them?"

Lilly shook her head. "The girls will be done in a minute or two."

We sat side by side, Lilly on the edge of the pool, me curled up in my chair. Amber and Jade dove and splashed, and I tucked my chin against the spray of water.

"Do you want me to tell you what happened?" I asked. I'd given her only the barest bones of the story the night before. She'd been too devastated to hear more.

She shrugged and then nodded. Suddenly, she rose. "Not here," she said. "Not in front of the girls." As if summoned, although Lilly hadn't called for anyone, one of the nannies appeared carrying thick white towels. She dried the girls off briskly and bundled them off to the house, presumably to play with Ruby and Isaac.

Lilly slipped her feet into a pair of plain white loafers and led me across the patio to a small stone bench set at the edge of the garden.

"Please start at the beginning," she said. "I need to understand everything. How it happened. Why."

I nodded. "Well, I guess it began a few years ago, when Blackmore brought Chloe to his clinic."

Lilly shuddered, and I put a hand on her arm. "Are you sure you want me to tell you this?" I asked.

"Yes," she said, inhaling deeply—steeling herself. "I have to know. But wait a minute, okay? There's someone else who needs to hear this, too. I'll be right back."

I nodded, and she got to her feet and headed to the house.

Within a few minutes she was back, leading Jupiter by the hand. His hair stood up on one side of his head, and his cheek was creased where he'd slept on it.

"Jupiter!" I said, surprised to see him.

He tucked his chin to his chest and smiled tentatively.

"I had one of the bodyguards go get him last night, right after you called. I didn't want him there, in that place. Not after I found out that Molly was the one . . ." Her voice trailed off.

Suddenly, something occurred to me. "But, Lilly, Jupiter was released to the custody of the center. If he leaves, the cops will consider that jumping bail."

She shrugged. "I told Wasserman and Dr. Blackmore to take care of it. They will. Especially now that Molly confessed. Wasserman says he's sure the DA will dismiss the case against Jupiter. And today he's going to arrange for Jupiter to check into another facility here in L.A. He'll be there by this afternoon."

She reached an arm around the only brother she had, and squeezed him tight.

"The two of you saved my life," Jupiter said to me. "Lilly, and you."

Lilly shook her head. "Oh, honey, I didn't save you. It's completely my fault all this happened to you in the first place. I'm so sorry." She looked like she was about to begin to cry.

He wrapped his arms around her. "It's not your fault. No one told me to sleep with Chloe. No one told me to keep using. It's not your fault, Lilly. It's mine. Recovery is about accepting responsibility, and that's what I'm going to do, from now on."

They leaned back slightly, away from each other, and looked into one another's eyes. Jupiter smiled his faltering smile, and Lilly returned it. Then they sat down next to me on the bench.

"Okay, Juliet. Tell us what happened," Lilly said.

I nodded. "Parts of this you know already. Blackmore was

one of Chloe's clients. I think he was sleeping with her, but I also think, although I can't prove it, that he intended to set her up with you, Jupiter, so she could be a connection to the CCU, and keep his clinic in the CCU's good graces. Chloe traded up in the ranks, however, and ended up marrying your father. That worked just as well for Blackmore. Polaris was indebted to Blackmore for introducing him to his wife, and the CCU kept sending clients to the clinic. And so things went for a couple of years. Except it seems that, at some point, Polaris started souring on his young bride. Perhaps because he realized that she'd never stopped using drugs, but maybe because . . . well, because he found out that she'd never stopped sleeping with his son.

"A few months before she was murdered, Chloe checked back into the clinic for an intensive therapy session. I guess her using had gotten out of hand, even for her. Maybe Polaris had finally given her an ultimatum. I don't know. But that must have been when Molly Weston told her about . . . about your mother."

At the sound of the name of the woman who had killed her father, Lilly moaned. I put a comforting arm around her.

"Did you know her, Lilly? Had you met Molly?"

"I knew who she was, of course," Lilly said. "Dr. Blackmore talked about her. And her name is on all those articles with his. And I think I might have met her once when I was up at the clinic. But I really don't know. Why did she want Chloe to blackmail me?"

"I don't think that's what she intended. I'm pretty sure that she expected Chloe to use the information against Polaris. Which Chloe did. Whatever the Very Reverend thought of her drug use, and her extramarital activities, he had to stay with her, or risk exposure."

"But why would *my* secret have mattered to him? Why would he care if it got out? Did he know it was Beverly? Or did he think I did it?"

I wrinkled my brow. "I'm not sure, Lilly. I don't think he knew the truth. I think he got to the room after it happened.

Maybe Beverly told him she'd taken the gun from you. Maybe he believed you had done it. We'll never really know for sure. Unless Beverly tells, of course. But whatever he knew or didn't know, Polaris had smuggled you out of Mexico without the police's permission. And he kept quiet about the case for all these years. His credibility as a religious leader would have been compromised if that had come out."

"But I still don't understand what *Molly* got out of getting Chloe to blackmail anybody."

"I think she imagined she was protecting Blackmore. She was in love with him. I should have seen it right away."

"He saved her life," she said simply. "He saved her, like he saved so many others. He got them off drugs, he helped them find their past."

"But not you, Lilly. He didn't help you find the past. He helped invent one that hadn't happened at all."

She didn't reply, and I continued. "Blackmore had tried to protect himself by setting Chloe up with Jupiter, but that was as far as he was willing to go. He wouldn't resort to blackmail, even to protect the center. Whatever his mistakes, I think your therapist is a fundamentally decent person."

Lilly nodded emphatically. "I know he is."

"But Molly is a different story. It probably seemed like a perfect scenario. She could use Chloe to ensure the center's future, and at the same time prove to Blackmore that the woman with whom he'd once been involved, the woman he'd slept with when Molly had wanted him to sleep with *her*, was even more corrupt than he'd imagined. But then, Chloe got more creative than Molly had anticipated. She blackmailed Polaris, sure, but she also started blackmailing you."

"And I got my father involved." Lilly's voice caught, and she swallowed hard.

I planted my hands on her shoulders and stared directly into her eyes. "This is *not* your fault, Lilly. What happened to Raymond is not your fault."

"He helped Chloe, didn't he?" she said.

I nodded. "He must have. He told her the truth, Lilly. He

told her that you never shot your mother. He told her that the real killer was Beverly."

She moaned.

"It's not your fault," I repeated. "It's not your fault your father gave up his career when his wife became the Speaker of the Assembly. It's not your fault he cheated on her, or that he was looking at the possibility of being left with nothing."

Lilly was crying now. "If I'd given him more money, he wouldn't have needed to use Chloe."

I wondered if this were true. I loved my friend, but she had some serious issues around money. Raymond probably knew full well that he wasn't going to get any help from her. Chloe's blackmail was a stroke of luck for him. He could use Chloe to fund his separation from his wife. I wondered what he and Chloe had planned to do. Split the blackmail money fifty-fifty?

"I don't understand," Lilly said, drying her eyes. "Why wasn't he afraid of being caught himself?"

"Maybe he trusted Chloe not to slaughter her own golden goose. Maybe he figured he was safe. If they were exposed, Polaris and Beverly would both face the ruin of their careers, whether or not they were extradited to Mexico. But your father had no career to lose. And he was, at worst, an accessory after the fact to a crime that happened a very long time ago."

"Beverly did it," Lilly whispered.

"Yes," I said.

"I didn't."

"No."

"Why? Why did my mother . . . why did Beverly . . ." Lilly bit her lip. The question in her heart was why had one of her mothers murdered the other. That was simply too difficult a construction to put into words, either semantically or emotionally.

"Jealousy, I think. Your real mother and Raymond had begun sleeping together again. Beverly might have talked a good game about free love, and breaking the conventional chains of marriage, but when push came to shove, she wasn't willing to share her husband, not even with the mother of his child."

"And then they blamed it on me," Lilly said flatly.

I nodded.

"Why?"

"Because you wouldn't have had to go to jail. And Beverly would have. She was protecting herself, and your father probably felt guilty. After all, he'd been in bed with your real mother."

"And then I made it all so easy for them," Lilly said bitterly.

I didn't reply. I didn't need to. We both knew it was true. Lilly had solved all their problems in a way they probably could never have anticipated by recovering memories of a murder she had never committed.

Suddenly Lilly stared at me, her face a twisted mask of horror. "Did Dr. Blackmore implant those memories on purpose?" she asked.

I gave her a reassuring squeeze. "No. No. I'm sure he was operating in good faith. He was just wrong. Disastrously wrong."

Lilly nodded, this one fact a fragment of relief in the catastrophe that had become her life.

"Tell me the rest," she said.

"Well, Raymond must have told Chloe what really happened, and she added Beverly to her list of extortion victims. Then, I assume Chloe made the terrible mistake of telling Molly how things were even more complicated—and lucrative—than even she had imagined. And that's what killed her."

"Why?"

"Because your doctor has built his entire professional reputation around the idea of recovered memory. You were his most famous case. Little Girl Q was the basis for virtually all of his journal articles. If it ever came out that not only hadn't Little Girl Q murdered her mother, but that he had, however unintentionally, implanted false memories of those events, then he would be exposed as a hack. Or worse. Molly couldn't have that. First of all, she was utterly dependent on him for her professional success. All the research and writing she's done has been with him. Without Blackmore, she's just an ex-addict with limited credentials. She knew that if he went down, she'd follow. As long as he was an international success, Molly could parlay their relationship into a successful career as an academic or a shrink."

Lilly nodded. "And she loved him. That's the other reason."

I nodded. "She couldn't bear to see him destroyed. Worse, she couldn't stand the idea of being the cause of his ruin. She had to make sure the story never saw the light of day. At first she trusted Raymond and Beverly not to talk. Raymond would never want his involvement in the blackmail to be exposed, and of course Beverly had everything to lose. But Chloe was another story. Chloe was never a particularly trustworthy person. She had never managed to kick her drug habit; she was a blackmailer. Molly couldn't risk that Chloe would let the story out. So she killed her."

Lilly sighed, and turned to her brother. "I knew you hadn't done it. I just knew it." Another ray of hope in her desolate landscape.

I watched the two of them for a moment, and then I remembered something. Why had Molly tried so hard to convince me that Jupiter was innocent? But had she? She'd told me how distraught he was; how much he loved Chloe; how devastated he had been when she had married his father. Molly had set him up with a motive, all the while pretending to be supporting his claim of innocence.

"Why did she kill my father?" Lilly said, her voice once again hollow with despair.

"My best guess is that once I started digging, Raymond began to panic. He was terrified that his involvement in the blackmail would come out and that he would become a suspect in Chloe's murder. He called the Ojai center the morning he was killed. At first I had assumed he called Blackmore, but now I think it's more likely that he was looking for

Molly. I'm guessing that he knew Molly was the source of Chloe's information, and he wanted to make sure she'd keep silent. I don't know if he suspected her in Chloe's murder. I tend to think not, because he agreed to meet her. Maybe he suspected Blackmore. Maybe he suspected you, Jupiter, or even . . ." I didn't finish my sentence.

"Even me?" Lilly asked.

"No. No," I said, although of course that was exactly what I'd meant. "Maybe he suspected Beverly. Whoever it was, Molly called him back and convinced him to meet her."

"Why did she kill him?" Lilly said.

"Probably because she was afraid he was getting closer to figuring everything out. She got rid of him, like she'd gotten rid of Chloe."

Suddenly Lilly stared at me. "How the hell did *you* figure all this out?" She sounded almost angry.

I said, "Actually, I didn't. I was wrong. I thought Blackmore did it. It was just a lucky break that Molly started to panic. She must have been thinking about what I'd told her about how close Chloe and her mother were and decided not to take any chances. Wanda picked up the phone and called me, and that's the only thing that saved her from the same fate as Chloe and your dad."

Lilly began to cry again. I wasn't sure for whom. Her father? Her mother? Even her stepmother? Or for herself?

Finally, she dried her eyes on a corner of her shirt. "What now?" she said.

I sighed. "Well, like Wasserman told you, they are likely to dismiss the charges against Jupiter, although you never know with the Los Angeles DA. They are often happier with a bird in the hand even if the one in the bush is quite clearly guilty. Thank God we have Molly's comments to Wanda, because Molly's not likely to confess. But even if the prosecution doesn't dismiss the case against you, Jupiter, you can bet Wasserman will be able to convince a jury of your innocence."

Jupiter nodded, his relief palpable. Lilly said, "I'm sure it won't get to trial, honey. They'll dismiss the case. I know they will."

I continued. "As for Beverly, I just can't say. She'll resign, don't you think?"

Lilly shrugged. It didn't seem like she cared.

"I'm sure they'll impeach her if she doesn't. As far as prosecuting her goes . . . well, it all happened a long time ago. The evidence was lost in a fire in San Miguel; most of the witnesses are gone. Maybe they'll try to reopen the case, but somehow I doubt it."

"They won't prosecute," Lilly said dully.

I frowned, not understanding why she was so certain.

"It's just my word against hers. And no one would believe me."

Once again I didn't answer. Lilly probably was right. I wasn't sure how Mexican juries worked, but I knew it would be nigh on impossible to convince an American jury to believe the testimony of someone who had lost and recovered her memory so many different times, and in so many different ways. Juana's testimony would help, but who knew if she'd be willing to go on the stand.

Suddenly, Jupiter got to his feet. "I'm going to go play with the kids, okay?"

Lilly raised her eyebrows at him.

"I want to have some time with them before I go back into rehab," he said.

She nodded, and he walked quickly back to the house.

"He just wanted to give us some time alone," she said to me.

Lilly and I sat together side by side. My friend's father was dead; her stepmother had murdered her real mother. Her own career might or might not be over—it depended on whether any directors and producers would be willing to deal with the notoriety with which she would now forever be plagued. But the stepbrother whom she loved would be spared execution, and she could finally rest easily in the knowledge that she had had nothing to do with her mother's murder.

Was it worth it? Only Lilly knew.

Suddenly, we heard squealing and the thumping of feet. The kids tore through the yard, heading in our direction, Jupiter bringing up the rear, laughing. I realized then that I'd never heard the young man laugh. It was a wonderful sound, full-bodied and joyful.

"The mommies are base!" one of the twins shouted. Within seconds the three girls were scrambling all over us, grabbing on to our legs, flinging themselves into our laps. I held tight to a wriggling Ruby and to the lower half of the twin who had lain herself down over both Lilly's and my laps. Isaac came up huffing and puffing, a much slower "it" in their game of tag. He scrambled up on the bench next to me and wrapped his arms around my neck. I bent lower to inhale his musty little boy smell and caught Lilly's eye. She had her nose buried in her daughter's hair. She smiled a sad smile, and then shut her eyes.

In the end, in a world that spins out beyond our control, all we can do is hold our children close, and breathe in the scent of them. That's all, and sometimes, if we're lucky, that's enough.